Battle of Eloas

Mystifying Book 2

Dorian Moore

Cover art by: Megan Moore

ISBN: 979-8-9871601-5-2 (Paperback)

ISBN: 979-8-9871601-6-9 (Hardcover)

ISBN: 979-8-9871601-7-6 (eBook)

Dorian Dedication: To cosmetology summer camp.

I still don't know anything about doing my makeup, but I met my bestie there, so I'll call that a win.

And to my siblings: Trey, Mike, Mackenzie, and Grace. You guys are way cooler than I ever was (and taller) and I'm totally jealous

Moore Dedication: To Nan and Poppy.

Nan, I love getting to share these books with you, and nerding out about fantasy things with you. I hope that this one brings you joy, I love you!

Poppy had the most incredible mind for creating things, from the intricate to the hilariously ridiculous…I like to think that some of the creativity for writing is my version of the imagination that I inherited from him. Miss you every day.

Chapter One

Erin sat at the edge of the pier and watched the sea lions play below. They barked happily to one another, ignoring the fog rolling in. People passed by, unaware of her, unaware that someone not quite human was so close. She could flick her wrist and have rocks block their path or vines wrap around their ankles. She could have flowers peek out from the cold ground for the passing kids to find and pick. But nobody saw her. December was settling in, and everyone was feeling the holiday rush.

This time last year she was going crazy catching shots of people in their monetary rush; the determined faces, the radiant smiles, the excited children. This year, she couldn't bring herself to look. She'd only had one person in her life who meant *anything*, and he was taken months ago. Gabe was the one person who always saw her. He shared her joy, eased her pain, shouldered her worries, even when she wouldn't tell him what they were. Now she felt invisible to the world.

She was getting too deep. If she got caught up in her thoughts and feelings, she would lose control. In the months since his death she'd spiraled more than once. One moment she'd feel strong and whole, and the next she couldn't eat or sleep without seeing him on the ground, his life leaving him while she was helpless to do anything. Her ability to heal had been weak when she'd needed it most, and that was not something she could easily move past. Erin rose quickly and walked into the mass of people bustling by. She matched their pace and made her way back toward her apartment, eyes on the ground instead of the life surrounding her. When she entered her building, she didn't stop to smile at her neighbor, just grabbed her mail and headed up the steps. The sight of *Mystifying's* stationary made her falter. The familiar pang squeezed at her chest as she held the envelope. Every time a reminder like this came across her path, it brought back everything she'd lost.

Erin refused to step foot in the store again. She'd ignored all of Ana's calls and Melody's texts. However, the elf refused to give up; she continued to send checks as if Erin still worked there. The first one came with a letter: "I understand you need some space right now. But your job is here when you are ready, as are your friends." This month's check rested inside the envelope along with a note in Ana's loopy scroll, reading: "Merry Christmas. Please come see us. You shouldn't be alone right now." Erin tossed all of her mail onto her kitchen counter and went to sit on her sofa, absently reaching for the necklace she wore around her neck. The amulet Gabe had when he died.

She looked at the small scar on her knuckle in the shape of an "x". It was *her* fault Gabe was gone. They went to Loinnir in order to rescue *her*. Gabe was the one to jump in to block Ana, because Erin hadn't been able to move. She'd been in shock from beating Bogor to death. The erebus had tortured her, threatened her, and those she loved. She'd lost control, and Gabe died. The small "x" wasn't the only scar left behind; Erin also sported a nice one across her cheek from Bogor hitting her during their final fight, along with all the internal ones that ripped open just from glancing at Ana's writing. She had the power to heal the physical ones; she considered it every day when she saw it in the mirror, or saw the lingering glances of strangers...but she needed it as a reminder. A reminder that she'd had true love in her grasp, and she'd *ruined* it. Just like everything else she touched.

A *thud* came from her bedroom and forced her to her feet, senses on high alert. Even though she'd stopped talking to Ana, she hadn't stopped practicing with her powers. Erebi were drawn to her power, and she'd had to fight off a few on her own. She was only too happy to send them back from where they came. Erin grabbed the dagger she kept in her boot and moved in a shroud of silence. The dagger, named *Willow*, was familiar in her palm. It was the same dagger she found in *Mystifying* so long ago, the dagger that had once belonged to her father. She saw a blur of movement and threw herself at it. She had them pinned with a blade to the throat before they knew she was there.

A human. She felt the soft, warm flesh, the racing heart. "What are you doing in my apartment?" Erin kept the dagger to his throat and didn't lessen the pressure she had on him. He was a teenager and gave her the queasy reminder of Joey, the boy who attacked her once upon a time in one of her foster homes.

"I...Someone paid me. I'm sorry!" He tried to press himself to the ground as much as possible to keep the dagger off his skin.

"Are you going to make me go through the list? Who paid you? What did they pay you for?"

"I don't know who, okay? I don't know! I was just supposed to come in and look for some necklace with a stone. You weren't supposed to be here! I'm sorry!"

"*Who* paid you?" Erin asked once more, her voice deathly quiet. She could feel his pulse racing under her fingers, could feel his body shiver with fear, but her heart was hard against him.

"He was in a cloak. I never saw his face. He didn't tell me his name! I swear!"

"What does your mystery friend want with my necklace?"

"He didn't-"

"He didn't say, you swear." Erin sighed and released the pressure from the kid. "You should really ask more questions before

4

going off to do questionable deeds. You can go back to your friend and tell him next time he should do his own dirty work. Now, get out of here before I call the police." Erin stood and watched the boy struggle to his feet. He ran toward the door, but Erin threw her dagger. It embedded in the wood just above the handle. "You might want to empty your pockets first."

Erin watched him pull the small amount of jewelry she owned from his pocket and drop it on the counter. She walked slowly and enjoyed–more than she should–the way he shook as she brushed against him to pull the dagger free. All the color was gone from his face and he wasted no time to run out the door as soon as she opened it.

"Have a nice day," she called in a sing-song voice. It was the second time someone had broken into her apartment. The first time was a month ago, but she'd walked in as they were going out through her fire escape. She went after them but hadn't been able to catch up. At the time, she'd assumed she'd just walked in on a burglar, but now she knew what they were after. Erin pulled the amulet from under the collar of her shirt and wondered why someone would be after it.

She'd tried to research it, wondering why Gabe had it, but so far her searches had come up empty. It didn't even look like the stone was from the human realm. She knew who she could go to, but her curiosity hadn't been strong enough to face Ana.

Slowly, Erin went to gather up the jewelry when her gaze fell on a velvet box. It wasn't familiar to her, so she popped it open. Her heart stopped. The other items she'd gathered slipped from her fingers and clattered to the kitchen floor as she froze and stared at the diamond gleaming up at her. Braided white gold made to look like vines wrapped around one circle diamond, with a few small ones scattered around the band to look like leaves. Erin walked back into her bedroom and saw her intruder had pulled open some of Gabe's dresser drawers and tossed aside his clothes. His items, remnants of his life, lay scattered across the floor. She hadn't been able to bring herself to move anything of his after he passed; now it was all glaring at her, the velvet box she never got, heavy in her palm. "Gabe..." His name fell off her lips.

Her thumb brushed over the ring she would never get to wear, and a dark haze filled her vision as her loss slammed into her like a sharp blade. The grief was unbearable. It made her want to rip at her skin and crawl into a dark hole. Tears didn't come. She wished they did; instead, tight bands seemed to wrap around her heart, and all she could do was slowly shut her emotions down. She took deep breaths - in for five seconds, out for five seconds - shutting down all emotion, and then closed the box like it was nothing. Erin picked up Gabe's clothes and carefully refolded them, putting everything back where *he'd* left it. She felt empty, but it was better than the spiral she'd been heading towards. She moved with precision until her job was done. With each breath, she slowly bricked up the gaping hole in her chest until she was numb again, and her apartment was clean once more.

She pointedly ignored the way her hands shook and the way her magic hummed under her skin, like it wanted to lash out at something.

.℘. .℘. .℘.

Though she typically would have gone home after class, Melody had several finals before winter break started within the week, so she had opted to study in the quiet of the library. The young witch studied often in the downtime at *Mystifying*, but she knew that if she went home now, she would have one eye on Ana the whole time. Ana wasn't grieving, precisely; instead, she was busy blaming herself for everything that happened while pushing herself too hard with work. The elf even continued to send Erin checks out of some sort of guilt; Melody had to bite her tongue every time she glimpsed the envelope in their stack of outgoing mail. The halfling wasn't the only one to lose someone, but she seemed content to sit back and blame Ana while taking her money.

Melody was drawn from her thoughts by the feeling of someone's gaze. Across the room she found herself caught in the stare of Liam, a classmate who epitomized *tall, dark, and handsome*. They shared a psychology class, but had never really talked. As soon as their eyes met, he rose from his chair and came over to her.

"Melody, right?" He kept his voice quiet, and he looked a little nervous. Her heart raced when he flashed her a shy smile.

"Yeah, Liam?" She said his name like a question, though she knew exactly who he was. "Did you need notes or something?" His breath huffed out in a chuckle and he shook his head.

"Umm, no. I actually wanted to know if you might want to go to dinner or something with me? I know there are finals and everything coming up, but maybe next week, after classes have ended?" He rushed to add in, "if you aren't seeing anyone, that is."

"No." Melody didn't have time to date. Being a full-time student, working at the store during downtime, and being a secret witch left little room for that weird thing people called a life. Not to mention, no one had asked her out since she started college. "I'm not seeing anyone." She hurried on when she saw his shy smile slide away. "I would like that." Melody wrote her number on an index card from her stack, and prayed she wasn't blushing. She handed it over and couldn't suppress the grin that spread across her face. "My last final is Thursday, so I'll be free after that."

"I'll call you Thursday night, then." He grinned, revealing a small dimple, and she thought she might melt. He gave a nod as he walked away, and Melody stared at her computer screen, trying to remember what she had been working on.

.℮ .℮ .℮

"Thank you for stopping in to see us today. Enjoy your tea!" Ana called with a smile as her latest customer left *Mystifying*. The second she was alone again, the grin fell and her shoulders drooped slightly. As much as she enjoyed her roommate's company and her help running things, the elf couldn't help but be relieved that Melody stayed at school after class. She knew Mel was worried about her. She loved her for it, but some days that concern was just unbearable. This was one of those days.

Ana busied herself with reviewing the accounts for the store, pushing all other thoughts away for a while. She was responsible for guarding the portal to this world; she'd taken over the duty along with the store she'd turned into a little magic shop. Yet, somehow in the past year, she'd lost one of her closest friends by sending her right into a trap. She'd taken a halfling under her wing to teach her how to use her powers, and let her get abducted by her oldest enemy. She'd found the brother she'd lost when crossing to this realm, only to make a mistake during battle and lose him to a blade. Once, she had thought she could help people. Now, she was an elven princess without a kingdom, and a protector who had failed at protecting those closest to her.

The weight of it all sat like a hard knot between her shoulder blades. She felt incredibly old for being as young as she was. *Enough, it does no good to dwell on what was.* She let out a deep sigh her mother would have chided her for, rubbed her temples, and then settled down to finish her paperwork.

Darkness had settled over the world by the time Ana finished her work. When she saw the street lamps lit outside, she realized her mind had finally given her a break from her loss and let her work in peace. Ana rounded the counter as if on autopilot to close for the night, feeling oddly refreshed. Then the stillness was broken by movement at the back of the store, and her throat tightened.

A stunning rust-red wolf was standing in the doorway to the office, and Ana felt as though her entire world shifted. She froze as the breath was stolen out of her. She knew that wolf, but it was *impossible* that they were the same. The wolf she knew was long gone. She'd been down at the stables when the erebi broke through the protections placed on the portal. She'd never found her way to her master's side as he tried to lead them to the portal to escape the realm. She'd probably been killed, just like her master and everyone else had been when the erebi came flooding in.

The wolf tilted her head curiously, watching her with all the familiarity of an old friend, and then turned and padded out of view. "No! Wait!" Ana scrambled after it, but by the time she reached the back of the store, the office was empty. She might have thought it had all been part of her imagination if she didn't still feel the portal pulsing with energy.

Ana rushed ahead, hoping she could follow the pull of power through the portal, but the wolf was too small of a creature to leave much of a mark behind. Even as Ana tried to step through, the energy dissipated. Why was she seeing this wolf? What could it mean? Ana thought of the wolf she'd seen after Toron's death, and believed they had to be the same. At the time she'd thought it had been something she'd imagined, but this time, *this time*, she knew what she'd seen. She'd *felt* the pull of the portal. The wolf was real; even if it couldn't mean what she hoped, someone was sending the creature through the portal to scout, and as protector, she would need to find out why. She knew she should move, start making a plan, but all she could think about was the way the wolf had looked at her; the familiarity that had been in that gaze, and how the wolf had been the perfect replica of her old friend.

"Aina, look!" Her brother called her from the past. His cherub face was upturned in a grin, his curls bouncing over his forehead as he raced after the wolf Ethelron had saved and brought home with him.

"You realize she is a wild animal, don't you?" A deep voice rumbled beside her, making the small hairs on her arms stand on end.

"Tell that to her. She looks pretty content to me."

The rust-red wolf threw herself to the ground, playfully tossing her young rider into the grass and rolling back to cover his legs. The boy squealed, his laughter echoing through the surrounding forest. Aina couldn't contain her affectionate grin, and she looked to see the same look fighting to show on the handsome face beside her.

"Ana?" Melody's concerned voice drew her from her memory, and the elf looked up to see her standing over the desk. She hadn't even heard the witch return. "Hey, you okay?" Melody asked, a frown knitted between her brows.

Ana nodded, running a hand over her face. "Yeah, I guess I just got lost in thought there for a moment." Ana swallowed back the information about the wolf. Melody needed to focus on her studies, and if Ana said she believed someone was sending a wolf through the portal to scout for them, Melody would go into witch mode. For now, until she knew more, Ana would just keep it to herself and let Melody have a moment of normalcy. Goodness knows the witch deserved that, and so much more. She was too young to have lived through and seen so much, and Ana knew she had been little help the past few months as she worked through her own grief. She shook her head. "How was studying?"

Melody gave her a skeptical look, but excitement seemed to bubble up from inside her chest. "Well, *studying* was lame...but the hot guy that asked me out? *Definitely* not." Her energy was infectious, and before long, the two women were gossiping like schoolgirls as Melody told her about Liam. The wolf, and the memories it stirred up, faded into the back of her mind as Ana let herself share in her friend's happiness for the first time in what felt like ages.

℘ .℘ .℘

Briar forced her eyes open to clear away the vision that was making her brain burn and blinked against the dry light that never changed in this realm. She sat at the top of a mountain, a place Doyle brought her to only a few months ago. The foreign land spread below her, dry and brown where her realm would have been filled with lush greens and bright colors not seen anywhere else. Briar's blue hair had faded since coming back, and lay in a braid over one shoulder. No wind pulled at loose strands. The sun blazed above in the same spot, but did nothing warm her skin.

She rubbed fingers into the base of her skull to try to banish the remnants of her vision. She'd tasted freedom for a moment, months ago with Doyle in her home realm. He'd walked with her and let her soak in the magic that flowed freely. The moment they returned here however, she'd felt that energy drain, returning her to the weaker version of herself. Doyle, the erebus with the long jagged scar across his otherwise handsome features, had noticed her start to fade, and he'd fought for her. Lyra had insisted she return to being locked away in her room upon their return to Skia, but Doyle insisted on a more permanent rune being placed on each of them so that she could have more freedom to roam.

She turned her wrist and looked at the intricate design that tied her to Doyle. She remembered how he'd stood up to Lyra, argued with her until she'd given in to some of his smaller demands. He'd given her hope with the way he'd stood between them, demanding she be given at least some wary trust, that she'd earned far more than that in what she'd done to help them so far. Lyra had relented, as long as Doyle was willing to take the hit if something went wrong. He hadn't hesitated when they were offered new, stronger runes than the one they'd shared in Loinnir. He now shared in her discomfort when she strayed from her room. If she ever tried to run, she would be incapacitated, and he would suffer right along with her until he retrieved her. They could now sense where the other was and - she wasn't sure if it felt the same for him - there was always a pull for her to go to him.

She knew he felt her visions, though a much duller version; she could see in his eyes when he felt the echo of her pain. He'd risked a lot for her, but she still saw the vision of him holding a knife against her. He was still destined to either love or kill her, and she hadn't been able to clear a path between the two.

"How's the view?" Doyle asked from behind her. He climbed from a small hole that led out of the mountain to the small perch that barely held the two of them. She'd felt him coming, so it did not

14

surprise her when he appeared at her side. If it wasn't for that connection, she wouldn't have heard him until he was speaking to her. They'd trained Doyle to fight and kill. He could move in silence over any terrain, but now he'd lost his ability to surprise her.

"About the same as always," she responded, not turning to look at him. Her neck still ached, and she didn't want to turn her head in fear it would explode with pain. Instead, she continued to look out at the surrounding land. The sky was always the same: thick, rust-colored clouds covered the sun that never moved. Sometimes she could make out something flying overhead, or people moving below, but all was quiet today.

He reached over and rubbed at the base of her neck. She almost jumped at his touch, but the gentle pressure slowly eased away enough of the discomfort that she felt it was safe to turn her gaze to him. She knew he was probably dying to ask what she'd seen, but he simply met her gaze in silence, and kept his fingers moving.

"I bet you regret taking on that rune now, don't you?"

"Never," he answered simply. That gave her a start, but his expression didn't change. "Your lot in life is not an easy one. If having a bit of freedom to roam is all I can give you, I'd be willing to sacrifice more than a mild headache in order to give it to you. You deserve far better and I'm sorry I can't give it to you." He let his hand fall back to his side after the muscles loosened in her neck.

"The halfling still has the amulet," Briar stated after a brief pause. She'd been keeping a close watch on the amulet and those connected to it. Because she'd held it in her hand, she could focus on the necklace, and draw images of it and everyone tied to it. She didn't know them, so the picture wasn't particularly clear, but it allowed her to continue watching the halfling after her lover's death. Part of her wondered if giving him the amulet had somehow led to his demise, but she hoped not. She'd watched the girl grieve over the last few months, felt her pain through the visions, and felt very connected to her now.

"Well, that's good," Doyle said slowly, clearly sensing something else in her words. They'd all been on edge the last few weeks. The queen had discovered the amulet was missing, and she'd been on a rampage, determined to find out what happened to it. Lyra was under close watch, and Doyle had been very careful about where he was and when. Queen Flereous had sent Malux in search of it, and it hadn't taken him long to find the halfling. It was becoming personal for him now, she could feel it. And after her last vision, she knew how his journey would end.

"Malux is in danger. His time is short." It hurt her to say it. She felt the pain Malux lived with. She knew that his very existence was a constant form of torture, but she liked to think of him as a friend, and she didn't want to lose him. He'd brought her blankets and helped when she'd asked for it. He'd listened to her and given her advice, and now he would die...and she had some hand in it. In pursuit of the amulet she'd put into play, he would lose his life, and she would have to live with that sitting on her shoulders.

"Is that good or bad for us?" Doyle asked after a moment. His scar sunk deeper into his skin as his brows pulled together in concentration. He'd known Malux far longer than she, and while she knew they were not friends, she'd felt no hatred between them either.

"I'm not sure. The queen has something over him that makes it so he can't go against her orders, but he has no love for her. He could have made for a great ally."

"I always thought so, but he also has no love for Lyra."

Briar kept her mouth shut on that one. *She* had no love for Lyra, either. She also had no intention of letting her take the throne, she just didn't know how to stop it from happening. "I suppose we will just have to wait and see how it all plays out." She said the words, but she was already wondering if there was something they could do to change Malux's fate. She looked sideways toward Doyle and wished she could confide in him.

Chapter Two

Melody stared into her closet and tried to remember the last time she went clothes shopping. Nothing stood out to her. Nothing made her feel pretty or special.

"How are you making out?" Ana peeked her head into Melody's bedroom, but Melody just groaned and plopped on the edge of her bed.

"I have nothing to wear. I wish I knew a spell to make my fairy godmother appear," Melody tried to joke even as she noticed Ana looked like she was losing sleep again. Melody knew something had been on her mind, but anytime she asked, Ana found some excuse to dodge the question.

"Well, I believe I am supposed to say something like...bippity boppity boo, but that doesn't seem very elvish to me. So I'll just say you deserve to have some fun. You need a break, especially after this last week with all of your finals." Ana reached around the door and pulled out a bag.

"You didn't!" Melody jumped up and grabbed the bag before throwing her arms around her. Ana returned the hug, then made it a point to press a loud kiss to her forehead.

"I hope you like it. Now hurry and get changed. He should be here soon."

Melody was always a pretty casual dresser. Either in sweats or jeans and a t-shirt, she never wore dresses, so she was thankful when she saw the dark teal pants and a long gray wrap sweater. It was dressy, but still *her*. Of course, Ana would know her well enough to find something so perfect. Paired with some boots and lipstick, she felt much better about the whole situation.

Melody added a silk teal tie to her hair. She was still getting used to wearing her natural hair in a puff style, but it was growing on her. After everything that had taken place in recent months, she'd needed a change. A change in her appearance gave her something tangible, fed the need to have some sense of control. Feeling that need had made her think of Erin, and her ever-changing array of hairstyles. She'd wondered if maybe Erin had always been running from her own lack of control and just hadn't realized it.

Ana gave her an approving smile when she walked back into their living room. "Okay, you have fun, but please text me if you are going to be too late, alright?" Ana took Melody's hand and slipped some cash into it.

"Ana, I have money," Melody argued.

"I know. It's just in case. I read it is very good for women to have multiple ways to get away if they need to. You shouldn't have to depend on him for a ride or money. But you can call me if you need me to rescue you. I'll be there."

"I know, Ana. I'll be fine. It's just dinner." Melody's phone rang and Liam's name popped up. Thursday night she'd gotten a text from him, and then he'd called to set up plans. This afternoon he sent her another text, just letting her know he was excited to see her. Just the thought of him gave her butterflies. "Okay, I have to go. I'll see you later tonight!" She hardly looked back as she rushed down the steps to meet him. She'd had her boy-crazy moments over the years, but now that she was in her second year of college, it felt *different*.

And there he was. He waited by a new-looking car, his dark hair styled to one side. He flashed her a confident smile that had her heart pounding in her chest. Liam took her hand and opened the car door for her. "You look beautiful tonight. I almost didn't recognize you without your nose in a book or behind your computer screen."

"Thank you. I'm so glad we are on winter break now. How did your finals go?"

"I was a little distracted, actually. I spent the entire semester staring at this girl in my class. Finally got the guts to ask her out."

Oh...My...God! "I'm sorry to hear that." She should've probably stopped grinning ear to ear to make her apology more believable.

When Liam pulled up to a restaurant she had never been to before, he ran around the car to get her door and take her hand. He didn't let go as they walked inside, but held tight to keep her close. She wasn't sure she could feel any more like a schoolgirl than she did at that moment.

℘ ℘ ℘

Doyle waited for Lyra, his hands locked behind his back, his chin held high, and feet shoulder width apart. His normal stance while in her presence. She'd summoned him, yet he stood waiting, and had been for over ten minutes. He thought about what Briar said regarding Malux and wondered if he should tell Lyra, but decided against it. If he was going to die, she'd find out about it soon enough, and they would all probably suffer for the queen losing her favorite pet.

"She's ready for you." One guard came from the room and motioned Doyle forward. He'd stopped trying to memorize the guards' names. They rotated constantly. Some were spies for the queen, some were playthings of Lyra's, only to be tossed aside once she was bored. He no longer cared.

He brushed past the guard and stepped into Lyra's sitting room. The erebus was mostly unconcerned with his presence, her lithe body draped over a man, copper hair flowing freely down one shoulder. Cat-like eyes lazily turned to him, and she gave a wide smile. "I've been hoping you would bring me some news after all the time you've been spending with the observer, but it's been silent on her end. If I need to start making adjustments to her freedom around here, I shall."

"She's been keeping a close eye on the amulet. Malux knows where it is, but Briar assures me it is in safe hands and is still the catalyst to bring down your sister."

"When?" She moved her leg from the man's lap and put her booted heels to the floor with a thud. Her ever-present daggers flashed under the light from the candles, and the sight felt like a warning.

"When it is time, I assume. If we are to get help from this group, then I suppose they have to be ready."

"This halfling has had the amulet for months now, and nothing has happened. The only change is my sister being up everyone's ass trying to find her missing jewelry."

"I understand, but without Briar, we wouldn't be this far. Without her, whatever path we'd be on would be leading to our deaths."

22

"According to her." Her eyes flashed, and she stood, her movements smooth and deadly. The man on the sofa got up and silently excused himself.

"I grow tired of having the same argument. You brought her in to help us bring down the queen. You either have to trust what she has to say, or you should free her now. Up to this point, she's done nothing to deceive us. She's helped us at every turn. I choose to listen to what she has to say, but if you are going to continue to doubt her, then there really isn't a reason to have her here." Lyra's eyes narrowed, but he refused to budge under the gaze. He'd been through this too many times before, and he'd watched Briar sacrifice far too much for there to still be such distrust.

"I need you to test the waters to see who would stand behind us once it *is* time. I need to know who will follow my sister to death and who is willing to switch allegiance. Do it slowly and carefully. We don't need anyone growing suspicious. And tell your little blue friend I need a timeline. Understood?"

Doyle gave a curt nod, but she didn't dismiss him right away. He could tell she was wrestling with telling him something else. The rune on his wrist burned to let him know Briar was out of her room, but he refused to show any discomfort while Lyra had him under such scrutiny.

Finally, she waved him off, so he gave a quick bow and left. He let his new "Briar tracker" lead his feet in her direction. Between her small glimpse of freedom and the feather he stole from her wings, she'd been able to have clearer visions without getting as sick. He could still feel when she had a vision though, and knew it had to be torture for her taking the full hit. He would get a mild headache and could feel the energy drain from him for a short time. But he'd seen how her whole body took on the vision and knew that, while she might have been born with a great power, that power did not come for free.

He thought of how quickly she'd gained power, color, and strength when they were in her realm for a short time. They'd hoarded food and water from Loinnir, but she'd since made her way through the supply, and he'd watched her fade away to the weaker version of herself all over again. He hated himself for doing this to her, but he'd already committed. If he'd wanted to free her, he should have let her go when she and her sister were trying to escape. He'd made his choice, and he was going to have to make the best of it. Keeping Lyra reigned in when it came to Briar was his first step. He would not stand aside while she hurt her like he had before.

It did not surprise him to find Briar sitting outside on the small ledge near the top of the mountain they usually resided in. She once told him it felt like the earth was pushing down on her when she was inside the caverns, and he could understand the sentiment. He felt the same way occasionally, and he was accustomed to his realm and living in the mountains. Briar however, was used to the freedom of fields and open sky. The only thing she was used to hanging over her was the thick boughs of trees, rich with color and life.

Doyle had just stepped out when his head exploded in pain as a vision coursed through her. He couldn't see anything, just felt a jolt in his skull. Briar went rigid before him, and he rushed forward to grab her before she tipped over and tumbled off the side of the cliff. Her gaze was distant, darting back and forth, not seeing him but seeing something far away. She screamed out, and pain shot down his spine. As abruptly as the episode started, Briar stilled in his arms, and he was left with little more than a dull throb of a headache. It took a minute for her eyes to flutter open, squinting against the never-changing sun.

After a few blinks, she focused on him. Her eyes darted to his lips, and he felt the gaze like a warm caress. There was a sudden pull between them, an intense urge to lift her up and taste her lips. He thought she'd taste like honeysuckle fresh from the flower. Then she pulled back and pushed herself back against the wall of the mountain, kneading away at her neck with deft fingers. That urge lingered, but the timing wasn't right.

"When did you get here?" she asked, pinching the bridge of her nose.

"Just in time to keep you from tumbling off the cliff." Doyle looked at the ledge where his foot rested, barely an inch from a sheer drop. If Lyra had kept him waiting a few minutes more, Briar really may have collapsed and gone right over. He shuddered to think of it.

"Well, thank you for that." She gave a wry smile, but her lips didn't quite pull up as much as they normally would. Her hands were shaking, and she struggled to pull in a deep breath. It killed him not to ask her what she saw, but he knew she was still struggling with whatever it was, and needed space. Her eyes were a little brighter when she looked up at him again; some of the immediate pain was fading. The scream that had torn from her throat, however, still burned inside his brain. He wanted to shield her from that pain, but he couldn't protect her from herself and her own power.

"Would you mind seeing me back to my room?" she asked finally. Doyle gave a quick nod, offering his elbow for her to loop her arm through. He helped her through the small doorway and they trudged back to her room. She was deep in thought, so he just led her in silence, letting her fall deeper into herself. As soon as they got back to her room, she picked up a sketch pad, and without a word started drawing. He took up his militant stance that Lyra had drilled into him and waited by the door. He felt like he should leave her alone, but there was something mesmerizing about watching her, and he wasn't quite ready to lose the moment.

After a few moments her hand slowed and, without looking at him, she said: "there is no reason to stand like that around me. I can't think of you as my scary guard anymore. You might as well be comfortable."

"Your scary guard?" The corner of his mouth twitched in amusement.

"Sure, isn't that what you were trying to be when all this started? The scarred erebus, willing to do what it took to save his realm? Even throwing me and my sister to the wolves?"

Her comment hurt him as only the truth could, and all the humor was gone. Briar must have sensed his pain, because her hand stilled and she looked up. "If you recall, I stated that I *can't* think of you that way. Not anymore. Now I know the truth."

"And what truth is that?"

"You are the type of person who would see my sister home safely, even though she could have been used against me. You bring me back food from my realm to help me keep my strength. You'd take on a rune that would cause you pain in order to give me a taste of freedom. We've been through too much for you to pretend you still hold some power over me."

"Don't I?" He moved closer, not missing how her eyes darted to his lips. Her features changed quickly, her eyes sparkling and her cheeks coloring just enough for him to notice.

"No." Her voice was deeper as he sat beside her on the bed. He was tempted to keep pushing her buttons, but decided to let it slide. He knew the truth: she held more power over him than he would ever want to admit. He held out his hand for her sketchbook and she passed it over without hesitation. *Malux*. His black cloak was a shadow on the ground, his eyes staring ahead, blank and emotionless.

"This is what you saw earlier?"

"Part of it." Her voice was quiet, and he felt pain there. He knew Maulx had become a friend to Briar. He'd stopped by more than once to find the two of them talking. When it first started, he'd been worried Malux was trying to use Briar for his own gain, to go against Lyra and himself, but it was never like that. Malux had told her about Skia, and those that resided within. She'd shared about Loinnir, and he'd even learned more of Malux's human life from the conversations he'd *overheard*. It couldn't have been easy for her to see his death. He still wondered if it would be better or worse for them for Malux to die.

"Have you seen my death?" he asked as he handed the sketch back.

"Many of them," she answered simply, setting the sketchbook aside. Her reply shocked him.

"I've had multiple deaths?"

"If you recall, I went into a trance for quite some time while I lived out all of us dying in hundreds of different ways."

"Ah yes, did you have a favorite?" She gave him an odd look, and after holding her gaze, he finally relented; "a joke. That is something I would call a joke."

"I'm glad to hear my time of mental torture is so funny to you. Now, did you come find me to discuss the time I saw you take hot pokers in the eyes, or did you come for something else?" She must have felt him flinch, because her mouth twitched. "What? That is what *I* would call a joke."

"Cute Blue, real cute." He couldn't help but reach up and rub his eyes, though. "I just finished speaking with Lyra and knew you were out and about, so I thought I'd see what trouble you were getting into."

"Ah, my favorite captor. And how is Lyra? I haven't seen her since Malux went on the hunt for the amulet."

"She wants me to identify potential deserters of the queen, and wants to make sure you are still working to find out how we overthrow her sister."

"Speaking of hot pokers, I'm curious what you've been drugging her with to keep her away from me. Everything seems to be at a standstill for the moment, and yet she hasn't come to breathe fire down my throat and beat the visions out of me."

He cringed at the image. Lyra had hurt her before, in ways he hadn't imagined possible. *Before* he'd really known Briar, the fact that she was being hurt had not been enjoyable for him. He'd hated every moment, and did what he could to end it. It had been the first time he'd really argued against choices Lyra was making. But now that he knew her, had seen how strong and stubborn she was and how bright and funny she could be, the idea of her being hurt was intolerable. Lyra was his family, but he'd stand between them and keep Lyra from touching Briar if that was what it came down to.

He couldn't tell that to Briar, though. He was trying to think of something to say when she grinned at him. "It's fine. You keep your secrets. Not to be rude, but would you mind leaving me? My head is quite angry with me and I want to lie down for a bit."

"Oh, of course." He stood quickly and linked his hands behind his back. He wanted to ask more about Malux and her vision, but he could see the crease between her eyes, and knew she needed space. He turned to leave and had his hand on the door when she said his name.

"Be careful poking around for information for Lyra. You poke the wrong beast and you'll lose your hand."

"Was that another one of my deaths?"

"Hopefully you'll never know."

.℮ .℮ .℮

Erin stood on the roof of her building and looked out at the city below her. Her father's dagger was gripped tightly in her hand, and the dummy she'd brought up for practice was in shreds at her feet.

With a sigh, Erin sat on the bench and looked at the garden she made. It was the perfect place for her to work on her fighting skills and powers. She'd grown each flower around her from a seed, and her powers kept them thriving even in the winter cold. Controlled vines were spreading out over the bricks, but she kept them tamed so no one would complain. She enjoyed using her powers and feeling her strength continue to grow. It was about the only thing that kept her moving anymore. She could still remember the feel of her powers while she was in Loinnir, how much stronger it made her feel to be in a realm of magic. It must have hurt her mother to give up such a beautiful place. But Erin could now understand how her mother suffered through so much pain and loss in order to be with Derek. She would give up anything, she would walk right into hell, if it would bring back Gabe.

"It's time you give up the stone."

Erin jumped from her bench and turned to see a figure completely shrouded by a black cloak. She wasn't sure how he got to the roof without her hearing or noticing, but that was the least of her worries at the moment. Her knuckles went white as she gripped her dagger and readied herself for a fight.

"You must be my visitor who likes to go through underwear drawers. What happened to your friend with the sticky fingers?"

The figure did not answer, but reached into his cloak and threw something at her. With a sickening thud, it landed at her feet. Erin looked down and saw the teenager's head, dead eyes staring up at her. Bile rose thick at the back of her throat, but she pulled herself together and reached her powers towards the surrounding plants.

"What do you want with the stone?"

"It was stolen. It must be returned to my master."

"Okay, who is your master?"

He pulled a large, curved blade from under his cloak and started toward her. Her eyes fell on one of the decorative rocks she had scattered around, and she used her powers to pull it from the ground and launch it at the stranger. The hood fell from his head, revealing a face that was only half human. The other half was covered in small blue scales, with a silver eye, and a bald skull covered in larger scales. He only paused a moment at her attack before he was moving forward again. "I don't care about you. I must return the amulet to my master. You can give it to me, or I can sever *your* head and take the amulet from your corpse."

Erin sent another stone into his chest and a third into his head. Unfazed, he reached her and swung an arm into her stomach, knocking her to the ground. Erin rolled back to her feet and gasped for breath. "Want to tell me a little about your master? I really don't understand the whole cryptic erebi schtick everyone seems so determined to do."

Vines wound around his feet, but broke easily when he shook them off. She leapt toward him, her dagger raised. He grabbed her wrist and swung her to the edge of the roof. She slammed the dagger into his arm, and he let her go with a growl. Erin swung her feet, knocking into his legs, and sent him to the ground.

"I'll take that back." She grabbed the dagger from his arm and went for his heart, but he waited until she was close and then threw her over the edge of the roof.

Erin screamed as she fell, landing hard on the deck below. It knocked the breath from her chest, and she had to struggle to get her lungs to take in air. The being looked over the edge of the roof before leaping down to land next to her. On his feet, unharmed, like a complete asshole. "This could be going better," Erin groaned. She rolled to her knees, preparing to fight again. His silver eye darted behind her, and with a short growl, he jumped from the ledge to the ground below. Erin peeked over and saw he'd landed safely six stories down and was now walking away.

Turning to see what he was looking at, she cursed when she saw the owners of the deck walking into their apartment. Quickly, she climbed onto the fire escape and struggled up the flight of stairs. Her whole body throbbed from her hard landing. This erebus was a lot stronger than the others she'd faced so far, and apparently jumping off the tops of buildings did nothing to him. He would be back. His *master needed the amulet back*. And Erin had the amulet.

It was time she got some answers about what the stone meant, and how Gabe got it before he died. She would have to go back to *Mystifying*, she realized with a groan of frustration. But first, she needed to rest for a bit - and take some Tylenol - before her body realized what had just happened.

Melody started picking at her food, but wasn't sure she could actually eat. Her stomach was a ball of nerves as she searched for something to talk about. She had little she could share with the average person.; there was school, and she could talk about working at a magic shop, but her topics ended there. The witch hardly went out to do normal college activities. She was afraid to drink around others in case she lost control of her powers, and most of the friends she'd made were part of a Wicca group with women of all ages; not to mention she fought erebi in her spare time.

Liam didn't seem to notice. He was being *perfect*. The man listened to everything she said; he engaged with the lame topics she brought up, and he seemed perfectly capable of talking about interesting things, even if she was just staring at him in awe. This could be a real problem. Melody was already contemplating how she would deal with a future of lies and secrets with him, and she was currently bombing their first date.

"Melody?" His voice broke through and pulled her attention.

"What? I'm sorry."

"Is your food okay?"

Melody looked down and realized her fork was hanging in mid-air, with shrimp dangling from it. "Oh, yeah. It's great." She gave a deep sigh. "I'm sorry. I'm a little nervous. You might have figured this out, but I don't date much."

"Well, I have been enjoying myself. Sitting across from you makes failing all of my finals worth it."

"I really hope you're joking." *Could he be any more perfect?* They continued to chat, and he reached across the table to take her hand. They spent the rest of dinner holding hands and talking about their classes. Melody steered away from difficult subjects, which was a little challenging considering she lived and worked at a magic store.

The bill came, and Liam snatched it before she could argue, and then asked if she wanted to walk by the pier. They were only a block away; but Melody thought of her boots and the heels and wondered if she would make it. But those brown eyes were staring straight at her, making her knees weak, and she couldn't resist. If she could fight the erebi, then her feet could survive a short walk in small heels. "That would be nice."

Liam led the way, keeping his fingers tangled with hers. Clouds and city lights hid the stars, but the moon was out, and it gave an eerie glow against the night. The air was chilly, especially coming off the water, but her sweater helped, and Liam wrapped his arm around her shoulder and rubbed her arm. "Maybe we should just head back. It's cold out and I don't have a jacket for you. I'm sorry, I didn't think that one through. Maybe next time we can go to the beach and walk around, really enjoy the view of the water."

"Next time, huh? I guess I wasn't such a bad date?" They got to his car, parked on a side road, but he didn't open the door right away.

"I had a great time. It was the perfect way to start off winter break." Liam brushed a hand against her cheek, his gaze on her a soft question. Then his lips found hers, and she wasn't cold anymore.

Warmth wrapped around her, but she'd expected a spark. The attraction was there, but she wasn't hungry for more. She started to worry that maybe she was doing something wrong. Just as those doubts settled low in her stomach, he pulled back. Something - *not desire*, she lamented - glinted in his eyes as he looked down at her. She'd messed up. He could tell she didn't know what she was doing, and now he would not be interested in her anymore. All the negative thoughts were running through her mind when she noticed three men coming at them from the alley.

She grabbed Liam's arm, wanting them both to jump in the car *before* they found out if the men had ill intentions, but Liam didn't move. He just looked down at her and pushed her hand off him. "Liam?"

"I don't like to get my hands dirty. I hope you understand."

The first man approached, and Melody thrust out her hand, knocking him back with a burst of energy. Her mind struggled to catch up to what was happening, but luckily her body reacted on instinct.

The second man grabbed her wrist and narrowly dodged her foot, swinging toward him.

"Liam! What are you doing?" Liam continued to stand with his back resting against the car, watching with boredom at the fight unfolding in front of him. The third man tried to grab her from behind, but she jabbed an elbow into his gut and focused her energy to call upon fire. When a small flame awoke in her palm, Melody grabbed the man holding on to her, and felt relieved when he let go with a scream.

She turned to Liam, ready to throw a burst of energy his way, but the first man recovered from her hit and swung something into the back of her head. She held out her hand, willing her powers to work, but her fingers were suddenly blurry, and then she was falling.

Chapter Three

Briar knew the time for Malux was growing short. The vision of a blade going through him still left an ache in her chest. He *had* to die; she'd tried to see a way around it, but she couldn't. There had been something else, though: after the pain of the death, she'd seen a flash of Malux opening his eyes and Doyle standing in the background. She tried to concentrate on that, to see if there was something she was missing in that brief flash, but she saw nothing else. She wondered if getting her hands on either Doyle or Malux would help her fall into another vision that would give her more information.

If there was a way for her to save Malux, she wanted to do it. She just didn't see how it was possible. When she'd first had the vision, she should have grabbed Doyle's arm and forced herself to *see* something else, but she hadn't had the energy. She'd needed to do something about her vision of death. Another glance at the sketch confirmed that there was nothing else for her to draw up. Doyle had been running around the last few days, trying to plant seeds and see who started speaking ill of the queen. The task Lyra'd given him was a dangerous one, but Doyle was smart and he knew his way through the politics of his realm.

Malux was her best chance to draw out more information. She hadn't seen him, other than in visions recently. He'd been running all over, trying to get the amulet back, and she knew his anger was growing as he continued to fail. It was possible if she sent a note for him, he'd come. They'd become friends of a sort, or at least she liked to think so. It was possible he'd come just to see if she'd had a vision about the amulet.

Feeling good about having something to do, she scrawled out a note and left her room to find a guard that always seemed to linger about. It only took her a few minutes of wandering to find one she recognized. Torik had long horns and pointed ears, his gray eyes reflected light, and he was quick to smile. He gave her a grin when he saw her and even gave a small bow.

"Miss Briar, looking for me?" His accent was thick, but she'd grown used to it. There weren't many guards she saw a lot of; it seemed they were often rotated, but Torik always seemed to be around.

"Yes, I was wondering if you could do me a favor, actually?"

"I'll see what I can do."

"I appreciate it. I was wondering if you could take this to Malux? You know I'm not allowed to wander too far and I haven't seen him lately."

Torik took the paper and put it in a small pocket at the front of his thick leather armor. "I'm sure I can find him. I'll make sure he gets it." He eyed her carefully. "How have you been, Miss Briar?" Torik didn't know exactly who she was or why Lyra kept her around. He had to know she had something that Lyra wanted to use, and he knew she had a short leash around the place, but he didn't know of the visions or all that Lyra had done to her in order to prompt said visions. He must have seen something in her face, and she didn't need him to start questioning.

Briar gave the best bright smile she could manage. "I've been fine, thank you, Torik." She waved and turned back toward her room before he could try to delve deeper.

She wasn't in her room long before there was a soft knock at the door. Malux stepped in, bringing along the chaotic energy that clung to every fiber of his being. She'd been seeing his face so often in her thoughts that seeing him in the flesh felt foreign. Her gaze was drawn to the human side of his face, making her wonder what his life had been before. She sensed softness in him, but it was clouded. He'd told her a little of his history, but it mostly revolved around him being changed.

40

"Malux." She stood and gave him a small smile in greeting. His eyes skirted around her room and froze on her table. The sketch pad they had given her for visions lay there face down, but his reaction made her uneasy. She wondered about his dragon eye, and if it could see through the pages. Part of her wanted to run over to cover the pages from his view, but she remained where she was and waited for his attention to return to her. "Have you had any luck retrieving the stolen amulet for your queen?" she asked, despite already knowing the answer.

He gave her a tight smile in response. "I know that is what your little team took. The day you sent me down to help them. I'm well aware that you don't want me to retrieve it."

"Then you know *why* I don't want you to. I'm not sure why you would want to get it if we need it in order to bring down the queen. You have no love for her, but you still help her." It was oddly satisfying to have a real talk with him without sidestepping their true meanings. He watched her for a moment, and she could almost feel the internal debate. "You helped me, you helped them. But now you work to undo it?"

"Why did you give the halfling the amulet? What did you see?" This was dangerous ground, and Briar knew it. It was possible he would run off to the queen and tell her all she was trying to accomplish. She didn't know what exactly Flereous held over him. "I didn't give the amulet to the halfling. I gave it to her lover. He was killed in Loinnir. She must have kept it when he died."

"But what did you see?"

"Giving him the amulet would tie his group to us and give us their help. Lyra needs it in order to bring down the queen."
He nodded, not giving away any of his thoughts. "I like you, Briar, and I know what you are trying to do. So I have to ask, do you really think Lyra is the right person to replace Flereous?"

"No, I don't." That got a reaction from him. He tilted his head toward her, and she watched him think through his response. "I want to bring them both down. I'm just not sure how to deal with Lyra quite yet. Flereous has to be top priority. She and her wars need to come to an end. Then we can work out who to put on the throne."

"This is a very dangerous game you play. What does Doyle think of you trying to keep Lyra from her crown?" He nodded as her silence spoke all the words she didn't dare to say aloud. "A very dangerous game indeed."

"I'm not the only one."

Something intense flashed in his eyes. "Do you know what it is like for me to be in this body? The war of selves within me causes constant pain. One day I was a human, and the next I woke up to my body on fire and this." He held up his scaled, clawed hand. "I've lived in blinding pain ever since. None of that compares to what Flereous did to me. The torture was one thing; the black magic used against me was another. Now I am under her rule. I can let things slide; I can watch you step out against her, but I cannot disobey a direct order from her. She could order me to cut off my own arm, and I cannot disobey. Everyone likes to call me the queen's pet..." His eyes shifted away from her and landed on her sketchbook once more. "I am her servant until death, no matter what. She has ordered me to retrieve this amulet, and so I shall. She has not connected it, or the halfling, to your little uprising, so I hope you can work around this."

"Malux..." What could she say? If he was bound to the queen by dark magic, then he had no choice but to retrieve the amulet. If he continued going after it, then his time was short.

"I hope you accomplish your goal. I hope you can return home once more. Just remember, Doyle is on Lyra's side, and it will be hard to turn him away." She felt the goodbye in his words. She felt his warning. There was so much she wanted to ask him, and so much she wouldn't learn if he walked away. "Till death, I am bound to this queen. I was born human. I never thought I'd live centuries as I have. If I'd known what that time would hold, I never would have wanted it. I should have died when I came across that dragon. There are worse things than death."

"Who would you like to see rule this realm?" She didn't want him to leave the room, desperate to save him somehow.

"I've never thought of a different future. It seems that the decision rests on your shoulders. The ancients won't accept just anyone. If they rise against a ruler, there is no hope of altering their decision. Lyra could pass. She does not carry ancient blood, but she is of this realm and has a connection to their bloodline."

"Doyle?"

He didn't seem surprised by her question, but shook his head quickly. "He's too good for this realm." She quirked a brow at that. "He'd fight hard to bring the best to this world and his people, but the ancients wouldn't accept him. He has too much love in his heart. Can I ask, what do you see of Doyle's future?"

"You ask for him, but not yourself?"

"I only have one future before me. You and I both know that. But Doyle...I've been around for a long time, but I've never quite been able to understand his motives. I'm simply curious."

"He has many choices to make," she conceded. "As of now, I'm just trying to keep us off the path that ends in our bloodshed. It does not leave me with many options." She wanted to tell him of the two futures she could see. If she succeeded in getting the queen off her perch, his future was split two ways. Malux was about to walk to his death and she still could not utter the words. She'd seen the tenderness in Doyle, felt the love radiating from him. She knew full well Doyle was not made to rule this world, but he wasn't the one she was asking for, not really.

"So the ancients need a ruler that they believe will be on their side. One who withstands this realm, wants the best for the people, but one who will not be ruled by the ancients as Flereous is. This realm needs someone who does not want it, or we fall into the trap of Lyra, and end up with someone who will grab at that power to our destruction."

"I suppose."

"Thank you, Malux. For everything." Understanding passed between them. This was the last time Malux would come to her room. The last time he'd be a pawn to his queen. He was ready to walk into his freedom, which would leave her to save a realm that wasn't hers. Malux turned to leave, but a sharp panic took her and she reached out to capture his hand.

She concentrated hard, and when the vision rose, she grabbed at it with both hands. Her head split in pain, but she held him to her and took in everything the vision offered. When it faded, she found his mismatched eyes inspecting her. The moment she let him go, he turned and left her alone to do what she had to do, with no questions about what she'd seen.

.℮ .℮ .℮

Ana flipped her ledger closed with a sigh, content with the fact that all of their bookkeeping looked just fine. She'd always been careful with the store's finances, but balancing the ledger always left her just a little antsy until it was finished. A quick glance at the clock told her it was only 9pm, but the elf couldn't help feeling a bit like an anxious mother. She knew she would not be able to sleep until Melody made it home, and Ana wondered if she was having a nice date.

Turning to head for her office, Ana jumped and yelped in surprise when she came face to face with a large, lean, red wolf. The same wolf that she'd thought she had seen several times in the months since Gabe's death; the one that left her feeling like she was losing her mind. Now, staring at the wolf in her doorway, she knew she *must* be going crazy. There was simply *no possible way.* "Sio?" The name felt strange on her tongue, foreign after so many years, but also so familiar.

The wolf whined and trotted towards her, and she couldn't breathe. The floor rushed up to her knees as the red wolf reached her, and Ana threw her arms around Siofra's neck, burying her face in the fur that smelled like *home.* Ana took a long moment to breathe in the painfully familiar scent, overwhelmed by the way Siofra instinctively curled around her. "Oh, my sweet and beautiful friend, I can't believe you're here." If this wolf, who had been such a constant in her life before being sent to Sula, was still alive, was *here,* it could only mean that—before she allowed herself to finish the thought, Ana was on her feet and running into her office.

As much as she'd been expecting it, she was still surprised by the looming figure in the back of her store, with a familiar face and painfully familiar armor. "E-Ethelron? You...h-how...what-"

46

"How very eloquent of you, Princess," he quipped dryly, stepping out of the shadows with a solemn face. Sio returned to her master, sitting obediently at his feet while his fingertips idly stroked her snout.

The taunt was so *him* that she couldn't suppress a sob as she threw herself towards him. The solid body beneath her touch tensed. Her heart swelled when his powerful arms finally wrapped around her with a tenderness no one would suspect. "I thought you were dead. How are you *here*?"

His chuckle reverberated through her chest, and they both pulled back to look at one another. Hazel eyes stared down at her. Ana took another step back in order to get a better look at the elf who had been her guard, and her best friend, throughout her childhood. Like her, Ethelron's aging had all but stopped, leaving him looking nearly the same as the day she thought she'd lost him. His eyes seemed harder, colder than she remembered, and the thought of what might have caused such a change made her chest ache.

"After your parents sent you and Toron away, we tried to prevent the erebi from following you. We were unable to keep them at bay, and were forced to destroy the portal to stop them. There was a possibility that we would lose the war, and could not risk it spreading to a place where you would be defenseless. If we won, we would rebuild it."

Ana took a moment to process what he'd said, and she stumbled back to rest against her desk. Ethelron looked as though he wanted to reach out to steady her. Instead, he crossed his arms over his chest and raised an eyebrow. Ana felt like she was on the verge of hyperventilating. *Her realm*...after seventeen years of thinking that everything she'd known and loved as a young elf was gone. Here stood the only proof she needed that she'd been wrong. "S-so...you won?" She cursed herself for sounding so young, so *timid*.

Something Ana didn't recognize flashed in Ethelron's eyes, and a muscle in his jaw twitched. Before she could wonder about it, his cool facade slid into place, and he smirked confidently at her. "I'm here. I've been searching for a way to get to you."

Ana raised a shaky hand to her face in an effort to gather herself before she spoke again. "This is...I think I need to sit down. Why don't we go upstairs, we...there is so much that we need to talk about." Ethelron tipped his head to the side, considering her in silence, before nodding. Ana pushed off of the desk and led the way upstairs, smiling to herself at the clicking of Siofra's nails as she padded along beside her master.

"I don't know how you lasted seventeen years in this realm...this place is so bizarre," Ethelron commented. Ana grinned, remembering how strange everything was to her when she first arrived.

"It takes some getting used to, but it's not all bad."

"I can see that. You seem to be quite comfortable passing as a *human*."

Ana tensed, halting just inside of her apartment and spinning to face him, hurt and anger flaring inside of her so suddenly that it caught her off guard. "Until ten minutes ago, as far as I knew, the only elves left were the ones who had been *lucky* enough to get out before Kali and her brother destroyed our realm. I had *no choice* but to pass as a human to survive here."

Ethelron hesitated at the top of the stairs. By the look in his eyes, he was just as surprised by her impassioned response as she had been herself. He raised a placating hand and stepped towards her. "I'm sorry, Ainadelothien...that was thoughtless of me to say."

Siofra settled herself against Ana's leg with a whine, and she couldn't fight the affectionate smile. "Lucky for you, just finding out that my realm still exists has left me feeling more forgiving than usual." She turned blue eyes to her friend, and her smile faded. Fear nearly stole her voice before she could continue. "My parents?"

"Alive."

Tears stung her eyes, and suddenly her lungs stopped cooperating with her brain. *Her parents were alive.* She *hadn't* lost all of her family...

A sharp pain in her hand startled Ana out of her thoughts. Sio had nipped her palm and was whining at her. Ethelron led her to her own sofa, his hands steady on her shoulders. "Breathe, Princess. Can't have you pass out on me. I don't know how any of your fancy technology in this realm works yet, remember? Some of us have been stuck in one realm for nearly two decades," he teased lightly. His thumbs were rubbing comforting circles into her collarbone, and she took several deep breaths to calm herself.

The laugh that bubbled up in her chest was breathy, and her hands grasped his wrists gently. "I'm okay, El. I just need some water. Would you like some?"

Without waiting for his answer, Ana lowered his hands back to his sides and maneuvered around him to the sink. She automatically pulled two glasses from the cupboard. A million thoughts raced through her head, and she dragged in several more deep breaths before turning back towards the living room. Ethelron had followed her, leaning against the doorway between the kitchen and the living room with his arms crossed casually. His face was an unreadable mask, his gaze tracking her movements. She settled her back against the counter and tried to take in every new aspect of him. *He was actually standing in her kitchen. He was* alive. Ethelron raised a curious brow, but he didn't interrupt her assessment.

He stood in dark green leather, layered over his chest and torso and shoulders, with sleek silver mail underneath. The buckles and embellishments identified the wearer as a warrior for her kingdom, and over his shoulder, Ana could see the hilt of his sword. The armor brought her back to the last day that she saw him. She remembered seeing him take a dagger to the exposed section of his arm between his gauntlet and spaulder and keep on fighting, fiercely determined as ever to protect the royal family. She'd lost sight of him shortly after that, and then she went through the portal and thought they lost him when he never followed behind her.

Now his gaze was harder, the old easiness between them gone. The additional runes covering his bare skin did nothing to lessen his intimidating look. Looping elven scrawl, protection runes, and moon glyphs worked their way up his neck and over one side of his face. "Do I need to worry about a jealous husband returning home?"

Ana nearly dropped the glass of water she'd been clinging to like a shield as she stared at him. Heat rushed up her neck and across her cheeks. Turning towards the sink to hide her flush, she shook her head firmly. "Not exactly easy to form honest, open relationships with most humans, particularly considering I will stay this age for quite a long time." Ethelron nodded stoically, and Ana had to shove down a wave of frustration.

"So, what exactly have you been doing with yourself all these years?" He asked, genuine curiosity clear in his voice. Once she was sure she'd regained her composure, she moved and settled herself into a chair at the table. Ethelron followed suit, not looking the least bit uncomfortable sitting in his armor. Elvish armor acted as a second skin, moving easily with the wearer, but remaining strong against attacks. It formed snugly around Ethelron's body, drawing her eye when she wasn't watching herself.

"Well, the portal that we came through, the same one that you found, opens into the office of this shop. The couple that owned it before me acted as protectors, intercepting beings that came through the portal to ensure that they did not mean harm to Sula. When I arrived, they took me under their wing, showed me the way things worked here. I learned as much as I could from them, and when they retired, they left the store to me. Mostly, anyone coming through the portal has been friendly. That has changed recently."

Ethelron nodded pensively. "How is Toron?"

The question was a punch to the gut. She'd known it would come, but that knowledge didn't ease the pain. She cleared her throat to force back the sudden lump that made breathing somewhat difficult. "Tell me about home," she insisted, her voice catching briefly. Ana recognized that he knew her too well to overlook the change of subject, but prayed that he would not push.

The prodding look in his eyes had her worried he would, but Ethelron broke the silence and began to tell her about the war. She could see him side-stepping different topics, but he recounted battles won and lost, and asked her more about the human realm. Time seemed to slip away as she held onto his every word.

.℮. .℮. .℮.

Erin woke on her sofa to the sound of a competitive cooking show playing in the background. Since Gabe died, she'd found it hard to be in a quiet apartment. The TV, that was hardly used before, was now on most hours just for noise.

Hardly able to sit up, she reached for the remote and hit the guide button so she could see the time. Seeing it was midnight, Erin decided she would go to *Mystifying* after a full night of sleep. But as she tried to move, her whole body screamed in pain. All her muscles were tight and her bones ached from her fall. Fear hit her hard. If the erebus returned, she wouldn't stand a chance. She *needed* to go to Ana right away.

Shuffling to her bathroom, Erin took two more pain pills and struggled to take in a full breath. Her body would heal; if it wasn't for her powers, she would at least be spending the night in the hospital, but the fae was afraid it would take far too long to heal for her liking. Ever since she'd failed to save Gabe, she'd struggled to control that power. She'd held it back from mending her wounds after their battle in Loinnir, and when she tried to test it once more, she'd had trouble drawing the warmth from inside. Her body still naturally healed quicker, but she couldn't just close her eyes and repair everything.

Erin drove to the store, all the while mentally playing out Ana's response to her showing up, unannounced, at such an ungodly hour, after avoiding the elf for months. Tension turned her stomach at the imagery. When she parked and saw that the main light to the store was still on, Erin grew wary. Ana had turned the sign to *closed* and hit most of the lights, but it was unlike her to leave the master switch on if she wasn't in the store. Erin tested the door and found she had at least locked up, so Erin went to the side stairwell for the apartment door. Every breath she drew in was a struggle, and each step sent a sharp pain lancing up her back. The steps went slowly, but the pain kept her from hesitating when she reached the door.

After two quick knocks, the door opened, and Ana faced her, shock quickly registering on her face. "I know, not who you were expecting, right? I'm sorry for the hour, but we *really* need to talk." When Ana didn't move to let her in, Erin turned to her frustration. "Listen *elf*, I was just thrown off the roof of my building. You can give me five seconds."

Erin pushed past, but stopped just inside the doorway when she saw a fully armored elf with dark hair and an array of tattoos standing in Ana's kitchen. Erin nearly started laughing at the unexpected sight, until an enormous wolf appeared and a low growl rumbled in its chest. She nearly jumped out of her skin at the sight of the beast. With a curse, she pressed herself against the wall and went utterly still. Flashes of her childhood flew into her mind until she didn't see the wolf any longer.

Instead, it was the dog from her foster home, being hit with a stick by one of the boys. Running toward her, teeth bared as the boy laughed. The pain of its teeth, the stitches, the nightmares she had for years. All of it came bubbling to the surface. Her chest tightened and her next breath was little more than a wheeze.

"Siofra." The male elf spoke calmly. The wolf stopped growling, but still looked ready to attack.

"Erin?" Ana touched her arm gently, but Erin couldn't take her eyes off the wolf.

"What the *hell* is that thing doing in your house?"

"I might ask the same question about you." The strange elf gave her a hard look, and Erin's confidence came flooding back as anger towards him replaced her fear of his *beast* pet.

"What exactly is *that* supposed to mean?"

"Erin," Ana cut in sharply, "what were you saying about being thrown off your roof?" Ana demanded attention with her tone as she stepped between Erin and her *guests*.

"Listen, I know you don't want me here, and clearly I'm *interrupting* something. I need Melody."

"She's not here. *What happened?*"

"Princess, who is this, and who is Melody?" The male cut in, sounding irritated that he didn't understand what was going on.

"What, did you send her away for your *date*? Do elves hang socks on the door handles?" Erin easily ignored him, crossing her arms over her chest, doing her best to shut out the pain that spread along her back at the movement.

"Erin, no, *she's* the one on a date. Why don't you just *tell me* what is going on?" Erin hated that she noticed a red flush form behind Ana's ears. The same thing would happen to Gabe when she was irritating him.

"I need Melody to do a spell on this amulet and tell me what it is. I've looked all over and I can't find anything about it. And now, I have some mobster erebus showing up and trying to kill me in order to get it. Since when do you let Melody stay out this late?" In all the time she'd known the two of them, Melody never seemed to have a life outside of school and being a witch.

"It's not that late," Ana glanced at the clock and surprise flashed over her features. Erin watched the elf search for her phone and when she looked up, her face was pale. "She would have texted or called me."

"*Who. Is. Melody?*" Ana's new friend bit out the words and was again ignored as Ana held the phone to her ear. Erin slowly moved as close to the door as she could get, giving herself as much space away from the wolf as possible now that Ana wasn't standing between them. Who the hell just had a *pet wolf*, anyway? Erin only pulled her gaze from the beast when Ana sat her phone down without having reached

Melody. Something was truly wrong, and Melody's absence suddenly took on a life of its own.

Chapter Four

Melody woke to a pounding head and a memory of the worst date in the history of dates. She moved slowly, finding her hands tied to chains anchored in the floor. She was in some kind of warehouse. At the center of the room, she saw an erebus sigil painted on the ground with what looked very much like blood. A quick glance showed her no one was around, so she stood to get a better look, pulling her chain until there was no more give. It looked like a "G" and "J" with a circle on one line. She closed her eyes and tried to remember the page of erebi runes.

"We will summon Hismael once we gather the rest." Liam's voice sounded from behind her. Melody turned and found Liam standing next to a woman in high heels and a skin-tight black dress. If

Erin were there, she would probably say something snarky about being a cliché.

Melody didn't care about being snarky, she just wanted answers. Starting with why the first date she went on ended up with her in chains, in an abandoned warehouse. Instead she went with something more practical. "The rest of what?"

"The rest of our offering, you are only one of many," the woman said, draping her long auburn hair over one shoulder.

"Liam, what is going on?"

"You think I didn't notice? I can *feel* the power radiating off of you. I spent most of the semester watching you, watching your little group of witches get together. Now it's time to actually use your powers for something worthwhile, like pleasing our master so he gifts us with his good will." Liam lifted his shirt and showed a tattoo of the same sigil from the floor inked onto his skin.

"Liam, this isn't a joke. Erebi are real and they rarely keep their word. You are going to get yourself killed."

"I was gifted eternal life for my last sacrifice. Now it is Liam's turn." The woman leaned forward until she sat in front of Melody. "You are so sweet to worry, but Liam is taken. He just did what he had to in order to get you here."

"That's fine. You can have him. Idiots should stick together." *Okay, maybe she wasn't completely above snarky comments.* Melody fell silent as a small group of men in shrouds entered, each with a girl struggling in his arms. They all had the same band around their wrists, and Melody realized it was blocking their powers, which explained why she felt foggy. One girl yanked herself free before her captor could react. The red-head threw out a hand and hurled a burst of fire toward the girl. She stopped just in time to avoid getting burned, but the man behind her took the opportunity to grab hold of her once more.

"Keep control! Their powers are blocked; it's not that hard!"

"Yes, Hela!" The man jerked the girl onward and found an open set of chains to tie her to.

Apparently, eternal life was not all Hismael gifted her with. Liam grabbed her arm and pulled Hela into a passionate kiss, making Melody's stomach turn. His eyes were wide open and staring directly at her, and he flashed a wink when he caught her looking. If she could, she would scrub her lips free of any trace of his touch. Hela moaned against his lips and Melody looked away, trying to find an escape. Then it hit her: Hismael, The Acquirer. He was one of the ancients. He had his wings ripped away after he failed to collect something. Melody remembered reading that he went crazy after they stripped him. Who knew what he would be capable of? She needed to get out of her chains before they summoned him and set him loose on the humans.

.℘ .℘ .℘

"I'm not getting any response from Melody," Ana huffed, tossing her phone to the table. Siofra flinched at the loud clatter and gave a dissatisfied grumble. Out of the corner of her eye, Ana noticed fresh tension in Erin's posture. When she'd first seen Erin on the other side of her door, she almost didn't recognize her. She'd lost weight, but it was clear she'd also gained some muscle. Dark circles framed her hazel eyes - which were almost a solid brown - like she forgot the word sleep, but her hair was the most startling difference. Ever since she first met Erin, the fae always had an extreme haircut and color. Now, it looked like she'd let her hair grow out over the past few months so that it rested just below her shoulders, a dark brown color that was likely natural.

Seeing how Erin eyed Siofra reminded her of a conversation she and Gabe had while he'd been telling her about his life as a human. Gabe shed light on his girlfriend's past, telling a story of cruel foster brothers and an angry dog. Erin's discomfort suddenly made perfect sense. Ana shifted to settle down in the chair that put her between Sio and Erin.

"How the hell are we supposed to find her?" Erin muttered. Ana caught how she winced when she tried to settle in the chair next to her, as far away from Sio as she could get.

"I actually have a simple solution for that," Ana said. "After everything that happened with you, Melody and I got matching runes that, with a spell, will lead me right to her."

Erin looked away at the mention of the incident that led to Gabe's death. Grief flared in Ana's chest, and she could see the same reaction in the fae. "Well, I guess that's a smart move."

Ana sighed at the bitterness in her voice. "I want *all* of us to have them so that we can protect each other more effectively. If it hadn't been for Sinopa-"

"*Stop*. Don't go there. Just...*don't*." Erin snapped at the mention of the fae who died in order to give them time to save Erin. Siofra stood at the sudden tension in the room, but Ana laid a comforting hand on the wolf's head. She murmured softly to Sio in Elvish, and the wolf settled beside Ethelron once more.

"I hate to interrupt, but I did not simply come here to chat, Princess," Ethelron interjected evenly.

Erin nearly growled as she turned to glare at him. "Look, pal, I'm sure Ana is happy to see you - *whoever you are* - but our situation is a bit more pressing right now."

Ana settled a calming hand on Erin's shoulder, doing her best to ignore how Erin flinched away from her touch. "Okay, let's take a step back and calm down. Erin, this is Ethelron. He was my guardian in Eloas." Erin's eyebrows shot up in surprise. "El, this is Erin. She is half-human, half-fae." She considered explaining their initial connection, but was not prepared to explain Gabe - *Toron*, just yet. "Melody is a human witch, and she is under my care. She was supposed to be home by now, so we need to find her to make sure that everything is okay. We can talk more after we find her."

Ethelron pushed himself away from the doorway. His focus landed on Erin, and the woman squirmed under his scrutiny. "We should leave the halfling behind if we are to go after your witch. She will slow us down with her injuries."

"Hey!" Erin barked indignantly, fury etched into the word. Siofra growled, the hair rising along her spine, until Ana moved from her seat to crouch in front of the wolf. She gave Siofra a low, stern command, once again in Elvish. The fae released a shaky breath when Sio whimpered and rolled onto her back submissively. "What did you just tell her?"

Ana rose to her full height once more, rubbing Sio's ear once the wolf sat up as praise for her obedience. "That you are not a threat to me or her master, so she is to treat you as one of our 'pack'. I apologize for her aggression. She will not harm you."

Once Erin nodded stiffly, Ana turned her attention to Ethelron, her protectiveness over Erin bringing out her fierce nature once more. Ethelron raised an eyebrow at her, dutiful respect and amusement warring on his face.

"I know you've been cut off from the other realms for a long time, but that gives you *no right* to disrespect the people that I care about."

The sharp tone of her voice chased any amusement from his face, and he bowed his head respectfully. "Apologies, Princess," he murmured sincerely. "To you as well, Erin." Ana glanced back at the fae and cracked a wry grin at the surprise on her face at his abrupt change.

"El, you know how much I hate when you call me that and actually *mean* it," she insisted, letting him know that he was forgiven.

"And *you* know that my duty to you and your family has been ingrained in me, *Highness*." He smirked at her exasperation. His sharp gaze then turned to Erin. "Perhaps I can help?"

"What?" Ana raised a curious eyebrow at him.

"I can help her, heal the worst of her injury."

"You can heal?" Ana whispered against the tightening in her chest.

"We haven't been idle for the last seventeen years, Aina." Her old nickname slipped from his lips, his tone soft. "I will take care of the halfling while you prepare the spell. The sooner the witch is safe, the sooner we can go."

"Go?"

"Just prepare the spell. Let's deal with one thing at a time." Ana turned to Erin, waiting for her agreement to Ethelron healing her.

"We need to find Mel." Erin nodded. Ana stood, moving away from the table so Ethelron could take her place. She watched, entranced, as he closed his eyes and began to work. She wondered about Erin. Ana had seen her heal more than one injury during their training, and knew she should have been able to heal herself. Yet, the halfling still bore a scar across her cheek and was half bent over in pain. She wanted to ask Erin why she hadn't, or *couldn't,* heal herself more thoroughly, but was afraid of the answer. Fae were emotionally attuned to their powers, and Ana could certainly think of a reason Erin may have lost control of her healing. She thought back to her mother, one of the strongest healers in Eloas.

"How did you manage to do this, Tor?" Faervel, the elven queen, chastised her son gently. Aina wrung her hands, guilt tearing at her for letting him get hurt.

"It's my fault, Mama."

"Oh no, my dear. Your little brother must accept responsibility for disobeying and running off; isn't that right, Toron?" The curly-haired boy pouted but nodded solemnly. The queen smiled affectionately and took his bleeding arm in both hands. Aina watched as tendrils of smoke danced around the wound before the skin knitted itself together.

"I won't hurt her, Aina." Ethelron's low voice drew her from the memory. She could feel his gaze tracking every emotion as she battled back her grief. Even after years apart, Ana felt like he could read her like an open book. Melody often seemed to have the same ability, but feeling Ethelron watch her, knowing all the little nuances of elven emotion, set her on edge.

She nodded, tucking away memories of her brother. Melody could very well be in danger, and she was not about to let something else happen on her watch. She hurried downstairs to get the candle she needed for the spell. Sio followed, nearly silent but for the soft tap of her nails against hardwood. By the time she returned, Ethelron was just finishing up, and Erin looked much more comfortable. Ethelron stood from the table, returning to his post in the doorway so Ana could sit down.

Ana removed the ring suppressing her elven nature and set it down. She heard Ethelron chuckle softly, and when she turned to question him, he was smirking. "Much better, Princess." Ana rolled her eyes at him with a smile of her own before becoming serious once more.

"Okay, here goes nothing."

Erin lit the candle for Ana, who held it in the palm of her right hand. On the inside of the same wrist, an intricate design of an eye began to glow, becoming brighter as she chanted the incantation to enact the tracking magic. A single bright pulse signaled the completion of the spell, and Ana hissed as the tattoo burned intensely. The candle flickered out, and suddenly she knew *exactly* where to find Melody.

"Cool trick," Erin commented.

"Looks like I'm not the only one with new talents," Ethelron mused.

"Now for my next trick," she crowed, waving her arms dramatically, and then uttered a brief incantation. Ethelron shook his head, but sucked in a sharp breath as they watched things *change*.

His hand flew to his ear, and he growled. "What did you do?" The women glanced at each other, and for a moment, the pain between them faded as she and Erin shared an amused grin.

"Just made sure you'd blend in out there. *Now*...time to get our girl back."

℘ ℘ ℘

Doyle woke in a cold sweat, his head pounding. *Briar*. The headache was just fading when the rune gave the slight burn to let him know Briar was up and about. *Now what?* Doyle rose and stretched, his muscles sore from the workout he'd done earlier. He'd sparred with a few others he knew, using the time to assess how they felt about the queen and Lyra. There wasn't a positive response about either woman, but it was only a small sampling, and the time hadn't been wasted. He'd gotten other names of those that hated the queen, too. Despite using sparring as an excuse to talk about the queen, the fights had been real, and his body was feeling the few hits he'd taken in the process.

There was no going back to bed, however, when he knew Briar had a vision and was now wandering around. He stripped down so he could grab fresh clothes, and had just pulled his pants on when there was a soft knock at the door. He felt her standing on the other side and froze. She'd never come here. He'd never shown her where he slept, and she'd never asked. He knew she probably just *felt* for him and followed the rune, but it was still odd to know she was *right there*.

"Doyle?" Her voice was unsure and muffled behind the thick door. What had she seen to make her seek him out? He moved then, worry coursing through him, and swung open the door. Her eyes widened when she glimpsed him. He still wasn't wearing a shirt, and he knew the scar on his face was matched by others across his chest and back. Years of fighting had earned him more than his share of battle wounds. It took a moment for her big purple eyes to look up to meet his, but she still didn't speak.

"Is everything okay?" He opened his door wider and motioned for her to come in. Once he closed the door behind her, he pulled out a shirt and threw it on over his head. It felt odd to turn around and find her standing there. No one ever came into his room, not even Lyra. If she wanted to speak with him, she just summoned him and expected him to come to her. Briar was looking around curiously, though he knew there wasn't much to see. There wasn't much difference between their rooms, even though he'd spent a lifetime in his.

"Yes..." She shifted her weight between her feet and he realized she was going to need a little more time to open up. He sat on the end of his bed and motioned for her to take the chair at his desk. "I...I

68

need some rare ingredients. Would you know where I can find some?" She wouldn't meet his eye, staring off into the corner of his room instead. Doyle felt trouble brewing, but if she needed something, he'd do what he could to make sure she got it. He owed her that, and so much more.

"I may know someone. Do you know what you need?" Her eyes flicked up to his. She handed over a folded piece of paper, crumpled from how tightly she'd held it in her fist. He looked it over and felt some pressure in his chest. *What was she doing?* "I can see what I can do. How quickly do we need it?"

"As soon as you can get it. There isn't much time."

"I'll wait until you are ready to tell me. I'm sure you have to work something out in your head before you can share, but can you tell me, is it for Malux?" Briar gave a quick nod. "Will it save him?"

"I think so."

"And that's what's best for the overall picture?"

Something crossed her features that he couldn't quite figure out. Then her eyes met his and held for a few long breaths. "I'm not sure. I just feel like I need to do it." Honesty. It wasn't something he expected. She could have told him yes, they needed to do it, and she'd know for sure he'd help her. But she was letting him know saving Malux could ruin their plans. She wasn't sure, and if they were going to save him, they didn't have time for her to have more visions to see where it would lead.

"Okay," he stood and held out his hand to her, "let's get moving." She hesitated before placing her small palm in his. Her skin always felt like a cool breeze.

"I can come with you?"

"Sure, just make sure you stick close to me. We'll be going deeper in the caves, and many of the creatures we'll pass are not friendly."

"I'll do my best."

He locked his room but kept her hand tucked in his. She didn't pull away, and it was calming to touch her. He wondered what it felt like for her, if the contact was mutually soothing. When he glanced sideways at her, she was chewing her lip and clearly working through something in her mind.

"Do you think you'd be able to go to Eloas?" She asked as they moved their way through a maze of corridors. They were traveling deeper into the mountain, and he could feel the air change. He wondered how she'd do since she preferred to be out in the open as much as possible. She'd told him how she felt the pressure of the surrounding earth; it was only going to get worse as they kept walking. She kept her pace steady with his, and didn't complain.

"I would just need permission from Lyra. As long as I tell her it will help our cause I don't see why not."

"The group will be there soon. I saw the halfling and someone new. If you could go, you could give the cure to Malux, maybe you could make the group's passage easier, make sure they don't have trouble with other erebi, and then bring Malux back..." She chewed her lip again. "I think we'll need to hide him somewhere."

"Why would he need to be hidden?"

"Because if this works how I think the vision was showing me, he'll die and you'll bring him back. We should just let everyone think he stayed dead."

"Briar," he stopped then and turned so he could face her, "what exactly did you see? I'll help you, I promise. I just need to know what we are looking at here."

"I see him die, but then his eyes open and you are standing behind him. I saw the vial in your hand and the ingredients. He dies, but as long as you get to him in time, you can bring him back. I talked to him Doyle; he is tied to the queen, and the only way to break his bond is for him to die. If he dies and then we bring him back, then those ties should be broken. He'd be free to help us. But if she finds out he's still alive, she'll do whatever dark magic she did before to connect them again. He said he can watch us go against her, but he cannot disobey a direct order from her. If he was ordered to kill me, he wouldn't be able to ignore the order, but once he dies..."

"You think he'll willingly come to our side if we sever that connection?" He always knew the queen had something over him, but he hadn't realized black magic actually tied them together. That would explain why he stood aside when he caught them breaking into the queen's room. Also, why he helped them after stealing the amulet but was now fighting so hard to retrieve it. It made sense.

"He has no love for Lyra. She doesn't go out of her way to make friends, but he wants to bring down the queen more than even Lyra does. I don't think he'll be helping us put Lyra on the throne, but he'll help rip Flereous *off*."

"Okay. Did you see anything else about the group?"

"Not really, just a flash of them. I know they will be there. Maybe if you are there, you can help make sure they get to where they are going. It won't help us if any of them are hurt."

He gave a curt nod and turned to lead them through the tunnels again. They would need a safe place to hide Malux until the time was right to use him. There was no guarantee that even if he brought him back, and the ties were severed, that Malux *would* help. It was possible Malux would just make a run for it, being "dead" and all. Either way, though, Doyle would help him. They'd get the ingredients, and he'd go to Eloas to make sure Malux could make his choice.

"Thank you, Doyle." He liked the way she said his name. Her voice had a musical lilt to it, and his name always seemed to roll off her tongue. It was an odd thought to cross his mind, but he couldn't quite shake it now that it was there.

"For what?"

"For trusting me, and helping me."

"Is there a reason I shouldn't trust you?" He said it in jest, but her hand flinched in his, drawing his eyes to her. She turned and gave him a grin. "Well, I have seen you die a lot. I think that shows a lot about a person. It's like I know all of your darkest secrets."

"Is that so? If that's the case, then I wish I had some more interesting secrets for you to delve into." It didn't escape him how she'd tried to jest after the small flinch. He was going out on a limb to help her with Malux; Lyra would certainly not be happy about it if she found out, but he knew she wanted to bring the queen down also, so she could help her realm.

"It's through here." They would have to duck down in order to get into the small cove he gestured towards. He waited for Briar to balk at the small space, but as usual, she surprised him by not even blinking in hesitation. He took a firmer grip on her, knowing the floor slanted, and the stone was slippery. She was light on her feet, though, and while she held onto him, she never slipped while his own feet seemed to slide down the smooth stones. He ducked down into another room and she followed. The room smelled of smoke and stale air. Candles flickered along the perimeter, giving the impression that the walls were moving from the way the light danced and reflected.

"Horace?"

"Humph?" The grunt came from the shadowed part of the room at the far corner. Horace rose from his seated position, his face catching some of the candlelight. Briar flinched when she saw him. He was not an attractive erebus, Doyle had to admit. His skin was slick and pale, his nose bulbous and pock-marked. He had yellow eyes that reflected the light and made one feel ill when looking into them. But the man could procure almost anything, and much of what Briar sought was in his stores.

Doyle released Briar and retrieved the piece of paper from his pocket, unfolding it before handing it over. "I was hoping you'd be able to help us with this list?"

Horace took the paper but didn't look at it right away. Instead, he looked between them, and then his eyes rested on Briar. Part of Doyle wanted to stand in front of her, protect her from view, but then he felt silly for thinking about it. Horace was harmless, even if he didn't look it. "She's new and powerful. You're rare; few have your power, *observer.*"

Briar's purple gaze snapped to the collector. She opened her mouth, but nothing came out. Horace didn't wait for a response, though. Instead, he gave another grunt and held the paper up to the light so he could see. Briar turned wide eyes back to him, and Doyle gave a little shrug.

"Yes, I have what you need. But I'll need some sort of payment for such rare ingredients."

"Did you have something in mind?" Doyle knew there would be a payment. There always was, but Horace never asked for the same thing twice. Nor did he ask for something that was impossible to retrieve, even if it might be something extremely difficult to give up.

"Did you know a spell can be done with the blood of an observer that can allow a person to glimpse into the future?" He continued on without giving space for either to answer. "Not many do. Even if someone came across the spell, observers are so rare, they wouldn't usually bother to think any more about it. But here is one standing before me." Horace held up a hand before either Doyle or Briar could protest. "It doesn't take much; if you'd allow me to take two vials, that would be enough for multiple spells, and I would be extremely grateful."

"Okay." Briar's voice was quiet, but she didn't hesitate. Doyle reached out and grabbed her arm, pulling her close.

"How are you planning on taking these two vials of blood, exactly?"

Horace gave a small shake of his head and a little smile. "A little human contraption I have. One little prick of her arm and I can fill my two vials."

"It's fine. You ask little for what we require. I appreciate your help." Briar sat in the seat Horace nodded to, and they left Doyle to stand by and watch as Horace leaned over her and did his work. He pricked her arm, and Doyle watched as the blood flowed into one vial and then the other. Horace topped them off quickly and then removed the needle. "Thank you, my dear."

A small drop of blood rose from the prick in her arm, but she reached over and held her finger to it for a minute. When she pulled away, there was only a small smear to show anything had happened. Horace went into the shadow where Doyle knew there was another doorway, which led to his collection. Once he disappeared with their list, Doyle took the moment to crouch before Briar. "Are you okay?"

"Sure, it didn't really hurt. I'd like it very much if we never told Lyra there is a spell to see the future and all she needs is my blood, though." She gave a little smile, but his heart clenched. He'd like to think Lyra wouldn't just use her as a blood bank so she could see the future for herself, but something told him if Lyra found out about such a spell, she'd be first in line to do more than a little prick to Briar's arm in order to make it happen. In fact, she'd probably be furious about all the blood spilled that they wasted by letting it fall to the stone. He couldn't really form a response past the lump in his throat, so he just nodded in silence instead.

Horace returned with a small covered basket. He sat it down and opened the lid so they could see the multiple vials contained inside. "Everything on your list." He raised a brow and looked between them once more. It looked like he was about to say something, but then gave a silent shake of his head, and handed Doyle the basket. "It was lovely doing business with the two of you. Visit me anytime."

"Thank you, Horace." Doyle let Briar lead the way while he took careful steps with the basket in his arms. They returned to Briar's room, and he watched in silence as Briar mixed up the ingredients into a larger vial. It turned a purple hue after she swirled it, and she grinned.

"You saw the whole spell in your vision?"

"I had to concentrate, but I saw it. I went into the vision looking for something in particular, so it helped me navigate. Like when I was trying to find the amulet. Do you think you'll be able to follow Malux into Eloas?"

"I have something else in mind. I'll come check on you later. I have a few things to take care of."

"Okay. Thank you again, Doyle."

"You can thank me once it's all over." Doyle left her and the potion safe in her room while he went in search of Lyra. He knew if they were going to pull this off; he was going to need one more thing for the trip, and it was going to take a bit of convincing to get Lyra to agree.

Chapter Five

Melody watched the rune on her wrist lighten in color. The tightness in her chest loosened, knowing that Ana was tracking her; she could only hope she would get there in time. Five other girls were now chained to the ground, their cries and screams keeping her unhelpful company. She did her best to block them out and focused on Hela, Liam, and the other men. It seemed the men were just there for muscle; Melody wasn't sure if they'd each captured their own girl to bring, or if Liam had drawn all of them out. She didn't recognize any of them from her Wicca group or any of her classes, but they all looked to be in their early twenties, and Melody could only assume they all had powers of some sort.

When Hela walked out with candles, she tensed. She *could* not let them start the ritual. Liam was creating the protection circle around the signal, so Melody called out to him. "So what, Hela just used you to get a bunch of girls together for her? She received immortality and powers already. What does she get this time?"

Liam smirked and fell for it, moving to stand over her. "She gets *me*. She's been alive for over eighty years, waiting to find someone like me to spend the rest of eternity with. Now that she has, she wants to call Hismael once more."

"I don't see it. I mean, I kissed you too, and she could definitely do better."

"I think you are just a little jealous; it's okay, I've heard virgins can get that way about the men that they like." He patted her head like a child and started walking away.

"You've been mistaken. I'm no virgin, so if that is necessary for this little gift basket to your friend, you might want another plan."

"Do you have any idea how hard it is to find virgins in this day and age? Add to the fact that they need to have an inkling of power in them." Liam shook his head. At least he was wasting time talking to her once more. "But you, my dear," he reached out to stroke her cheek, "were an easy mark. I've never seen someone get as flustered as you did when I asked for your number. All I had to do was give you the smallest push, and you were falling all over yourself. It's a shame I won't have time to show you what that body of yours can do."

His words shouldn't have hurt her, but they did. Deep down, she knew he was right. She'd been eating out of the palm of his hand.

She should have known better, but she'd let him get the better of her. Hela called him, so Liam left her and returned to his work. He finished with the circle and Hela surrounded it with candles, lighting each one as she went. Melody tried once more to pull some power from within, but the enchanted band around her wrist held all her powers at bay. If Ana didn't get there soon, Hismael would be summoned, and they would face a much bigger challenge than breaking her out of there and freeing the rest of the girls.

.℮ .℮ .℮

"Can you sit still?" Ana groaned as Ethelron twitched in the seat beside her. Erin watched the two from the backseat and wondered what their relationship was, *exactly*. Ethelron was having issues dealing with the changes in himself from Ana's spell, and spent the entire drive reacting to every sound and touching the top curve of his ears.

"So what, did you two date or something back in the good old days?" Ethelron tensed, and Ana's knuckles turned white.

"No, Erin. And we are about to walk into who knows what, so maybe we should just focus on getting Melody out of whatever danger she is in right now."

"Trust me, I know how your rescues go." Erin's eyes filled with tears as she sat back in her seat. She shouldn't have said that. She knew immediately after the words left her lips. Erin hurt herself with the memory, and she'd hurt Ana too, but there was no taking them back. Ana sighed deeply, but didn't argue with her, which only made it worse. Ethelron glanced at Ana, who refused to look back at him. It didn't seem he knew about Gabe.

"You didn't have to come," Ana whispered. The wolf whined at Erin's side, and Erin nearly jumped out of her skin at the sound. She had not been a happy camper when the wolf tried to climb into the car with them, but it seemed she and the elf were a package deal. Unfortunately, with his freakish elven height, Ethelron didn't fit in the small back seat of Ana's car, and Ana was the one with the built in tracking device, which left Erin to sit with the beast. Before they left, Ana placed a hand on her fur and told her something elvish and assured Erin that she wouldn't move, which - so far - had been true.

"Of course I did. I came to you and Melody for help. I wouldn't just sit by knowing Melody is in danger." *She's worth saving.* Erin just wished she could go back and stop Ana and Gabe from coming to save her. If Ana had listened when she told them to go back, Gabe would still be alive. He could be getting to know his sister and building the life he'd always deserved. "The points aren't going to come back until Ana lifts the spell. Just stop already," Erin lashed out when Ethelron reached up to touch his ear again. As she watched him, a conversation with Ana resurfaced. Ana had told her of a man she'd had feelings for but had never confessed to before she lost him with the rest of her realm. "Wait a minute...*he* is the one you told me about, from when you were young, before-"

"*What*?! No...definitely *not*, I-" As if realizing that the more she protested, the worse the implication, the elf's mouth snapped shut. A vibrant blush colored her ears, growing brighter when her *former guardian* stared at her quizzically. Ana cleared her throat, and Erin had to smother another taunt. Ana was far too easy a target right now, and this was not the time to joke about love lives.

"This must be it." Ana, abruptly donning a mask of seriousness - one that Erin assumed she'd only been able to master because of her time as a princess - pulled into a dark street with a large abandoned building taking up most of the block. *Convenient timing*, the fae thought to herself as she watched her friend completely ignore the questioning looks from both of her companions. With a final smirk, Erin redirected her own attention to the admittedly serious matter of heading into danger to save Melody.

"Of course it is, abandoned building in the worst part of town..." Erin opened her door when the car stopped. "So, can we all agree that Melody is grounded from dating in the near future?"

"Do you feel that?" Ethelron spoke up as he climbed out of the car, Siofra leaping out after him.

The air was heavy, like a cloud had settled over them. Then the ground under them shifted and nearly sent Erin to her knees. Ana grabbed her arm and steadied her just in time. "Earthquake?"

"Something much worse." Ana took off running, followed by Ethelron.

"Why doesn't anyone just give a straight answer anymore?" Erin ran after them until they found a door on the other side.

"Remove the spell." Ethelron's voice had a demanding edge to it that seemed to surprise Ana. "There is a fight waiting for us, you *know* that spell changes the way we move and hear. I need to be able to protect you."

"*Don't* try to protect me. We just need to get Melody out of there," Ana argued, even as she reached out to reverse the charm. Ana slipped her own charmed ring from her finger and the two exchanged a silent nod. Then Ethelron was busting through the door, and their small group ran inside.

The screams of women echoed through the building, and Erin wondered how they hadn't heard them from outside. But her gaze wasn't on the women chained around the room. It was on the center, where the floor seemed to have opened up and given birth to twelve feet of *ugly*. Black pits for eyes, and what looked like long tentacles hung around where a mouth should be. On his head stood a crown of bones. The body was large and muscular, with arms like tree trunks and claws that quickly reminded her of the infection erebi. But he stood alone. He was nothing like the erebi she had come across so far. This creature was *pure* erebus. An erebus of old. He turned his back, revealing clear markings of wings that had been ripped from his body.

"What in the hell is that?" Erin whispered in shock. Siofra gave a low growl at their feet and her fur fluffed out to make her look larger. Erin didn't even flinch at the wolf's appearance; all her fear was concentrated in one direction.

"Where is Melody?" Ana's voice grew desperate as they searched the faces of the girls, but didn't see her right away.

"She must be on the other side." Ethelron nodded to the other side of the large erebus.

"I don't remember inviting guests." A woman appeared, her eyes dancing with fire. "Take care of them." She absently flicked fingers in their direction. "Liam, bring me the first one!" The woman didn't seem too worried about their presence; the reason became clear when five men came from the corners of the warehouse and started toward them.

"Humans. I got them. You get the girls free!" Erin jumped in front of the others and grinned. She had a few frustrations to work out. Ethelron seemed skeptical, but Erin reached down to touch the ground at their feet, and the concrete rose up before the men, blocking them from getting to the elves. Ana darted past as a man appeared, pushing a struggling girl toward the erebus.

Siofra rushed forward, grabbing the woman's attention, who turned on the approaching elves. With a cry of fury, electricity sprung from her fingers and shot out at them. They were both able to move out of the way without getting hit, but the air burned with the smell of it. "Free them. I've got her." Ethelron drew his sword and started toward the witch, not leaving Ana with the chance to argue.

Erin made sure the men could not break free from the thorny vines tying them together. For good measure, she brought a circle of earth above their heads so they couldn't climb out, even if they did somehow slip the binding. She left the top uncovered; as much as she wanted to bury them, she couldn't kill the humans. She already experienced once with Bogor how quickly darkness could overwhelm the soul. Siofra reached the man - Liam - pushing one of the young women, and her jaws clamped down on his ankle. He lost his grip just long enough for his would-be victim to kick her leg out and unwittingly break the circle around the erebus. Two other girls raced past her and out of the building as Ana freed them. Ana was just about to disappear around the ancient being, hopefully to find Melody, when the erebus let out a roar of freedom.

"Hela!" Liam called when the beast started toward the red-head. Ethelron froze in his tracks as the whole world seemed to pause. The erebus had broken free from his circle. Nothing else mattered. Liam released the struggling girl in his arms and ran toward the witch. She grabbed hold of him and quickly backed away from where the erebus stood. Two long strides later, however, the erebus hovered over them. "I am Hela! I brought you my sacrifice. You have blessed me with life and power. I am forever grateful!" Then she pushed the man out in front of her and ran. The erebus didn't pause; his claws dug into the man's chest. He pulled out a heart, and his tentacles reached out to grab it and shove it into its mouth. Erin let out a quiet curse as she watched, unable to blink or look away.

Everyone kicked into high gear then. Ethelron grabbed Hela before she could get away. "Send him back!" He shook her when she just stared at him in fear. "How do you send him back?"

"My-my book!" She pointed, and Ethelron dragged her over to it. Erin rushed ahead to release the rest of the girls and met Ana in the middle, standing there with Melody.

"Go, help her finish the incantation to send him back. We can't let him get out of here!" Erin pushed Melody forward before sending the concrete and ground into the air before the erebus. He turned toward them, and Ana and Erin took separate routes to draw him away from the witches and their spell. Ethelron threw his sword and struck the erebus's arm. Ana moved quickly and retrieved the sword, tossing it back to the other elf with ease, and Erin gaped as they seemed to do a well-rehearsed dance. They each moved on either side of the beast and kept drawing his attention away. Siofra joined in, circling around his feet.

"Erin, fix the circle." Melody tossed her a container, drawing her attention away from the fight happening before her.

She ran to the gaping hole in the floor and started to recreate the circle while the two witches ran forward. Melody began to re-light the candles while Hela continued to chant. Erin finished her part. "Now what?"

"We have to get him back in." Melody's eyes were wide.

"Okay, just keep her chanting and be ready to re-seal the circle if we break it getting him in." Erin shoved the container into her hands, rushed toward the elves, and told them what they needed to do.

"El?" Ana called over and a silent conversation seemed to pass between them. The dance continued as they drew the erebus toward the circle. He didn't seem to want to go near the hole that would send him back to his corner of hell, so he lashed out an arm and hit Ethelron square in the chest, knocking him to the ground. Siofra gave a low growl and lunged at the arm, taking hold with her jaws and refusing to let go, even as the erebus shook her. Ana stabbed him from the side, trying to draw his attention. Erin sent a large piece of concrete hurtling into the erebus' chest. Ethelron was back on his feet, and with a short whistle, Siofra released her hold. Ethelron didn't hesitate; he ran straight into the beast, knocking him off balance, and Ana used the moment to send the erebus falling back. Melody dashed forward to re-salt where his feet dragged, and the erebus was sealed within his trap once more.

Hela's voice halted, but Melody grabbed her wrist. "Send him back, or one of my friends will throw you in with him and *I'll* send you *both*!" Erin gaped at Melody in awe, wishing she was close enough to high-five.

Hela pulled her wrist free and finished the chant. The second her words stopped, the earth rumbled again, and the erebus was sucked into the ground. Then, Hela began screaming, and the book fell to her feet. Erin watched in fascinated horror as the witch grew old right before their eyes. She fell to her knees, while Melody looked down at her aged figure with disgust. She grabbed the book from in front of her, lit it on fire with a candle, and threw it into the pit before it sealed.

.℮ .℮ .℮

Briar was only just waking when she heard a small knock at her door. She could feel Doyle's energy, and wondered if he'd come to say goodbye before leaving to trail after Malux. She opened the door and his eyes turned up to her hair. An actual smile pulled up at his lips, making his eyes a little brighter. "Did I wake you, Blue?"

"No, I was awake, just not *out* of bed yet." She connected what he was looking at and reached up to touch her hair. "How bad is it?" She asked, trying to run her fingers through the tangles.

"It's perfect, actually." She could *hear* the smile in his voice this time.

"Ugh, come in." She turned away and went to the small mirror over the desk. Her blue locks were sticking up in every direction. She didn't have a brush, so she just combed her fingers through and tried to fix what sleep had done.

Doyle came into view in the small mirror, his features amused as their eyes met through the glass. Something in his gaze made her heart race and her hands fell to her sides.

"Are you leaving soon?" she asked through a sudden lump in her throat. She turned away and started idly braiding her hair to the side.

"Well, I have some news. I am leaving soon, but not quite yet. I was wondering if you would like to go for a walk with me?"

"Are you leading me to some trap or something? Trading some of my blood for votes for Lyra?"

"No telling how the day will end." He gave an easy shrug, and she couldn't get over how his eyes were dancing today. Briar nodded that she'd go, and he held out an elbow for her to loop her arm through. She hadn't eaten yet and was a little hungry now that she was up and moving, but she doubted their walk would last too long. She was guessing he wanted to ask more questions about Malux so he would know what to expect when he left the realm. Doyle led her down a path she hadn't taken before and the air turned cold and wet as they traveled deeper into the mountain. Though she moved with ease over the smooth stone, Doyle pulled her tight against him, and even his thick-soled boots seemed to slide against dampness with every other step. She heard the water before she could see it.

Doyle must have noticed a change in her, because he gave her a small smile. She could get used to him smiling at her. Finally, they came to a cavern and she actually let out a little gasp, releasing his arm so she could walk in deeper. The ceiling opened above them, and a waterfall cascaded from the sky to a pool at their feet.

"Don't touch the water." Doyle warned, stopping her in her tracks.

"Do I want to know why?"

"It's beautiful, but poisonous." He walked to a spot where the wall jutted out near the floor and sat, pulling out a basket from under the natural stone bench. "Are you hungry? I thought you might like some breakfast."

She stared up at the dark ceiling above and wondered how far up it had to go for her not to see any light at the top. Then her stomach reminded her of daily needs, and she went to his side. He opened the basket and offered her some bread. She missed the bread from home, covered in honey and so fluffy it was like air. The bread here was tough and stale, but it was food, and she was growing used to it after being here for so long. She ripped off a chunk and started to tear smaller pieces to eat.

"This place is beautiful. How did you find it?"

"Oh, this was my playground. I know all the little entrances and hidden coves. I spent most of my life running around these mountains. I always liked it here, though."

"Please tell me someone told you the water was poisonous, and you didn't find out the hard way."

"Well, unfortunately, I can't say that. When I found it, I decided to dive right into that pool and stand up under the waterfall. It wasn't a pleasant experience afterwards. Took me a while to venture back, but at least I knew to be more careful after that."

"Well, thank you for the warning, so I didn't have to repeat mistakes." She finished the triangle of bread he'd given her and sat back to just watch the waterfall. If she closed her eyes, the sound reminded her of home. She could almost feel the water that was always perfect, whether to swim in or drink. It helped her forget just how far away she was.

"So, I spoke with Lyra and made some arrangements."

"Hmm." She didn't want to open her eyes yet. She didn't want to reenter this world of politics she'd fallen into. She could almost hear her sister laughing from the edge of the lake...

"How do you feel about getting another rune?"

"What?"

"Well, the rune we share will only work in this realm. We'll need another one if you are going to Eloas with me."

"What?" She stood and turned to him. "What do you mean?"

"Well, I can't go there on my own. How would I keep track of Malux? And what about the group you want me to keep an eye on? If you think it would be good for me to make their passage safer, then I'll need an extra set of eyes, especially ones that can tell me when and where I need to be."

She gaped at him. "How on earth did you get Lyra to agree to that?" He gave a shrug, but she knew it couldn't have been easy. It wasn't home, but it was a lot better than sitting around here alone in her room. She would get to help save Malux. Briar might get a glimpse of the group she'd been keeping such a close eye on. She would get to enter another realm. She'd be alone with Doyle and hopefully get more of his smiles.

Without thinking, she threw herself into his arms. "Thank you, Doyle!" She clung to him, and after a moment, his arms came around her too. A flash of one of her visions crossed her mind: his lips on hers, claiming her as his own. She almost turned her mouth to meet his before she caught herself and pulled back, her heart pounding in her chest.

"I'm glad you're happy about the news," he stated gruffly, giving her hips a squeeze before he released her.

"I am. Now, when do we leave?"

Chapter Six

"Yes, I believe there is some kind of strange satanic ritual happening in one of the abandoned buildings." Erin gave the address over the phone to the police and shot Melody a wink. Clearly Melody had missed a lot while on her date of a lifetime. Erin was standing in the same space as Ana and neither looked like they were about to murder the other, so…progress? She was more interested in the man hovering at Ana's elbow, like he was ready to shield her if needed. He'd come with them, of that she was sure. Everything in the warehouse had been a blur, but he'd arrived with Ana and he was clearly an elf like her. She had missed *so much*.

"So, is anyone going to tell me when we picked up another elf?"

"Let's talk in the car." Ana eyed the building, but Melody refused to turn her gaze towards it. Her date had turned out decidedly bad, and she didn't want to think of the man that had asked her out and dragged her there. Everything had been a lie. Her first real date hadn't been all that *real* after all. And now he was dead.

"It looks like the other girls are gone. I don't see them anywhere. They got away safely at least." Erin gave Melody a small smile, and Melody felt like there was an apology hidden in that simple gesture. She was going to need more than a smile to feel better about the last few months, though. The color in Erin's face abruptly drained away when the wolf Melody had seen inside came out of the shadows and put herself between the elves and Melody and Erin. "Let's get this over with," Erin sighed unhappily and opened the back door. The wolf hopped right in and took the far window seat. "You go next. I'm not sitting next to her if I don't have to." Erin actually cringed, which didn't exactly make Melody feel better about her situation.

When she moved to climb into the car, Ana caught her arm and pulled her into a suffocating hug. Ana held her there and Melody couldn't even return it, her arms pinned at her sides. When the far off sound of sirens made it to them, Ana released her, gave her arms one more squeeze, and then slid into the driver's seat.

Melody waited until Ana pulled onto a main road before trying again. "So...who is this guy? And where did you two learn to fight so well together?"

"That was like riding a bicycle, wasn't it?" Ana turned her head to grin at the male elf.

"Excuse me? Riding a *what?*" When Erin let out a snort in response to his question, he turned on Ana. "Ainadelothien, you have spent far too long in this realm. Remember, I am not privy to ridiculous *human* metaphors."

"Hey now, human back here," Melody complained with a raised hand. "Still don't know who this guy is," she added with mounting frustration.

"Melody, this is Ethelron. He was my guardian in my realm - which apparently did *not* collapse like we thought it did. Next to you is his wolf, Siofra. Sio for short. They arrived in the middle of your little date-slash-party back there."

"Woah…That's a lot of major news to take in…"

"Yeah, you're telling me. Ethelron, this is Melody, or Mel. She's been with me for a few years now. She's pretty sassy, so don't mind her."

"I take offense to that," Melody grumbled. Normally she wouldn't mind a little teasing, but she'd had a long night, and was presently cramped in the car like a sardine.

Ethelron turned and gave her a respectful nod, but his attention turned away quickly. "Princess, now that we have retrieved your friend, w e need to focus on why I am here. Your kingdom needs you to return. Your parents need you."

"The war is won, so now they think it's safe to return?" Ana's voice was quiet but held an edge that Melody recognized.

"I never said the war was won. We've held the castle, but not without loss. Other kingdoms have fallen to the erebi, and many have taken refuge with us. We have not been able to rid our realm of the erebi and..." Ethelron looked away, but there was no escaping whatever he needed to say. Ana would make sure of it, even if she had to drive the whole state of California before she let any of them out of the car. "Your parents have been leading the war for far too long. They are tired. Your father...your father was infected early on. Your mother is a great healer and has been able to keep the infection at bay, but not without weakening herself. They need their children to return and take over. The realm needs the hope that your return would provide."

The car fell silent. Melody wanted to be happy for Ana. Her realm still existed. Her parents weren't at full strength, but they were *alive*. She'd lost her brother, but she could have her people and her home back. But Melody had made Ana and Mystifying *her* home. If Ana left, where did that leave her? Ana had taken her in when she had no one else. They'd been friends, and sisters, and mother and daughter. Their relationship had always been complicated, but there had always been love and the sense of *home* between them. Now Ethelron was showing up and taking that away from her?

She *was* happy for Ana, and she would only show her support, but a little piece of her heart cracked at the thought of losing another family. She hadn't thought she'd survive her parents abandoning her just because of who she was. Yet she had. She'd stood on her own and endured the best she could until Ana found her. She would survive Ana leaving, too. She'd know that Ana was home and surrounded by people that loved her, and Melody would be okay.

Ana pulled into her usual parking spot and led the way up the side stairs to the apartment. "Why don't you guys get some rest? We have a lot to discuss, but it's been a long day for all of us. Our talks can wait a few hours while we recover, and we can sort everything out in the morning." Ana sounded defeated; that was the only reason Melody didn't argue. Instead, she grabbed Erin by the elbow and led her to her room.

"I'm so glad you can show up when I've been kidnapped, but you haven't been able to answer your phone for months." Melody turned on Erin the moment they entered her bedroom. "How did Ana even get a hold of you? How many times did she have to call you in order to get you to answer? Did she just show up at your apartment?"

"Melody-"

"No, I know you've been hurting. I understand that. You had a great loss. But you cut Ana out like it was her fault and that's not fair! She lost her brother!"

"I know that, okay!" Erin burst out, cutting off Melody's tirade. "I don't blame Ana. *I'm* the one who got kidnapped and needed saving! *I'm* the one who got so caught up in getting revenge that I wasn't able to stop Kali from attacking Ana. Sinopa, the only one who would have been able to tell me *anything* about my parents, got killed saving me. It's all *my fault!* There are so many times I could have made a different decision and changed the way that played out." The crack in Erin's voice softened Melody's anger a touch. "I haven't been avoiding Ana because I blame her! I was angry! Angry that she brought him to save me, angry that I walked into her shop and my world came falling down around me, but it wasn't her fault. I've avoided her because every time I see her, I see Gabe. Every time she talks, I am reminded that *I* should be the one who is dead and she should have her brother. I have no one. *Gabe was it.* I'm an orphan who never trusted anyone enough to let them in. Except Gabe, and even him, I kept my most important secrets from. It's *my* fault, Melody, and I am keenly aware of that."

"Erin..." Melody held her arm and led her to the bed, forcing her to sit down. "You have *us*. That's why Ana kept reaching out to you. The two of you knew Gabe and feel his loss. She thought you should carry that loss *together*. Instead, she's put all the blame on her own shoulders, while you've put all the blame on yours. There is no blame, there is just loss."

They sat in silence for a minute, while the words sank in between them. "Melody, are *you* okay? After everything that happened with your date?"

"Yeah...I just thought if any guy could be trusted, a guy found in the library could be." Her mouth twitched in a wry, bitter smile.

"True." Erin sat up straighter. "I came by before Ana realized you were in trouble. There is an erebus after the amulet that Gabe was wearing. I don't know why, he just says he has to 'return it to his master', whoever that is. I've tried to find information about it but I can't. I thought maybe you could do a spell or something to find some answers."

"May I see it?" Melody waited while Erin seemed to debate removing the necklace. She brushed a finger over the stone before finally handing it over. The weight of it surprised her as it warmed in her palm. She felt an odd impression of Gabe. That could happen sometimes when someone died in a tragic way; things around or on the person could take on some of their aura. While there was the feeling of Gabe, there was also an oily presence to the amulet. Melody had the sudden urge to put it down and wash her hands. Instead, she walked to her desk and placed it in the center before surrounding it with crystals and grabbing a candle from a shelf hanging above the desk.

Melody could feel Erin hovering around, but it was easy enough to ignore her as she lit the candle and concentrated her magic on the amulet. Melody could feel it reaching out towards the stone, but the moment it brushed against it, her magic pulled back, whipping back into her. She knew better than to force her magic somewhere it didn't want to go, so she released her concentration. Her stomach roiled from the darkness her magic had briefly touched. She couldn't pick the amulet back up to hand it back to Erin, so she just left it sitting on the desk and blew out the candle.

"I don't know why Gabe had that, but there is a dark power attached to it. I can't tell you anything more about it. There is something protecting it, pushing away my powers, but I can tell you this: you shouldn't be wearing it. The darkness I felt was dangerous, and until we can find out more, I think you should put some space between you and that amulet."

Erin only hesitated a moment before she reached around her and picked the necklace up from the desk. "There is some erebus after this, and, for some reason, Gabe had it with him. I can't just leave it sitting around. So, until we find out more, I'll keep it with me."

Melody didn't like it, but she nodded. "Fair enough."

"I just don't understand why Gabe had it. Do you know when he got it?"

"No." Melody looked at it once more. "We were together when we traveled through Loinnir. He didn't have it before we passed through the portal, but I don't know when or how he got it. I didn't see it on him until...after."

Erin nodded absently, her fingers brushing over the stone before she tucked it beneath her shirt. "Well, if you are okay with me crashing in your room with you, I guess we should get some rest. I feel like there will be a lot to discuss tomorrow. By the way, what did you think about Ethelron?"

"Well, he helped save my life, so he's under the friend column in my book. I'm happy for Ana. She will have her people and her home back."

"Yes, but from what we overheard, I don't think it will be as simple as all that." Erin sighed and sat on the corner of the bed again.

"Nothing ever is, is it?" Melody sat beside her, doing her best to mask her own worries over Ethelron's appearance.

"Not in my experience. I just wish Gabe was here to be with his sister through this."

"Me too. But none of us wish he was here *instead* of you. Just make sure you remember that."

℮ ℮ ℮

Doyle watched Briar carefully. His body still ached from going through the portal, but she seemed to have recovered after only a few minutes. He watched how the realm took hold of her and brought her back to life. If he could, he'd find a way to leave her here, where she'd be whole and have the taste of magic on her lips once more. How he wished he could. Already, color was returning to her, and they weren't even in Loinnir. Her eyes were becoming more violet instead of the pale purple they were in his realm. And her hair...as he stared at her, he could see the color deepening. A rosy blush tinted the bronze skin of her cheeks, and her lips - he tore his eyes away then. The soft pink of her grin was far too inviting, and he had no right to want that from her.

He was the reason all these terrible things had happened to her; he would not forget that, and he knew, even though she showed him nothing but kindness, there was no way she'd be able to forgive him for the part he'd taken in her capture. If only he had the power to see the future, he would have let her and her sister go through that portal to the safety of Sula. But he was going to have to live with the choices he'd made since he couldn't take them back now. Doyle drew a deep breath and took in Eloas. He'd only been there one other time, but he could feel a change in the air. The erebi being here for all these years was draining the realm. It still had the magic that kept the realm alive, but it was fading, and it would only get worse if the war did not end soon.

He knew, since Kali's death, her brother was taking a harsher approach. He wanted it over and he wanted the realm for himself. The war was going to change quickly, one way or the other.

"It's so beautiful," Briar sighed. The sound made his chest ache.

"Well, it's not the waterfall I showed you, but it'll do." She swung her arm out and swatted him in the stomach. He looked at her

102

with surprise and found her grinning and shaking her head. "How long do we have to find Malux?"

"A day or so I believe. It's hard to tell from the visions, but Malux left to follow the group. They will be here soon."

"Do you think you'd be able to pick out where we should camp out to wait for them?" Briar nodded slowly and walked a little farther, letting her fingers trail over the greenery she passed. He couldn't take his eyes off her as she moved, more in her element here than in his own realm. She took a deep breath and then turned to him, her eyes bright. Then she silently held out her hand to him, and he knew what she needed. He reached out and took it, opening his mind to her.

Her skin was cool against his, and after a moment, her grip tightened and he felt a dull ache at the base of his skull. Her eyes stared blankly into whatever vision she was having. Finally, she blinked at him and came back to the world. She continued to hold his hand, and he didn't release her. Something stirred in the pit of his stomach, and he did his best to ignore the effect she was having. She clearly just needed another minute to come back to herself.

"We should head north. They will need some help with the infection erebi. They will move much quicker if you help clear the way for them a bit."

"It's odd that the group we need for help are the ones to kill Malux..."

"Yes, but Malux is working under the queen's orders. He has no choice, and he gives them no choice other than to kill him." She slipped her hand out of his and took the lead. He hastened to cover her back. Doyle could sense other erebi nearby and the last thing he wanted was for Briar to get herself hurt. He touched the sword at his hip and glanced down at his left boot to make sure a dagger was still strapped to it.

"Maybe you should take the dagger," he said quietly, eyeing her and realizing she had no weapon. He should have thought of that sooner, but packing his own weapons was second nature, and he wasn't used to making sure others had weapons. Briar shook her head, though. The only thing she had with her was the vial with Malux's cure. "I trust you to keep me safe, and I've never been much of a fighter. I never had to learn before, and now I'd likely stab myself before something else."

"You should train with me when we get back. At least to learn the basics." She glanced back at him and he swore her cheeks flushed the tiniest bit.

"What do you think Lyra would think of me learning to fight?"

Doyle felt the familiar twinge at the base of his spine at the mention of Lyra from Briar's lips. She always said the name like she was talking around something unpleasant. He couldn't blame her, and that made it worse. "*I* think it would be good for you. You should know how to protect yourself."

"There." She stopped abruptly and pointed toward a shaded area deeper into the forest. He could see how the leaves browned at the edges, and felt a familiar wave of unease that he usually got around the infection erebi. He might also be an erebus, but there were many different kinds, and the infection erebi were dreaded by all. They used to be rare, but Kali and her brother found a way to control them, and bred themselves an army. It was one thing Lyra had been against and tried to talk to her sister about, but Kali had won that argument. No one else wanted to fight Kali's war, so they were perfectly content to let mindless infection erebi be fodder for the elves. "A group of five. Do you think you can handle that many?"

"You saw them there. What was the outcome?" He grinned when he saw the flash of a smile. "Then I guess I've got it covered. Stay here. I don't want you stabbing yourself." He drew his sword and moved forward. He heard their hissing as he moved from Briar and rolled his shoulders to loosen up. Five. He trained daily to make sure he could handle whatever came his way, but five was a little more than what he would ask for on his own. The moment he spotted the first, though, he fell into it, instinct taking over and moving his muscles before his brain even processed what was before him.

The first erebus let out a screech of pain as he dove forward and stabbed it before it knew what was happening. A second turned to him and he ducked, avoiding claws that would infect him, and brought his sword up into its chest before it made a full turn. It actually felt good to have a proper fight. The guys he sparred with were good and wouldn't hold back, but it was never the same as an actual battle. The last three infection erebi tried to be smart; circling him, hissing, but keeping distance. He watched carefully, waiting for his opening, when he saw the flash of blue hair and then something heavy hit one of the erebi in the back. The thing reared back with a hiss of pain and turned. He didn't hesitate. Doyle sliced through its neck, and then turned in time to plunge his sword into the stomach of the one darting toward him.

Briar yelled from the side; his heart stopped, thinking she was being attacked, but when he looked up, he realized she was distracting the last erebus to give him a moment. It worked a little too well, though, because the creature saw an easier target and charged her. "Shit!" Doyle was on his feet and racing after it, keeping the shadow-like creature in his sights before he lost it between the trees. Briar darted out of the way just before claws caught her, and his blade found its mark. Gasping in a breath, he watched as the creature faded to black smoke and disappeared with the rest of its comrades.

"What were you thinking?" He looked up to Briar as she came back into view, a little paler than before.

"It moved a little faster than I was expecting." She held out a hand to him, and he took it even though he didn't need the help. He just wanted to feel that she was okay.

"The claws didn't touch you at all, did they?"

"No, I'm fine. I just didn't want you to get overwhelmed. I didn't think it was going to run at me."

He rubbed his eyes and then took another deep breath. "Let's try not to do that again, okay?"

"No promises." She grinned when he groaned at her response.

Chapter Seven

Ana woke after only a few hours of sleep to the sound of movement outside her door. Dagger in hand, Ana inched the door open, and found a startled Ethelron and Sio waiting for her on the other side.

"Are you often attacked in your own home, Princess?" His eyes fell on her dagger with amusement.

"Do you often lurk outside of women's bedrooms early in the morning?" She suppressed the twinge of discomfort at the thought and nearly preened when he shifted uncomfortably. Then Ana noticed the pillow he had propped up against the wall across from her. Had he spent the night outside her door? She'd set him up on the sofa in the family room before she'd escaped to the quiet of her own room. They'd talked a little more before she'd left him for the evening, but she'd been so drained from all the news and events that she'd gone to sleep not long after they got back.

"This world is strange and noisy. I kept worrying that something might attack. I'm sorry if we woke you. Sio was starting to get antsy. I should take her outside."

"Give me a minute. I'll join you." Ana closed the door on him and ran to brush out her hair and braid it back. A quick change of clothes and she was ready. She led them down the stairwell when Ethelron laid a hand on her arm to stop her.

"Aren't you going to *charm* me?"

It took her mind a moment longer than it should have to realize what he meant. She looked him up and down and shrugged. "Hopefully there won't be too many people out and about this early. When you are dressed like *that*, your ears and aura aren't the things that are going to draw attention." Ana lived a short walk from a park, so she led them there and watched Sio take off gratefully. The wolf was used to her open spaces and forests to run through. Ana thought Sio would love Muir Woods.

The heaviness of the task ahead weighed her down until she came to a stop and decided to sit in the grass. She felt Ethelron's gaze on her once more. She hardly recognized him now with his features set in a hard line, his gaze glazed over in seriousness and wary perusal of their surroundings. Elvish ink covered his exposed skin and spoke to the battles he'd seen, the ranks he'd moved up in the guard over the years, and highlighted scars. There had been a time he experienced amusement in her presence. He'd been her friend and, even though he always took his position with the guard seriously, he'd also visibly resisted laughing when she'd teased him, or joining in when she played with Toron. He'd always stood a little closer than necessary, and stared a little longer, his gaze flashing with fondness.

That part of him, though, seemed to be gone. One part of her longed to see that boy on the cusp of manhood once more, but a larger part of her just wanted to get to know *this man*. This man that had seen too much, that now kept space between them even as he took up a seat beside her, and didn't quite meet her gaze as he once had. This man that still fought by her side like no time had passed between them. She longed to reach past this new rift between them and find out who he had become.

"What is it?" She wished she knew what he was thinking, but he kept his mind closed and his face devoid of readable emotion.

"It's hard for me to imagine you here, like this." He gestured to her ears before a crease formed on his forehead. "You lose your light when you wear that ring. It's still there, simmering underneath, but it's not the same."

"Well, if we are to return to Eloas, then I won't need my charmed ring any longer. And this world isn't all that bad. It's different, and took a while for me to get used to, but it's been my home. I've found friends and family along the way."

"You'll miss it?"

"Does that surprise you?" Their shoulders touched while Sio ignored their presence and began chasing a squirrel.

"You belong in the forest, Ainadelothien, Princess of the Elves; you were born to rule there. It's just hard to see you here, and know that the realm I'm going to return you to is not the one you left behind." His voice was weary, making Ana's stomach turn. It was a gift to find out her home was still there, people she loved still alive, but she knew it was going to be painful to see how her kingdom had fallen, to face what she had abandoned. She wanted to ask how bad it was to prepare herself, but she knew she would see for herself soon enough.

"Thank you for your help with healing Erin, and saving Melody yesterday."

"What happened to him, Aina?" His voice was a soft caress, but his question still hit her like daggers in the chest.

Ana let out a shaky breath and leaned away, needing as much space as she could get. Ana knew he was asking about Toron, and she knew she needed to tell him. But speaking aloud about the loss, especially to someone who knew him and knew it was her duty to protect him, was the last thing she wanted to do right now. "We were separated leaving Eloas. Kali stopped me from entering the portal with him, and when I finally made it through, he was nowhere to be found. I searched for him...for *years*. Eventually I had to accept that he was gone, and pray that he'd made it through safely and had managed to find a *normal* life for himself. I never stopped feeling responsible that we'd been separated, and I never allowed myself to accept the thought that he was dead. A little over ten years later, I found Melody, and our friend Aria. Together we were a mis-matched family.

"And then, about a year ago, we lost Aria because Kali was trying to get my attention. I didn't realize that at the time, or know about the war breaking out in Loinnir. Then Erin walked into my shop. With Erin came *Gabe*. I didn't know for sure right away, but Erin noticed my tattoos one day, and said that her boyfriend had some of the same ones. He was Toron. It turned out his memories were erased when he went through the portal, and he'd lived his life as a human. I removed the spell that had kept him human all along, and I had my brother back." She paused to take a shuddering breath, jumping when the weight of his hand settled onto her shoulder, giving a reassuring squeeze. Ana leaned into his touch, grateful for the strength he offered. "Kali took Erin to draw me out. We went after her...and Toron jumped in the way of an attack meant for me. He'd come back to me, only to be ripped away for good. It was my fault."

"Princess, he died a heroic death. He saved the woman he loved, and he saved his sister. That is no small thing." He paused, some understanding flashing in his gaze. "Erin's scars...she received them during this battle?"

"Yes. Why?"

"She wouldn't let me heal her until she made sure I wouldn't heal them. I'm not a strong enough healer to have taken away old scars, but she was determined that they remain. I wondered what it meant, but now I understand." He held up his own forearm, showing her a long scar. "I was supposed to go through the portal with you and Toron. I was supposed to stay with you and protect you. But I got caught in battle, I was injured, and wasn't quick enough to catch up to you. If I had...well, then maybe none of this would have happened. Your mother, along with a few other healers, offered to mend the wound, but I wouldn't allow it. I failed you and Toron, and I've done everything I could over the years to make up for it."

"Ethelron, you gave us an opening for escape and you've stood by my parents fighting this war all these years." Ana reached out and touched his arm near the scar. The size of it let her know just how badly he'd been injured at the time. The thought of what it could have done had her quickly blinking away the sting of tears. "You are annoyingly stubborn to not allow them to heal this. You could have bled out."

"*You* could have died. And Toron did." His expression was grim as he looked down at her.

His deep gaze did something to her and caused an aching in her chest. "We should head back. Get some food and get started. I'll need to talk to Erin and Melody about my plans to go back to Eloas." The two sat together in quiet for a few more minutes and watched the city slowly come alive. Ana tried not to think about saying goodbye to Melody and leaving her behind. She knew Melody would be okay, and she was going to ask that she and Erin look out for one another, but the idea of not having Melody with her felt like another loss she wasn't ready to live through. Once the sun was up, Ethelron stood from the grass and called Sio over to them so they could start back towards home. As they walked, Ana sensed his walls rebuilding, and was grateful for the glimpse of the Ethelron she'd depended on for so many years.

.℮ .℮ .℮

Briar led the way to a good place to camp. Doyle cleared two other small pods of infection erebi, which made her feel better about the group that was to follow them. She felt like they would find Malux tomorrow, but wished it was still another day off. The energy from the realm filled her. It was so very different from her own, but still *alive*. She couldn't stop reaching out to touch all the green as she passed it. Briar had never been connected to nature like her sister, but she still felt the wonder at seeing something other than stone. It made her chest ache for home. She was going to enjoy every moment in this realm while she could.

Doyle set up a fire with an ease that made her smile. He had it roaring to life before she'd fully made herself comfortable. The flames danced over his features, and watching him made her mouth dry. She yearned to reach out and touch him. She wanted what she'd seen in her visions, and being alone with him, *truly alone*, was making her thoughts stray into dangerous areas. His dark red eyes turned to her, and she wondered if he was starting to have any of the feelings she knew he was capable of. His gaze lingered longer than usual, looking over her features with slow interest, and her stomach muscles tightened.

"Thank you for bringing me along. I'm sure it wasn't easy to convince Lyra."

"I'm glad I could. Being in a realm with magic does wonders for you. I could literally see you coming to life when we got here." She felt heat creep into her cheeks at that. "Briar, I vow to you, I will make sure you make it home. So much has happened to you, and it's my fault. I'll do everything I can to protect you from harm, and I *will* make sure you go back to your realm."

She wasn't sure what to say to that. She could feel his determination and see in his features how serious he was. Hope swelled up within her, and she couldn't bear to tamp it down. "I believe you. And I don't blame you for any of this; you did bring me to your realm, but only because you saw me as a way to help your people. You didn't know what was going to happen, or what choices Lyra would make."

Something heavy hung in the air between them, but then he broke eye contact. "We should try to get some rest. We still have a lot to do on this little trip of ours before it's over."

He laid out on the other side of the fire, so she did the same. She didn't feel tired, though. Her body was alive with wonder at the realm, and a new yearning for Doyle. She stared up at the sky peeking through the branches, and couldn't help but smile at the stars twinkling down at her. It was different from home, but there were actual stars instead of the thick reddish clouds and dull sun that never changed in Skia. She never wanted to leave, but she believed Doyle would do everything to get her home when this was all over, and she hoped they were growing closer to the end.

She was just drifting off, the cool grass under her, the fire keeping her warm, the air fresh in her lungs, when she heard something rustling nearby. Briar sat up, and her small movement had Doyle awake and on his feet, sword in hand, before she'd even looked around. They both heard the noise growing closer and Doyle motioned for her to stay.

Then the world seemed to explode around them. It was hard to make out the infection erebi at first. They didn't look quite solid when they were fully infected, more like wispy smoke from nightmares, but the firelight caught them and she sucked in a breath.

"Take this, don't let them scratch you." Doyle handed her his dagger and took a protective stance in front of her. She had no idea what to do with it. She'd never learned to fight, never had to. Why hadn't she seen this attack? This kind of danger would have been a good thing to have some kind of warning about. There were too many, she could see that. There had to be at least fifteen of them, with their long claws and glowing eyes reflecting the fire. Doyle's entire body was tense in front of her. He rolled his shoulders and neck, and then he darted forward, leaving her to watch, frozen in her spot. He ducked and dodged claws and then swung his sword and stabbed one. Without losing momentum, he brought the sword through the neck of the next one, but more just kept coming.

She couldn't just stand there, she had to move forward and help him. Her feet finally seemed to listen, and with adrenaline pumping through her, Briar swung the dagger into the back of one trying to circle Doyle. While the thing looked like smoke, it was solid under the blade, and she felt the jarring up her arm as she connected. It went down, and she went for another. Hissing filled the night, but she could hardly hear it over the pounding in her ears. Something solid hit her back, knocking the air from her lungs in a startled gasp. She fell to the ground and horrible memories of being locked in the mountains with Lyra's henchmen came to her, freezing her muscles even as she tried to struggle back to her feet.

"Briar!" Doyle's voice sounded panicked, and it grounded her. She couldn't leave him alone, or he'd die. They'd *both* die. Claws wrapped around her arm and brought her to her feet like she weighed nothing. Without thinking, she kicked out and hit the erebus in the chest, loosening its grip. Then a sword pierced where her foot had just struck and the hold disappeared as it turned to smoke to return to Skia. Doyle's eyes held a crazed glint when they met hers.

"I'm okay," she gasped out, and ducked when she saw his gaze dart behind her. He swung the sword and connected with whatever was trying to sneak up on her. Doyle grabbed her arm and dragged her to her feet, pushing her behind him as he faced down the last of the erebi. There still had to be about eight left, but it was hard to get an exact count when the tendrils of smoke seemed to blend into each other and the darkness of the night.

Doyle moved forward again, diving at the closest erebi, but two slipped past him as he engaged the others. Briar backed up two steps to give herself space between the two coming for her. She could do this. She'd had her wings ripped from her and survived, she could take down two erebi. The fae thought of everything she'd been through, and let the rage she'd pushed down for months fill her. She ran for the one closest to her and, probably from pure luck, it didn't move in time, letting her dagger find its mark. But the second erebus was not as slow, and it struck her right across the cheek before kicking out and knocking her back to the ground.

"What in the hell are you two doing here?" A familiar voice called out in the night and she saw Malux standing on the other side of the erebi. The moment of distraction was enough for her attacker to cover the space between them, and she let out a little scream as she tried to scramble backwards. The thing reached out and gripped her neck, cutting off her next breath. She wanted to be thankful it hadn't scratched her, but as stars started dancing before her eyes, she couldn't find it in her. The dagger fell from her hand as she reached up to try to pull the vice from her throat. Her feet left the ground, and the world started to dance before her. Sounds from the fight faded as a buzzing filled her ears. Then she was on the ground, her legs and throat pulsing in pain. She struggled to pull a breath through her swollen windpipe, and then Doyle was in front of her, his hands holding her cheeks in the most gentle way.

"Briar?" Thumbs swept over her cheeks and she forced her eyes open to look at him. "Shhh, just breathe, okay?" Then he did the strangest thing and rested his forehead against hers. She could feel him shaking, but didn't quite understand his reaction. He took a deep breath. like he was showing her how, reminding her body how to draw in air. Her throat loosened enough so her lungs could fill, and Doyle's next breath came out ragged.

"Are you hurt?" The words grated against her sore throat, but she knew he shouldn't be shaking like that. He might have gotten scratched, and she knew that was very bad.

"No, I thought I wouldn't get to you in time." His gaze searched hers. "You weren't scratched, were you?" She knew better than to talk this time, so she just shook her head. Her heart was pounding in her chest and she felt warm where his hands rested.

"Does anyone want to tell me why you are here?" Malux brought her attention back to reality, and she broke from Doyle's gaze. Malux had helped clear the rest of the erebi, just in time too, or she would probably have been killed.

"Just out for a stroll, how about yourself?" Doyle responded after a moment, though his eyes stayed on her.

"I have things to do. Just try not to get yourselves killed, okay?" Malux's eyes fell on her then, and she felt the cool gaze of the dragon eye. He was running to his death, and they would need to be ready to save him once he did. She could tell he was trying to assess something about her, but then he turned back to Doyle. "Take better care of her. You've let Lyra use her as a play-thing already. She doesn't need more harm done to her." Then he turned and left before Doyle could form a response.

She heard him let out a shaky breath before he turned back to her. Her heart ached when she saw the hurt in his gaze. "He's right. I should have taken better care of you. If he hadn't shown up..."

"It's not your fault. I should have seen them coming." She reached up to hold her throat, hating how raw it felt.

"You're sure you weren't scratched?" She started to nod, but he gently moved her hand away from her throat and brushed gentle fingers over the tender skin. Then his touch moved down her arms and back up to cradle her face. The pain was forgotten. Goosebumps rose under his gentle touch, and her tongue darted out to wet her lips. His eyes were drawn to the small movement, and his gaze grew hungry. The tension between them bloomed into something different. She could feel them on the precipice of something great and she stopped breathing, waiting for it to happen.

"Briar...I have no right...but," his thumb brushed over her bottom lip and her heart tried to leap from her chest, "I'd like to kiss you right now." His thumb moved to the corner of her mouth and she felt dizzy from the touch. Briar realized he was waiting. He wanted her permission to kiss her. She'd never been kissed before. She'd always been wanted for her visions; in Loinnir, she was held in high regard, basically untouchable. The male fae gave her a wide berth until she was to be matched with one of them for procreation.

When she didn't answer him immediately, he started to draw his hand away, but she reached up and pressed it against her skin. She turned her mouth to the center of his palm and placed a soft kiss there. She must be doing something right, she mused, because he drew in a sharp breath. "I think I'd like that." Briar answered quietly, trying to push down the nerves building within her.

Doyle's hand moved to the back of her head, tangling in her hair. He kissed her cheek first, then the corner of her lips, and then he found her. The kiss was soft at first, leading her into the motion. When his free hand came around her waist, she let out a small moan, and his whole body grew tense around her. His tongue reached out and had her opening for him, tasting him. She let instinct take over, reaching her arms around his neck to bring him closer to her. He left her breathless when he pulled back from her lips. He rested his forehead against hers once more, and she could hear him struggle to catch his breath.

"I knew it would be life-altering to kiss you, but I still underestimated it," he said with a voice that sounded deeper than usual. After he seemed to get his bearings, he pulled a little farther away so he could see her face directly. She liked how the fire danced in his eyes, and how his gaze warmed her to the core. "Did you see this? Did you see a future like this?"

"Does it matter?" She wasn't sure how to answer him.

"No, I guess not. I was just wondering if you knew this whole time what we could have."

"You know my visions don't work that way. I never really know." Briar didn't want to tell him. She didn't want to say how she'd seen love and devotion in his gaze, but she'd also seen him choose Lyra over her. That he could be her end. She just wanted to enjoy this moment, the feel of his skin against hers.

He leaned in toward her again, slowly, giving her the chance to turn away. But she didn't. This time, she leaned forward to meet him, and let herself get lost against his lips for just another moment.

Ana and Ethelron returned to the apartment to find Melody and Erin sitting at the table, breakfast laid out on the table already. "Thought we might need nourishment for our chat." Melody grinned. Ana noticed the sad tilt to her lips, though. She was only going to make it worse by telling her she would have to return to Eloas. As long as Melody was here, Ana would find a way to return to her. She just didn't know how long it would be before she got to see her dearest friend again.

"It seems Eloas is still there, but in serious danger." Ana dove right in, wanting to get the conversation over with, and knowing they didn't have much time. "I'm going to go back with Ethelron today to help fight. There isn't time to lose. But Erin has been attacked and is also in danger, so I would like it if the two of you stick together. You can watch each other's backs while I'm gone."

"That will be kind of hard, Ana, because there is no way you are going to war in Eloas without me."

"Mel-"

"It's okay. I'm going to make this easy. How about you just keep watching our backs, and we'll watch yours, like we have before." Melody arched a brow and crossed her arms. Ana was too stunned to speak, but she turned her gaze to Erin. She knew there was still so much anger there, and while Melody seemed determined to come with, Ana couldn't see Erin wanting to travel with them. Not after spending months doing everything she could to avoid them.

"Princess, we cannot bring them," Ethelron interrupted, his tone demanding they listen. "They did fine in the fight yesterday, but we are talking about *war*. The elves are having a hard enough time keeping the kingdom alive. We are in a hurry, and we can't drag along a *human* and a *halfling*."

"But you think it's okay to drag Ana into the middle of a war?" Melody barked.

"She is the princess. Her family *needs* her." He turned his attention back to Ana. "They didn't want me to come. They thought it would be a fruitless search, given how long its been and how vast the realm. But *I know* they need you."

"Well, we are family, too. And *we* need Ana, just as much as she needs us." Melody's voice weakened at the end, and it broke Ana's heart to hear. She went around the table to pull Melody into a tight hug. She didn't want to put Melody in harm's way, but she didn't want to leave her behind, either. Knowing that Melody would stand up to Ethelron and demand she go with them showed just how much love was between them. Melody was her family, even if Eloas still existed.

"She's right, Ana," Erin spoke up. "I'm not about to let you fight for your home alone. We are in this together. We will *all* leave together." Erin looked pointedly at Ethelron, and Ana caught his look of exasperation from being overrun by a room full of women.

"Erin..." Ana's eyes grew misty.

"I don't blame you, Ana. It wasn't your fault. And now I'll be there to help you save your home, Gabe's home."

Ana released Melody to pull Erin into a hug. The other woman resisted for a moment before giving her a light pat on the back. Ana turned back to Ethelron and found a war of emotions crossing his features. "We need an hour to prepare, then we can leave. Melody, call Marissa to see if she and Asher can watch over the store. Both of you prepare a small pack for travel, and make arrangements for being away. I don't know how long we will be gone."

Both women nodded and departed to start their own preparations, which left Ana alone with a very quiet Ethelron.

"As a leader, you are expected to make the choices best for your people. Bringing a group with us to Eloas is not the best choice. It will slow our travels, and you are putting your friends in danger-"

"They *are* my people, too. The sooner you get used to the idea, the easier this is going to be. Melody and Erin are strong. They can hold their own. And they are willing to help us win back our realm. You should be happy to have two extra sets of very capable hands. Now, I have a few things of my own to prepare. Why don't you eat so you have your strength once we are ready to go?" Ana gave him an overly sweet smile, then, after stealing a breakfast sandwich from the center of the table, she went to her own room.

Chapter Eight

The hour passed quickly as all of them rushed to prepare for a few days of travel before they would reach the protection of the castle. Everyone met in Ana's office to stand around the portal, ready to cross over. As she stared at the gateway, her pulse started to quicken. She was about to go back to Eloas. *Back home.* Toron should be standing at her side, and his absence was a knife to her heart. "Princess, are you ready?" Ethelron's voice drew Ana from her anxious spiraling.

"Of course." The elf squared her shoulders. "Ladies?" Everyone nodded, and Sio rubbed against Ana's legs. They all joined hands, and Ana cursed the tremor in hers. Ethelron swiped a thumb across her palm in reassurance, then spoke the words to cross over, which would help guide them to the correct portal on the other side.

The swirl and jerk of the portal hit them all. Just as she was sure her head would split, they landed in Eloas, and she immediately pulled her ring off and tucked it away. Erin stumbled beside her, but Melody helped her to her feet right away and held her steady.

Ana stared, devastated by the utter destruction around them. Her breath caught in her lungs, and she knew it would come out as a sob if she let it. She ached for the beauty that once typified her realm, the vibrant life that radiated from everything. In the outreaches of the kingdom, where the elves had clearly abandoned the fight, the erebi had taken a stronghold and feasted on the magic from their world. The trees were dying; the air lost the hum of magic that once filled their world. If the elves lost the fight, if the erebi drained all the magic from the world, the realm would collapse upon itself and the edges between the realms would crack or collapse all together. The erebi would spread out across all the realms and leave destruction in their wake.

As she took in their surroundings, determination settled into her bones. Ana squared her shoulders and turned to face her companions. "We need to get moving if we don't want them to figure out that we are here."

"What *did* all of this?" Melody breathed, still distracted.

"This is what it looks like when erebi take control," Ethelron explained solemnly. "We have managed to keep them outside of the boundaries of the kingdom, and as of yet, this portal is unknown to them, but there are areas that are utterly destroyed. Even at our most heavily guarded spots, they have begun to gain ground."

Melody and Erin glanced back, and realized that the portal was nowhere to be found. "But...how?"

"Elves are able to sense portals that other beings cannot. After Ainadelothien and Toron escaped through the primary portal of this realm, we destroyed it in an attempt to stop Kali and her erebi horde from following them to Sula. This one was hidden and away from any of our major towns or cities, so we are able to keep it shrouded from them for now. Ainadelothien and I sense where it is, but it is invisible to the erebi just as it is invisible to the two of you." The two women glanced at Ana, who nodded before gesturing towards what she knew to be her kingdom in the distance. She adjusted the pack on her back and they began their trek.

The group traveled in silence for some time, with Ana leading them towards the nearest tree line. Once-vibrant greens and browns of the foliage throughout the realm were darkened by the black veins left behind by the erebi. The thought of surrounding herself by the constant, blatant reminder of how she'd failed her people made her nauseous, but she knew that if they left themselves exposed in the open fields, they would be spotted for sure.

"You are not to blame for this, Princess."

Ana's eyes slid shut to bury the tears that burned in her eyes at Ethelron's low voice in her mind. *"Aren't I? I ran away."*

"You were sent *away to protect your brother."*

Ana scoffed bitterly. *"And look how well* that *turned out."*

"Okay, are you two having some kind of silent conversation or something?" Melody questioned in a whisper, stopping in between the two elves. Ana's gaze dropped to the ground, and Ethelron's frustrated gaze locked on her. Melody turned to face Ana. "I have no idea what you two were *thinking* about, but I know that look on your face. I also know that no matter how many times any of us might tell you that it's not your fault, you won't listen unless you are able to fix it somehow. So how about, instead of dwelling on what got us here, focus on saving your people and getting us *out* of here."

Ana blinked at her before nodding. "You're right, Mel. I-"

"Hush," Ethelron hissed suddenly. Ana's eyes snapped to his and followed the direction of his gaze to Siofra, who was suddenly alert and ready to attack. She closed her eyes and focused on listening to the forest, understanding immediately what had Siofra upset.

"Erebi, ahead of us," she murmured. With a quick gesture, the group adjusted direction to head deeper into the woods. Sio shifted to come alongside them, keeping herself situated protectively between them and the potential threat. Ethelron drew in closer to the women, tightening up the group and listening intently. They moved slowly, careful to make little noise. Even after Siofra began to settle down, joining her master in the back, they were all on edge from their close call. They walked until it began to get dark, grateful for the fact that they did not have any further encounters along the way.

"We should stop, eat, and get some rest. There is a secluded cave nearby that we can use for cover," Ethelron suggested. All the women nodded, happy to stop for the night. The guard led the way around several dying trees, fingertips brushing the blackened bark. Ana's mind conjured up memories of the times they'd played amongst those very trees as young elves, wondering if his mind was thinking the same thing. They reached the cave easily, and Ana paused at the opening while the others took a look inside. All of them ate some snacks while they settled in.

"How did you know this was here? You two use this as a secret make out spot or something?" Erin inquired with a sly smirk to Mel, who snorted.

"A secret *what* spot?" Ethelron looked at Ana suspiciously, like he knew she understood what they were talking about and was having a laugh at him.

"*Nothing,*" Ana hissed, glaring at the fae with a flush burning her cheeks. She was quickly regretting letting the two of them tag along. She'd once been very much in love with Ethelron, but she'd practically been a child and the years that had passed between them had not been easy ones. Ana couldn't deny that her eyes kept straying to him, taking in all the small changes like new scars and markings, and she also noticed so many of *his* glances.

They'd both changed, but she sensed that they were still the same people at their cores. The more time they spent together, the more certain she became that he was very much still *him*, her confidante and protector, with the same fiercely loyal soul she'd fallen in love with. Ana had never made time to try to find someone in the human realm; she hadn't seen the point considering who (and what) she was. Now, the man she thought she'd lost stood before her. Unfortunately, she had no idea if he'd ever cared for her the same way, even before the years had separated them.

"Why don't you tell them how you found this cave," she insisted, praying that he let the matter go and moved on. He watched her with a skeptical look in his eyes, but eventually complied. Ana sighed in relief as he told Melody and Erin the story of how he'd been out exploring one day when they were young, while the royal family was entertaining their council, and heard yelping from within the cave. She remembered the excitement on his face when, later that evening, Ana's mother helped heal the wolf pup that had drawn his attention. As he spoke, Ana's eyes settled on the now-grown wolf in question, settling protectively at the mouth of the cave.

"*Where has that mind of yours wandered off to now?*" Ethelron's comforting presence beside her drew Ana from her thoughts, and she offered him a half-hearted smile. "Sio will watch over us. Rest, Princess. We are going to need it." Their eyes met and held, neither wanting to look away, both remembering the simpler times in which they'd shared this space before.

"Goodnight, El," Ana murmured softly. She settled herself down beside Erin and Melody, and watched silently while Ethelron set up his pack just far enough inside of the cave to be hidden from outsiders, but still able to defend them at a moment's notice. He laid down with his back facing the women, and Ana finally closed her eyes.

℮ ℮ ℮

"Aina, watch me!" A young Gabe, Toron, *with curly blond hair and huge eyes, grinned at his sister. When he found her ever-patient eyes resting on him, he started climbing up the tree as fast as he could.*

"Be careful, Toron!" Aina stood at the bottom of the tree and watched as he leapt from branch to branch. He peeked his blond head from the branches and waved.

Erin stood in the forest with them, watching the memory as she had watched her mother's memories. She wasn't sure exactly how long ago it was, but Aina looked younger, and Toron looked to be around five or six. The forest was alive, *the trees a vibrant green, the air was thick with the smells of earth, moss, and rain.*

"Aina!" A deep voice called to the young elf and Erin turned to see two men approaching. One was clearly a young Ethelron, missing the runes that now decorated his skin.

"Papa!" Toron saw his father and cheered. As soon as the elf got to the bottom of the tree, Toron leapt from his perch and landed in his father's arms, making the older elf grunt as he caught him. Erin saw Aina's cheeks turn pink when Ethelron came to stand beside her. He didn't say anything, just gave her a small bow and stood stoically, watching the royal family interact. Aina's smile faltered as she watched the guard, before she turned her attention to her father.

"What are you doing out here, Papa? I thought you had leaders from the other realms coming today."

"I have just been working on some training with young Ethelron here. If I am to trust him with my family's protection, I want to make sure he is at his best."

"Did you see how high I got?" Toron tugged on his father's armor, demanding attention.

"I did. Did Aina give you sugar leaves? You seem to have a lot of energy for an elfling who has been playing in the forest all day."

Toron's eyes quickly flicked to his sister, and Erin watched with amusement as her head gave a small shake. "No, Papa," a solemn shake of his own head as he lied to protect his sister.

"I'm not sure I believe you." His father gave his nose a loving flick before he settled him down on the grass. "Ethelron, we should continue. I'll see you both at home for dinner." He brushed Aina's cheek gently and ruffled his son's hair before *leading the way deeper into the forest, the young guard-in-training following after with a stiff back and serious expression.*

"When I grow up, I'm going to be just like Papa!" The elfling hugged his sister before running for the tree again, a high squeal of laughter filling the forest when she started to chase after him.

Erin woke with a start. Her heart ached as the image of the carefree Gabe slowly faded from her mind's eye. Sio raised her head and looked at her in the darkness, her head tilting to one side before laying her head back on her paws and staring off into the darkness outside the cave. Everyone else slept on, but Erin couldn't close her eyes again just yet. She wasn't sure how she connected to Gabe's memories. Maybe it was just being in his home realm, but she was raw with fresh loss. Tears blurred her vision, but she didn't want to cry here. The last thing she wanted was to wake one of the others and have them find her sobbing in the cave. As quietly as possible, Erin rose and stretched, feeling her body work out the kinks from sleeping on the hard ground. She tiptoed out into the woods, trying to stay as far away from Sio as possible as she left the mouth of the cave.

Gabe had been a happy child. Different from the one she met in the group home. When Erin met him, he had been broken, memories of his happiness and family wiped away. His true self was hidden away so deep even *he* couldn't find it. It made her wonder if she even knew him. She always thought she had, but she hadn't had time with him after his memories returned. Erin didn't get to see who he was after he reclaimed his true elven self.

Now she stood in his home. In his forest. He could have climbed the tree that now stood dead in front of her. He could have picked flowers for his mother and sister in the field that was now filled with dried grass and weeds. Tears were silently falling down her cheeks now. She moved a little farther away from the cave and touched the tree closest to her. She felt the familiar ball of warmth in her stomach as her powers buzzed inside her. The tree started to come alive under her fingers. Leaves sprouted, bark covered the trunk once more; she felt the age of the tree and its will to live. The second she pulled her hand away, however, the leaves disintegrated and fell like ashes to the ground. The color faded, and it was dead once more.

Things already dead could not be brought back. If anyone should know that, it was her. The child in her sleep had so much love and happiness. He wanted to grow up and be like his father, a king to the entire elven realm. He never got the chance.

Everything went still when a branch cracked nearby. Quickly she twisted so she was hidden behind a tree. Searching the darkness, Erin tried to find what caused the noise. She reached down and grabbed the dagger strapped to the side of her leg. She now carried and reached for that blade as she once had done with her camera, the familiar handle molded to the inside of her palm. They'd spent an entire day walking, and she hadn't seen one animal, or sign of life other than the erebi they'd heard. It would be just her luck to try to get a little air and run right into a pack of infection erebi. Then she caught the silver glint of an eye peering at her from the forest. Her heart stopped, and a curse slipped from her lips.

"You have something that belongs to my master." The erebus from her rooftop stepped out into full view. No cloak to hide his scaly skin this time.

"How did you even *get* here?"

"I followed you." The human side of his face formed a smile. "I told you I will have that amulet back. I will give you one more chance to hand it over and keep your life." Erin felt the weight of it around her neck. She hadn't moved so far away from the cave that they wouldn't hear her if she called, but she didn't get the chance. He moved swiftly, grabbed her arm, and slammed her to the ground. Erin kicked out at him and jumped to her feet, moving away before he could get in another hit. She tried to swing her dagger, but he grabbed her hand mid-air, forcing them into a battle of strength. She felt the moment her energy wavered, so she did the only thing she could think of, and cracked her head against his. Instant pain shot through her and she wondered why all the heroes used that move in the movies. It was *stupid* and probably hurt her more than it hurt him. It did allow her the chance to get in one good swipe; she stabbed him in the side of the leg and got in a punch to his face.

With a growl, he lunged at her once more, and one of his claws cut at the skin of her arm. Her yelp was cut off when he let out a grunt of his own pain and released her, struggling with something in the darkness. Then Erin heard the low growl from Sio and saw the wolf had her teeth locked into the calf of his leg. He tried to kick her away, but she refused to let go, even as she whined against his attack. He moved to dig his claws into her side, but Erin hit him before he could find his mark.

His eyes went wide in surprise, and Erin gasped when she found the tip of a sword poking from his chest. He looked down and grabbed wildly for the weapon.

"I'm free..." Blood gurgled from his mouth, but a smile touched the corner of his lips before he fell to the ground.

"What?" Erin tried to understand, but Ethelron pulled the sword out with a sickening squelch and the erebus grew still.

Ethelron looked at the erebus carefully. "It's very odd to see his kind here. He was once human and was infected with dragon blood. I've seen his kind once before, but they are incredibly old and rare. They lived at the same time as dragons..." Ethelron's gaze fell on her in question. "Yet he was here, and just happened to be in the same place as *you*."

She couldn't say anything. Erin felt the question in Ethelron's gaze, but she could only watch as silver blood covered the ground. The body didn't disappear, but Ethelron drew her away before she could try to ask more questions. He had been trying to kill her, but at the last moment, when his eyes lit with freedom, she knew there was something more to his story. She wished there was a way they could have helped him instead of killing him.

"You protected Sio." Ethelron's voice broke her silence.

"She saved me first." Their eyes met in the darkness and a silent truce passed between them. The wolf, however, ignored her and started back toward the cave now that the danger had passed.

"You are lucky she was here. You could have gotten yourself killed." His voice turned angry, and their truce broke almost immediately. *So much for that.* "What were you thinking, leaving the cave? You are lucky it was only one and not a team of infection erebi."

"El, what's going on?" Ana stood behind him, the noise from the scuffle waking her. "Erin?"

"I'm not a child!"

"Yet, you needed saving." Ethelron turned his back to her and glared at Ana in the darkness. "I told you not to bring your friends. This isn't a tea party, this is war. I will not be held responsible for their lives as well as yours. Try to keep them in check." He tried to storm into the cave, but Ana put a hand on his chest before he could pass.

"I am well aware of what is at stake here. My *friends* are a team. If you want me, you get them too. You'll do well to remember that."

Erin watched with surprise as Ana held his gaze until he gave a sharp nod and stalked off toward the cave. Her eyes softened when they landed on her.

"You're hurt." Her blue eyes fell on the cuts on her arm.

"I'm *fine*. I didn't *need* saving. I was holding my own." Erin touched the wound on her arm. Her body would slowly heal it, but she wished she had power over her healing abilities so she could take the sting away. She was not about to ask Ethelron to heal her, though, and she hadn't told the other women that she didn't have control over that ability any longer.

"What happened?"

"The erebus that was after the amulet followed me here. He said he had been watching me since he attacked me on the roof. He must have seen me go off alone and thought it would be a good time to get it. I didn't mean to cause an argument or anything between you two."

Ana shrugged. "He can be a bit of a hot-head. He takes his duty as guard too seriously sometimes. Why *did* you wander off, though?"

It was the first time the two had actually sat together and talked in a long time. It felt good to not have to argue with the elf, but Erin wasn't sure she wanted to bring up the reason she needed air. With a deep sigh, she decided it was better for Ana to know. "I had a dream, but it was a memory...of you and Gabe. You were younger. I think about two years before you had to flee. He was climbing a tree." A smile played at her lips as she remembered. "You were both so happy. Your father showed up with Ethelron. Gabe lied to him about you giving him sugar."

When Erin saw Ana's face, she knew it was a real memory. A mixture of emotions flitted through her eyes in the darkness. "We had a great childhood before the war started." Her voice was quiet and thick with emotion.

"He really looked up to you, Ana. I wish..." Pain squeezed her chest. "I wish I could have known him once he'd gotten his memories back." Erin's voice broke and she had to stop talking. Ana took her hand and the two sat in silence, carrying each other's pain. "He had a ring," Erin finally broke the silence, needing to get everything off her chest. Ana's gaze flicked to her face with sorrow. "It was beautiful. We never talked about marriage, you know. We had never *seen* marriage. I didn't even think it was something I wanted. But I found that little box and thought of all we could have had."

"Erin, I'm so sorry."

"I don't even know if he would have loved me." There, the truth was out. "I didn't know him, not really. I knew a different version of him, one without memories or family. We were both broken. But he wasn't like that, not really. And I didn't give him the chance to really know me, either. I had powers and memories of my parents and I didn't tell him. There's no way to know what would have happened to us if he lived. I may never have seen that ring."

"He *loved* you, Erin. I saw him and talked to him after his memories came back. All he wanted to do was rescue you and tell you how sorry he was for what he said to you. He was still the Gabe you knew."

"Look at me, you lost your brother and I'm...I don't even know." The elf pulled her into a tight hug, even as Erin resisted. Then she broke, and returned it, knowing the elf needed the support as much as she did.

"Come on, we should get some sleep. We have a lot of walking ahead of us tomorrow, and Ethelron will only complain if we slow him down." Ana flashed her a quick wink and grin before leading the way back.

.℮ .℮ .℮

Doyle let Briar rest by the fire, but he couldn't find sleep for himself. He'd been thinking of her in dangerous ways for some time now, but he'd never allowed himself to think there could actually be anything between them. She *had* to hate him for the part he played in her capture; but when he thought of how she'd melted against him and returned his kiss, he understood hate wasn't the feeling she had for him. Lyra would not be happy about this development, but he had zero interest in Lyra's opinion. He was growing pretty tired of Lyra when it came to all things having to do with Briar.

He looked at her now, the fire dancing in her blue hair, her side rising with each steady breath she took. When he'd seen the erebus lift her off her feet by her neck, his world stopped. He'd sworn to keep her from harm, but she'd come away from the fight bruised, and it would have been far worse if it hadn't been for Malux coming across them. She seemed okay now, though he was sure her throat was still raw. Luckily, her body would draw the magic from the realm and help her heal quicker. He wanted to kiss her again. He didn't want to *stop* kissing her, and that could be dangerous for both of them.

Her breathing changed suddenly and then she sat straight up with a gasp, her gaze wild. He reached over to touch her shoulder, but she recoiled, so he lowered his hands and moved a little farther back. "It's okay, it's just me. You're safe." His heart broke for her when she reached up to her throat and rubbed at the skin there, but her eyes cleared from the nightmare and she gave him a small nod to show she was okay. He was afraid to move closer to her again; he didn't want to startle her when she was already out of it, but he didn't have time to worry over that because his head exploded as she doubled over, clutching at her temples.

Doyle dove forward to support her while she endured whatever vision was attacking her mind. She gave a moan of pain while he held her. He moved her hair over one shoulder and rubbed between her shoulder blades until she stopped rocking. His own head felt like he'd taken a dagger through his skull. He'd never felt the pain of her visions so strongly, and he wondered if this one had just been that much worse, or if it was because they currently had two marks connecting them.

"It's time to go to him." She rasped out after he felt her take a few deep breaths. When she looked up at him, her eyes were wide and filled with tears. He brushed away one that escaped, and she leaned into him.

"Are you okay?" He combed his hand through her hair and gave her another moment to gather herself. Finally, she nodded and pulled away from him to stand.

"Malux needs us."

"Okay." He stood and put out the fire. Then he made sure they had everything before he started following her down whatever path she was seeing to lead them to Malux. Her shoulders were tense as she made her way through the darkness of the forest. He kept his gaze moving to make sure they weren't ambushed again, but knew it would be hard to make out the infection erebi when it was so dark out. Briar stopped suddenly in front of him, so he darted the extra two steps to come up to her side.

"There," she nodded her head, and he made out a figure on the ground. He didn't hear anyone else around, but he still moved forward slowly. He wanted to make sure they were not about to come across the ones who killed Malux. It was hard to see Malux on the ground. His cloak swirled around him, drenched with his blood. Oddly enough, the expression on his face looked almost relaxed, like his last moments had been without pain. Briar stayed a step behind him. He was sure she'd seen his body enough in her visions and didn't really want to get up close and personal with the real deal.

"Here." She handed over the vial, but he took an extra second to clasp her hand when he saw how it shook. Briar gave him a small smile. "Pour half over the wound and the other half in his mouth."

He nodded and looked over the body. Even in the dark, it was easy to find the wound. He was careful with the vial, making sure not to pour out too much. Then he opened Malux's mouth and poured in the rest. They both waited in silence, watching for any change. He was wondering if they'd been too late, when Malux's mismatched eyes opened. He lurched upright, his hand going to his chest where he'd had a gaping sword wound just moments before.

"What?" Malux looked between the two of them and Doyle leaned forward to squeeze his shoulder.

"Welcome back."

Briar fell to her knees beside him, leaning forward to touch Malux's face. "Do you feel her control any longer? Were you broken free from her bond?"

"No...I don't feel her...I'm free." Malux actually grinned. Doyle had never seen anything stranger in his life. The urge to punch the other man hit him hard when Malux leaned forward and kissed both of Briar's cheeks before pulling her into a tight embrace. A sharp pang of jealousy coursed through him so suddenly that he was making a fist before he even realized it. "How did you do this?" Malux asked, pulling away and releasing Briar.

"We just had to wait for you to get yourself killed." Briar shrugged and stood. Malux moved to follow her but fell back to his knees with a grunt. "You'll probably still be weak for a while." Briar's eyes met his, so Doyle put an arm under one of Malux's while she took his other side. "We should camp out for the rest of the night, let him rest as much as he can, then we can head back for the portal later tomorrow."

"Agreed." Doyle took on most of the weight and started leading them back to where they'd made camp. It was slow going through the brush with the three of them in a line. They'd brought him back from death; but now he was going to have to figure out how to hide him from Lyra. They reached their camp, so he helped Malux lean against a tree that would be close to the fire, and then worked to relight it. Briar sat close to Malux and pulled some berries from her small bag to hand to him.

Doyle watched Briar carefully. Her eyes were bright with the firelight, her hair so full and vibrant. He couldn't think of sending her back to his realm, where he'd have to watch all that life drain so quickly from her all over again. Her lips were pink, and he wanted nothing more than to lean forward and claim them once more. She was consuming him and they weren't even touching.

It came to him then, what he had to do. His decision would probably get him killed, but he hoped they had enough in the works to bring down the queen. It didn't take long in front of the fire for Malux to drift to sleep, and Briar got up to sit beside him. "Thank you for helping me save him," she whispered, bumping her shoulder into his. He thought of telling her his plan, but knew he was running out of time alone with her, so instead he cradled her face, relishing the feel of her soft skin under his calloused hands. Her eyes widened, and he watched the color rise to her cheeks.

He was about to ask her if he could kiss her again, if he could keep kissing her until the world fell down around them, but she didn't wait for the words to leave his mouth. Instead, she leaned forward and drew him against her. She smelled like honeysuckle and tasted just as sweet. She sucked in a sharp breath, and her back arched when he nipped at her bottom lip. He forced himself to release her and back away. His own heart was pounding against his chest.

"What are we going to do?" she asked with a shaky breath that sent his blood pressure skyrocketing.

"With Malux?"

"No...I..." The blush spread down her neck. "I just meant you and me..."

"I'd like to do more of what we were doing." He tried to joke, though his voice sounded different even to his own ears. He knew what he wished they could have, but he also knew he was going to have to let her go, and he was not ready to do so just yet.

Chapter Nine

When Melody woke the next morning, tension was crackling in the air. Everyone ate their breakfast in silence, and no one seemed to make eye contact. Ethelron and Sio kept their distance from the girls, but Ana and Erin seemed oddly close for people who had avoided each other for the last few months.

"Okay, is anyone going to tell me what I missed? How long was I *sleeping*?"

"We should get started," Ethelron cut in. He didn't look in their direction, instead kept his eyes on the forest outside their cave.

"I had a run in with the erebus after the amulet. Apparently, he followed us into this realm and waited until I was alone before attacking last night."

Melody didn't think that fully explained the tension, but it didn't seem like the guard was going to wait around for the entire story to be told. He was already packed and moving with Sio outside the cave.

Ana's gaze followed his large form. Her blonde hair cascaded around her shoulders as she shook her head before turning back to Melody. "Just give him some time; he'll cool off."

The young witch raised an eyebrow at her, hating to be out of the loop but knowing her friends would tell her if it was important. The three of them finished loading up their packs and followed Ethelron into the woods. Instead of Siofra taking the lead and Ethelron bringing up the rear like they had done the day before, it seemed Ethelron was content to stay ahead of them. Ana gestured for Melody and Erin to go ahead of her, exasperation towards her guard clear on her face. They trekked in silence for a while, and Mel took the opportunity to observe. The farther they made it into the realm, the less devastation seemed to be taking over the forest. The trees were still lined with black veins of infection, but here there were more signs of life.

"All erebi will drain small amounts of magic from realms. They need magic to thrive, but they do not create their own. If we all lived in one realm as we did in the beginning, there could be a balance between our kinds. My father spoke of it often; the erebi would live much brighter lives if they could reach magic, and it actually *helps* to have a small drain on the magic. It's like a pruning, which helps the magic stay pure. Keeps it from becoming too wild. However, the infection erebi are different. The ancient erebi created them. They exist solely for destruction. Their kind drain magic like we breathe air. They also infect the land and people around them, which then goes on to drain more magic. Magic is the lifeblood of the world, so if this kind of draining continues to spread..." Ana shook her head sadly, "it could destroy everything in the end." As she spoke, Ana's eyes never stopped scanning their surroundings, though Mel wasn't sure if it was for danger or signs of life.

She watched her friend, not used to seeing her without the cloaking magic for so long. *Elf* looked good on her. Frustration towards her own kind surged in Melody; humans were *so quick* to judge what they didn't understand. It was why she'd come to live with Ana in the first place; it was why Sula *needed* a protector standing watch at the portal. Ana shouldn't be forced to suppress her true nature, and neither should she. She had a rare power that humans once carried with pride. She remembered how cool and collected Ana was about Sinopa's shocking arrival. It was *normal* amongst other realms for other beings to arrive in their true form. *Magic* was *normal*. Melody envied that and wondered if that would ever be the case for Sula. *For her.*

"Sir!"

Melody jumped at the voice. The witch glanced at Ethelron, who looked past her to Ana, and instantly shifted his body to be between her and the newcomer. She sent a look to Erin, who clearly noticed the same thing. "Even pissed at her, she's his first concern. How chivalrous." Melody muttered under her breath. Erin smirked at her comment.

As he approached, the group seemed to exhale all at once. His armor gave him away as a member of the guard, but as he took in the rest of the group, it became apparent that he did not recognize Ana. "You found another portal? We have been searching for you for days. The queen was starting to worry."

Ethelron glanced at Ana, who drew in a sharp breath. They seemed to have another one of their silent conversations before he turned back to the newcomer. "I did. It is not safe. The area is overrun, but I found one. I need you to go back and let the king and queen know that I will not be far behind you. We cannot risk any more resources being wasted on me."

"Who are these people with you, sir?" It was clear to Melody that the scout was young. He stared at Erin and Melody like he'd never seen someone that wasn't an elf before. *Probably only ever seen elves or erebi if he's too young to know who Ana is.* At least, that's what she hoped he was wary of. Were there elves with dark skin like her? Maybe she should have asked questions like this before going through the portal. Ethelron hadn't seemed all that surprised by her, so maybe she was safe. She'd have to ask Ana when she had a moment with her, though.

"I will explain everything once we get to the castle. *Go*, Myriil. You will get there faster alone than we can together." With one last wide-eyed glance at all of them, the young elf nodded, bowed respectfully to Ethelron, and was gone. The guard sighed heavily and ran a hand over his face.

"Why didn't you tell him about Ana?" Erin asked. "Don't her parents have the right to know that their *daughter* is home?"

"They *will* know, as soon as we arrive," he snapped. "Myriil is an excellent scout. He can become virtually undetectable when he is focused. He was born just before Aina and Toron were sent away, which is why he did not recognize her. Knowing that the princess had returned, Myriil would have become distracted and over-eager to get the news to the king and queen as quickly as possible. Distraction means greater chance of mistakes, greater chance of being caught by the erebi. If *they* knew that Aina returned, we would never make it back to the kingdom."

Erin nodded her understanding. "How far are we from your kingdom?"

"Depending on how much trouble we run into? A day or two. Myriil will make it back by nightfall at the latest." He sent a pointed look to Ana, and Melody rolled her eyes.

"Maybe we should stop for a while. Sio hasn't been able to hunt for a while, and we could use the break. It looks like we're far enough in that we can settle here for now without being seen," Ana murmured. Melody glanced at her and noticed a distant look in her eyes.

Ethelron must have noticed the same thing, because he sent Sio away with a low command and nodded. They ate in tense silence, Ethelron sitting just far enough away to separate himself from the group, and Ana staring blankly at the ground as she ate.

"Okay, whatever is going on between you two needs to stop. Now is not exactly a good time for you to be on different pages here," Melody finally complained, unable to deal with the tense silence any longer.

"El?" Ana spoke gently, ready to make amends. He silently continued to pick at his food. Erin and Melody turned to Ana and watched her huff in frustration and get up to walk away from the group. That got his attention, and his eyes remained trained on her until he realized she wasn't going to stop walking.

"About time," Erin muttered as he finally took off after her.

ℰ ℰ ℰ

Briar and Doyle stood on either side of Malux the next day as they slowly made their way to the portal. "Do you think the group will be okay?" Doyle asked.

"I hope so. You cleared part of the way for them, I'm sure they will manage from there." Malux was silent between them; she knew it would take some time for his energy to return, and he seemed focused on not collapsing on them.

"Do you ever wonder what it would be like to live in a world that wasn't split by the portals? If that witch had never torn the world to pieces...can you imagine what a world like that might be?"

Doyle's question startled her, and she glanced around Malux to see his expression. Doyle's mouth was set in a thin line, but his eyes warmed when they fell on her. She could really get used to this new way between them. She thought of how easily she'd fallen into his hold the night before and how ready she was to do so again. Their time together could be very short, and he could still turn against her, but she wanted to enjoy what they had while she could. Her life had been a large question-mark since her mother's death. She might as well take what good there was while she could.

"I believe the world would have more balance," she said slowly after thinking through his question. "If not for greed and obsession with power, your kind could still safely enjoy the magic created by mine; those with rare powers - like mine - would be left to live in peace. Humans and elves would live amongst their kinds in peace. But even within our own realms, we all oppress those we consider weak and glorify those deemed strong, allowing them to hoard powers at the expense of anyone and anything they see fit. By the time the beings in a realm realize how extensive the damage has become, the ancient erebi and their army have gained too strong a foothold, and it is too late to fight back." Briar shook her head and felt weary. "We can't go back, and even if we could, I can't say which way is better. It seems we are all built for war, and it doesn't matter if we choose to fight each other or ourselves."

"I always dreamed that if the realms were whole again, we would have the chance for better lives and more choices. We could all share in magic and strength and knowledge...but I'm sure you are correct. If we all lived together once more, we wouldn't have the chance to share all we have, because we'd be too busy trying to *take* instead of *give*. I suppose all we can do is try to make our own space a little better, right?"

"I think if more people thought like you, we could make a world for everyone." The energy of the portal started to tug at her. They still had a small hike to make it there, but it was nearby. She wasn't ready to return to Skia. She wasn't ready to feel the weight of the mountain all around her again, and she wasn't ready to lose Doyle to Lyra. He'd been more at ease with her here; he was lighter outside of his realm. Doyle said that the magic of the realm brought her to life, but it brought *him* to life, too.

He would thrive in a world where all the realms and beings lived as one. "So, how do you think we can get Malux through the portal and hide him? Almost anyone in your realm will recognize him with only a glance." Doyle's stance changed. His face hardened as he glanced at her, but wouldn't meet her eyes. Unease chilled her. There was something he wasn't telling her. "Doyle?"

"The easy answer? We can't. You're right. One glance at him and anyone would recognize him. Word would immediately get back to the queen, and she'd put him right back under her spell."

"There has to be some way to disguise him or something. Maybe if I went through with just him and he was cloaked, people would think it's you. I can get him to my room and then you come through-"

"I'm not taking him back to my realm." Doyle stopped, which made her lose her balance since Malux had been braced between them. Doyle took on the weight and helped Malux lean against a tree. Malux let out a groan but rested his head back and closed his eyes, using his time to gather what strength he could.

"Then what are you planning on doing with him?" Panic rose in Briar's throat. Was he already turning against her? This wasn't how her visions had gone. He'd only turned against her once he found out she was working against Lyra. They should have more time. She should have more time to convince him to turn against Lyra instead. Without thinking, she took a step away from him. His expression softened.

Doyle moved toward her, the heat of his gaze freezing her to her spot. "Briar, I told you I'd help you save him. I'll not go against my word." He reached her and cupped her face with his palm. "I also promised I'd see you home. I think it's time to do that. You've helped us, you've given Lyra enough information. We know who we need to get on our side to help us overthrow the queen. You've helped put the wheels in motion to do just that." His thumb brushed over her lips and his words scrambled in her brain. What he was saying didn't make sense.

"I can't take you back there. I can't watch you fade away again. I...I can't hold you as I have this past day and then take you back to a realm that will eat away at you, make you less of yourself. I'm going to take the two of you back to Loinnir. You can bring Malux back to full strength there, then maybe you can send him to help us in this fight if he's willing to join-" He was still speaking. She could see his mouth moving, but his voice faded out. Home. He wanted to send her home. He was going to free her.

Her heart was beating so hard in her chest that she was sure he could hear it. His eyes were warm like sunshine against her, and she could already smell home. She could feel the moss under her feet, feel the water from the lake against her skin and her lips. She wouldn't be going back as the same person she'd left, but he wanted to take her *home*. Tears pricked her eyes, and she fell into him, wrapping her arms around his neck and holding him so tightly she thought they'd somehow become one being.

"I'm not ready to lose you, Briar, but I'd be selfish if I took you back to my realm. I never should have brought you there in the first place. I never should have let Lyra lay a finger on you. I'm so sorry for the part I played-" She stopped his words with her lips. She claimed his mouth as her own as she gave him everything she had in her.

Her body seemed to catch fire when he made a growling noise in the back of his throat and pressed her body flush against his. She wanted to tell him to come with her. Briar wanted to tell him to run with her and make a life with her. The words were on the tip of her tongue, but she wasn't ready to pull away from him yet. She showed him instead; she poured all the love she'd seen them share; she gave him the forgiveness that he still felt he needed. She gave him the longing she had for him. Briar put all she could behind that kiss. His hands were fists at her waist, and there was no room for air to escape from between them. He lifted her off her feet and pressed her against a tree as he dragged teeth across her bottom lip. Her hands moved to touch his face, then her head exploded with pain.

"Briar?" She heard his voice, husky from their kiss but filled with worry. Somehow they were both on the ground, his form dancing before her, and then the vision came to her in an explosion of painful stars, and she was falling.

.℘. .℘. .℘.

"What do you think you're doing? It's dangerous; you can't just go wandering about!"

Ana spun to face Ethelron as he reached her, her frustration finally boiling over. Ethelron took a step back to avoid running into her. "If it was the only way to get you to talk to me, I would have started yelling for the erebi to come and get me. You are acting like a *child!*"

"This isn't a joke, Princess! Many have died from these erebi. Our world is coming down around us. We are already delayed because of the size of our group."

"You're being ridiculous. I want to get to my parents as quickly as you do. I want to end this war just as badly as you do. But you *have* to *stop*. You aren't my guard any longer. It's been almost eighteen years since you've been my guard. I thought you were *dead*. I thought all of this was lost. So, I tried to make a new life, and you keep holding it against me."

"What?" His eyes widened with surprise. "I would never hold that against you."

"You do! You look down on my friends, you act like I can't handle myself. Do you have any idea what those girls have been through? Melody was abandoned by her family because of her powers. She was living on the streets. You might think *I* saved her, but she saved *me.* I was drowning in my new realm. My brother was lost, and *every day* I was reminded of all I left behind. Then she came around and made me smile again. I found myself actually *enjoying life* again. I had a reason to wake up without dread, grief, and self-loathing every morning. Then Erin walked into my store. Her parents both *died* fighting to keep the erebi from entering Eloas. They left their daughter to try to help a world that was not their own. She grew up with no idea what she was. She and Toron met in a home for children without families. Every story Toron told me of growing up involved her."

Tears filled her eyes, so she started to pace, not wanting to break in front of him. "You should have seen how his face lit up around her. They were in *love.* Erin is in pain right now at his loss, but she came anyway. Her parents died fighting this war, but she *came anyway.* You see them as something slowing us down, as proof that I became *human* while I was away, but both of them would die for me if it came down to it." She took a steadying breath. "And I would sacrifice myself for them without question. If you want to be angry at me for running all those years ago, go ahead, but stop putting everything on them."

When she finally turned to look at him, his eyes were soft and his face was openly tender. He squeezed her shoulders to halt her pacing. "Princess, *Aina,* I am not trying to make you feel like I blame you or judge you. I apologize that I did. I just know it is important to get you back, and it is my duty to keep you safe."

"I am more than a *duty*, Ethelron." Ana fought back fresh tears as, once again, he reminded her just what she meant to him. She was *so tired* of his propriety and *duty*. She wanted to be his friend again. She wanted him to look at her like she was a *woman*, not just some task he had to check off his list.

"I-" Siofra's howl cut him off, shattering the moment. Both elves turned in the direction of her call and they were quickly joined by Erin and Melody.

"What is it?" Erin asked, standing on her toes as she tried to see into the distance.

"Let's move." Ethelron took the lead, leaving Ana to make sure everyone stayed together. Another howl pierced the air, closer this time. Erebi appeared up ahead and Ethelron turned, his eyes meeting hers, only to find all three women right behind him, weapons ready. Ana gave him a small nod to show that she and her friends were more than ready.

A circle of infection erebi stood before them, but their attention was turned elsewhere. Siofra bit at them and dodged their attacks, and when she moved one erebus out of the way they saw Myriil at the center, warding them off with a long elven blade.

"Stay here, I'll get him," Ethelron demanded.

"Nice try, guard. But you are greatly outnumbered."

"Erin's right. Melody, can you do the protection spell on us again?" Ana turned and found the witch already one step ahead. The spell cover her like a cloak, and she saw that Ethelron and Erin felt it too.

Without a word, Erin sent a boulder crashing into three of the erebi, giving them an opening to join the scout at the center of the fight. Ana ran ahead before Ethelron could try and argue. "Are you hurt?" Erin called out to the scout as they joined him, everyone automatically pressing their backs together to protect each other.

"They came out of nowhere!" Myriil stabbed an erebus and the forest filled with its hiss of pain. A new one came from the shadows to take its place, and everyone froze at the sight. Clearly, it had once been an elf. Still wearing elven armor, its skin was now taking on the wispy shadow look from the infection. Hollow black eyes stared at them and the start of claws jutted from what used to be slender elven hands.

Myriil tried to stab it, letting out a curse, but the elven armor blocked the attack. The scout narrowly missed getting hit by claws and Erin shot out a hand, breaking the earth under the erebus' feet. In a panic, Myriil broke from the circle and ran, leaving them to fight off the remaining erebi. Ethelron took out two, but Ana got to the elven erebus first. Erin covered her side, killing off a few of the infected on her own, when they heard Melody scream and felt the cloak of her protection spell drop. Distracted, Ana turned to see what happened to the witch, and in the next heartbeat something hit her arm.

Intense agony shot through her like nothing she'd ever felt before. A dark fog filled her mind, and even though the pain was radiating from her arm, her whole body suddenly felt like it was on fire. Her strength waned, and the elf stumbled.

"Princess!" Ethelron grabbed her, and his touch felt like a white-hot poker pressed against her skin. She screamed as Ethelron turned her away from the fight, protecting her with his body, leaving Erin to fill their space.

"Ana!" Melody's voice sounded far off even though Ana saw her standing nearby. "It scratched her! Is she infected now?" Melody's voice rang out in fear, and *that* made Ana pay attention. Sio's wet nose brushed her uninjured arm, but she recoiled from the touch. The wolf whined, but Ana couldn't stand anything else touching her.

"Mel, a-are you okay?" Ana struggled to find the words, *was her mouth going numb*?

"I'm fine, the scout ran into me while he was trying to run away. I'm so sorry, I lost my concentration. It's all my fault!"

Ethelron's support left her, and Ana found herself in Erin's arms instead. The abrupt movement left her feeling unbalanced, and she leaned heavily against her friend. "You idiot! You nearly got her killed!" Ethelron grabbed Myriil by the scruff of his cloak and lifted him completely off the ground in his anger.

"Ethelron *stop*! What about Ana? Is there something we can do? The wound is starting to turn black!" Ana could almost taste the panic in Erin's voice. Ethelron dropped the scout and lifted her from the ground; he held her against his chest with such tenderness. A younger version of herself was probably falling over herself at being held this way by Ethelron, but her present body protested against being touched, pain radiating from every point where their bodies touched.

"Cover me." His words were sharp as he carried her away from the rising smoke of the erebi bodies breaking down.

Chapter Ten

Briar's body felt like it was ripping into pieces. She hadn't experienced pain like this from a vision since she'd lived through almost every way the group of them could die, when she first started looking into ways to bring down the queen. She'd been stuck in a coma while her body tortured itself. Now every one of her limbs felt disjointed, her muscles stretched, and her skin seemed to be peeling from her bones. She was screaming. She knew she was screaming. Her throat was raw, and she wondered when her voice would fail. She didn't see anything though, just felt the agony.

Everything around her was black. She felt like she was floating, and then her body slammed to the ground and bones cracked. Bright light flashed across her vision, making her eyes constrict so quickly it was painful. Heavy chains were around her wrists. She felt one around her neck, weighing heavily and rubbing her skin raw. Flames shot out in front of her and, when she tried to kick away, Briar realized the chains were too tight for her to move. The flames started inching closer while a laugh broke out behind her. She knew that laugh. She'd heard it so many times before. Lyra was there, her cat-like eyes flashing.

"You had the runes removed. You let her go..." A sharp boot flashed into her ribs, knocking the air out of her. The next breath she dragged in was full of smoke and heat. "You betrayed me. You betrayed our plan. Maybe," Lyra squatted down until she was eye level, "I should have treated you more like my sister treated Malux. Then you wouldn't have betrayed me for some blue-haired trinket." Another sharp kick to the ribs. Briar looked at her chained arms and saw the cuts and bruises, and realized they were not her arms. She knew who she was right now. She knew, because before she'd fallen into this nightmare, those very arms had been holding her like she was the center of the world.

It was enough; she knew what was to happen if he betrayed Lyra. Briar understood, and she didn't want to be trapped in this vision anymore. She tried to surface, tried to find a way out, but there was nothing. Just flames roaring toward her, ready to lick at her skin. Lyra left her then - left Doyle - and the flames heated the chains and burned where they touched her skin - his skin. Briar wanted to scream, but she held her back stiff and tried to pull against the chains. Nothing would give. Lyra was going to kill Doyle because of what he wanted to do for her. Maybe in his plan to send her home, he believed Lyra would forgive him, but there was no forgiveness in Lyra, only control and hate.

The flames reached skin now and the scream that tore from her throat racked her whole body - Doyle's body. The pain kept growing worse as the flames moved farther. She hoped she'd black out or something, but it wouldn't end. She was ready to beg for death when finally, the blackness closed in again.

Abruptly, she was herself, and she was in her home realm. Her feet were dangling in the stream, and Malux sat beside her. He was still weak, but slowly gaining strength. They'd talked about what to do about the queen. Malux was ready to help, but while they were in Loinnir, it was hard to know the current state of things. Then something in the air changed. Malux was on his feet, but it was already too late. Briar caught sight of erebi just before Malux found himself surrounded. Lyra stood before them, her head cocked to the side, her teeth gleaming.

"Well, well, look what I've found here. My sister's little pet and my missing observer fae. Kill him." She flicked her fingers, and Malux was overtaken by numbers he had no hope of fighting off. Then Lyra moved like the wind and had her hands clasped around her neck. Briar wanted to scream out, but there was no breath left in her to do so.

"You are coming home with me and I will beat every vision I want out of you. And now," she cooed, breath hot in Briar's ear, "your little knight in shining armor will not stand between us. He freed you and turned against me, so I had no more use for him. But you, my dear, I see many years of use ahead of us-"

The vision swirled again, and Lyra stood before her with a crown on her head. Briar's body ached, and when she tried to draw in a breath, her ribs protested. Chains hung from her hands and weighed down her neck. She saw years of Lyra's reign, with her chained at her side, spread out before her.

.℮. .℮. .℮.

The fire was spreading like poison through Ana. Her vision danced as Ethelron got them to a spot he must have felt was safe and then laid her gently on the ground. Despite his care, the jostling nearly brought her to the brink of unconsciousness. *'I'm so sorry…hold on, Aina…'* His voice in her mind sounded so young, so scared. Had she imagined it? Imagined or not, the soft plea drew her focus enough to stay awake. She heard crying and wasn't sure if it was coming from her or someone else. Ana hoped no one else was injured. She thought Melody had said she was okay, but now all of that seemed fuzzy.

"Is she going to be okay?"

That was Melody; her voice was thick with tears and worry, but Ana knew it like she knew her own.

An unfamiliar warmth spread through her, easing away the fire. "If caught early enough, the infection can be drawn out. The queen taught me how to do it. Any elf with the ability to heal has been trained. If the infection spreads too far, though, there is no stopping it. It can sometimes be held back-" His voice faded from her for a moment as the pain flared where she'd been scratched. She was *so stupid* to have let herself get injured. Fear for Melody had distracted her, and she'd failed. Again. This time she'd done so in front of

Ethelron, which was painful to her ego, but at least it had only been *her* that was injured.

Finally, relief washed over her as the pain left her body like it had never been there to start with. A gentle touch ran over her cheek and the point of her ear. When she blinked, she found Ethelron staring down at her, his skin looking oddly pale, the runes on the side of his neck and face standing out starkly.

She slowly sat up, but held her head once she was upright. Everything felt heavy, and her equilibrium was off kilter.

"Princess, how are you feeling?" Ethelron placed a hand on her arm to slow her down, but she needed to stand. She needed to get away from the mistake she made.

"I'm okay. We should get moving again. We should get a little farther before it gets dark. Where did the scout go?" Ana asked after taking a slow - and somewhat unsteady - look around the small group and finding everyone, including Sio, surrounding her.

"He continued his journey back to the castle." Ethelron's voice, so close to her ear, made Ana keenly aware that his hands were on her, helping her stand upright. As much as she wanted to lean into his touch, draw on some of the strength he was silently offering, her pride would not allow it.

"Okay, let's move." Ana ignored the skeptical look in Ethelron's eyes and did her best to ignore the matching gazes she was getting from Erin and Melody. Her blood still seemed to burn as her elven magic fought off the remnants of infection, but it was the fog in her mind that was truly hindering her. It was like a black cloud over her vision that made her mind buzz. Drawing on her deepest reserves of strength, though, she pushed through it. Sio took the lead, while Ethelron walked directly beside her, ready to catch her if she fell. Erin and Melody took the rear, weapons still in hand, ready for another fight if needed.

After the third time Ana stumbled, Ethelron held out a hand for everyone to stop. "You are weak. We won't go any farther tonight."

"I'm *fine*. We need to keep moving."

"Aina," the nickname slipping from his lips actually gave her pause, "the darkness is not going to clear from your mind for a few hours. We should rest for the night. You'll be stronger in the morning."

"We could all use a break," Erin cut in before Ana could argue. "The fight took a lot out of all of us."

Finally, Ana relented and sank down. She leaned her back against the nearest tree and struggled to hold her head up. Siofra took off for another hunting trip, while Melody started a fire for them. The leaves next to Ana rustled, and strong hands gripped her shoulders, tugging her to lean against a solid body rather than the tree. She might have argued, but deft fingers found the tension points on her head, and the smoke in her mind began to swirl with the movement. She relented with a soft exhale, allowing herself to relax against his chest.

It was oddly satisfying to feel the practice of elven healing once more. It had been years since elven magic was used on her. For the first time since returning to Eloas, Ana actually felt like she was *home*. He wasn't able to take away the shroud of darkness, but it helped to relieve her a bit.

Surprisingly, he didn't release her once he was finished. Instead, he began to knead her neck and shoulders while he turned his attention to Erin. "Could you tell me about Toron?"

"What?" Erin looked up from the fire, her eyes wide and instantly filled with grief.

"I'm sorry. I understand it may be too painful. Ainadelothien told me you are the reason she found him again."

Erin glanced at Ana. The elf quickly looked away, not wanting to force her to speak. "I knew him as an elfling, I just wanted to know more about his life in Sula," Ethelron finished.

The camp filled with silence, but then Erin started speaking. Her voice was heavy with grief at first, but quickly grew lighter at the memories.

"It couldn't have been long after he left Eloas that we met. I was the first one to speak to him when he came to the group home. He was scared. Most kids are when they first get there. But he was much better at being there than I was. He made friends easily and always seemed to look on the bright side of every situation. I wasn't like that. I found it nearly impossible to make friends. He was really the only one I felt connected to."

Melody silently passed out food to everyone, and paused to give Ana's hand a light squeeze when she found the elf hanging on to every one of Erin's words.

"Gabe was caring and always looked out for everyone. He'd let you cry on his shoulder, or talk his ear off. He didn't try to fix everything, he would just listen. I...I was attacked once, in one of the homes. When I came back, everyone was judging me, like it was my fault. He snuck up to my room. He could have gotten in a lot of trouble because the boys weren't allowed in the girl's dorms. But he did it anyway, and he cracked a joke. He even stole scissors and helped me cut off all my hair when I said I wanted to chop it off.

"We were separated for a while, once we aged out of the system. But when we found each other, he was still so *open*. It was like the world couldn't get him down, you know? He was quick to forgive..." Erin's voice trailed off then. Finally, she smiled again and began to tell a story about working all summer to earn money to buy himself a bike, only to spend it on a camera she fell in love with.

"Thank you," Ana spoke up some time later as Erin and Melody drifted off to sleep. They'd talked late into the night, listening to Erin share stories, and each of them sharing a few of their own.

"For what?" Ethelron was still pressed against her side. Sio had returned from her hunt and laid on Ana's other side, head resting on her lap.

"Healing me, asking about Toron. I always wanted to hear stories of his that I missed. He told me a few, but our time was limited. It was nice hearing about him from someone who loved him."

"Go to sleep now, Princess. The hour is late." His voice was soft, lacking all of the demand he usually had. The quiet tenderness in his gesture made her smile. She leaned her head back and closed her eyes. It didn't take long for sleep to find her.

.℘ .℘ .℘

Erin was standing in a beautiful room filled with light. Glass windows surrounded her, held by delicately woven metal. Aina was in front of her, a book in her lap and her mind clearly preoccupied.

"Aina!" A young Toron came tumbling into the room, breaking her quiet study. She looked a little annoyed at the interruption, but her brother's excitement was contagious, and she couldn't help but smile. "You won't believe what happened! Ethelron brought in a young wolf! She was hurt and Mama healed her! You have to come see!" Toron took her hand and tried to drag her from her seat. Finally, she set the book aside and rose to follow him.

Erin walked through the halls behind them, unable to take her eyes off the intricate working of metal and trees that made the walls. Trees with thin trunks and branches intertwined and let in light. They entered another room and a wolf pup was running around, Ethelron standing in the center of the room, watching with obvious delight.

Erin thought it odd to see that expression on his face. But his eyes fell on Aina and the emotion vanished, the perfect image of a royal guard once again.

"Toron, wait! You can't go running up to a wolf!" Aina grabbed the scruff of her brother's shirt.

"He's perfectly safe. I wouldn't let any harm come to the young prince."

"Just the same, she is a wolf," Aina argued.

Ethelron's eyes danced with some secret, and he smiled. "Give it a try," he nodded toward the pup, who tried to stop, and slid on the smooth floor. Aina knelt and reached out a hand. The pup ran right for her, but she knew Ethelron would not let harm come to her, so she resisted the urge to flinch. She was rewarded by an onslaught of kisses from the wolf's wet tongue.

"I want to pet her!" The young prince jumped in his spot.

"Be calm and she will come to you." Ethelron stood next to the boy and knelt down to his level. The wolf abandoned Aina and went for her master. "Go ahead," the guard motioned that it was safe for the prince to pet her, and she sat calmly while the elfling stroked her red fur.

"What's her name?"

"Siofra," Ethelron answered after a short pause.

"You are going to name her 'elf'?" Aina giggled, reaching out a hand to join her brother in petting the pup.

"Well, she seems to think she is one, or at least enjoys being around them. It seems fitting."

Sio moved away from her master and threw all her weight into Aina, her tongue hanging from her mouth as she enjoyed every second of her belly rub.

"I think she likes me more," Aina teased.

Erin watched her cheeks flame when he answered, "I can't blame her."

Erin woke in the morning to the sound of Sio barking.

"They are like children!" Melody laughed and Erin looked up to find Ana and Ethelron throwing a branch back and forth, Sio trying to catch it in mid-air.

Erin sighed in agreement but couldn't help a smile. "Good to see Ana's feeling better. What do you think about those two?"

"We've seen my dating track record as of late. I don't think I can be a good judge. Besides, I don't think *they* know. I've never seen Ana like this, though. She's never shown any interest in dating, but she seems more alive around Ethelron."

"Yeah, I can't tell if it's just that they've known each other for so long, or if there is something there. All I can say is, if there is *something,* they shouldn't run from it. Life is too short, even if you are supposed to be 'semi-immortal'."

"We should start moving." Ethelron approached the camp, but his eyes were noticeably lighter than usual. The group packed up and started moving, but it didn't take long for the sound of erebi to reach them.

"Again?" Melody groaned.

"Honestly, I'm surprised we haven't come across more."

"Do you think the scout got through?" Erin asked quietly, waiting for the view of the erebi to reach them. Her question was met with a grunt from Ethelron, clearly he was still upset that Myriil ran from the fight and nearly got Ana killed.

"There!" Ana pointed into the distance and they finally saw the dark erebi emerging from the cover of trees. Two infected elves followed.

"They have weapons. I haven't seen any of the infection erebi with weapons. Do you think they still retain some of their *self*?"

"There is no way to know for sure, but we've seen them before. They never talk, and even when they are faced with loved ones, they don't show any recognition, or mercy," Ethelron whispered, his hand tightening his grip on his sword. "They are harder to kill since they have elven armor. It's going to take a few direct hits to get through it."

The lead erebus hissed and suddenly turned toward them. "Melody, can you do the protection spell again? It helped last time," Ethelron asked. Ana's eyes turned toward him at his words.

"Yeah, be careful." Melody started her chant, and the other three ran ahead to meet the approaching erebi. Erin leapt toward the full-fledged infection erebus, with its long finger-like claws and wispy looking body. She wondered if they'd all been something else at some point. Maybe the longer a being was infected, the more shadow-like they became. The elven erebi were newer and still retained the elven body. After her second hit, she stabbed the erebus in the heart and watched him sag to the ground. Her dagger came back covered in dark blood.

Ana and Ethelron were each working on one of the elven erebi. They kept their backs to each other, but seemed to move as one. Ethelron took down his erebus first, his long sword working better to penetrate the armor. He didn't have the chance to turn and help Ana, however, because she finally broke through the armor of her own creature and sank her dagger into its chest, leaving this battle unharmed.

"Am I the only one with the urge to eat some popcorn and watch a cheesy movie on my sofa?" Erin asked after everyone caught their breath.

"I'm thinking of some rocky road ice cream," Melody joined in.

"I'm not sure I understand any of the words you are saying, but I believe I understand the sentiment. Personally, I'd go for a glass of elven wine."

"Look at that, he's one of us!" Ethelron seemed to catch himself before smiling, but Erin didn't miss the way Ana grinned toward him. Her chest ached to see the look, so she turned her attention to cleaning her blade until everyone was ready move again.

♇ .♇ .♇

When Briar came out of the vision, her body ached, her head pounded worse than she'd felt in a long time, and she was quietly sobbing. She felt arms around her, the ground hard beneath her, but she couldn't get her eyes open to see who was holding her, or where they were. Briar shook with her sobs and ached from what she saw. She'd been so close to going home, so close to being free, but she knew now it wouldn't end well for any of them. Even if she hadn't just seen herself enslaved to *Queen Lyra,* she wouldn't be able to go home knowing what kind of future awaited Doyle.

Finally, she came more into herself and surfaced from the vision. She was acutely aware that a hand was moving in steady circles over her back, and that Doyle's deep voice was strained and anxious as he tried to repeat calming words to her. "How-" She started to talk, but her throat was raw and burned when she tried to push the words through. Doyle jumped back from her, his face haggard as he leaned back to look at her. "How long was I out?" She kept her voice low this time, so it didn't hurt as much.

"Briar…" Her name was a beautiful whisper on his lips. His hands came to her cheeks, and he held her like he never wanted to let go. Then his lips found her forehead before he pulled her back against him. He was shaking.

"Doyle, how long?"

"Two days, Briar. I've been so afraid to leave you to even search for food or water. You've been screaming, and I had to fight off infection erebi." He leaned forward and kissed her cheek before letting her go. "I've been afraid to touch you, that I might be making the vision worse, but then you screamed more when I wasn't with you…" He ran a shaky hand through his hair.

"I'm sorry, Doyle. I'm sorry I left you for so long, and that you had to deal with that. Are you okay? I know you feel my visions, too."

Doyle was on his feet, pacing before her. "How in the world could you have just spent two days sounding like you were being tortured and worry that *I* might have gotten a migraine?"

She wanted to stand, but felt weak and lightheaded. The moment she even moved, her head exploded in pain. At her small groan, he was at her side again. "Shit, I'm sorry. What can I do?"

"Is Malux okay?"

Doyle looked down with a sigh like he found her exasperating, but then he nodded, like he understood answering her was the only way. "Malux is fine. He's been doing his best to help me, but he's still weak. He fought an erebi that got past me, though, and kept it from you."

"Is there water?" She was parched and her throat was still burning. He left her side and came back a minute later with a small pouch. It hurt to tilt her head back, but the water helped bring her back to life.

"I didn't think you'd have a vision that strong while we were here. I thought my realm made them worse for you." He let out another shaky breath, his red eyes meeting hers in desperation. "I thought you were dying, Blue."

"I don't think it's from the realm, but from the vision itself." She reached out and stroked his scarred cheek. She could smell his flesh burning and wanted to cry again. Lyra beat him, chained him, and burned him. The woman who had once saved his life and kept him at her side had turned on him so easily.

"What did you see?"

She flinched at his question, but wasn't surprised. She wanted to tell him; how could he stay on Lyra's side if he knew how she could betray him? But something held her back. Instead, she just said the words that would break her heart. "I can't go home. Not until we bring down the queen." *And Lyra*, she added to herself.

Chapter Eleven

"My dagger against your sword is not a fair fight. I'll try to be gentle."

Ethelron raised a questioning brow toward her as Ana twirled her blade gracefully. He glanced down at his sword and then back up at her, his hazel eyes bright with mirth. "You sound so sure of yourself, Princess. Do you forget that while you have been playing shopkeeper with the humans, I have been honing my skills, trained by *your father*? You have fought well, I will give you that, but I do not believe that you are capable of besting *me*."

Erin, Melody, and Siofra sat near a tree while Ethelron and Ana sparred. When she'd challenged him, the guard had initially been hesitant, citing her recent injury as a reason to take it easy. Ana scoffed at him, taunting and teasing and dancing nimbly around him until he finally caved. She couldn't say for sure what sparked this surge of energy, but it seemed to have started when she and Ethelron had been playing with Sio. Maybe it was surviving the infected elf's hit, maybe it was Ethelron's healing and care afterwards, she couldn't say for sure. Either way, she needed to settle herself and get rid of some extra energy, hence challenging the other elf to a harmless match.

"You assume that I did not train and have battles of my own while living in Sula." He blocked her first swing easily and then pushed her back with a lunge of his own.

The clang of their blades reverberated through the clearing, and both elves stepped back. Movements perfectly in sync, they danced around one another, reading moves before they were made and reacting gracefully. As they circled, Ana narrowed her eyes at him, focusing on a move she wanted him to *think* she was going to make. If the twitch of his lips was any indication, he'd read her exactly as she wanted him to. As he swung his blade at her, Ana dropped the hand brandishing her dagger, and latched onto his fighting arm with the other. Before he could react, she twisted the hilt of his sword free, forced him to turn, and pushed him chest-first into the nearest tree. Instinctively, her body pressed against his back, pinning him in place, and she grinned triumphantly at the grunt driven from his lungs by the impact.

"Woo! That's my girl, show him how it's done!" Melody cheered from the sidelines while Erin joined in with clapping of her own.

Ana glanced over her shoulder at the others with a grin.

The next thing she knew, his foot hooked around the back of her knee, and she was falling, her own dagger suddenly pressed against her throat. "Distracted there for a second, *Princess*?" Ethelron hovered over her with a smug grin on his face, but when she tried to shift, both of them froze. He'd landed straddling her hips, and they found themselves in uncharted territory.

Ana only took seconds to decide what to do and shifted her weight to flip them. She pinned his hand with the dagger over his head, gripped his throat with lax fingers, and leaned in to let her breath dance across his ear. "You tell me, *Guard*." She couldn't help but grin wickedly as she reclaimed her dagger and stood in one fluid motion, leaving him scrambling to regain his composure. She winked at Erin and Melody, who looked almost as shocked as Ethelron. Ana grabbed her pack without breaking stride and whistled to Sio, who leapt up and followed happily.

A few steps later, she glanced over her shoulder to see Ethelron pushing to his feet, and her friends laughing at one another as they fell into step behind her. "Let's go, slow pokes, we're wasting daylight!"

"That was great, lunch and a show." Erin threw her own pack over her shoulder.

"What exactly happens when one is healed by an elf? Did you drug her or something when we weren't looking? She's so...hyper." Melody waited for Ethelron to catch up to walk beside them. He didn't answer, though, and when Ana turned, she found his dark gaze focused on her.

"So," Erin said some time later. "Siofra means elf? I guess you *do* have a sense of humor." They made good ground for the day and Ethelron told them they should have the kingdom in view by nightfall.

"You were teaching her elvish?" Ethelron looked at her, but Ana shook her head.

"How did you know that?"

"I saw another memory. I saw when Gabe first took you to see her." Erin watched the silent looks everyone seemed to exchange. "What?"

Ana stopped walking so she could give Erin her full attention. "Erin, did you do another memory spell or something before we left? Like you did with your mother? They can be very dangerous if not done properly." She thought of stories of people getting lost in memories and not being able to return. It wouldn't surprise her if Erin had been desperate enough for some connection to Gabe that she tried to do the spell on her own from memory, and possibly made a mistake.

"What? No! I don't know why I'm seeing his memories. It didn't start until I got here. I don't know...I didn't really think anything about it." Her voice became defensive, so Ana relented but hung back so she was walking beside Melody.

"Were you able to do the spell on the amulet before we left? I was so caught up in everything happening that I never asked."

Melody nodded, her eyes dropping to the ground. Ana knew instantly something was wrong. "A strong, dark magic was blocking me from being able to find out much about it. I told Erin it was full of darkness, though. She didn't seem to think so, because Gabe had it."

"Is something the matter?" Ethelron's voice pushed into her mind. *"The fae can see into the past?"*

"Not exactly. I'm not sure what it means quite yet."

"Erin, when the erebus followed you here, did he say anything else? Hint at who he was trying to get the amulet for?"

"No. I guess I might still have to deal with that when I get back home. Whoever sent him will probably send someone else."

Ethelron stopped in his tracks and turned to look between the women. "The erebus with dragon's blood? He was after you?"

"It was the same erebus that attacked me in my apartment. That you healed the injuries from. He said he had been watching me and followed us here."

The guard's eyes darted quickly to Ana. "Aina, did I just lead more erebi into our realm by bringing her here? Why didn't anyone say anything?" His question was an angry growl. She caught his use of her nickname again and became irritated that he only seemed comfortable enough with her to use it when he was terrified she was injured, or when he was annoyed with her.

"It was just him. No one else was following me. I don't think they would know where we went or how to even get here," Erin interjected before Ana could snap back at him.

"May I see it?" Though it was phrased as a question, he held his hand out, demanding she hand over the amulet. Ana nodded reassuringly when Erin's eyes flicked toward her. Slowly, the halfling unclasped the chain and laid it gently in his palm. He studied it, turning it in his hand and brushing a finger over the smooth finish. "I've never seen such a stone."

"Neither have we," Melody spoke up. "I was trying to find out what it was for, but the spell didn't quite work..."

"You wear an amulet around your neck and you don't know what power it holds?" His growl had returned, and Ana watched something come alive in Erin as she nearly hissed back at him.

"It was Gabe's. He was wearing it when he *died*." Erin snatched it from his palm, her brow creased with worry for the safety of the piece. Quickly, she bound it around her neck once more, but kept hold of it, like she was guarding it in case someone decided to rip it from her.

"Ainadelothien..." Ethelron's voice held a warning, but the elf stepped forward and laid a reassuring hand on his arm.

"We are close to the kingdom. Once we are there I will show it to my mother. Maybe she will be able to tell us more. Erin has been wearing it for months, and no harm has come to her. I'm not sure how Gabe got it, or why the erebus was after it, but it should be fine for now. Let's keep moving." Ana nearly pushed him forward before resting a reassuring hand on Erin's shoulder. When her eyes fell on Melody, however, it was clear the witch had her own worries about the stone. Fear glinted in her gaze as Melody watched Erin.

.℘ .℘ .℘

They stayed in the realm an extra day to give Briar time to recover from her visions, and to figure out how to get Malux hidden away safely without being noticed. He pried more than he usually would to try to find out exactly what Briar had seen. There had to be some way around the clearly horrible outcome she'd seen, so that he could still send them to Loinnir, but she was set against it and there was no changing her mind. She wouldn't tell him what she'd seen, but he'd witnessed her reaction to it, and the toll it had put on her body. He knew it hadn't been good.

They decided the best option was for her to go through with Malux and for him to follow after. Malux had gotten a few extra days to recover; he was still weak, but he'd have enough strength to protect

Briar if they faced something on the other side of the portal. He also knew the unused passages just as well as Doyle, so he'd be able to keep them out of sight as much as possible. The only thing that worried him was how their runes would react to going through the portal separately. He hoped, since she was going to Skia, it would be okay, but there was no way to be sure until they did it. Doyle wouldn't be able to give them much of a head start if the rune reacted badly to the separation. He and Briar would both end up in too much pain for him to stay away if that happened. And while he knew it would hurt for him, it would be worse for her. He was meant to be punished if they got separated, but her rune was spelled to incapacitate her until he caught up to her.

He told her as much, but Briar shrugged it off. "I'm sure I've been through worse. I just have to get Malux hidden and then it will be okay. If it reacts badly, then you'll feel it too, and you'll come through sooner." She paused and looked down at the pair of runes on her arm. "How were you planning on getting them off if you'd sent me home?"

"I was going to go with you into your realm. There is a fae there that has the power to remove runes. I looked into them when Lyra had me helping Kali before. I figured I'd find them, have them remove the runes, and then I'd go home." Doyle stopped himself from asking about her vision again, but it wasn't easy. He wanted to take a minute, pull her aside, and claim her lips once more while she was still vibrant in this realm. He wasn't ready to see her colors fade when they returned. Doyle didn't want that for her, but if she wouldn't tell him what she'd seen, there was nothing more he could do.

"Why are you looking at me like that?" She asked, though from the way her eyes danced, he had a feeling she knew *exactly* why he was looking at her in the way that he was.

"Do you think if I kiss you right now, you'll fall into another vision?"

"Well, we certainly can't live our lives worried about something triggering a vision, now can we?" She came to him easily, and he had to wonder about it. Their relationship had somehow changed, and he was not going to complain, but he wasn't sure how to deal with it. He hadn't expected it. The desire for her was there. It had been for some time. How she'd overcome so much, how she stood up to Lyra even after what Lyra had done to her, how she smiled and worried about everyone; it had all taken hold in him. Like roots settling in and spreading out, and the moment he'd kissed her, those roots had tightened around his ribs and refused to let go.

He took her lips slowly at first, tasting her and drinking her in like a man dying of thirst. She shivered when he touched the small of her back to pull her against him, and he had trouble taking the kiss slowly after that. The hunger for her bloomed in his chest as she gave him everything and more. Then she took for herself, and that was enough to drive him insane.

190

"How long have the two of you been so affectionate exactly?" Malux's dry tone broke them apart, but Doyle wanted to drag her right back to him, especially when he took in her swollen lips and pink cheeks, her eyes dark with desire.

"Not long enough." Doyle answered without hesitation, keeping Briar pulled to his side, not ready to let her go completely. Malux rolled his eyes, which was odd to see with the dragon eye. "If you are done, are you ready to go through, Briar?"

Doyle let her go and went to Malux, grabbing his arm. "You'll be able to get hidden quickly?"

"Yes, there is a tunnel not far from the portal. The moment we are through, we'll head straight there. I'll keep my hood up. Once we are in that tunnel, we should be fairly safe."

"You'll watch her? If the rune reacts...it will be extremely painful for her."

"I'll keep her at my side. I promise I'll watch her until you reach us. She saved my life." Doyle squeezed the man's shoulder and nodded. Then he turned back to Briar and lost his breath at the sight of her.

"You'll be okay?"

"Doyle, I know this rune may not make this easy. But you'll feel if it goes bad. We just have to get out of sight and then you can follow right through. If there is pain, it won't last for very long. I'll be fine."

She pressed her hands to his chest so she could get the leverage to meet his lips. The kiss was fast, but it warmed his skin. "I'll see you soon."

She tucked her hand around Malux's elbow, and after Briar glanced back at him once more, they stepped through. They'd only just faded from sight when Doyle's rune shot hot pain up his arm.

☙ ❧ ☙

Already things were changing. Melody used to be the one to comfort Ana when she was upset; for so many years, they'd only had each other. She could feel the anxious energy coming off her friend, but apparently she wasn't the only one. Ethelron came to Ana's side. He didn't say anything; he didn't touch her, just stood at her shoulder. He was like a silent statue of comfort. Ana's posture relaxed ever so slightly in his presence. Melody wondered if they were silently communicating in their elven way, or if they even needed to.

Night had fallen over the realm, and after fighting off another small group of erebi, Ethelron had settled them in a spot he felt would be safe enough for the night. It hadn't been an easy setup for camp. They were close to the castle now, and when Ana had seen the devastation from years of war, she'd almost lost it. Melody looked at it all with fresh eyes, but she could see where plants had once grown in lush fields. Whole groves of trees now stood dead from the draining that had taken place from the erebi. She could only imagine what it was like for Ethelron and Ana to look out at a land that was once vibrant and alive and see it as it was now. She could make out the castle in the distance, a thick circle of erebi at its base.

"The erebi have been trying to keep us trapped within the castle. The last few months, they have become more aggressive in their strategy." Ethelron appeared at her side, and she realized that he must have followed her gaze.

"I just don't understand. If Kali was leading the war in the other realms, why is there still fighting? We killed their leader. Shouldn't they have withdrawn or something?"

"Kali left this realm some time ago. She left her brother, Zepar, in charge of this fight. The erebi have just *been here* for the most part over the years. They make attacks, especially in smaller towns and the weaker kingdoms, but I think Kali just wanted to keep us out of the fight. She knew by cutting us off, she'd be making us weaker. That gave her time to take over the other realms and then come back for us." Ethelron glanced at Ana, who was now sitting and petting Sio. "Kali and Zepar have always wanted the elven people to suffer. Their mother was an ancient erebi of chaos. When the realms were created, she was one of the first to cross the portals. She was killed by elves, and her children have never forgotten. At the time we didn't know why, but now the increase in violence makes sense. Zepar knows his sister is dead, and it seems he's done playing with our people now." He sighed.

"*Now*, he wants us dead. That was one reason I felt it was so important to bring the royal children back. We need to end this war, and our people need a reason to remember a time before it. They needed something to celebrate so they could gain the strength to make the final blow to the erebi forces."

This close to him, Melody could see the exhaustion on the guard's face. He hid it well behind his mask of duty, but the man was *tired*. The entire realm must be tired. "It won't be easy on her. I know it hasn't been easy on anyone, but you are bringing her here as a display of hope in a time when she's been feeling very little. Losing Gabe changed her. We've lost others...she's lived through *so much* loss in her life, but Gabe hit her differently. Now she's going to have to face her parents, people she's loved and mourned, and she will have to tell them that he's gone."

"You care very deeply for her."

It wasn't a question, but Melody felt the need to answer, anyway. "Of course I do. We are family." She reached out and touched Ethelron's arm. "I hope for Ana's sake, you stop acting like you are just her guard, and you treat her as a friend, at the very least. She's going to need someone at her side, someone who understands this world and its dynamics. She cares for you, and not because you were trained to protect her." Before he could respond, Melody stepped away from him and went to Ana. She wasn't sure what to say to her. What *could* she say? Instead of remarking on all the damage they could see done to the kingdom below, or discussing the dying land they walked on, Melody laid her head on Ana's shoulder and let out a small puff of breath.

"What do you think my second date will look like? If my first date ended with an ancient erebus being summoned and multiple deaths, it's going to be really hard to top that."

"Hmm...you did set the bar pretty high. Maybe you could just portal hop right into Skia for takeout?"

"I'll keep that in mind as an option." They sat quietly, and Melody watched Ana pet the wolf absently. She wanted to pet Sio too, but she also thought it might be better to keep a safe distance. The wolf seemed to accept them well enough, but Sio also clearly favored the elves. "So, random thought. I've seen exactly four elves in my lifetime." Melody pursed her lips.

"Well, once we cross that circle of erebi tomorrow, you'll have seen more than four."

"Yeah...and will there be any elves with a darker skin tone? I'm just wondering if I'm about to be put on display for my amazing shade or not. Because so far, one-hundred percent of the elves I know are white."

The laugh burst out of Ana so suddenly that Ethelron and Erin both turned to look at her. "What? It's an honest enough question."

"It is, I'm sorry. Elves come in all shapes and sizes, and colors, too. We are very much like humans in that respect. Just to point out, half of those elves you've seen were related, so not the best sample of the population."

"Well, to be fair, we thought all other elves were dead. So, until recently, it was believed that one hundred percent of elves *were* white. *Thank you very much, Princess.*"

"Hush up, brat."

Melody chuckled, but the ease that she'd created around them broke when Ethelron approached. "We should all try to get some rest. Tomorrow we have to make our way through *that*." He nodded to the view below. "I'll take the first watch. We are too close to the kingdom to just leave Sio on guard."

Ana shook her head. "No, I'm not going to be able to sleep yet. I'll take the first one. I'll wake you next, though."

Melody watched as Ethelron assessed Ana carefully. Finally, he gave a curt nod. "Wake me as soon as you need, Princess." Melody gave another soft snort at that and got Ana's elbow to her ribs.

As soon as Ethelron settled down, Melody turned to Ana, a big grin already taking over her features. "Yeah, *Princess*, you can wake him up *whenever you need*. Wonder what you'd be waking him up fo-*ouch*." Ana flicked her right in the forehead, but it didn't stop Mel from laughing. It felt good to laugh, and Ana joined in quietly.

"How are you feeling about getting through those erebi?" Ana asked.

"There are a lot. I feel stronger here, though. Like in Loinnir, my powers seem to take in some of the magic around me, making me stronger."

"That makes sense. Sula has very little to offer in magic. It is there, but it's not the same as here and Loinnir. Here, you'd be able to draw some of the magic from the realm into yourself as a power boost, basically."

"Wouldn't that make me like the erebi?"

"Not all erebi are bad, and taking some of the magic wouldn't be wrong. If you were trying to siphon the magic into yourself and purposely draining the realm, then that would be an issue. If you went to Skia, where the ancient erebi have done exactly that to their own realm, you'd probably feel weaker than usual. Your magic would feel more faint because it doesn't have anything to draw from." She let out a tired sigh. "Enough of all that. Head off to sleep. The sun will join us in no time."

"Ana, they'll be happy to see you. They'll know it wasn't your fault. You just have to remind yourself that Kali took him away. *His death isn't your fault.*" Melody stood, but leaned down to give Ana a soft kiss to her forehead as Ana had done for her so many times. Then she went to find rest on the hard ground. Tomorrow she would be sleeping in a bed in an elven castle; she could get through one more night sleeping on the ground.

Chapter Twelve

Doyle found them in Briar's chambers not long after they crossed into Skia. Sweat coated his brow from pain, which finally faded once he was in front of her door. When he entered, he found Briar on her bed, her knees pulled up to her chest and her head resting on them. Malux was pale beside her. "I came through as soon as I could. I wanted to give you enough time to get out of sight..." Doyle whispered, the pain returning with a vengeance when he saw how her body was shaking.

"We weren't seen. We took the back way, and no one was in this hall. I...I had to carry her, but she kept from screaming."

"Briar?" Doyle sat on the other side of her and placed his hand on her back.

"I'm okay." She whispered, her voice barely loud enough for him to hear. She glanced at him, face pinched and pale. He brushed his thumb over her cheek, scooting closer so she could lean into him.

"Malux, are you okay? I know you still aren't back to normal strength." Doyle worried about how pale the dragon being was.

"I'll be fine. I'm just going to lie back and rest for a bit, if that's okay?" Malux didn't wait for an answer. He went to the floor and leaned on the wall near the end of the bed. It seemed he was asleep after a few deep breaths. Doyle knew they'd have to move him some place other than Briar's room, but for now, they all needed some rest. Doyle kicked off his shoes and then squatted on the floor in front of Briar to remove hers. She watched him silently, her eyes wide. When he finished, he climbed in beside her on the bed and pulled her against him, laying them both down. "Is the pain fading yet?"

"Yes, it's just, my blood feels like it's both on fire and has ice running through it."

"I'm sorry, I should have just come through with you...we should have risked it."

"It all worked out. I'm okay. Now we have to figure out a better place for Malux, and what we are going to tell Lyra."

"Well, we'll tell Lyra we managed to clear some pods so the group could get through easily, and, thanks to your visions, you saved my butt against one pod." He kissed the top of her head as she melted against him. He could lay in this bed beside her forever and be quite content. The shivering left her body and her breathing became steady. He knew he should get up, check in with Lyra before she heard he was back and came looking for him, but he didn't want to move. Briar had her head on his shoulder, her arm draped over his chest and one leg over his. He held her tightly against him, his senses filled with her flowery scent.

He'd wanted to send her to her home realm. He wanted to see her completely free from this life he'd dragged her into, but it would be a lie if he said he wasn't happy to be holding her. If they'd stayed with his plan, he'd have returned alone and he'd spent *so much* of his life alone. After finding Briar, he didn't want to be alone anymore, but he'd give up his own happiness to make sure she was safe. And he didn't think she'd ever be fully safe while she was with him.

℮ ℮ ℮

Ana hadn't slept well. She was fully prepared to stay up the whole night, but Ethelron had woken on his own to take his watch, and ordered her to rest. She knew she needed to, but it had taken her forever to shut her mind down enough to sleep. Even then, she'd woken at the first whispers of sun on the horizon, feeling like she hadn't slept at all. In the last moments of stillness, the elf watched her companions silently and tried to prepare her mind and body for what was to come.

Ethelron sent Sio off to find the weakest spot in the circle of infection erebi before cleaning up their small camp. Melody woke at the sound of everyone else moving around. She'd seemed more energetic since being in Eloas, the magic of the realm filling her instead of the *magical caffeine* provided in Sula. Melody silently fell into helping Ethelron, leaving Ana to wake Erin. Erin seemed dead to the world around her, but when Ana got close, Erin let out a painful moan.

"Shh," Ana dropped to the ground next to her, shaking her friend awake. When Erin blinked blearily, her hazel eyes were so dark they almost looked black. "Erin, are you okay?"

"Yes..." Erin gave her head a little shake. "I'm sorry." She reached up to massage her temples. "I saw another one of Gabe's memories. When Eloas first came under attack. And when he went through the portal, I felt his pain. His head felt like it was exploding. I'm so sorry, Ana. It was so scary, seeing the infection erebi all over, and trying to get through the portal-" A piece of Ana's heart broke hearing one of her worst memories being spoken aloud by Erin. She pulled her into a hug, knowing Erin was still living through memories she'd had years to process. Knowing she was also feeling the loss of Gabe all over again with each of his memories. Ana still didn't understand what it all meant; she hoped her mother would be able to help, but until then, it seemed Erin would carry this piece of Gabe, even if it broke her a little to do so.

"Can I get in on that?" Melody spoke up behind them, and when Erin looked up at Melody in confusion, Melody just shrugged. "What? I like hugs too." Erin gave a silent nod and held out her arm to welcome Melody into their circle. It was odd to see Erin allowing affection from them, even welcoming it, and it made Ana wonder if something was finally shifting in Erin's head. "You want in on this too?" Melody called out to Ethelron, who was looking down at the kingdom below, ignoring them. He barely spared them a glance, his eyes lingering on her only a second, before he turned back without responding. "Your loss," Melody called again, not quite letting him off the hook.

Ana soaked up the comfort their embrace gave her. She was so happy to find out her realm was still here, that her parents still lived, but another part of her was terrified to pass through the erebi surrounding what had once been her home. She wasn't afraid of the fight ahead of them, but of facing her parents, her *people*, and telling them that her brother was dead. Eloas had been falling to war when she'd left. Her people had been left behind to fight when she did not, because she'd been tasked to protect Toron. No matter what anyone said, *she'd* failed at her duty.

"Siofra went to scout for us. She'll be back any minute. Is everyone ready?" Ethelron called, breaking the moment and drawing

Ana from her thoughts. The girls pulled away from one another. Ana squeezed both of their hands before letting go with a silent prayer that she was not about to get her friends killed too.

"I won't be able to fight and keep the protective cloak over everyone."

"It's okay, Melody. You just blast anyone you can away, okay?" Siofra chose that moment to come running back toward them. She nuzzled against Ethelron's leg for a moment before starting forward, waiting for him to follow. Ethelron looked back to make sure everyone was ready before taking the lead behind the wolf. Ana took the rear as they traveled a winding path that led around the back of the castle. The closer they drew to the enemy, the more evident the destruction, and it took all of Ana's willpower to keep her breathing steady. How many times had she taken this same path with Ethelron, lighthearted and carefree as a young elf? Flowers that once lined the walkway were long-dead, and trees were blackened husks of what they'd once been.

Walls had been fortified against the erebi, but it was clearly a last defense. It didn't seem the erebi were actively attacking the castle; they were simply posted around it, keeping elves from leaving, from gathering any food or seeking help. Sio led them to the edge of where the erebi circled. At the thinnest point, it was still about twenty erebi deep. As soon as they took out one, another was there to press in.

"Move quickly. Just fight off the ones nearest to keep them from hitting you. Keep moving. Once we get through, we can take cover,"

Ethelron instructed sternly. The ease with which he took on the tactician's role reminded her of why he'd been her father's favored amongst the guard, and it stoked a flame of determination within her chest. Suddenly, the anxiety and grief were gone, replaced by righteous fury. On the other side of the erebi, her people needed help. *Her family* needed help. "Are you ready, Princess?"

"Let's move."

As soon as the words left her lips, Ethelron nodded and broke into a run, going right for the erebus ahead of him. Sio gave a long howl and followed, lunging at the ankles of the erebi around her, thrashing and ripping at their bodies. Erin plunged her dagger into the nearest erebus and pushed it back into the ones behind it and then situated herself back-to-back with Melody.

Ana found herself the most vulnerable of the group as the one guiding them through the mass of erebi. Her back was exposed, and Sio seemed to know it. The wolf danced around her, lunging at any erebi that managed to get too close. Before long, though, the horde of erebi became impenetrable. Panic rose in Ana's throat as the air filled with the cacophony of erebi hissing and growling around them. Any time one was killed, another moved forward to take its place. Ethelron tried to kill erebus after erebus in a desperate attempt to keep inching them forward, but it didn't seem to do them any good. Erin shot out her hands and called vines from the earth. They twined around the nearest erebi and she tried to force them back, but it was useless.

Evading a wicked set of claws, Ana stumbled back into Ethelron's solid chest. He promptly dispatched the attacking erebus and righted her, nodding with a grim face, when she immediately threw herself back into the fight.

They could hear some elven warriors join the fight from the other side, trying to help clear the way. Ana hoped they'd be enough, but there was still a wall of erebi blocking them from view. Then Melody dropped her dagger.

"Mel?" Ana called to her, terror threatening to freeze her where she stood. The witch had gone pale and stiff. "Mel! Are you hit?" Ana killed another erebus, preventing it from hitting Melody. The witch's whole body began to shake. Ethelron stopped, trying to move forward to cover Melody's right side, while Ana took her left. Erin met Ana's eyes, sharing a concerned glance over her head.

Without warning, Melody's hands shot out before her and a dazzling light formed a ball between her palms. With a loud warrior cry, she clapped her hands together, and the ball of light exploded. The force pushed the small group back, but the erebi in front of them flew into the air, parting a small path for them to quickly push through.

Melody sagged, all her energy gone, so the two elves supported her on either side and Erin quickly took the lead, using her powers to create walls of vines around them. Ana shoved all of her emotions down to be dealt with later, and was glad she had when Erin was met by four elven warriors, covered in the dark erebi blood. They continued to fight so the small group could completely escape the grasp of the erebi.

"Keep moving!" Ethelron called when Erin started to slow. Ana felt for the fae, obviously shocked and disoriented by everything that was going on in such an unfamiliar place. Sio caught up and led them toward the far right castle wall. The wolf disappeared, down the hole that used to be so familiar to her. Erin looked lost, so Ethelron pointed down into the darkness that had just swallowed Sio.

"Jump in, then I'll pass Melody down to you."

Her searching gaze found Ana's, and the elf tried to be as reassuring as she could. As if the single look had given her strength, Erin took a deep breath and straightened her spine. The four elven warriors were quickly approaching, the erebi close behind. They were out of time. "Here goes nothing…"

℘ ℘ ℘

Briar woke to a hard chest under her cheek. The familiar scent that seemed to cling to Doyle filled her and made her want to burrow in. She blinked and found she was tangled up with him, their legs entwined and his arms wrapped securely around her torso. Something funny happened in her chest. The pain was gone from her body now, but the energy she'd gotten from Eloas was also gone. She was back to feeling sluggish, which she didn't like.

She was debating just snuggling back into Doyle when his arm tightened around her, and his breathing changed. She looked into his face and found his dark eyes watching her, a glint of mischief dancing there. "I could get used to this," he said with a grin before kissing the top of her head. Something seemed to lodge in her throat, or she probably would have responded that she could, too.

"I shouldn't have fallen asleep, though. I need to check in with Lyra. Then we need to figure out where to keep our new dragon pet." He sat up, so she followed along, glancing over to Malux, who was still passed out on the floor at the end of her bed. "Don't say I never get you anything." Doyle flashed her a roguish grin, and she slapped his arm. Doyle gave a playful tug of her hair to bring her closer to him so he could place a tender kiss on her lips.

"Be careful," she whispered when he pulled back. He flashed her a wink before he left her to go in search of Lyra, and she turned back to sit on the edge of her bed.

"Why did you save me?" Malux's deep voice made her jump. He let out a little huff before standing and coming to sit next to her on the bed. "You saw my death. You could have just let me be. Why did you and Doyle save me?"

"I..." Briar didn't have a real answer. She hadn't had a particular vision other than a way to save him. But she had a *feeling;*

something didn't sit right with her about him dying. Maybe it was nothing more than the fact that he was kind to her. Maybe he'd play a key role in bringing down the queen. "I don't really know. It didn't feel right to let you die."

They sat in silence for a few minutes before he leaned over to knock shoulders with her. "Well, I appreciate it. I suppose I owe you now, and I'm guessing you'll ask for my help to bring down the queen."

"I don't think Doyle or I would complain about your help. I'm sure you have knowledge we could use against her, but neither of us will force you to help. If you want to leave and make a new life for yourself...you deserve that."

"I don't think I'll ever be able to have a real life for myself. I certainly can't go into any other realm and expect to be accepted. This is my home now, and if I intend to stay, then I'll have to make sure the queen gets brought down." Briar watched him as he straightened his shoulders. "I'll help you in any way I can, but I don't plan on stepping aside and watching while Lyra is put on the throne. She will be just as bad, if not worse, than our current ruler."

"I don't plan on seeing a crown placed on her head, either." She felt both of Malux's eyes on her, and feeling the dragon eye resting on her made a shiver run up her spine. She always felt like he could see *through* her with that eye.

"I don't believe you've told Doyle about your feelings toward her yet." Her silence seemed to be enough of an answer, because he let out another little huff. "You certainly like to play the game dangerously, Briar." She thought of the tender kiss Doyle had left her with, and the ways she'd seen him kill her when he found out about her betrayal. Malux had *no idea*.

.℮ .℮ .℮

"Won't the erebi just follow us?" Erin asked. Ana glanced back as the halfling looked to the hole all the elves had just come piling in through.

"It's protected. No one infected can come through," one of the warrior elves reassured her. "You know, Ethelron, I've spent years wondering if you had working parts. After all, you've never so much as batted an eye, no matter how many times I've offered to...cook you a meal. And it's not just me, you haven't spent any time with the womenfolk-".

"Ryo, please stop talking." Ana's heart was racing after their ordeal and her worry over Melody, but the exasperation in Ethelron's voice caught her attention. She got the feeling Ryo teased him often like this, and somehow that made her feel a little better. It was good to know that there had still been some lighthearted fun in Ethelron's life over the years, not just constant war. Sometimes it was the little things that kept someone *alive*, and she found she liked Ryo already, even if he *was* flirting with *her* guard.

"But now," the new elf, *Ryo*, raised his voice over Ethelron's protest, "you show up with *three* gorgeous women. Where have you been hiding such delicious figures? No wonder you haven't had energy for anyone else-"

"Ryo. Unless you wish to find yourself being offered up to the beasts outside our gates, you will kindly lose your ability to speak. Very. Quickly. Are we understood?" Ethelron nearly growled at the other guard, but Ryo simply raised a brow. The elven warrior tucked away his two blades and smiled at each of the women before him. His silver eyes glinted with mischief when they landed on Erin, who looked ready to claw them out.

"Is Melody okay?" Ethelron asked, turning his back on the silver-haired elf and focusing his attention on the witch, who was still leaning heavily on Erin. She was surprised by the edge of concern in his voice. They must have grown on him during their short travels.

"I'm fine," Melody groaned, but her voice was weak.

"I think she just wore herself out. That was quite a trick you pulled up there." Ana stroked Melody's forehead to check her temperature and looked her over to make sure there wasn't any hidden damage.

"Sometimes I surprise myself. Are we safe now?" Melody stood to support herself, but kept a hand on Erin's shoulder.

"I'll be happy to show you ladies up to a room," the charismatic elf spoke once more, his voice thick with suggestion, his too-handsome face begging for attention. Erin barely hid an eye roll. Ana fought to suppress a grin, knowing the restraint it must have taken her friend to bite back whatever response was going through her mind.

"Ana, I can watch over Melody. I'm sure you want to see your parents as quickly as possible. Ethelron can take you, and the other elves can take care of us for now," Erin suggested.

With a nod, Ethelron placed a hand at the small of Ana's back, the feel of it a warm comfort, and started to lead her down the tunnel before them. He paused, and Ana glanced up at him curiously. The stoic elf glanced back over his shoulder with a firm stare. "Hands off, Ryo. Don't let me hear otherwise." The grin wouldn't be smothered this time.

Chapter Thirteen

"Just breathe."

Ethelron's hand was a steady presence on her back, but Ana couldn't loosen her muscles. She was about to go into full panic mode at the idea of seeing her parents after all these years. She should be happy and excited, but all she could think about was her own failures. Her parents left her brother in her care, and she lost him and then watched him die. She failed them-

"Aina." Ethelron stopped walking and waved away the other guards that were in the hallway. Once they were alone, he put his hands on her shoulders and made her meet his gaze. He took a deep breath, and her body followed in response, matching his breathing until some of the panic edged off. "Your parents will be overjoyed to have you returned to them. They love you and have ached for you every day."

"And Toron," Ana found her voice. "They also loved *Toron* and ached for *his* return. He was just a little kid when they last saw him, and I-" Her voice cracked and her vision blurred. Then she was breathing in the scent of leather as Ethelron pulled her against him. She was so stunned he was hugging her that everything else faded away. She looked up at him and he wiped away the tears staining her cheeks. Something flashed in his gaze that sent warmth spreading through her.

"Yes, they loved Toron. They will mourn his loss. But they will still love *you*. You did not fail them. His death is not your fault. His death will not steal their love from you."

She nodded and pulled herself back together. "Stay with me?" she asked quietly. If it was anyone else, she wouldn't dare to show this weakness, but she wanted Ethelron's strength at her side and knew he wouldn't judge her for it. "Please, El. I just need someone in there that already knows." She watched as any of his arguments fell aside at her request. He gave a curt nod and led her through halls that should be familiar, but looked so different after her years away.

The changes told a devastating tale. The stone walls now stood bare. Long gone were the flowered vines and beautiful paintings that once brought their people joy to see. Stones had fallen loose from the walls, likely from the multitude of battles that had happened over the years, and they replaced the beautiful stained glass windows that used to let in light with boards. Ethelron led her down a long hall to what she remembered to be a tutoring room in happier times. He waited outside the door until she gave a small nod, and then he opened it for her.

Ana fought to maintain her composure when she saw the familiar profiles of her parents leaning over a table in the center of the room. Breathing became a struggle, and her vision seemed to narrow. After all these years thinking them dead, they were mere *feet* away. The gentle nudge of Ethelron's hand on the between her shoulders was all the encouragement she needed to take off at a dead run towards them.

"Aina?" her mother breathed, turning just in time to catch her daughter in a fierce embrace. "What?" Her mother shook as she squeezed her harder. "Oh, my sweet girl, you've made it home!" Both mother and daughter wept, unwilling to let one another go. Surrounded by her mother's warmth, flooded with memories at the smell of that subtle fragrance she'd always loved, Ana felt like she was a child again, seeking comfort after a nightmare. In some ways, this reunion *was* like waking up from a nightmare; spending so long thinking all of her loved ones were dead and finally having tangible proof of the contrary.

In other ways, though, returning to Eloas had been the worst kind of torture. So much life and joy had been destroyed. Every streak of black infection was a taunting reminder of how she'd abandoned her people, her realm. She would soon have to reveal her failure in protecting their prince.

Her father chuckled tearfully behind her. When Ana turned in her mother's arms, she found him standing next to Ethelron with his healthy hand on the guard's shoulder. The sight was nearly as familiar as her mother's embrace, and yet so jarringly different. Where her mother looked just as royal and proud as the day she'd left, her father was a shell of his former self. His once-straight back was hunched, right arm braced against his chest and covered by a long glove. She remembered Ethelron warning her of his condition, but nothing could have prepared her for the sight of how frail he had become. "Papa…"

"I am so sorry you had to come back to this, Aina…but your return is a wonderful light in this dark time." King Brannor cradled her jaw with his good hand, and she curled herself against him. "Brave Princess, no more tears. You are home. We are together."

"When Myriil returned to say that he'd found Ethelron, we had no idea that you were with him." In her peripheral, she noticed Ethelron tense at the mention of the scout.

"I-I'm sorry," a small voice stuttered from past Queen Faervel. Ana's eyes snapped to the young elf in question, surprised to realize that there were several others in the room that she hadn't noticed in her excitement. "I did not know who you were, Your Highness."

Ana leapt into Ethelron's path before he even moved, pressing a hand to his chest and wrapping the other around the exposed skin of his arm. His furious eyes locked on Myriil, his rage palpable. Ana stared up at him.

"I am fine, El. He is young, he has much to learn."

Ethelron's gaze turned to hers, and the passion in his eyes nearly stole her breath away. *"That may be, but not at* your *expense. You could have died!"*

The hand on his chest slid up to his jaw when he tensed as if to move around her. *"I didn't though, did I? You healed me, and I am okay."* Ana waited until he nodded and stepped back to drop her hands and turn back to her parents, who were watching the pair with inquisitive eyes. She flushed and ducked her head when she realized how that exchange must have looked to them - comfortable and familiar touches, and an intense conversation without speaking a word? She was sure she'd be hearing about it before long.

With a quick gesture from the queen, the other occupants of the room shuffled out. "Come, sit. There is so much to discuss." Ana's heart raced as they did so, and she was grateful for Ethelron's continued presence at her side, lending her strength. Excitement and joy warred with apprehension and dread within her; would they appreciate the person she'd become in the years they were separated? Would they even want to look at her once they learned the truth about their son? That question turned her stomach, and she forced herself to breathe.

Her parents sat in front of her in awed silence. Both of them seemed to drink in her image, which just made her want to burst into tears. Before she broke, her mother finally spoke to Ethelron, giving Ana the chance to rein in her emotions. "When Aeron told us that you'd found a portal, we thought you would be gone for a day, two at the most. When you still hadn't returned by the third, we were afraid something terrible had happened," Faervel explained. "I didn't even allow myself to hope that it was because you'd made it to Sula, to *Aina*, that you were gone for so long." A fresh wave of tears spilled over the queen's cheeks as she reached out for her daughter's hand. Ana squeezed her mother's shaking fingers tightly, using the touch to ground herself in the moment as much as she could.

"How did you find her?" Brannor asked. Ana smiled as she thought back to that first time seeing Siofra in her office.

"I sent Sio through first, using a piece of the princess' armor to remember her scent. She scouted and came back almost immediately…we didn't have to search for long." Ethelron glanced at her, something akin to pride in his eyes. *Interesting. Filing that away for later*, she thought to herself. "She lives and runs a business there to watch over the portal in Sula."

"Does Toron live there with you? Where is your brother?" Faervel questioned brightly, glancing behind them to the door as if the mention of his name would bring him to her. Caught off-guard, Ana inhaled sharply, and Ethelron reached out to take her free hand. Faervel watched the interaction, and Ana felt her eyes fill with tears. Her mother noticed and raised a shaking hand to cover her mouth. "Oh...Aina, no…"

"I am so sorry...I am so, so sorry. I couldn't keep him safe," Ana whimpered.

"I don't know what happened," Brannor was the first to fight through his grief and find his voice, "but I *do* know that you would *never* allow something to happen to your brother without doing everything in your power to stop it." Ana looked at her father, who reached out to cradle her face. "When?" The single word came out cracked and broken, all of his kingly training falling to the side in his grief.

"Just a few months ago..." Ana tore her heart into pieces and recounted their tale to her parents. She told them how they'd been separated and he'd lost his memories. She told them of Melody, and how her friend helped give her a reason to continue on. Ana told them about Erin, and how she and Toron had grown up together and fell in love. Every word was like a cut against her soul, but she needed to share all of it with them. They needed to see how she'd failed in her duty.

Almost as soon as she thought of the blame on her shoulders, Ethelron moved in and rested a hand there, giving her a small, reassuring squeeze, as though he were lifting the weight from her. "We were trying to rescue Erin when he was killed by Kali, with a blade meant for me." Silent tears fell as she spoke, forcing her voice past a growing lump in her throat. "Melody and I gave him as much of an elven burial as we could," she finished, as though burying him with tradition would somehow relieve the pain of his loss. Her mother finally lost control and let out a heart-wrenching sob. Her father pulled his wife against him, placing a tender kiss on her forehead as he did his best to comfort her despite his own pain. Ana moved out of her chair to drop to her knees between her parents and hugged both of them tightly. "I wish he could have been here with us, that you could see how happy he was with Erin."

"I need to meet her," Faervel murmured past her tears. Ana drew back and offered a tired, pained smile.

"She and Melody have both gone to rest for the evening. The trek was trying for all of us, but I will introduce you to her in the morning."

Faervel nodded, gingerly wiping at her eyes. "Very well. Ethelron?" Ana felt him tense behind her. "Thank you for bringing our daughter home safely. You both look exhausted, and we still have a great deal of turmoil ahead of us. Go rest with your friends. We will talk more in the morning."

Devoid of any gumption to argue, Ana gave her parents each one more tight hug, kissed them on the cheeks, and stepped back. "Goodnight, Mama, Papa. I have missed you desperately."

"As we have missed you, Aina."

Ethelron bowed respectfully, and offered his arm to Ana. She stared at it for a beat before turning tired eyes up to meet his gaze. "Come on, Princess. I don't bite."

That's unfortunate. The immediate thought surprised Ana, and she blinked a few times. Praying that her embarrassment at the thought was not clear on her face, she curled her fingers around his elbow and allowed him to lead her away from her parents.

While her parents' insistence that she was not to blame for Toron's death alleviated much of that particular guilt, stepping back into the battered halls was like sprinting into a wall. Maybe it was exacerbated by her bone-deep exhaustion, but at the sight of the first boarded-up window, tears burned Ana's eyes and blurred her vision. She clenched her jaw and blinked several times to try to force them back; Ethelron wouldn't let it go if he noticed.

"It has been quite a day," he commented with forced nonchalance. *Too late.*

"It has," she agreed. Teeth worried her bottom lip as she worked up the nerve to voice what she already knew deep down. "The gardens are all destroyed, aren't they? And the galleries?" So much of their rich history, documented in beautiful artwork…how much of it had been lost?

Ethelron stopped and turned her to face him. Compassion and mild confusion warred in his eyes. "The gardens, yes. I think the devastation you've been able to see is proof enough that nothing green has survived out there, Aina." He settled his hands on her shoulders. "Though the outer grounds of the castle have been destroyed, and the buildings that housed the galleries with them, we transferred everything to the vaults for safekeeping not long after you left."

Though what Ethelron had just said was good news, and should have brought comfort, all she could process in that moment was *'after you left'*. Emotion curled like a vice grip around her throat, making it hard to breathe, and the tears she had been trying to keep at bay spilled over. *What right do you have to be emotional? You ran when they needed you most. You expect to be queen when this is over - if you manage to survive - and you can't even face the fact that you abandoned your people to this fate?*

"Ainadelothien!"

The sharp, commanding voice in her ear startled Ana out of her panicked spiral. When she looked up, she realized they were in the library…and much of the room looked untouched by the ravages of war. "I'm sorry…"

"Where did your mind go, Princess? I've never seen you like that before." Concern shone in Ethelron's eyes as he searched her face for some kind of clue. Ashamed, Ana shook her head and tried to pull away from him. Fingers tightened around her biceps. "No, do *not* shut me out. *Talk to me.* What just happened?"

Frayed nerves made her laugh sound a little hysterical. "Coming from the *king* of stoicism and emotional distance…" Even as she said it, Ana knew it wasn't fair, and she cringed. Ethelron simply raised a surprised brow. "Sorry. I'm sorry, you've done absolutely nothing wrong." This time when she pulled away, he let her go, and she paced in front of the rows of bookcases. She wondered if she looked like the caged animal that she felt like at that moment. "I have no right to this warm reception from any of you! *I ran away*...I abandoned all of you in the middle of a war, and look at all the damage that has been done. What kind of princess flees when her people need her most?"

Ethelron was thunderstruck. "You *what?* Aina, you didn't *run away!* You were *sent* away. Your parents made the decision that was best not only for their children, but for our people...it gave them hope to know that the princess and prince had made it out safely, and might make it back to us one day." He stepped in front of her to stop her pacing and cradled her face in his large, warm hands. "And *you have*. We ache with you that Toron didn't, but we rejoice that *you* have come home."

With a sob, Ana threw her arms around Ethelron's neck. His response was immediate, the embrace closing around her and pulling her against his solid form. The steady rhythm of his heartbeat was barely tangible under the thick vest of his armor, but it was enough to ground her. "El..."

"No one thought that you abandoned us, Aina," he murmured into her hair. Deft fingers massaged the tip of her ear, and Ana thought

222

she might fall asleep right there in his arms. "If anything, I hated myself for not being strong enough to follow you and protect you." She smiled tiredly at the image his words conjured. Ethelron would have made quite a sight in Sula with his tall, proud posture, wide chest, and thick muscles honed from years of training for battle.

Ethelron nudged her back enough to look in her eyes, and the unabashed affection that he wore stole away her breath. For the briefest moment, she thought he might kiss her...and he did. On her forehead. If she were less exhausted, maybe she would've been less disappointed, but he didn't give her the chance to think on it much longer before pulling her towards a rather comfortable looking sofa in the corner. "El, I-"

"Princess, you have been through enough chaos today. You will rest better without any more reminders tonight of what awaits us in the morning." It didn't escape even her exhaustion-fogged mind that he forewent any option of sleeping somewhere else himself, and settled onto the couch first. Ana nestled herself into his chest without hesitation, unable to resist the urge to inhale his comforting scent. Ethelron's chuckle reverberated through her body. If she were any more awake...

℮ ℮ ℮

Melody felt lost in her body as she walked beside Erin. She was beyond exhausted after her little light show. Her magic felt drained, but there was also a low hum in her veins. There was power, an energy she didn't recognize. Erin walked stiffly at her side, their shoulders brushing, and Melody had the feeling the other woman was ready to catch her if Melody's body decided to stop working mid-step, which felt like a real possibility. The silver-haired elf, Ryo, was talking as he led them, but she couldn't concentrate on his words as she took stock of her body. Ever since entering this realm she'd felt different, *stronger*. Ana told her how it could work, being in a realm of magic. She'd felt it in Loinnir too, but they hadn't been there very long. They'd already spent more time in Eloas.

"So, I've known Ethelron all my life," the elf was saying. He was so attractive that looking at him almost hurt. He had some of the same markings as Ethelron, an intricate tattoo on the side of his neck and on his exposed arm. His hair was long, falling to his shoulder-blades, and was a shocking silver. He had that same glow about him that all elves did, but more than that, his eyes danced with a manic energy. She got the feeling he was the type of person that couldn't sit still for very long. His fingers hung over the twin blades strapped to his hips, like he was forever ready to dive into battle. He probably was. Most of his life had been lived during a time of war. He looked younger than Ana, but not by much. She wondered if he'd been a kid when war came knocking at his door. "He's got that broody, dark past thing going for him. He's always been deliciously mysterious." Erin elbowed her in the side and raised her brows. Melody could just imagine the thoughts going through Erin's head at the words *deliciously mysterious* being said about *Ethelron*. She was probably working out ways to fit it into conversation in front of him. "And *now* he shows up with three beauties that seem to have materialized out of thin air. Care to share what's happening?"

"Not much of a sharer," Erin muttered in response. They were walking down a narrow corridor now, but Ryo stopped to face them. His freaking eyes seemed to *glow* with mirth.

"Well, isn't that too bad? Missing out on half the fun." His hand actually reached out to touch Erin's arm for half a second before he dropped it to his side, almost like he remembered Ethelron's orders to keep hands off. Another elf turned sideways to get past them and kept going while Erin and Ryo stared each other down. They were sizing each other up over something, and Melody felt like an awkward third wheel. Erin glared at the elf, her arms crossing over her chest, and Melody felt her retreat into herself for a beat before a little smirk broke out on her lips.

"Ah, I see," the halfling whispered with a little nod to herself.

"Not yet, but I'd be happy to show you whatever you'd like." He flashed a sultry wink.

"And you think I'd be interested in *anything* you might have to offer?" Melody noted the first bite of weakness in Erin as she taunted back. Whatever game the elf thought he was playing at needed to stop. He was walking right into the minefield of pain that Erin had bottled up in her chest.

The elf's gaze shifted between Erin's eyes, reading something in her gaze, and Melody noticed when his lips turned down. The witch clearly didn't know much about men; her shiny dating record was enough to prove that. But she had the feeling he used flirting and teasing to get to know people. He wasn't trying to harm, but he seemed to sense that he had hurt Erin. He actually took one step back, putting a comfortable space between them. "No, I guess not. I'll just have to keep chasing after Ethelron then. I'm curious though, what *do* you see?"

"You might know how to wield those blades and fight off the erebi. You know how to crook a finger and have someone ready to spend the night with you. But you don't know a *thing* about love. I'm sure there's some family member out there you love, but you have never been *intimately* in love with another. You keep giving away pieces of yourself to whoever will take it, but you've never ripped your heart and soul in half and tried to fit it with someone else's. You are still a little boy who thinks love is a game played in the bedroom." Erin grinned then. "It's going to be really fun to see you fall apart when you find the person you are meant to be with. It's not Ethelron, but please, *please*, keep giving him a hard time. I find it highly amusing."

"And who is to say it isn't *you*? I mean, how am I supposed to find this magical person if I don't ask around a bit? It could be you, or your friend here." Ryo turned his gaze on her. He was still teasing, even after Erin told him off. A lesser man might have cowered under Erin's stern, yet amused voice. Instead, he seemed entertained by her.

"How about you go back to sniffing around the people you were entertained by before we showed up? Our little group - we aren't here to play with you. We are here for the big kid camp. You need to stay in your kiddie pool."

Ryo flashed a grin, giving his head a playful shake. "I'll just point out my room on the way, in case anyone changes their mind. I wouldn't be an excellent host if I let you get bored in your *big kid camp*."

Ryo walked them through the castle, showing them how to get around and where important meeting places were. He grabbed them food and drinks as they walked, and while he did point out his resting quarters as they walked, he only flashed a quick wink at the two of them before moving on. Melody was dead on her feet by the time he brought them to where they would be spending the night. He placed a gentle hand on her elbow when Melody tripped over her own feet in exhaustion.

"You okay?"

"I'm fine. Just tired."

"Well, I'll leave you ladies to get your rest. I have to check in for my own beauty rest. You don't get to look like this without doing the hard work." He wiggled his eyebrows shamelessly. Erin just rolled her eyes, making a little shooing motion, but Melody couldn't stop a small laugh from slipping past her lips. That earned her a grin from the elf before he made a flourishing bow and closed the door behind him.

"How about that, a tour and entertainment." Melody nudged Erin before going to the nearest bed and collapsing.

"I'll say this, I'd pay good money to see Ryo call Ethelron delicious again in front of Ana. *That* would be entertaining."

Lyra hardly spared Doyle a glance before sending him on his way to gather more intel about who would be on her side if they started an uprising. Doing so was easier said than done. Everyone knew who he was to Lyra, which made it hard to broach the subject with anyone inconspicuously. Add to the fact that his thoughts were really focused on Briar and what to do with Malux, he wasn't exactly all in when it came to being Lyra's little spy. While he worked on making small talk with some people he didn't completely distrust, his mind was on where to keep Malux so he wouldn't be found.

The best option was going deeper into the mountain and having him take up residence in one of the hidden caverns there. Not many bothered to venture that far unless they were going somewhere specific; it was far too easy to fall or get lost.

Everyone he spoke to was on edge. The queen, it seemed, was on a rampage. She'd felt Malux's death, and wanted to make anyone who crossed her path pay for the loss of her favorite pet. She also wasn't over the death of Kali and the loss of Loinnir, so she was now determined to back the war in Eloas to bring them down as quickly as possible. That made him worry over their little group, which they were apparently going to depend on. They'd traveled into Eloas, and he could only guess that they were there to help end the war. He'd have to ask Briar to try to keep an eye on that.

After a few hours of wandering and speaking to anyone he came across, he headed back to his room. He wanted to shower and change and maybe catch more than a few hours of sleep. There was still so much to do, though; he needed to get Malux out of Briar's room. It was far too likely Lyra would go there, or send someone to retrieve Briar, and Malux didn't have anywhere to hide in her room, other than her small washroom.

He didn't get very far, however. Doyle came up short when he came into view of his doorway and found Lyra leaning where the wall curved not far from his door. "We need to talk, and I don't need those guards around us when we do. I was hoping you'd come back to your room soon."

His spine straightened just at the sight of her. He didn't like her near his room. She never came here, and the memory of Briar standing in his space was still fresh in his mind and not something he wanted overpowered by Lyra. There was no denying her, however, so he opened the door and motioned for her to step inside. She kept her arms crossed and her eyes were sharp as they took in each corner of the room. "My sister is on a rampage, and she's had her eye on me. All the work we did to show her we were *playing nice* has gone out the window since she's lost her jewelry and her little dragon pet."

"Is there something we can do to gain her trust?" He took his normal stance around her, which felt odd to do in his own room. Somehow, she was making him feel out of place in the only area that was actually *his*.

"I wish we hadn't given up the observer's wings already; they would make a nice gift right about now. Or if we still had her sister, we could gift her away. Unfortunately, Briar is too valuable to hand over, or I would."

He thought he might break his teeth from clenching his jaw. The idea of handing over Briar, or her little sister, to the monster they called queen made him want to punch a wall. She seemed oblivious to him, however, and kept right on talking. "I may have to offer my services in the elven war or something. I don't even think offering you up like last time will help." She released a heavy sigh. "How did your talks go today?"

His hands were fists at his back, but he shared how his few discussions went, which hadn't been great, and then he waited to see if she'd leave his space. He wanted to get to Briar, and they needed to get Malux hidden.

"Well, keep digging. And how did our observer fare in Eloas?"

"As I said earlier, she helped me clear some infection pods so the group could get through easier. She felt they were safe when we left."

"And has she had any other visions of interest lately?"

"She saw the group in danger and got us there to help them. Other than that, I don't believe so."

"I grow impatient with this game, and I am not prepared to go play servant to my sister." She leaned against the wall, but nothing about her spoke of ease.

"Fully bringing the queen to her knees and placing the crown on your head cannot be done overnight."

"Yes, yes." She waved him off and straightened, crossing her arms over her chest. "I shall speak with my sister tomorrow and see if there is something I can do to get her off my back. But you keep digging around for who would stand against her, and keep me apprised of anything the observer sees. I want to keep us moving forward."

"Of course." He gave a curt bow when she finally left him. He broke his stance the moment the door shut behind her and paced his room for a moment to shake off the anger from her comments about

Briar. She could never know that he'd grown to have feelings for the fae. He could see that. He wanted to start training Briar that instant, as he'd said he wanted to do while they were in Eloas. There was something in Lyra's eye that made him worry for her, and he didn't like it.

He stripped down so he could take a shower, then he'd go to Briar and they would get Malux moved this evening. At least then he would have one less thing to worry over.

Chapter Fourteen

"Hey, did you guys get sleep last night?"

Ana looked up from her conversation with some guardsmen to see Erin and Melody approaching. The princess excused herself from the discussion and felt Ethelron follow. She narrowed her eyes at the mischievous glint in Erin's eyes. "As well as can be expected, I suppose." Ana thought of how drained she'd been after the emotional conversation with her parents. "Melody, how are you feeling today?" She eyed her friend and couldn't find any trace of the exhaustion that had been there when she saw her last. Melody had saved their lives yesterday with her show of powers. She'd always known Melody was strong; she'd seen her use her abilities time and time again, but she had a feeling yesterday was just the beginning of what Melody could do when surrounded by magic.

"Much better after getting some food and sleep. Actually, more energized than I think I've ever felt."

"Yeah, your elf warrior friend fed us and led us to a place to sleep...after showing us where we could find his bed, in case we got bored," Erin deadpanned. Ethelron stiffened at that and took a step closer.

"Ryo did *what?*" His question was hardly more than a growl.

"Well, after we wouldn't tell him any of your *delicious mysteries*, he offered to show us a good time, but I told him he should keep working at breaking your tough exterior."

Melody tried to cough to cover her laugh, but Ana caught it, and nearly started laughing herself. If she looked at Ethelron now, all would be lost. Erin, however, just stared the guard down, one eyebrow quirked expectantly at her teasing.

"Ryo is harmless, but if he goes anywhere near either of you, I will toss him from the highest window. You have my word." That had Ana turning to face him. He was staring at two of the most important people in her life like he'd shield them from an attack with his own body. Somehow, over the course of their travels, her girls had gotten under his skin. It seemed he was now seeing them as part of their team. She wondered if either of them realized what it meant to have Ethelron as a protector.

"I handled him just fine," Erin grinned. "But we were a little worried about you, Ana. We knew you were going to have a difficult chat with your parents and then you didn't join us."

"El and I walked a bit after my parents retired for the night...I needed to clear my head if I had any hope of sleeping." She glanced at Ethelron and had to fight not to roll her eyes. After his affectionate behavior the night before, it was as though none of it had happened once they stepped out of the library. *Typical.*

"Ah! Your Royal Highness!" Ana turned just as the silver-haired warrior sauntered up to her, having no idea they'd just been talking about him. "Forgive me for not addressing you properly when you arrived last night. I was too captivated by your beauty to realize that I was in the presence of the future queen." Ryo took her right hand in his, gave an exaggerated bow, and pressed a kiss to her knuckles. "It is a pleasure to meet you, Princess."

The air behind her suddenly seemed to vibrate with Ethelron's disgust and outrage. *"That is enough, Ethelron. Ryo is being polite."*

Despite sending her message telepathically, the elf behind her grumbled something along the lines of "polite my ass" in response. Erin and Melody glanced at one another with knowing grins, but Ana could only bring herself to be bemused by her territorial guard. She expected the conversation they'd just had didn't help.

"Ethelron," Ryo's attention left Ana, and she watched as he shifted his body towards her guard. "If you are going to growl at me, I could think of more interesting ways to implement that. You are free to invite any of your lovely companions to join us-"

"Ryo, I may tolerate your mouth when it is directed at me, but you will not speak of these women in those terms if you value your neck. Are we understood?"

"Ah!" Ryo flashed her a wink and Ana almost died right then and there. She glanced at Melody and found the witch biting her lip as she watched the interaction. Erin looked like she needed popcorn so she could sit back and enjoy the show. "A jealous man. You want me all to yourself, then?" Erin actually chuckled, and Ryo grinned, clearly pleased to have gotten a laugh.

Ana laid a hand on Ethelron's arm and felt how tense he was under her palm. As entertaining as she was finding all of this, she thought she should do her best to save her guard before he did something he would regret. "Ryo, this has been a pleasure, but we were just going to get some breakfast, and then change into more appropriate attire, so-"

"Good morning Aina, Ethelron. Ryo. These ladies must be your travel companions?" The group turned in unison when the king and queen entered the hall. Awe filled her as Ana watched them approach. It was still so hard to believe they were alive. They were standing right in front of her.

She stepped forward to embrace them before gesturing towards her friends. "These are my parents, King Brannor and Queen Faervel. Mama, Papa, these are my friends, Melody and Erin."

Her parents approached Melody first. Ana watched as her mother took Melody's hand and cupped it between her own before she placed a kiss on her knuckles. "It is such a pleasure to meet you. Ana told us so much about you and how you have become a family for one another. We hope you will think of us as family, too." Her mother swiped a finger at a tear that must have broken loose and tracked down Melody's cheek. Ana knew what that meant to her. To have someone accept her so quickly, when her own family had pushed her away...it made Ana love her parents all the more. Her father pulled Melody into a one-armed hug, giving his own quiet greeting. Then Faervel turned her full attention to Erin.

"It is a pleasure to meet you both. Erin," her mother's voice went soft as she stood before the woman her son had loved. "Would you walk with me for a moment?" The fae in question glanced at Ana, eyes a mixture of terror and hope. Ana gave her a reassuring nod, knowing they needed a private moment to talk about Toron and get to know one another.

"Mel...we have some guardsmen waiting to take you down to the armory to get you into some armor. While you're there, see if there's a weapon or two that speaks to you. We need to be well-prepared for what's coming next. Apparently my old armor is still here, so I'm going to go find out if it still fits as well as it did when I had it made." The witch nodded, her eyes brightening with excitement, and Ana pointed out the elves waiting for her. "Grab something to eat on the way!"

"Ever the protector, Highness. Do you ever allow anyone to take care of you for a change?" Ryo asked, his voice velvety and sweet. "Allow me to assist you with securing your armor?"

Ana gave him a polite smile in return and had to smother a chuckle when she heard another low growl behind her. "I appreciate the offer, Ryo, but Ethelron is familiar with how complicated my suit is, and hopefully remembers better than I do how it pieces together. Would you mind waiting here for Erin to return and then showing her where to go to prepare?"

The warrior bowed respectfully and turned to engage another elf in conversation while he waited. Ana turned and pushed Ethelron back towards her family's armory. He stalked ahead, but Ana's hand lingered between his shoulder blades. Even through his armor, she could feel the tension thrumming in his body. Her skin heated with frustration, and as soon as they reached the room, she latched the door behind them.

"What is your problem?" Ethelron started pacing while Ana grabbed her undershirt and pants and stepped behind the privacy divider to change. He didn't respond right away, and when she stepped back into the room, he'd gathered the armor she hadn't worn in years.

She was grateful she'd been fully grown before everything had become chaotic. "El," she pleaded, his angry silence cutting at her.

"You are the *crown princess* of this kingdom. You deserve better than an obnoxious warrior whose reputation with men and women is just as well known as his reputation with a sword. You *owe* that to your kingdom."

Anger flared, and Ana took a step away from him. She snatched her jerkin from the table beside them and shrugged it on. The weight of the long leather vest was comforting, as if the armor could protect her from the emotional turmoil building between her and her guard. She wanted to scream at him. How *dare* he tell her that she deserved better - presume that he had a say in who she chose to be with - after keeping her at arm's length all their lives? "Firstly, I do not owe my kingdom anything when it comes to my love life. I will spend my time with whom I wish, and I will lead as I'm needed to. The man I choose to be at my side will be perfect for that position because of his love for me-"

"And you think *Ryo* would truly love you in the way you need? He spends half of his time in the bedroom and the other half trying to get someone to join him there."

"I suppose I should keep it all about *duty* like you, hmm?" She didn't bother to mask the anger in her voice; after biting her tongue so many times, she was done. He drew her close only to slam his walls in place repeatedly, the night before a prime example, and Ana wasn't sure her heart could take much more of it. Instead of allowing him to see her hurt, though, she lashed out, a storm against his walls.

"Excuse me?" Ethelron snapped, stepping into her personal space and forcing her to look up at him. His eyes were dark, and Ana wasn't sure how to read him. The thought terrified, excited, and annoyed her all at once.

"If it should be all about what is *proper*, why *don't* we consider Ryo? After all, he was sent to help us get back through the horde around the castle, so clearly, he is one of the best fighters in the realm. He is polite and respectful - albeit a *bit* of a relentless flirt - and he is one of the Royal Guard, meaning he is liked by my parents. Perhaps I *should-*" The blonde elf gave a soft noise of surprise when he silenced her with his lips. *Claimed* her as his own in one possessive motion.

Despite her surprise, Ana took only the length of a heartbeat to react. The soft sigh of relief was an unconscious response. He surrounded her, the woodsy scent of him, the taste of spices on his lips, and a bite of possession as his hands got lost in her hair and *she* got lost in him. He seemed to come back to himself and started to pull away, but she grabbed the nearest buckle of his armor and tugged him close.

"Aina, wait, I'm sorry-"

"Oh no, you are *not* apologizing for that," she hissed, shoving him back abruptly. He was warring with himself, and Ana wanted nothing more than to smack some sense into him. He'd *finally* allowed himself to be impulsive and kiss her, and the idiot couldn't even give himself *five seconds* to enjoy it.

"But you-"

"So help me if you say that it's wrong because I am the *princess*, I will knock you out, Ethelron. You have always preached about me needing to be with someone who can command the respect of the people. Someone who is *approved* by my *parents*, who can be both diplomat and best friend. Someone who would lay down his life for mine, and someone who can set that aside and *play* in the quiet moments. El...it has *always* been you. You have to see that." She held his gaze unflinchingly. "*Who better* to stand beside me than the man who has already been there all along?"

Ethelron brushed fingers over her cheek before taking a step back, dropping his hands to his sides. When he shook his head, her heart broke. "We can't do this, Aina. *I* can't. Now, let's finish getting you ready. They will be waiting for us."

.℮ .℮ .℮

Briar and Malux spent the day holed up in her room. She left once to get some food, and they shared it in silence. Malux was still tired, and she knew it could still be some time before he came back to full strength. He had *died,* after all. He asked her about the vision she'd had, and why she hadn't gone back to Loinnir. Doyle had asked a few times, too, but she hadn't felt good about telling him. Malux knew that she wanted to keep Lyra from the crown, however, and she thought it might actually feel good to get the terrible vision off her chest, so she told him everything. He'd sat in silence and listened before nodding. "Yes, I suppose that was a good reason to avoid home," was his dry response to everything.

"Do you have an idea of a good place to hide? Doyle knows the caves very well, and I'm sure you know just as much."

"Yes, there are a few places that would be good. No one ventures deeper than they have to. Creatures like to hide and attack those who wander."

"Doyle and I walked to a few places, and I didn't see anything."

"The queen doesn't like them and keeps them pushed deep into the mountain. But trust me, I wouldn't go wandering anywhere you don't know if you don't have Doyle with you. Depending what you come across, they can be vicious and they don't care who or what you are."

"And you are going to reside among them?"

He lifted a shoulder. "I've lived with worse." He gave her a smile, and she tried to think if she'd ever seen him actually smile before. Suddenly, his back straightened, then he jumped to his feet. "Someone is coming."

"Go, go." She stood and started pushing him towards the washroom, the only option she had to hide him. She left the door open just a crack, as it had been before, and raced back to her bed where she still had some food laid out. Her heart was still pounding when her door flew open without so much as a cursory knock. Lyra stepped in, her yellow eyes sharp when they fell on her.

"Ah, my little pet observer. It seems you've been enjoying yourself." Lyra swayed toward her. She always had the look of a predator about her, from the way her eyes darted around the room, down to the way she swayed her hips while moving. "You've been having some adventures, but it doesn't seem you've been doing a lot for *me*." Lyra stopped before her and reached out to catch some of her hair between her fingers. Briar wanted to pull back, but refused to show any emotion around the erebus. Her blood ran cold at the memory of her visions, but she would not give an inch, not to Lyra. She straightened her spine and stared her down.

"I think Doyle has been too easy on you. He's too trusting and soft, and I'm tired of being patient. I let him try his way, but my sister is still on her throne, and it doesn't feel like we are any closer to bringing her down than we were *months* ago." Lyra suddenly gripped the section of hair and yanked it to her, sending a burn through Briar's scalp. "I think it's time we go back to my way of things." She twisted the hair around her hand and pulled Briar off the bed. She had to bite the inside of her mouth to keep from crying out as she slammed onto the floor. Then Lyra released her and two guards stepped in and grabbed her arms.

"Lyra, I'm doing everything I can. We protected the group. We have to wait until they are in place though-" Lyra slapped her, and her eye exploded with pain.

Lyra leaned forward and captured Briar's face in a tight grip. "I think you are just stringing me along. The whole thing with the group is probably a wild goose chase. I need other answers, and you are going to show your worth." She jerked her hand and released Briar before nodding to the two guards. "You know where to take her."

Briar knew it would be useless to struggle, so she let the guards lead her out of the room. Fear filled her when Lyra did not follow immediately. The last thing they needed was for Lyra to go poking around and find Malux stuffed in the washroom. She actually gave a relieved smile when Lyra's boots sounded behind them and her door slammed shut.

.℮ .℮ .℮

Doyle finished his shower, changed, and then wandered deep into the mountains, weapon in hand. He needed to find a good route for Malux. Getting him out of Briar's room would be the worst area; after that, they could get into a passage and keep fairly hidden from there. Feeling as confident as possible about the plan, Doyle turned back to head to Briar's room. He wished they were still in Eloas, where he felt free to hold her; here they would have to watch their every step. He knew it wouldn't be good for Lyra to find out he had feelings for her, and she had as many spies as the queen.

He got to Briar's door and knocked softly. No one answered, but he heard movement inside. Doyle realized then that he didn't feel Briar's presence there. He'd been so caught up in his own thoughts, he hadn't noticed that the pull of her was in another direction. He gave another quick knock before entering into an empty room, panic twisting low in his stomach. There was a piece of bread sitting on the bed and a few more scattered on the floor. "Malux?"

The door to the washroom opened, and he knew from the grim look Briar hadn't just wandered off for a stroll. "What happened?"

"*Your* queen struck Briar and told her it was time to go back to *her way* of doing things. She had two guards drag her off somewhere. I'm sure to serve her some tea and biscuits."

"Shit-" Doyle sent his fist into the stone wall, but didn't even feel the broken skin. He should have known Lyra was going to do something after their talk.

"You know you are going to have to choose between them at some point, don't you? You truly believe Lyra will take the crown and then let an observer go home, when she could keep her chained at her side for all of eternity to warn her of any uprisings or trouble? She could know which battles to fight and which to avoid. She'll. Never. Release. Briar."

Doyle had no interest in hearing all of that. He needed to figure out where Lyra took her, and he needed to stop Lyra from laying a finger on her. He'd seen the damage done to Briar in the past, and he was not about to stand aside and watch it all happen again.

"Doyle, you can't really think Lyra would be a better queen than the one we already have?" Malux continued despite his lack of response. "She's just as power hungry, and she'll tear down anyone who stands in her way. Do you know what Briar saw that kept her from taking your offer and going home?"

That grabbed his attention. All the times he'd asked Briar, and she hadn't told him. He knew it was bad, but she hadn't shared the vision with him, yet she'd told Malux? "What?"

"Lyra tortured and then killed you. Then she went to Loinnir to get Briar. She found and killed me and then locked Briar in chains at her side and beat visions out of her for the rest of Briar's days. *That* is who you want to put on the throne. A woman who would kill *you* for standing against her."

"I get it, okay? Just shut up for a minute and let me *think*!" The foundation he'd built his life upon was crumbling at his feet. He was off balance, his mind whirling. But none of that mattered. The only thing that mattered now was getting to Briar.

"If you go after Briar and stand against Lyra, you may be chained right up next to Briar."

"I can't let Lyra keep hurting her!"

"Then you may be going to your death."

Doyle looked down at their shared rune instead of responding to that. He knew exactly how to find her; he'd be able to just follow the rune to her. "We need to get you hidden, and then I'm going after her."

.℘ .℘ .℘

Queen Faervel was silent as she led them through winding halls before settling them into a small room, warmed by a blazing fire. The silence gave Erin the chance to get a good look at the queen, *at Gabe's mother*. Of course, she had seen the queen in his memories; Erin witnessed how much she loved her children, and how much she was willing to give up in order to protect them. Her heart nearly ripped in two when she thought of how the queen had gathered her son into her arms and soothed him.

Faervel looked the same today as she had in the memories. Her blond hair was pulled back into a complicated braid, all twists and knots at the back of her head. Her eyes were older, darker after years of watching her people suffer and being separated from her children.

When the queen settled in a chair across from her and set those eyes on the fae, Erin nearly stopped breathing. Having the motherly gaze upon her, knowing that it was her fault the woman's son was not there, wiped away the hard wall of sarcasm she usually cocooned herself in. She was soft and vulnerable under the royal gaze, and if the queen struck out with her words, it would break her completely.

"My son loved you very much." A sad smile finally settled itself over the elf's features.

Startled by her words, Erin could only stutter "what?" in response.

"He loved you very deeply, and his aura is still all around you. You wear it like a protective shroud."

Her vision blurred as she shook her head in protest. "If he did, I didn't deserve it. It's my fault he was killed in the battle. I know Ana blames herself, but *I* made the mistake during the battle. *I* kept us there longer than I should have, and *I* was distracted, leaving only him to block Kali's attack-" A sob escaped and Erin clamped her mouth shut. She ducked her head and let her plain hair fall over her face as a shield. Faervel had lost her son, her *family*, and yet she managed to keep her composure. Erin was the reason he was dead, she had no right to grieve before the queen. She struggled to pull herself together enough to make an excuse to leave the room, before she embarrassed herself further, but didn't get the chance. Soothing hands found her shoulders and Erin suddenly found herself in the queen's warm embrace.

"His death is not your fault, my dear. You still grieve for him, but don't let that grief turn into blame. Shh." She pulled Erin's head against her and softly stroked her hair.

The motion, pure motherly affection, broke her. Tears flowed freely down her cheeks, and she didn't bother trying to fight against the flood. If Gabe had lived, the woman could have become her mother. Erin would have had a *family*. She should have *known* that wouldn't have been allowed. It was too much for her to have the love of her life *and* gain a family in the process. Not after a lifetime of rejection. It was almost like the queen could read her mind, for she made another soothing sound, and even pressed a light kiss on her forehead.

Erin grew stiff at the sentiment, unsure how to handle such an outward show of love. Queen Faervel pulled away slowly, her blue eyes glistening with tears of her own. "Toron may be gone, my dear, but it doesn't take away his love for you. He may be gone, but it would still be an honor to consider you part of my family."

Chapter Fifteen

Briar was obstinately refusing to have any visions. She was done playing Lyra's game, and while she could have focused and tried to fall into a vision just to get Lyra and the guards to leave her alone, she decided she would let them beat her to death first. She wasn't sure what made her feel that way, but something snapped inside her, and she was not going to give in this time. Even if she did fall into a vision, she was not going to share a single detail.

While one guard decided to pick up a whip and test it on her back, she focused on the memory of the tender way Doyle held her in Eloas. He'd been afraid for her, cared for her. She'd had the smallest taste of what they could have, but she knew there was so much more. There was an ocean of love that they could dive into, but not while they were stuck in the middle of all the politics of this realm.

"Does my little observer want to play at being tough today?" Lyra purred near her ear, forcing her back into the moment, back into her aching body. She knew tears were streaming down her face, her throat was raw from crying out in pain, but when Lyra's face came into view, Briar did something she'd never thought to do before: she spit on Lyra's cheek.

"I always thought you were feisty," Lyra said, almost in awe, as she wiped away the moisture. Then she scraped nails down Briar's face until blood joined the tears. "I think it's about time we tame that out of you." Another lash shot across her back and only the chains held her up now; her legs had given out, and she wondered if there was even room on her back for another lash. She *had* to be running out of skin. Briar hadn't told Doyle what Lyra was capable of, but if he saw them now, Lyra was going to turn him against her all on her own. Or at least she hoped so.

The lashes stopped, and the guard walked around to the front of her. It took all her energy to raise her head so she could meet his eye. The chains at her wrists were cutting into skin, but she had no strength to get her legs back under her. "You should try to have a vision here soon, or things are only going to get more interesting."

Lyra grinned at her from behind the guard, and Briar met her gaze. "I'm not your dog to kick around. I could have a vision of step-by-step instructions on how to bring down your sister, and I'm still not going to open my mouth while you are treating me like this. I've done nothing but help you, now I'm done. You can burn in the pits for all I care." Briar forced a sweet smile onto her face, thinking she'd probably just signed her own death warrant.

Something glinted in Lyra's eyes. "Maybe I'll just have to send someone to Loinnir to get your little sister, then. She didn't do too well in this realm, but it could be fun to pull her nails from her little fingers and pluck strands of her hair until *my sister* is off her throne." Lyra turned on her heel and walked out the door, leaving Briar to the guards and whatever *interesting* things they had in store for her.

℮ ℮ ℮

Ana entered the war room with Ethelron at her back. It was taking everything in her to act like she wasn't falling apart. She'd finally said the words, put herself out there, and handed her heart over to Ethelron, only for him to tell her he couldn't be with her before going into a brooding silence while he speedily finished with her armor. If he didn't want her, he should just say so. She'd been away for years and didn't know his personal life. He could be in love with someone else for all she knew; it wasn't like he'd been particularly forthcoming about, well, *anything* since they'd reunited. She could let it go if he just didn't return her feelings.

The problem was, she felt like he *did* share her feelings. She'd caught his lingering gazes, she'd seen the flicker of longing that matched her own, and felt his touches that danced along the edges of 'platonic.' Not to mention that *kiss*. He was just too bullheaded to make a move. He wouldn't stop just looking at her as a princess, as a duty, so he could see her as a *woman*. A woman who was very much in love with him. She had been since she was a teenager. It had always been him, and she didn't want to waste another moment pretending otherwise. But she couldn't force him to love her, or to act on that love.

He touched her elbow to lead her to a set of chairs that were still open, but she saw a single seat across the table between Melody and Ryo. Needing space from him after he turned down her declaration, she withdrew from his touch and sat herself down in the empty chair, leaving Ethelron to sit alone.

"Look at you, all fitted out in armor." Ana leaned into Melody, taking in the sight of her dear friend looking ready for an all-out war. They'd spent plenty of time fighting side by side, but seeing the armor on her made it feel more real. More dangerous.

"You owe Erin an apology." Melody tilted her head towards Erin, who was sitting on the other side of her. Erin heard and leaned forward to glare at her before her eyes shifted to the silver-haired elf on Ana's other side. She'd sent Ryo to lead the girls to the armory, and clearly Erin wasn't happy about it. Ana gave a small grin of apology just as her parents entered. Everyone stood to show their respect until the king and queen were seated. The quiet conversations that had been going on silenced, and all attention went to the queen as she stood once more.

"As you have heard, we are overjoyed to welcome our daughter home. Princess Ainadelothien, and her friends, fought and killed Kali, now they will help us bring down Zepar and rid our realm of the invading erebi." She paused, allowing those around the table to slam their fists down in a show of support. Ana sat straighter and felt Melody and Erin do the same. "Our son, Toron, was taken from us at Kali's hand. So many of our people have been lost to this war, and now it is time we end it. I would like to spend a short time bringing Princess Ainadelothien and her friends, Melody and Erin, up to speed on our efforts. Aeron, could you please lead us through how our defense stands, and Zepar's current moves?"

Ana recognized the dark-skinned elf that nodded and stood from his chair. "Of course, Your Highness. We now understand that Zepar has increased his attacks because of his sister's death. In the past, they have been enough of a problem to keep us away from war outside of Eloas. They were content to keep us occupied and spread their infection through our home. Now, they wish for our destruction, and they want it quickly. As the Princess saw on her arrival, they have surrounded our castle, keeping us locked within, making it difficult for anyone to come or go. This is making it hard for us to get supplies, fight back, and gather information. Our main goal right now is to push back the erebi circle, but the attempts so far have only led to more infection erebi to replace those killed." Ana listened intently as Aeron covered how the erebi first came through the portal and spread as quickly as they could.

Unlike Sula, Eloas' portals are mostly centralized in one area. This made it hard for the erebi to get a good footing through the realm, making it easier for the other kingdoms to defend themselves and, eventually, many of them came to help the areas most infected. Over the years, they kept the erebi pushed back, which explained how some areas of the forest were completely dead, while other parts were only starting to show signs of infection.

"Zepar is looking for revenge, and the fall of the elven kind for good," Ana observed. It was overwhelming to have all this information thrown at her, but it felt good to have the broad strokes of what had happened to her home and people over the years.

Once they were caught up, no one got up to leave; instead other conversations started up again. Discussions of how they could push the erebi back and keep it that way, how they could find Zepar's location and bring him down for good, and training schedules all reached her ears. She was trying to follow all of them when Ryo leaned close, his breath warm against her neck as he whispered a dirty joke in her ear. She couldn't stop herself from laughing. After all the serious talk of war and destruction, having someone make her laugh made her feel a little lighter.

The sound died on her lips, though, when she caught sight of the dark gaze watching her from across the room. There was a large table between them, but she could feel that stare down to her toes. *Possessive* was the only way she could describe it. Her spine straightened. Heat traveled from the tips of her ears, down her neck, and across her cheeks. Ethelron seemed to follow the signs of that heat, his gaze drinking her in.

Ryo chucked at her side. "My, oh my. The leader of the guard looks like he wants my head to decorate his bedroom." The elf leaned back with ease, completely unbothered by the murderous look that was now shooting in his direction. "Do make sure he finds some way to retain my looks, won't you, Your Highness? So many would miss the beauty I bring to the world."

Ana wanted to tell him he had nothing to worry about, but Ethelron was now looking at Ryo like he was debating throwing his weapon at his head. That reaction really bothered her. She'd just laid all her feelings out on the table, only for him to go silent. He had no right to look at Ryo like he wanted to end him. He had no right to look at her like she was his next meal. If he wanted her, she was his for the taking, but if he wouldn't claim her, then he needed to free her.

"I'm curious what our Princess has done to her poor guard to bring out this side of him." Ryo placed his arms on the table to lean forward, turning his whole body to face her. She must not have been hiding her emotions well, because Ryo searched her features, and his gaze softened. "Try patience with him. He has suffered these years, and he's never looked at anyone as he is looking at you now. I understand how hard it can be to wait, but he will get there. In fact," he canted his head and dropped his voice, "if I were to lean in now and kiss you, I'm sure your guard would launch himself across this table and murder me in a breath." He glanced away to look at Ethelron, and Ana caught Ryo flashing him a wink. Ethelron's hand became a fist on the table. "Leave the room and he will follow." His eyes flashed with mischief, and his words pushed her into action.

He was right, Ethelron *would* follow her. It would give them the privacy for her to tell him she needed space from him. She couldn't love him like this: to have him in front of her, but still out of reach. She'd been lonely for too much of her life. He needed to understand that she would respect his decision to not be with her, but he was hurting her by just leaving her hanging like this, and looking at her as he was.

"I'm going to step out. Will the two of you be okay?" Ana asked Melody and Erin. Both were listening to the talks happening around them and seemed content to stay for the time being. Melody nodded and gave her a shooing motion with her hand, so Ana stood and walked to her parents, leaning down to let them know she was going to step out. Her father kissed her hand before dismissing her.

Ryo caught that same hand as she walked past him and his mouth tilted up in a grin that seemed to ask her to bed. "I'd walk out with you, but I do like my head attached. Make him fight for you, Princess." Ryo released her hand and leaned back in his chair once more. When she looked across the table, she found Ethelron was standing, watching them, his jaw tight as his gaze fell on the hand Ryo had just been holding. Without acknowledging him, Ana walked out the door.

She was just reaching the end of the hall when she heard his footsteps. He kept a distance between them, and that broke something else inside her. He'd only followed as her guard. She kept walking, wanting more space from where everyone else was. He was her silent shadow, even as she led them upstairs and headed towards a balcony she had used on many occasions to escape when she wanted fresh air. She and Toron had even spent time laying on their backs there, finding shapes in the clouds. Mostly, she'd snuck away on her own, though, using the space to read or study without interruption. Relief hit her when she reached the door and stepped onto the familiar platform. Her chest tightened with memories, but when the door shut behind her, Ana pushed the comforting feeling away and turned on Ethelron. Had she been waiting for him all these years? Maybe some part of her heart had always known he'd been alive and had refused to beat for another.

Ethelron stopped in his tracks, his eyes searching her face in question. She wasn't even trying to hide any of her feelings. He must be seeing a war taking place across her features. "Princess?"

258

"Don't." She actually choked on the word and gave herself a mental shake. She would *not* cry, not now. "You *can't do this*, right? You don't want me? Fine. I accept that. I understand that, for whatever reason, you can't be with me in that way." Surprise flitted across his face, but he quickly tried to tuck away his feelings. "You don't want me romantically, but I don't want you as my guard. I will speak with my parents and ask for someone else to be assigned to me. You've spent years without me here, clearly thriving as the leader of the guard; you don't need to fall back on old habits. There is no need to undo the years of work you've done to get where you are now. You did your duty well. You protected me, brought me back home, and now it's time for you to give me space. Because I love you, Ethelron. And that's not fair to you. It's not fair for me to have carried these feelings all these years and put them on your shoulders now.

"You don't want me, and I accept your feelings on the matter. But I can't have you as my guard. I can't have you look at me like you were back in the war room. I *can't*, because it's hurting me. I know the last thing you want to do is hurt me, El. So please." She drew in a shaky breath. She was almost done. Then he'd leave her here alone and she could mourn the loss in peace. "Please, just let me go." She normally used silence as a shield. She could have locked away her emotions and pretended that sending him away as her guard was just about not holding him back. But she knew if she showed him her pain, let him have one more piece of her, he'd see how staying close to her was hurting her, and he'd give her the space she needed. Ana wasn't giving him the chance to fight back.

Ethelron stood frozen between her and the door. His gaze met hers, probably recognizing how her eyes were filling with tears, before shifting down to her lips. She thought of the kiss they'd shared, and how she'd been so full of hope for mere seconds as they stood together in that room. "Aina…" Ethelron took a step towards her, and it took all her strength to keep from moving. "I don't deserve you. I don't deserve your regard, or your love."

"But you have it all the same. If you don't want it, then you *have* to step away. You deserve all that is good in this world, Ethelron, but so do I. I want us to stand together, but if you don't, then that's okay. But I need spa-" His hands were on her hips, pulling her flush against him while his mouth came down on hers, cutting her off for the second time with a kiss. He dragged her across the balcony, pressing her back against the castle wall so he could explore her more thoroughly. She let him claim her, and in return, she gave him back all the love she held for him. She let him feel it in the touch of her hands, and in the way her lips danced with his. Hope flared alive in her chest once more; surely he wouldn't kiss her like his right after her little speech, not if he didn't mean to make her his. He was not a cruel man.

"Princess…" He drew back just enough to speak, his lips still moved against hers as he said the word. "I'm yours. I've always been yours. If this is what you want, if this is what you are choosing, then

I'm here with you." He drew her lips to his once more, drinking deeply from her.

"Ethelron, I don't need you. I can stand on my own, but I don't want to. I trust you, I love you, I *want* you. I *choose* you." She followed the tattooed markings on the side of his face with her fingertips. He gave a quick nod, showing that he was hearing her, that he understood.

"I won't leave your side, Aina. You will always have me. You will have my sword, and my love. I've been devoted to you with everything in me since I set eyes on you for the first time. You are beautiful, intelligent, and brave. Far braver than anyone else I've ever met." His nose brushed against hers and she melted at the small touch. When he rested his forehead against hers, as she'd seen her parents do so many times before, the intimacy wrapped her in a new shield. One forged of love.

.℮ .℮ .℮

Doyle acted as guard to make sure Malux got from Briar's room and into a hidden passage without being seen. From there, the two of them found a hidden cavern for him to make his home and they fought side-by-side to get the small space cleared of soul-feeders that liked attaching to their victim's face and draining their energy until

261

nothing remained. "I'll come back with some supplies and food to make this more comfortable." A fine sheen of sweat was starting on his brow, and it wasn't from anything he was doing. His body was beginning to shake with pain. It was worse than when Briar got visions. He was feeling her pain, but he knew it had to be extreme for it to be affecting him, and he was all too aware of the fact that he was only feeling a shadow of what she was. He wanted to double over and be sick as his body tried to fight against the intrusion, but he swallowed it down. Doyle had to get to her.

"Go on, I'll be fine. Briar is the one in danger right now."

Doyle left him without argument and let his instincts lead him. He didn't have a plan, other than when he found Briar, he was dragging her out of whatever place she was in, and he was taking her back to her room, where he'd stand guard over her to make sure no one hurt her ever again. If Lyra had a problem with that, then they were going to have to come to an understanding. He couldn't continue to support her if *this* is what she would do to those helping her.

Doyle followed a winding path before he felt Briar nearby. His pace quickened when he heard a cry rip from her throat. Even through the tunneled walkway he could hear the raw emotion in that cry, and he broke into a full-on run. He didn't need the rune now; her screams led him right to the door she had to be behind. He didn't bother to try the knob. Instead, he kicked it off the hinges and saw red.

His heart stopped beating, and he thought he might faint. The pain he was feeling was nothing. *Nothing.* He thought he felt a shadow of her pain, but he felt a paper-cut compared to what her body had clearly been put through. He could almost feel his blood draining from his face as he spotted her hanging from chains shackled around her wrists. Her legs were limp, her head bowed. Every inch of her seemed to be shaking, and blood pooled at her feet on the ground. He was aware that there were two guards near her, one holding a knife, but he didn't even see them. He didn't see who they were as he drew his sword and cut them both down before either could even think to fight him.

He fell to his knees in front of her, reaching up to touch her face. She jerked back and let out a little sob from the movement. A stream of curses fell from his lips as he rose to look for the keys for the shackles. He found them on the small table behind her, and when he turned, he got a good look at her back. Her shirt hung off of her in shreds, showing all the lashes criss-crossing over her skin. His stomach turned, and he nearly lost it right there.

Doyle gave himself a small shake. First, he had to get her down, and then he had to get her safe. He couldn't leave her there, shaking and bleeding. He had to keep it together so he could keep moving. "Briar, it's me. I'm here. I'm going to do my best not to hurt you, but I have to get these chains off and move you. Okay?" He crouched again and gently touched her chin, trying to get her to look at him. He hoped if she saw him, then she'd know she was safe.

Fuck. Like she was even close to being safe around him. *He'd* done this to her. Her eyes opened, so bloodshot he could hardly make out the purple irises. "Hey, Blue. I'm going to get you down, okay?"

"Doyle, she'll be mad at you." Her voice was weak and he had to lean closer to hear her.

"I don't care." He wanted to kiss her cheek, to do something to comfort her, but he couldn't even see a spot that looked like it wouldn't hurt her to touch. One cheek was swollen and bruised, the other had nail marks down it. Instead, he kissed the tip of her nose and moved to undo the chains. Every small movement made her whimper, and every sound she made tore at him. He wished he hadn't killed the guards so quickly. If he could, he'd go back and make their deaths slow. He let the keys clatter into the puddle of blood as he moved to support her weight. There were cuts up her arms, and her back was hardly even a *back* any longer, so he wasn't sure the best way to hold her. He had to move her, but it wasn't going to be pleasant.

"She said she'd get Fern...I can't let her bring her here..." He swept her off her feet and into his arms, knowing it was going to hurt her back, but not seeing an easier way. She let out a little cry before her head lolled back, and he knew she'd fainted. It was almost a relief; he could get her moved quickly without causing her more pain.

He didn't go back to her room. He took her right to his, surprised that no one stopped him along the way. It would be hard to murder them while he had her in his arms, but if anyone thought to stop him, he'd find a way. The moment he got to his room, he laid her on the bed face-down. He hurriedly gathered everything he had for taking care of wounds and put it on the small table next to his bed. Then he ripped away the little that remained of her shirt. His hands shook as he tried to look past the injuries and just make quick work cleaning and wrapping the lashes before she woke. Normally, she'd need a lot of stitches, but he knew her body would heal. She just needed a little time. Luckily, he still had some salve that Horace had made for him, which helped wounds heal faster. He saw every small mark on her body and raged.

"Doyle?" Her voice whispered against the pillow. He crouched next to the bed so he could meet her gaze.

"Don't move, okay? I wrapped the wounds on your back until they heal, but if you move it's going to hurt."

"You can't let her take Fern. I'll go back, but she can't hurt Fern."

"I won't let her, I promise. And she's not coming anywhere near you. This is the last time anyone lays a finger on you."

"Doyle." She gave him a watery smile. "You can't stand against her. She'll turn on you-"

"I know. Malux told me about your vision. I'll deal with her, okay? Now try to get some rest. I'm not going anywhere."

"Where's Malux? I was afraid they would see him."

"They didn't find him. He's moved. Now hush. Stop worrying about everyone. You need to rest so you can heal." He placed a kiss on her forehead and watched as her eyes closed.

Finally, her breathing evened out, so he stood and draped a light sheet over her and sat one of his shirts on the table in case she got up and wanted it. Then he changed out of his own clothes, which were soaked with her blood, before he went to stand guard outside his door. He knew he was going to have a fight on his hands, but he was not going to let anyone even see her until he made it known that if anyone wanted to speak with Briar from now on, they could go through him. He knew Briar was worried about Fern, but he also knew Lyra. She wasn't going to send someone after the girl; it was too much work, when she thought she could just break Briar on her own. But she was not going to be happy to hear he killed two of her guards and took Briar off without her permission.

ℰ ℰ ℰ

Melody thought of her powers, and wondered if there was something she could do about the erebi circling the castle. If there was a way for her to use that burst of energy again, and control it enough to make sure she only blasted away the circle, she could solve the main problem they were currently facing. She'd been so deep in thought that she didn't notice the queen sit at her side until she felt Erin straighten beside her.

"Melody, it is so lovely to meet you." Queen Faervel looked at her with the same eyes as Ana. Her smile was soft and motherly, and her voice had a musical quality to it. The stray idea that the queen probably had a lovely singing voice flitted across her mind as she searched for how to respond to a *queen* talking to her. She was not prepared for this kind of life. She'd never once thought of Ana as a princess. Ana had never been royalty to her, even after she'd learned that she was, in fact, elven royalty. "Please don't look at me like that." The queen grinned at her openly. "You look frozen in place, dear. There is no need for worries between us. You are family. You have been family to my daughter, which makes you family to me. No need to stand on ceremony."

"Thank you, I appreciate it. I'm so happy that Ethelron found Ana and could bring her home. I know it means so much to her to have been reconnected with her family and people."

"Yes," Faervel's blue eyes went misty, "it is a true blessing to have her returned home. I wish we could have ended this war for her, but she is no longer a child. She's clearly grown into a strong warrior, and I think she is exactly what we need to end this once and for all. I just wish she didn't have to be. I wanted peace for her, but I suppose she's never really had it, has she?"

"No, but maybe she's a step closer to it now."

The door opened to the room and the separate conversations were cut off once more as a female warrior entered. "Your Majesties, we have received word from one of the scouts that they believe they have found where the queen is being hidden away. If we can get to her, the portal that the erebi are coming through should be nearby. If she can be killed and the portal destroyed, we will cut them off."

"I'm sorry, what queen?" Erin asked, glancing at Ana's mother.

"The infection erebi swarm around a queen." Ryo spoke up to answer her question. "You can only gain control of them by enslaving the queen. They keep her hidden and keep moving her. She has control over a different kind of portal. It moves with her and seems to only work for the infection erebi. It's like a way for the queen to call her minions to her. Only those infected can actually see the portal, but it can be sensed."

"There wasn't a queen though when we brought down Kali. Once she was killed, the erebi escaped back to their realm, leaving the fight." Erin glanced at Melody for confirmation. The witch gave a slight nod to show she was correct, knowing Erin had not exactly been in her right mind after that fight.

"They are likely from the same swarm. Once Kali was gone, they had no reason to stay far from their queen. They either came here or returned to Skia once she was killed," Ryo countered.

"So the goal now is not to go after Zepar, but to take down the infection queen?" Melody asked.

"Yes, if we kill Zepar, the infection queen will be released from her enslavement. Right now the erebi are actually being controlled for the benefit of war. The queen could easily let the erebi loose, and we won't be able to fight against them. Zepar doesn't want the realm destroyed because he wants to rule over it." This time Aeron answered, standing from his spot at the table. "We need to move quickly. The queen is never kept in one area long. If we lose this chance, it could be some time before we find her again."

"Ryo, please find my daughter and Ethelron," the king spoke up, also standing from the table.

"I would love to, but I don't think that is the best idea." Ryo shifted uncomfortably.

"Oh, for the love of the realm!" One of the other females at the table stood, sending a pointed look at Ryo. "We should start some kind of countdown of days you went without causing trouble, Ryo."

"Nelel, darling, could we do it by the hour instead? Otherwise, I'm not sure anyone would ever do any counting." Ryo grinned with ease, but he stood and checked his weapons. Even though his features remained relaxed, something about his stance changed. Before Melody's eyes, he went from rogue to warrior.

Melody stood too, and tried to check in with her magic. She could feel it at her center, stronger than she'd ever felt it before. She held on to that knowledge as everyone prepared to go to war. Erin nudged her arm with her elbow, her gaze questioning. They were in this together, for Ana and her home.

Chapter Sixteen

The small group of warriors followed the scouts out of the tunnel to leave the safety of the castle. Twelve warriors, plus a wolf. They still had to get through the wall of erebi around the castle, but with the larger group, it was a little easier to keep the erebi from pushing in on them. Ana made sure her group was together, pushing Melody to the middle so she could place a protection spell on everyone. It did not take them as long to break through to the other side of the erebi, but quite a few broke from the circle to follow them.

Ryo stepped forward, both swords raised. He cut through three of the erebi while another warrior, the female Nelel, that had come to get her and Ethelron, shot arrows to take down the other four that tried to follow them. Ana felt the tension. They needed to get to the queen. If they didn't get to her, take *her* out, the erebi would just keep coming.

Ethelron took the lead behind the three scouts, so Ana and her group quickly followed, leaving the other warriors to take the rear. After about half a mile, the scouts slowed and talked quietly to one another. Even with her sharp elven ears, Ana was finding it hard to understand all they were saying as they began to discuss the best direction to come from. Then she felt a firm hand on the small of her back and lost her focus for just a moment. Every small touch from Ethelron set her skin on fire. *He was hers.*

"It is just behind the abandoned blacksmith's forge." The nearest scout, Arasson, pointed toward an old stone building, crumbling but for one wall that continued to stand tall, as if it were another tree in the dying forest.

"Your job is to feel out where the portal is and get it closed. Who knows exactly how the erebi are going to react when the queen is killed. We don't want more to swarm from Skia," Ana spoke quietly to Melody, but the witch shook her head.

"I should focus on keeping a protection spell up around everyone. The queen is going to be strong. People are going to get hurt."

There was a fierceness in the witch's eyes. It gave Ana pause, and she forced herself to look at each of the surrounding faces. Elves who had spent nearly eighteen years fighting for their survival. Living

272

off scraps of food because they had to make everything they had last for as long as possible. Now they were all focused on her. Ethelron might be the leader of the royal guard and a well-respected warrior, but she was the princess. *She* had royal blood, and she was the one who might have to make the decision about who would live and who would die.

Ryo, the fierce warrior with mischievous silver eyes. Arasson, the blue-eyed scout, who moved through the forest as if he was a deer frolicking, two elflings of his own to care for. Myriil, the young elf who argued to come so he could redeem himself. The list went on, and she was responsible for them all. They were *all* hers.

"Just focus on the portal. Erin, Ryo, you cover Melody. Keep the erebi from her so she can focus." Ana caught the hard look Erin flashed her at the mention of the flirty elf, but Ana knew he was a true warrior and would keep the erebi at bay. "The rest of you, the focus is the queen. The other erebi will get in the way, but handle them quickly. We cannot allow the queen to move." She'd had to play catch-up after abandoning the meeting. Nelel filled her in on the importance of the infection erebi's queen. Ethelron filled in gaps as they had moved to catch up with the rest of the group. It was jarring to be declaring love for one another in one breath, and preparing for battle in the next, but she didn't regret the few stolen moments she'd had with him.

Each elf met her gaze and nodded. Her blue eyes lingered when they fell on Ethelron, his eyes dark with the coming fight. He reached out and his fingertips brushed over her palm. Just a small movement, but intimate, speaking volumes. She nodded. It was time.

ℰ ℰ ℰ

Erin kept near Melody's side, a dagger gripped in each hand. She was in no way adept at using her left hand for fighting, but it gave her something to slash toward an opponent. She felt a gaze on her and turned, finding Ryo grinning. "Trying to prove yourself, halfling? It's not easy work, fighting with two weapons at once. Only the most *skilled* can make magic with *both* hands." Melody gagged beside her, the stress lifting for just a moment as he flashed a dangerous wink.

"If you keep it up, I'll show you exactly what I can do with a blade. The princess is my friend, she'll forgive me if one of her warriors disappears."

"Oh, were we still talking about weapons?" His mouth turned up on a wicked smile, but an erebus interrupted whatever witty remark he was preparing to add, and the battle began in one swift breath.

"How do we know which one is the queen?" Erin asked, but then she understood. There was no denying which one stood as leader over all the others. Opposite from the black swirling energy of the infection erebi, the queen stood a foot taller than the rest, bright white energy swirling around her like liquid, licking at the air. Erin couldn't even make out the features of the face, the light she was giving off far too bright. But, when the queen sensed the surrounding danger, she wailed out a high-pitched scream that seemed to fill the forest.

The shadow erebi swarmed, hissing in warning as they all came to protect their queen. Ryo and Erin surrounded Melody. "Melody, you need to focus on finding the portal! I don't think we will have much time." Erin blocked one erebus coming at them full force.

Sio rushed past her, the fur of the wolf brushing against her leg, but she didn't spare the wolf a second thought. She had nothing to fear from the beast, and even if she did, she didn't have the energy to spend on her old fear. Erin stabbed the erebus and kept pushing Melody forward. Ryo might enjoy annoying anyone within a fifty-mile radius, but he *was* a skilled fighter. He moved with confidence, his body using a natural grace to pull him in the right direction. Four erebi were at his feet by the time Erin stabbed one. He kept his body between the erebi and Melody with each movement, never straying from her side.

"There!" Melody pointed toward the standing wall. "The portal is over there!"

"Let's move, then!" Ryo started to clear the way, pushing erebi aside, leaving Erin to cover Melody's back. Three erebi jumped at them as they neared the queen. Melody thrust out her hand and a ball of fire shot from it, slamming into the chest of the nearest erebus. Erin tried fighting the other two while Ryo was still clearing away erebi ahead of them. Her left arm was almost worthless however, forcing

Erin to drop the second dagger and put all her force behind one. She narrowly dodged an attack before she stabbed one. She was pulling her dagger free when she looked up at the sound of a sword and found Ryo cutting away the arm of an erebus about to dig its claws into her. Before she could thank him, he grabbed her arm to bring her back to her feet and had them all moving again.

.℮ .℮ .℮

Out of the corner of her eye, Ana saw Ryo shield Erin from an attack. The halfling might not have been happy to be paired with him, but at least Ana knew she'd made the right decision. It looked like the trio had a destination in mind, which meant Melody knew where the portal was. She couldn't keep track of where everyone was; after the queen's cry, the erebi closed ranks and blocked her view of many of the elves. She just had to focus and keep moving toward the queen at the center. Ethelron pressed to her side so they could work together to clear a path.

She lost sight of him as well when claws hit her armor, knocking her back into a small swarm. Suddenly, she was surrounded, with no ally in sight. She fought back quickly, trying to keep them from overwhelming her, and took out two before another fell at her feet, stabbed from behind. Ethelron's face appeared and his hand grabbed her arm roughly, pulling her back to his side. She could feel the tension in his muscles, but she didn't have time to reassure him. The queen stood before them and swiped an arm toward Ethelron. She knocked into his shoulder but didn't cut him. He dodged the next attack, and Ana took the opportunity to stab her dagger toward the queen's arm.

Ana's arm reverberated as she met diamond-hard resistance. Ana moved quickly, ducking under an attempted attack, and tried to stab again, this time striking the queen's stomach. Again, there was no softness to the skin. Ana knew that when a creature was first infected, their skin would turn hard as they went through the final stages. After the infection took full control, however, the skin would become pliable once more. That did not seem to be the case with the queen. Ethelron met her gaze as they tried to figure out how they could kill her if they couldn't stab her.

"Maybe she is weak over her heart," Ana sent the thought to Ethelron. He gave a curt nod before letting out a high-pitched whistle, calling Sio back to him. The wolf came dodging through battling figures to reach her master's side. He pointed to the queen, and she seemed to understand him perfectly, moving to draw the queen's attention so Ethelron could line up an attack. The queen hardly moved to watch the wolf, however, and knocked Ethelron back at the last second. Ana jumped to his side before one of the infection erebi could attack him, stabbing one in the heart. She reached out a hand to help him to his feet, but he pulled her down on top of him, holding her

head still between his hands. The sound of his racing pulse overwhelmed the sound of battle, until she heard the whizz of an arrow above her, followed by a high-pitched scream. Both elves rose to their feet to find the arrow lodged in the queen's heart. The energy that swirled around her pulsed with her agony.

Then the whole world erupted in chaos.

♪ ♪ ♪

"Mel, how's it going there?" They reached the portal, and Melody immediately began chanting, working to close the portal off. Ryo and Erin stood at her back to fight off the erebi that came to protect the magical area. Erin threw out her hands and brought the surrounding earth up to make a shield between them and the erebi for a few breaths. It gave them time to gather their strength and buy Melody a little more time. The sight of Ana and Ethelron near the queen made her lungs seize in worry, but she pulled her attention back to her own fight as the erebi broke through the dirt. The earth around her was so alive even as the magic was being drained by the erebus hoard. Still, her veins buzzed on the magic she felt, and she wished beyond anything that she could share these powers with Gabe. She wanted him at her side so she could show him what she could do. She wanted to fight for his realm and see him stand in the world he was born in.

She held off the erebi closest to her, making sure to keep her body between them and Melody. The air was crackling with dark energy and battle sounds. It made the hair on Erin's arms stand on end. "Come on, halfling! Have a little fun, will ya?" Ryo had a huge grin across his face as he fought any beast that came in his direction. "We are alive. That makes for a good day!" His eyes drew away from hers. "Shit!"

Erin followed his gaze, just in time to see the queen calling out in agony, an arrow sticking out from her chest. Another arrow followed, and the queen fell. "Hurry up, Mel!" Melody's chanting took an aggressive edge, and Erin got the feeling the witch was telling her off with her tone, since she had to continue the chant. The magic felt like a lightning storm at her back. Static energy fizzled as Melody tried to undo the portal. She worried that, with the queen injured - or possibly dead - the erebi would swarm the portal, and the power radiating from Melody. Only she and Ryo could protect the witch. Everyone else was too far away.

But the erebi didn't swarm to the portal, nor were more summoned from the other side. Instead, all the erebi stilled as one before their hissing became unified and aggressive.

"Nelel!" Ryo left his station at Melody's side and ran as the erebi moved toward a violet-eyed elf. Erin realized she was the elf that shot the arrows, and remembered that Ryo had joked with her at the meeting. Ryo was attempting to help her, but it was already too late. Nelel didn't even have time to scream for help before she was overwhelmed, claws digging into her as all the infection erebi converged in a single attack. Ryo reached them and began ripping erebi away in desperation. Ana and Ethelron moved forward as well, working to clear away erebi so they could at least get to the elf's body.

"Got it!" Melody's voice rang out behind her, and Erin turned her attention back in time to see the wall glow with a red light before it expanded and retracted into a small pinprick. Then it was gone. "Oh god." As the portal came to a close, the erebi turned their attention towards them. Most of them hovered around Nelel, but about ten of them broke away, and it was just Melody and Erin.

Melody shot out a hand and blasted three of them back with a burst of energy, and Erin pulled up the ground again to block a few off. Ryo was moving back toward them, seeing their danger, and took out the three that were tripped up by Erin's powers. More of the infected broke away and came at them. Erin hardly had time to think *this was her last breath* before she and Melody were surrounded. Erin sent vines into another small pocket heading their direction, trying to buy them time for help to arrive, and killed the first to make a leap towards them. Her dagger slipped in her palm from her own sweat. She barely kept hold of the blade as Melody killed the next. Another came from the side and knocked Melody back, slamming her into the wall, her head bouncing off the stone. Erin stepped in quickly, covering her with her own body.

A claw dug into the skin of her arm as she swung her dagger to stab the next erebus in the chest. She screamed. She had no control over it. Her body pulled in on itself in agony, but Melody was hurt behind her, and Erin had to keep the erebi at bay. Struggling, she took out another erebus as Melody regained her feet and shot a ball of fire into the chest of another. Ryo finally reached them, his blades never stopping.

"Erin?" His voice was distant as darkness filled her head. After spending days being tortured by Bogor, she thought she knew pain, but nothing compared to this. It felt like her body was ripping itself apart while on fire.

"Gabe?" His name tumbled off her lips. Her body was pulsing with agony, and she wondered if she was dying. She heard her name being called, too many voices for her to sort through. But she saw Gabe's face smiling at her from her bed. A book in his hands as he read aloud to her, stroking her hair. She tried to say his name again, but felt numb and wasn't sure if he heard her.

.℘ .℘ .℘

Briar woke slowly with an aching body. When she moved though, it wasn't the sharp pain that went right down to her bones, rather more of a soreness that spread through each muscle. She wondered how long she'd been out, to have healed enough to not pass out from the pain. She saw her shirt shredded on the floor, covered in her blood, but she was covered with a sheet and bandages. Slowly, she sat up, aware of every inch of her body, keeping the sheet wrapped around her. She was in Doyle's room. Briar remembered him whispering to her, taking care of her. She remembered him telling her he wouldn't leave her, but she didn't see him.

Her eyes fell on the shirt left on the nightstand. She assumed he'd left it for her, so she pulled it on over her head and breathed deeply as his scent enveloped her. "Doyle?" She whispered, wondering if he was in the washroom. The door to it was opened, so she entered and found a small mirror reflecting a pale version of herself. One side of her face was still a little discolored from a faded bruise and the nail marks down her cheeks were just pink against her skin. She wondered how bad her back still looked, but she wasn't going to take the bandages off herself.

"You cannot be here." Doyle's voice was muffled, but it was close. She turned and headed to his bedroom door and felt the pull of his presence.

"Last time I checked, you took orders from *me*, not the other way around." The sharpness of Lyra's voice had her stopping in her tracks and she hovered by the door, afraid to move any further. A thin sheen of sweat coated her skin at Lyra's voice. Her body reacted to it, sending her heart into a galloping race. "You know, I left the observer to stew with fear over her sister, and I came back to find two of my guards killed and the observer gone. Those do not seem like actions taken by someone loyal to me."

Briar knew he'd taken her from the room, but she didn't remember the guards being killed. She just remembered how gentle he was when he'd touched her face and kissed her nose, and the pain that felt like it would kill her when he moved her.

"I've been loyal to you my whole life. But I don't agree with your actions towards Briar, and I won't accept it any longer. She's done nothing but help us, yet you continue to torture her. I won't allow it."

"You *won't allow it?*" Lyra chuckled, and Briar could almost imagine the dark look in her eyes as she did so.

"Lyra, if you want her to be of any use to us, killing her isn't going to help. You know I've stood at your side for years. You know me and trust me. But I won't stand aside and let you hurt her again. If you want my help and my loyalty, then you'll leave her alone. She has no problem being an advisor, and she *wants* to bring down your sister. Torturing her for visions does not work, though. If anything, you will turn her against us! Why would Briar want to put a crown on *your* head if you do nothing but bring her pain? You are my only family. You've been family to me since I lost my parents. But you are being stupid about Briar, and I won't stand aside and let it happen."

Briar wanted to puke. All she could see was Doyle, chained down while flames slowly licked at his body. He was making a stand for her, even if it meant losing Lyra. Something warm swirled in her chest, and she wanted him to come into the room so she could kiss him. She wanted to hold him and thank him. She wanted to see if there was still a future where he would turn against her, or if his ties with Lyra had been severed by his feelings for her.

"I hope you don't live to regret this choice, Doyle. Maybe I should have done to you what my sister did to Malux. Tying you to me by dark magic certainly would have made you less trouble. But I never thought I had to worry about you standing against me. I thought I'd earned your loyalty after years of caring for you. I guess a pretty face and a pair of legs to settle between is enough to change that, though."

"Lyra-"

"No, you can have your little plaything. As long as she continues to present me with her visions. They'd better be useful, dear, or not even *you* will stand in my way."

"I'll make sure that she does."

"I'm not done. You stood against me. You killed two of my guards. I'll not let you carry on without punishment. Come to me in an hour to face the consequences of your actions. If I have to send someone after you, they will drag your pet along as well."

"I understand. I will be there in an hour."

Doyle was just going to walk freely into whatever punishment Lyra thought he deserved? He had *no idea* what it was he might face, but he didn't even hesitate to accept her terms. She was still frozen there when the door opened, and Doyle looked at her slowly. He didn't seem surprised to find her there, so close to the door he'd almost hit her with it. Instead, his eyes traveled over her intently, probably checking for injuries, though something changed in his gaze when he reached out to tug on the bottom of the shirt he'd left out for her.

"You look good in this." His voice was deeper than usual, and the way he gazed at her made heat rise to her cheeks. "How are you feeling?" He let his hand drop away and his gaze fell to her cheeks.

"I'm better. Really sore, but that's about it. My back is tender, but I think all the wounds are closed. I just couldn't get the bandages. Doyle-"

"Let me take a look." He took her hand and led her to the bed, sitting her at the edge while he settled behind her with his legs stretched out on either side of her. "Is this okay?" he asked as he started to lift the shirt so he could see her back.

Something was stuck in her throat, so she just nodded and reached up to hold the shirt out of the way for him. His hands moved slowly, tracing her exposed skin and prodding gently at the edges of the bandages. He worked slowly at peeling them away and she did her best not to make a noise. Her skin was tender and it hurt to remove them, but she knew if they were left there, it would just make her itch.

Doyle was clearly being as careful as he could, and when he was finally done, he moved gentle fingertips over her skin. "The wounds are all closed, but it's still very red." His voice was rough. "How does it feel?"

"I'll be okay. I'm sure by tomorrow it will be like nothing happened. But Doyle…" She turned now, letting the shirt fall back into place. He wouldn't quite meet her eyes. "You can't just accept whatever punishment she has in mind for you."

His hand came up to cradle her face. "Do you think she can do worse to me than she did to you? I can handle whatever she's preparing. But I'm not letting anyone near you again. They shouldn't have been able to get to you yesterday. Lyra came to talk to me here and she never does that. I should have known something was going on."

She leaned against him, and it took him a few seconds before the stiffness left his body and he held her close. "I can't apologize enough for what happened-"

"Shhh, it wasn't your fault. You stood against her…I wasn't expecting that." She felt him start to talk, but didn't want to waste the time they had before he had to go to Lyra to answer for what he did. Instead, she met his lips with hers. The kiss began slowly, soft and questioning, but as he joined her, he brought heat that set her aflame.

286

The horrors from the day before burned away and were replaced, one by one, with thoughts of hope...and of love.

Chapter Seventeen

Ethelron finally reached Nelel on the ground, but it was far too late. It looked like the erebi were trying to turn her, replace the queen that she killed. Her veins were glowing white and her skin was already beginning to harden. He moved swiftly, leaping forward to stab Nelel in the heart before her skin fully hardened and made her nearly impossible to kill.

Ana knew he was killing the elf in order to save her, before the infection took full control and made her something else, but she also knew he would carry that death on his shoulders. Erebi were forcing their way in, and she had to turn her attention away before she could try to offer him some form of comfort. She would make sure he had whatever time he needed; she would protect his back with everything in her.

Ana didn't know where anyone else was anymore; she sensed other elves and magic around her, but the loss of the queen was sending the infection erebi into a frenzy, and it was taking all of her focus to hold them back. Then Ethelron was there, taking up his stance at her side, his lips set in a grim line as he helped fight them. The other elven warriors were around them, trying to take out as many erebi as they could when the energy shifted. The energy coming from the portal collapsed, leaving behind an empty feeling at the loss of magic.

"Aina, we need to move!" Ethelron grabbed her arm, and she turned to search for Melody and Erin, remembering where she saw them last. She wasn't the only one. At the collapse of the portal, all the erebi were now turning to them, seething with a thirst for revenge. Even worse, she caught sight of Ryo in the center of battle instead of by their side. Ryo must have seen what they were looking at, because he took off running back towards her friends, but there was already a circle of erebi between them. Melody shot off a spell and Erin raised the earth.

Then her view of them cut off, and she just tucked herself in behind Ethelron as he rushed them forward. He didn't stop until she caught sight of a pale Erin fighting off erebi, Melody on the ground behind her. Claws hit her armor from behind, making her stop to take out the dark shadow trying to attack her. The moment she was free from it, Ethelron had them moving again. Then he was shoving her in front of him so he could protect her back while she went to her friends.

"Erin?" Ana ran forward as Ryo caught the halfling before she hit the ground. The blood was gone from her face. When she got closer, Ana saw the cut on her arm, already beginning to turn black.

"Cover my back!" Seeming to ignore the chaotic buzzing of the leaderless erebi around them, Ethelron dropped to his knees beside Erin as Ryo eased her to the ground. Ana watched as he laid steady hands on her, trying to draw the poison from Erin's veins as he'd done for her.

"El?" Ana tried to keep the panic from her voice, but she didn't like the way Ethelron was shaking his head.

"I can't get it all! Ryo, take her to the castle!"

"What?" Ryo looked nearly as panicked as she felt.

"The wound is too deep. It will spread if it's not dealt with right away, but there is too much poison for me to draw out. Her natural healing powers are trying to fight it, but I'm not strong enough to help her. Take her to the queen, now! We'll keep the erebi from following you, the warriors at the castle will help you pass through. Melody, you go too. Keep a protection spell over them so they don't get hurt."

"Melody?" Ana asked when she didn't respond. She looked over Melody's exposed skin; she didn't think she'd been infected, but Melody looked like she might be sick.

"Yeah, okay. Let's move!" Melody waited for Ryo to gather Erin into his arms, then placed the protection spell over the elf and halfling before drawing her weapon, ready to protect them if needed, even while holding the spell.

Ana dove into battle. She would use her body as a shield for them, giving them all the space they needed in order to make it back to the castle. Everything else fell away: the sounds of battle, her worry for Erin, the woman her brother had loved. All she felt was the desire to end this, to take out each of these wispy figures until her body gave out.

"Aina, stop. Just breathe. Your mother will help her." She didn't answer or acknowledge him. She didn't even slow. But she felt him make a change in his own fight to keep up with her. He kept his thoughts to himself, but his presence acted as a beacon of light for her to find her way once her work was done.

$$\mathcal{C} \ \mathcal{C} \ \mathcal{C}$$

Melody held the protection spell over Ryo and Erin with everything in her. She was paranoid the whole run that something would appear out of thin air and attack them. Instead, she found that the circle around the castle was broken, many of the erebi were gone, and those that remained were scattered, making it easy for them to get through. Melody dropped into the tunnel first, but another elf came up to take Erin as Ryo handed her down. Neither of them spoke on the way back to the castle, but Erin murmured Gabe's name a few times as she cried out in pain. Each sharp breath the fae took did well to remind Melody that Erin got hurt protecting her.

"Come on." Ryo took Erin back into his arms, even though he'd already carried her the entire way back to the castle. He led them through the passages, seeming to know exactly where to find Ana's mother.

The queen's bright eyes fell on Erin, and she didn't even pause. She was on her feet and leading them past a row of beds, clearly set up to treat the injured, into another set of doors which led to a private room. Ryo laid Erin on the bed with such care, Melody worried Erin might be more frail in this state than she thought. They exchanged no words. The queen understood what happened with a glance and knew there was no time to waste. She found the wound and immediately hovered her hands over it. If Melody wasn't so close, she would have thought her quite unaffected, but from where she stood, she could see the slight tremor in her hands.

The sight before her brought up thoughts of the king; his arm useless from the infection, spending every day of his life fighting it from spreading. Ethelron had drawn the poison from Ana, but he hadn't been able to do it for Erin. Ryo placed a hand on her shoulder to stop her pacing, and the witch turned into the embrace. She needed the

292

comfort; Erin had been injured protecting *her*. If she couldn't be healed...it wasn't something Melody was ready to come to terms with. She might not have always gotten along with Erin, but when it came down to it, Erin had been there when she was needed, and she'd pushed past her pain and loss in order to help Ana.

"I'm sorry. It was my fault. I shouldn't have left your side," Ryo finally whispered, hugging her a little tighter against him. She looked up into his face and found his eyes watching the queen work, the ever-present smile oddly missing from his features.

Then it started. Melody broke from his comforting embrace to move forward and watch. It looked like smoke was rising from Erin's veins as the queen began to draw out the poison.

.℘ .℘ .℘

Gabe stood before her, just as she remembered him. His green eyes were bright after his workout at the gym that morning. She knew they needed to get ready; she was going into the store, to learn more about who she really was, and to gain control over her powers.

"So, Jason found a new roommate, which means..."

"You are free from sock patrol?" She couldn't help herself and earned a reproachful look. It was staggering how quickly their relationship moved and amazing that she wasn't trying to run in the other direction. After their first night

together, he almost always spent his nights with her at her apartment, and she didn't want it any other way. So after only a month and a half since they'd found each other again, she asked him to move in. She went from a person who avoided relationships to someone who now found it impossible to fall asleep without the sound of his heart beating under her ear.

"It means," he quickly invaded her space, pressing her against the kitchen counter, laying his palms on either side of her. His eyes were dark as he looked at her, making it hard for her to breathe, "that soon I'll officially be living here...with you."

"Uh huh..." She nodded, but couldn't form any other words as his lips trailed kisses down her neck, resting at the hollow of her shoulder, knowing full well how that made her whole body quiver. "How will we deal with being around each other all the time? How does one pass the ti-" Her words cut off when he playfully nipped the sensitive skin of her neck.

"I have a few ideas." His voice was a dark promise.

"I'd like to hear them. I like to have a plan." The playfulness left them when he took her lips. The air changed dramatically as he pressed his body against hers, leaving no room for escape. Luckily, escape was the last thing on her mind. Instead, she wrapped her arms around the back of his neck and deepened the kiss, letting him surround her completely.

"I love you." The words tumbled from her lips when she came up for air. She didn't think about them, or worry over saying them. They were the three simplest words she'd ever said. He lifted her from the ground completely, leaving her to wrap her legs around him and hold on while he carried her into the bedroom. The bed was

soft against her back, but he could have laid her on rocks and she wouldn't have minded. Not when he was looking at her like that.

"You are my life, Erin." His fingers brushed over her cheeks. The warmth in his gaze had tears springing to her eyes. How could she handle being loved like this? It was almost too much; she was too vulnerable. If he left her, if he walked away, she wouldn't be able to breathe.

"I love you, Erin." His lips fell on her temple, "I love you," on her collarbone, "I love you," then her stomach. She was on fire.

She was on fire. She was screaming; Gabe's face was lost in a sea of dark smoke. Erin was running, trying to find him, reaching out for him. Finally, her hands found other hands, his *hands. He was reaching out for her, pulling her to him. She was solid against his chest once more, but when she found his gaze, his eyes were black. When he opened his mouth, it came out as a hiss, and she was screaming.*

.℘ .℘ .℘

Leaving Briar alone back in his room was no easy task. He knew she was still in pain, and every inch of her skin looked tender. Yet *she* was worried about what Lyra might do to *him*. He wasn't sure if there was anything she could do that would be worse than walking into that room and finding Briar chained with a pool of blood at her feet. Having been in Eloas recently, combined with the healing salve he'd used, probably helped her heal more quickly than she normally would have, for which he was grateful. He did not have such healing powers, so whatever he was about to walk into would stay with him far longer than it had for Briar. It didn't matter though, he would accept his punishment. And he would keep her safe.

He came to Lyra's door and paused outside of it. Briar told him once that he made it easier for her to see visions, because he opened his mind to her. He *wanted* to make it easier on her. Now, however, he didn't want her looking into whatever was about to happen. He didn't want her sitting alone in his room, worrying over him and falling into a vision to feel whatever it was he was going to feel. With a deep breath, he tried to imagine a door in his mind and closing it on her, placing locks on his mind, hoping it would help keep her out. Then he straightened his spine and clasped his hands behind his back to take up his normal stance before he walked into the room.

Lyra stood with her back to the door, speaking with three of her guards. He knew she was aware of his presence, but she didn't turn to acknowledge him right away. She finished whatever their conversation was before turning slowly to him and tilting her head. "Ah, you came."

"I said that I would."

"The guards you killed were with me for a long time. I lost out on years of service." She paused, and he wasn't sure if she was expecting him to apologize for the loss. He'd kill them all over again if she placed them in front of him. "It turns out, between the two of them, I had twenty-five years of trusted service." She nodded toward him, and the three guards stepped forward. Two of them took hold of his arms while the third led them toward the door to the side. When he opened it, Doyle saw the chains hanging from the ceiling. "You will get a lash for every year those guards were with me, plus another ten for standing against me." She watched while he was chained, and then she turned from the room and closed the door behind her.

ℰ ℰ ℰ

Ana pushed through the castle, ignoring her own sore and protesting muscles as she made a beeline for her parents and her friend. Now that the adrenaline of the battle had worn off, worry had taken over. Siofra was like a shadow, and she heard Ethelron behind her, deflecting questions and attempts to draw them into celebrations.

Without hesitation, she yanked the door open and took in the private healing room: Ryo and her father were standing behind her mother, who was busy healing a still-unconscious Erin. Melody paced anxiously at the other end of the room. "Mama?" Melody and Ryo turned at her voice.

"It is working, but the wound was deep, so it is taking time."

"She's going to be okay?" The princess couldn't bring herself to care about the way her voice sounded like a child.

"Your mother is doing everything that she can. Be patient, my little bell," her father answered with a reassuring smile.

Strong hands settled onto her shoulders, and Ana immediately turned into Ethelron's embrace. His arms curled around her, tucking her head under his chin and pulling her close. Exhaustion from the battle, guilt over the lives lost, and concern for Erin all crashed over her, wrenching a sob from her chest.

"I have you, Princess. She's strong, she'll be okay." He stroked her hair tenderly, giving soft reassurances as she wept.

"I am sorry about Nelel," she eventually whispered, leaning back in his arms to look into his eyes. He brushed away her tears with his thumb and gave her a sad smile.

"She gave her life protecting her realm, and her princess. I wish I could have done something to save her, but she died a warrior's death."

Bracing her hands against his chest, Ana raised onto her toes to press a brief, affectionate kiss to his lips. Ethelron's grip tightened, fingers flexing against the back of her head.

The gentle clearing of her father's throat was like a shock to Ana's system, and she immediately buried her head against his chest. *"I'm sorry, El...I wasn't thinking."*

"No turning back, remember? At least I don't have to worry about how I am going to tell them anymore." Ethelron let her turn in his arms, but he

kept her pulled against his body, his hands going to her waist, his thumbs making small passes over the dip of her hips.

"Well," Ryo drawled, watching them with an amused glint in his eyes, though some of his elven glow seemed dimmed, "I guess I have the answer to *that* question." Melody flashed her a reassuring smile, but her parents were back to concentrating on Erin. Erin would be okay. She would wake, and *then* Ana could take the time to speak to her parents about Ethelron. He might be worried over their reaction, but she knew they already loved him, and would only love him more knowing how she felt.

"I've healed the infection. She should wake soon," Faervel announced. She sat back, swaying in her chair. Ana rushed forward to catch her, but her mother had already righted herself. "I am fine, Aina. Simply tired. The trek back allowed time for the infection to spread." The queen then turned her attention to Ryo. "Thank you for bringing her to me."

"I was simply following orders, Your Majesty." Ana raised a curious brow at his uncharacteristically humble response.

The room was silenced by a soft noise from the halfling lying on the bed, and all eyes turned to watch as Erin shifted fitfully.

℘ ℘ ℘

"Gabe! Gabe!" She was screaming for him, reaching out to find him once again. His hand found hers once more, and she prayed his eyes would be *his* again. But when she forced herself to look, she found a glint of silver staring back at her.

"About time you woke up. Not sure who Gabe is, but I can be him if you want me to." Erin scrambled to sit up, pushing at him. Her mind was still clouded, and she couldn't quite make out what was happening.

"Don't touch me!" *Was he clawing at her?* His hands were on her and she was trying to get out of his grasp. "Where's Gabe?" *Was he lost in the darkness?*

"Erin, why don't you tell me what makes this Gabe so special?" Silver Eyes...he had a name, but she couldn't place it. He was holding her steady, so she pushed again. Then he was gone. She watched as a blur moved. *Ethelron.* He came out of nowhere and punched Silver Eyes, sending him to the ground.

"*El!* What are you doing?"

"Ana!" Erin's mind finally locked into place. She wasn't sure *where* she was, but she knew who was around her. Melody was standing with her back against the wall, eyes wide as she gaped at *Ryo* on the ground. Ethelron loomed over him, and Brannor was kneeling down to check on him. Faervel looked stricken as she stared at Erin, tears shining in her eyes.

"What's wrong?" Erin turned to Ana, who was now standing beside her and rubbing her back. Ana drew her eyes away from Ethelron and followed Erin's gaze to her mother.

"You were calling for Gabe. Are you okay?"

"What in Skia was that for?" Ryo was getting to his feet, the back of his hand pressed to a bloody nose. His silver eyes were trained angrily on the elf responsible for his injury.

"She told you to get off of her, and you decided to make jokes about the man that she loves? You thought *that* was a good time to mock the fallen prince?"

"What?" Ryo's eyes flicked between Erin and Ethelron. Realization dawned on him when he saw the queen's expression. He quickly turned apologetic. "I was just trying to calm her down...I didn't know. I'm sorry." He gave a quick bow to the queen and king. "Truly, I had no idea that Gabe was Prince Toron. Or that he and Erin..." His words fell away as certain facts seemed to connect in his mind.

"Ethelron, Ryo saved Erin. He got her to my mother. Let it be, no harm was meant." Ana placed a hand between Ethelron's shoulder blades until he finally turned his attention back to Ana and Erin.

"You saved me?" Erin turned eyes on Ryo as he slowly approached her bed, sending a nervous glance toward Ethelron.

"I'm sorry, it's my fault you were injured in the first place. I should have stayed by your side. If I had, you wouldn't have been overrun. You wouldn't have gotten hurt."

"The elf...you were trying to help the other elf," Erin searched for her name but couldn't remember. She just remembered her eyes, a vibrant hue like purple flowers, and that she killed the infection queen. "Did she make it?"

"There was no way for us to help. The erebi swarmed to turn her, trying to replace their queen." Ethelron answered, his gaze shifting to the ground.

Erin nodded sadly before swinging her legs over the edge of the bed. She felt off balance, but her mind was growing clearer every second. She caught the king's eye, and her heart faltered. He had the perfect reflection of Gabe's eyes, and he was watching her with a look of complete understanding. Was he suffering through the burning pain and clouded mind all the time? She hadn't thought of it before, hadn't experienced it before. The queen had to sit with him every day to keep his infection at bay, but the smallest amount of poison caused *so much pain*. Erin could only imagine what he must endure every moment of the day.

She turned her attention back to Ryo, who was still looking at her with an odd seriousness written across his features. "Thank you for getting me here. It's not your fault I was hurt. I'm sorry you lost your friend."

"I'm sorry for what I said."

"You had no way of knowing." Erin reached out a hand and felt the warm energy rise in her stomach. His nose stopped bleeding as she healed him.

℗ ℗ ℗

Briar woke the next morning after only managing about two hours of sleep. Doyle hadn't come back, and she'd tried her best to concentrate on him so she could force a vision, but nothing came to her. She showered quickly just to wake herself up and then started pacing.

His room was sparse, devoid of any personal touches, which was odd because she knew it had been his since Lyra first brought him there. Most of his life was spent in that room, and there was nothing that really spoke to who lived there. He'd left his dagger and sword behind, placed in a way that made her feel he left them the same way whenever they weren't attached to him. The room held his scent, but if it wasn't for that and the weapons, she could have been in any other room in Skia. She thought of him, the jagged scar that ran down his face, and the way it deepened into his skin when he smiled. She thought of how his dark red eyes always seemed to follow her when she was in a room with him, and how they'd raged when she was hurt, even as his touch was as gentle as could be. He was too good for the life he'd been born into. He just wanted to bring peace to his people, but he'd been trapped in a political game, a life full of grief and guilt.

Briar wanted to fill him with love and desire instead. She wanted to help him bring peace to his people, *and* her people. She wanted him to choose her when the time came, and to stand by her side and help her put the crown on someone who would actually *change* the realm for good. Make it worthy of a man like Doyle. Briar felt him near and darted to the door, swinging it open to find him pale but smiling.

"Did you miss me?" He raised a brow at her, but she ignored his teasing and threw herself at him. She hadn't realized just how worried she was until she finally saw him. Some part of her was worried Lyra would never return him; that he'd be lost to her forever. He grunted even as he caught her and wrapped his arms around her, lifting her from the ground like she weighed nothing. She folded into him, breathing him in and feeling his heart pound under her hand. Doyle carried her back into his room and kicked the door shut behind them, and then his mouth found hers. He claimed her lips with a desperation she hadn't felt from him before. He needed her, so she gave all he could take.

Briar didn't know how long they stood there, but it didn't seem long enough. He cradled her face and deepened the kiss, exploring every part of her, drawing out her soul until he held it in his palm. She didn't mind; she knew he'd keep it safe for her. Only then did he release her and rested his forehead against hers. "I couldn't see you. I tried, but I couldn't see what was happening." She traced his face with soft fingertips and felt him shiver under her touch. He gripped her hand and pressed a kiss to her palm. "What happened?"

"I earned a few lashes for myself. They already treated and wrapped them. A friend of mine brought me a salve that will help with pain, and help heal it a little faster. I used the last of mine when I brought you here. I'll be fine, just a little sore for a few days." He traced her lips and gave her a smile that he only seemed to have for her.

"Now, Blue, I promised Malux I would return with some items of comfort and some food. Would you like to join me and check on your patient?" A part of her needed to see his back and how bad it was. He'd stood up for her and was punished for it. She should share in that punishment. But the way he was looking at her made her heart flutter. So she nodded silently and let him lead her, his hand still warm and possessive around hers.

Chapter Eighteen

"How are you feeling?" Ana questioned softly as she sat beside her friend, who was munching on some fruit, still in the healing room. Melody shuffled over to join them as well, settling silently on Erin's other side. Erin looked up at Ana and smiled, glancing over her shoulder to where Ethelron was talking with Ryo and the king.

"Almost back to normal...just can't quite shake the fog." Erin blinked slowly, like she hoped that would help. "So, are you going to tell us exactly what happened with your man or continue to hold out?" Ana dropped her eyes with a timid smile before her gaze found Ethelron.

"I just helped him to realize that there is more to life than responsibility and duty." Blue eyes returned to study Erin. A pang of sadness hit her; in moments like this, it became painfully obvious that her brother was missing. The halfling should have been doted on by the love of her life after recovering from a near-death experience. *Gabe* should have been there, sitting by her bed and holding her hand. Her heart ached for the opportunities that were ripped away from them. "If you rest, it will help you get rid of the lingering haze."

"I may be able to help that along." All three women looked up at Ethelron's offer to see that he and Ryo had joined them, leaving the king and queen conversing quietly in the corner.

"Will you teach me?" Ana murmured, rising to her feet. Ethelron gave her a tender smile and nodded.

"Erin, it would be better if you are laying down or sitting back against something." He offered the fae his hand and helped her to her feet. Once he was sure that Erin was steady on her own, he turned to Faervel as if to ask permission to teach her daughter. The queen nodded, a light shining in her eyes. Ana watched them intently, overwhelmed with affection.

"Okay," Ethelron huffed as he approached Erin, now resting back against the wall on the bed. "If this were anything more than helping clear her mind, I would not be teaching you now. Until you are experienced with it, healing is draining, and therefore needs to wait until there is time to recover." He guided Ana by her shoulders to where he wanted her. "Contact is not entirely necessary, but helpful, and makes it easier when you are first learning. So for now, I want you to touch your fingers to her temples and close your eyes. Our healing abilities come from the light inside of us, the *core* of our magic, which is why it can be draining. You need to sense the edge of your power, which I am going to help you with."

"Help me?"

"I am going to help you become more sensitive to your magic, so that you can see what you will eventually be able to feel without help. Once you have drawn what you need, focus on Erin, and you will feel the lingering darkness under your fingers. Extend your power through your hands and draw that darkness away." Ana nodded, feeling strangely nervous despite the confident smile on the guard's face. "Lean back against me and focus all of your attention on your power and Erin."

Ethelron stepped up behind Ana, pulling her back against him and then settling his hands over the sides of her head. Both closed their eyes, and Ana drew in a long breath to steady herself when she felt his presence envelop her. Their surroundings fell away, and though she could not *see* him, she could sense him guiding her. Light radiated around and through them, and suddenly she understood what needed to be done. The elf shifted her focus outward, leaving the warmth of Ethelron's light and pressing forward into Erin's mind. The lingering dark energy was easy to find, and she called on her own power to draw it away from her friend's mind. She drew back carefully, afraid to lose her grip. As soon as she separated herself from Erin, Ethelron instructed her to *let go* of the dark energy and relax her mind.

Ana snapped back into full awareness. The force of the shift left her dizzy, and Ethelron's hands immediately dropped to her waist to steady her. Ana's hands covered his, and she allowed herself to lean her weight against him until her balance returned. "Whoa…"

"*That* would be why I had you lean against me," he murmured in her ear. The deep rumble of his voice implied other benefits of having her pressed against him. "How do you feel?" His fingers kept a gentle dance over her skin as he asked.

Taking quick stock of everything, Ana grinned. "I feel great. Erin?"

Her friend was leaning back with her eyes closed, and Ana's stomach dropped. *Had she done something wrong?* "So much better. I didn't realize how bad that was messing me up until it was gone."

Ana couldn't contain her excitement. She hugged Erin first, relieved that her friend was no longer suffering. As soon as she released her, Ana spun and threw her arms around Ethelron. "Thank you!"

"Slow down there, Princess," Ethelron chuckled. He held her back at arm's length, growing serious. "This does *not* mean that you are ready to heal an injury. If you do that before you have been properly trained, it could kill not only you, but whoever you are trying to heal as well. Do you understand?" Ana nodded, his warning doing nothing to dampen her optimism.

.℮ .℮ .℮

Erin stared at the wall across from her and tried to push away the memory her injury had brought to the forefront. Would she ever learn to *breathe* without him again? She was just as afraid of having the pain lessen as she was of it remaining this intense for the rest of her life. She loved Gabe. Even if he was gone, that love still made her stronger. What would happen to her if she woke one morning and *didn't* roll over expecting to see his face?

She rose from her bunk in the room they had been given, and decided it was time to ask the queen about the amulet. It had been forgotten with everything going on, but Erin still wanted to know how Gabe got it and what it meant to him. She thought about waiting for the others to return from getting dinner, but then decided it might be better if she found out the information alone. So, she made her way towards the sitting room, hoping to find Ana and Gabe's mother there. The door was closed with an elf standing guard on either side of it, but they made no move to stop her as she stepped forward to knock. She entered when she heard the queen's voice summon her. Queen Faervel was sitting in a chair next to King Brannor, her hand resting gently on his arm, eyes closed in quiet concentration.

"I'm sorry," Erin whispered and began to back away from the room.

"It's quite alright. She has grown used to healing me during meetings. The world does not stop moving. What bothers you, my dear?"

"I should be asking you that. How do you deal with that feeling every day?" That wasn't what she came to ask, but seeing Gabe's father sitting before her, clearly in pain and frail, was breaking her heart.

"I don't have much choice, unfortunately. *You* narrowly avoided the same fate. I was injured during a battle, three large gashes across my arm. I couldn't leave my people on the field, so I stayed longer than I should have. By the time I got to Faervel, there wasn't much she could do." His eyes fell fondly on his wife, giving Erin's stomach an odd turn. She wondered if Gabe would have worn the same expression when looking at her. "It takes a lot out of her to do this for me, and she does it twice a day. There is always some pain, but it becomes highly muted after she heals me. She contains the infection, but the longer I go without her healing, the farther it spreads; the pain worsens, and the darkness closes in." He brushed a hand gently atop his wife's palm, and Faervel stole a glance at him.

"It's worth it, my king, to see your pain lessened." Finally, she pulled away, her work done. Erin could see how pale she was. Her inner glow faded to the point of distinction.

"You didn't come to talk about me, though. Where are the others?"

"I'm sorry. I really didn't mean to disturb you. The others went to get food to bring up to the room, and they wanted me to stay behind and rest. But Gabe," she gave a quick shake of her head, reminding herself who she was speaking to, "*Toron* had an amulet on him when...when he-" The queen rose and gave her hand a quick squeeze.

"Erin, you do not have to call him Toron simply because we do. He was always Gabe to you. You don't have to try to change his memory for our sake."

"He had an amulet on him, but we don't know where he got it, or what it's for. Ana thought you might be able to tell us." Erin reached behind her neck to free the chain before handing it over. The second it landed in the queen's hand, her eyes went wide and her lips pressed into a confused line. Erin and Brannor exchanged glances as the queen sat and continued to stare at the stone in her hand. She turned it over a few times in her palm, but when she looked up, Erin knew she didn't have an answer.

"I can almost *feel* him in the stone. Sometimes, when someone dies, an item of theirs can take on part of the spirit. I have never seen a stone like this before, but there is dark energy in it too. I wish I could tell you more." Instead of handing the stone back over, she stepped behind Erin and pushed her hair to one side so she could clasp the necklace for her. Once again, Erin was struck with a feeling of wonder at having someone act motherly around her.

"I'm sorry." The queen stood before her and looked into Erin's face. "It makes you uncomfortable to have someone dote on you, doesn't it?"

Erin now understood how Ana ended up being so intuitive. "Not uncomfortable; I'm just not used to it. It makes me a little sad, too. Being around you both reminds me of what I never had. My parents died not long after I was born. You should know, Gabe was my best friend. He was..." tears filled her eyes, but she kept her voice even, "caring and strong. He never let the world get him down. You would have been proud of the man he became."

Faervel reached out to brush away a tear and pulled Erin into a comforting hug. Brannor quickly joined in. The tears became heavier when he kissed the top of her head, also accepting her as part of his family.

A knock at the door interrupted the quiet moment, and Brannor broke away to answer it. Erin glanced at the queen to make sure she was presentable and didn't look like a blubbering idiot. Faervel swiped away another tear racing down Erin's cheek before giving her a reassuring smile.

"Is Erin in here? We brought her food but she-" Ana stepped into the room and found who she was looking for.

"You are all free to join us here to eat." At Brannor's gesture, Ethelron gathered chairs from the wall and placed them out for everyone. Ryo and Sio were gone from the group, but everyone else took seats. Erin took her food gratefully, realizing how hungry she was.

"What did Toron's name mean?" She asked, remembering that Siofra meant "elf".

"It means forest." Faervel smiled sadly. "From the first time he blinked his eyes open, they were a deep forest green. He looked like he belonged amongst the trees. As a child, he always smelled like the forest too."

"The boy knew how to climb trees, too. He'd be at the top of the oldest, tallest tree before I could draw three breaths," Brannor added.

"I always thought he smelled like the forest." Erin grinned, her heart warming at the memory of his scent and how it always made her feel like she was coming home.

The world outside the castle walls suddenly exploded in noise and Ethelron was on his feet and out the door, leaving the others to stare in confusion. Brannor followed but both returned quickly. "The erebi are going wild," Ethelron announced.

"I'm surprised they stayed calm for as long as they did after their queen was killed. Zepar is losing control of them now." Brannor began to pace while he worked through their next move.

"I can lead a group to fight the erebi back. If Zepar lost control, nothing would stop them from attacking the castle at will. They've done it before. We can hold it, but they will leave destruction in their wake." Ethelron stood tall, keeping his eyes trained away from Ana, clearly trying to keep her from joining.

Ana must have noticed the same thing. With a huff, she stood at his side, but the king stopped them both before an argument arose. "You have all just returned from battle. Others can fight this time. You should all rest, finish your meals and sleep for the night. We can't have everyone fighting for all hours, or we will lose more people. You are all confined within the castle walls for the night. Do you understand me?" His eyes turned to each of them to make sure he had everyone's agreement. Only Ethelron looked ready to argue, but years of training had him biting his tongue.

"Good," Brannor nodded when he saw they would rest for the night. "I shall send forces, but for now, I simply want the castle walls protected. I don't want to send anyone out into battle just yet. Let's see what the erebi do on their own."

.℮ .℮ .℮

Briar spent the next week walking down with Doyle to spend the day with Malux. Sometimes Doyle would stay, other times he left to speak to others about Lyra and the queen. A few times they came across beasts she'd never seen before - and could go the rest of her life not seeing again - but Doyle kept her safe and by his side. Today, she and Malux sat alone after two days of Doyle joining them. She could feel Malux watching her, and knew he wanted to ask her something, but she waited for him to speak first and broach whatever subject he was thinking of.

Finally, he stirred and spoke her name. "Have you had any other visions recently?"

"No, not since Eloas. I suppose she'll be bothering Doyle soon, though." That worried her. The last thing she wanted was for Lyra to decide to torture Doyle in order to get her to see something.

"Have you thought of how to overthrow Lyra yet?"

"No, but I'll not help crown her." She watched him and felt that there was something he was holding in. This was clearly a conversation he didn't want to have with Doyle around. "Malux, what are you thinking?"

"I was a slave under Queen Flereous for centuries. I know that she is not an easy foe to take down. No simple blade will kill her. She's been devouring dark magics for far too long. Her body is protected against most attacks."

"Does one in the group have something that could bring her down?"

"I have not seen your visions of this group, but I believe they will simply help provide a distraction for Lyra to get in front of her sister in order to attack."

"I would agree with that. I've seen that they are needed to get to the queen, and I believe they will help in the fight. If Lyra went against her alone, she would fail. We would all fail. She needs them in order to win, but I didn't see how the queen dies or if one in the group actually kills her."

"They can't. Whoever kills the ruler will take the crown. If they are not strong enough, the dark power that will transfer would eat them alive. Whoever kills her will not have a choice about taking on the crown, and the power that goes with it."

"So we have to have the correct ruler in place to actually kill Queen Flereous..." She felt the weight settle heavily onto her shoulders again.

"Yes, and that person must have the correct spell cast on their blade, or they won't be able to kill her."

"What spell?" She felt breathless from all this new information. Malux watched her carefully, before closing his eyes and holding out his palms. She took them and tried to search his mind, tried to let the vision he wanted to show her take hold. Then, with a jolt, she felt her stomach turn as she fell into it, pulling her deep into Malux's mind.

Chapter Nineteen

"You are making me antsy. *Relax*, Ethelron. There's nothing more we can do tonight, so just *sit down*," Erin insisted. Ana watched him silently as he stared towards the door, fists clenching and unclenching in sync with the twitch of his jaw. Sio followed his every move, and Ana felt bad for the wolf, feeding off the tension of her master. They had all removed the majority of their armor, but the guard still had an air of intensity and strength about him.

When he didn't respond, Ana stood and approached him, stepping into his line of vision. "Hey, I know you want to be out there fighting with the others, but my father is right. We can't run ourselves into the ground...not yet. We don't know how long this fight will last. Everyone needs to *rest*."

"I am meant to be leading the fight. How do I allow others to risk their lives while I am inside sleeping?" His eyes drifted shut and his chin dropped to his chest.

"By remembering that you cannot fulfill your duty if you are dead, *you stubborn elf. Aeron has been stepping up well as your Second while you've been with us. He and my father will not send out warriors who have already been fighting...they will send a team that has been* waiting *for this. Tomorrow morning, we will regroup, fully rested, and take on Zepar and the erebi side-by-side."*

Ethelron's eyes snapped open, determination burning in them as he stared hard at her. "No." He filled one syllable with such demand that a weaker person would have fallen to his will.

Ana, however, did not blink. "We have made it this far together. We are not going to stand by and watch as they attack *my home.*"

Ethelron took her face in both of his hands, and she felt a slight tremor. "Aina, I *cannot* lose you."

She covered his hands with her own. "That goes both ways, El. Luckily, I outrank you. We are *all* going to fight together." He held her gaze, clearly warring with himself. As soon as he sighed and nodded in resignation, Ana turned her head and kissed his palm. She laced their fingers together and tugged him back towards where the others had settled themselves for the night.

None of them were prepared to be separated from each other. The cacophony outside had all of them on edge, and they'd seemed to silently agree that they would just bring pillows together and sleep on the floor. Ana waited for Ethelron to sit before following suit, curling herself against his side. Siofra settled at their feet, draping her tail across her nose. Ana looked around her, feeling the nervous energy of her friends and watching them fidget. "Erin, Mel...you have done so much for a world that isn't yours. You have risked yourselves and given of yourselves far more than I had any right to ask. The erebi are significantly less of a threat to Sula now that the queen is dead and Zepar is losing control…"

"Do you *honestly* think we are going to leave you guys to fight the rest of this battle on your own? *Now?*" Melody rolled her eyes. "You elves can really be dense sometimes. I've kept you alive this long; can't leave you high and dry now, can I?"

Ana chuckled, grateful for the witch's humor. Ryo, who seemed to be following Erin around after she'd been hurt on his watch, flashed Melody an appraising look. Erin nodded her agreement, though she stayed silent. Ana knew her thoughts were on Gabe, the amulet that still had no answers, and on the memories she'd relived. Once this war was over, she would make sure they used everything at their disposal to solve the mystery of the amulet. If they had to travel back to Loinnir to discover the answer, she'd be the first to stand at Erin's side. But for now, they needed rest, and they needed to prepare for what she hoped was the final battle to save her realm.

.℘. ℘. ℘

Doyle felt a change in Briar, but couldn't quite figure out what it was. She and Malux had been talking when he arrived to retrieve her, but they grew quiet when he approached. "Are you up to something?" He teased as he pulled her hand into his and started walking her back through the tunnels. She'd offered to walk by herself, but they'd run into trouble a few times, and he was not about to let her out of his sight if he could help it.

"I just might be," she said under her breath, drawing his gaze. Instead of taking them back to his room, he walked them to the waterfall so they could sit with the sound of water instead of the stuffiness of his four walls.

"Anything you want to share?" When they entered the cave, he stood behind her and curled his fingers around her hips to pull her back against him. She gave a small sigh and melted against him, making his chest ache. He'd never known he could feel this way for someone, but everything about Briar drew him deeper into her.

"What might I get in exchange for this information?" Her voice was a little tighter than usual, which made him grin. He liked knowing he had a physical effect on her, just as she did on him.

"I could think of a few things." His hand slid under the hem of her shirt to touch the soft skin at her hip. He reached with his other to move her hair to one shoulder and grazed his lips down her neck. They were slowly entering dangerous territory. He could feel every inch of his body respond to her small moan. Doyle didn't care about what she and Malux had been talking about; he didn't care about any of that. All he cared about was the scent of honeysuckle and the sweetness that lingered on his lips after touching her skin. He wanted to touch more of her-

"Malux knows a weakness of the queen and he shared it with me today."

Dammit, that wasn't something he could ignore. He drew back and turned her in his arms so he could look down at her. Her purple eyes were bright from his touch, and he drew her lips to his, momentarily distracted, before pulling away to find out what she was talking about. "He gave me a vision. The queen cannot be killed by regular weapons, but there is a spell that can be done on a blade in order to kill her."

"Did you see how to do the spell?"

"No, but I think your friend who took my blood might have some information about it. I think we should tell Lyra and let her try to find out what she can."

For over a week, Doyle had done everything to keep her away from Lyra. He didn't even want Briar crossing her line of sight. His muscles tensed at the idea of walking Briar into a room that Lyra occupied. He didn't like that Lyra had put him in a position to feel that way towards her, but it didn't change his need to protect Briar from her at all costs. "I can go to her and tell her about your vision." He stroked her jaw and almost pulled away when he remembered the bruises that marred her fair skin.

"We go together, Doyle."

"Not just yet, though. I've been away all day, running her errands, and right now I'm thinking of some other things I could be doing." He didn't want to waste more of his day thinking about Lyra and bringing down her sister. He didn't want to think about all the things that he'd spent his whole life worrying about. Maybe he shouldn't allow himself this, but Briar brought about a new way he could live and, for just the evening, he wanted to pretend that the war was over, and he could just come home to find Briar smiling up at him.

"What might that be?" She leaned closer to him, waiting for him to claim her lips.

"Come back to our room?" From the way her eyes brightened and her cheeks flushed, he knew she understood what he was asking. He was asking for everything, and when she nodded slowly, shyly, his world tilted. Tomorrow, they could worry about Lyra and everything else. Tonight he wanted to show Briar just how much she'd given him and changed him.

They walked back to his room, hand in hand. Her skin warmed against his, and he swore he could feel her pulse beating against his palm. She'd shared his bed with him this past week. She'd slept with her head against his chest, her body curled against his in perfect trust. They'd kissed, and it ignited like fire between the two of them, but he hadn't dared to ask for more.

"Doyle…" Briar waited for him to close his door before stepping up to him. "I love you." She spoke quietly, but the words made him soar. He was itching to touch her, but he wanted to move slowly and drink in every moment. "I just thought you should know that." She gave him a small smile and his thumb reached out to touch where her lips tipped up.

"I love you, too." Then he claimed her lips and started working to show her.

℘ ℘ ℘

Melody lay awake, surrounded by friends but feeling alone. Her magic was whirling inside her like it sensed what was coming. Her chest tightened against the power, making her worry the energy built up in her would eventually explode. Sleep had not found her easily. She'd been restless, and every small sound that reached through the castle walls woke her with a jerk. Others in the room were beginning to wake now. She heard the sound of breathing changing, small rustles as whoever it was moved around, while trying not to disturb everyone else. Melody could get up, but she wasn't quite ready to face the day. She felt pinned to the floor by her worries and the weight of her magic. Something in the air was different this morning, and she knew in her soul, today would end the war. One way or another.

When she heard the soft voices of Ryo and Ethelron, she finally sat up. Both men looked at her, giving her almost identical nods, before returning to their conversation. It must have been Ryo moving around, because he was crouched near Ethelron, who was still laying down with Ana on his chest. Seeing Ana so peaceful in rest hurt her heart. Soon, *the princess* would be waking to face down her enemy once more. Erin also sat up, and looked like she got about as much rest as Melody. The witch watched as Erin's gaze lingered briefly on Ethelron and Ana before darting away.

Ryo moved to Erin's side when he noticed her waking up. He'd become her shadow, and Melody knew he blamed himself for leaving their side during the fight with the infection queen. He'd hardly made any jokes towards her or Erin. Melody wondered if Erin somehow now held some life debt over him. *Was that a thing for elves?* She wasn't sure; maybe she could ask Ana.

"Were you ladies able to get some sleep?" Ryo asked, looking between them and drawing Melody from her thoughts.

"Enough, I guess." Erin rubbed the bridge of her nose. She'd been rocking dark circles under her eyes since she'd helped rescue Melody from the worst date of the century, but they'd worsened since arriving in Eloas. She thought it probably had to do with her reliving so many of Gabe's memories. Her hair was an odd length and mouse brown, which also made Erin look like a different person than she'd met; the person that discovered her powers and learned to hone her skills. In a way, Melody supposed she was.

It made her think of Aria. So much had happened since the death of her friend, and reminiscing over everything brought a surge of guilt. If Aria had been here, maybe none of this would have played out the same way. Kali *had* taken her away, though, as well as Gabe, and now Melody wanted to be part of the group that took down Zepar.

"Melody?" Ryo was watching her intently when she met his silver eyes. She wondered how *she* looked. Probably not well-rested. A shrug was all she gave in response, but she didn't miss the crease of worry that formed between Ryo's brow. He looked like he might say something, but then the background noise from outside grew utterly still. The world just fell *silent*. Whatever he was about to say was lost as his warrior role took over.

"Aina." Ethelron sat up and tapped Ana's shoulder. "You have to wake up. Something is wrong."

Everyone was on their feet, the slow, quiet morning left behind. Sio circled the room, and Melody caught Erin eyeing the wolf wearily. In the midst of battle, the halfling didn't seem bothered by her, but being in such close quarters seemed to be making her nervous. They worked together to get ready, helping each other with armor clasps, handing weapons to their rightful owners, and then they moved as one to leave the large room.

It didn't take them long to find King Brannor, who, it turned out, was on his way to them with his wife. "They have retreated. We believe Zepar got control of them once more and pulled them to him. We think he's trying to gather his forces once more for a large-scale attack. Everyone is meeting in the war room to discuss our defense. I have a few others to gather, but food is being brought up for everyone there."

"I can fetch whoever else you need," Ryo volunteered. King Brannor looked to Ana and Ethelron, who were openly holding hands. The warrior elf was clearly trying to give Ana a moment with her parents and Ethelron.

"We'll come with you. It will be good for us to stretch our legs a bit to prepare for what comes next." Melody stepped up beside him, dragging Erin with her. The king nodded gratefully and directed Ryo to his task before sending them on their way.

"Were you actually being thoughtful?" Erin frowned at Ryo, who feigned shock.

"No, in fact, this is purely selfish. Ethelron and Ainadelothien becoming an item erased all of my chances of ever winning him over. So, I suppose I'll treat my heartbreak by spending more time with you two beauties."

"You know what I think?" Melody asked, tucking her arm into his before doing the same to Erin, making them a tangled line as they walked down the hall.

"I don't, but I'm growing more curious by the second."

"I think you ship the princess and her guard more than anyone else in all the realms. Don't think I didn't overhear the things you said to Ana in the council meeting. You know, right before they finally got together. You are just a hopeless romantic-"

"Who talks too much," Erin added with a big grin.

"I have no idea what you're talking about. I would never put them on a ship. What does that even mean?" Ryo looked down at her, his silver eyes glinting in the early light. Erin snorted beside her, and Melody couldn't hide her own grin. Ryo tracked their amusement before shaking his head. "You humans are odd creatures."

℘ ℘ ℘

"Zepar has managed to regain control of the erebi, and they have returned. The damage that they did last night has allowed them to get further into the castle. They have breached the inner barriers. We don't have much time; we need to get out there and help the warriors." Aeron, the tall dark-skinned second-in-command, clad in armor similar to Ethelron's, looked up as the group approached, and gave Ethelron a respectful nod before bowing to the princess. The fact that no one was *sitting* at the large table in the war room was a testament to how tense the situation had become.

"How many entry points have been breached?" Ethelron asked.

"As of now, two. They are pushing for a third, but we have been able to keep them at bay."

"Good. Take your men there to ensure that it remains in our control. Where are the breaches?"

As she watched the interaction between the two, Ana couldn't help but be impressed at how seamlessly Ethelron and Aeron worked together; Aeron had never complained about taking the lead while Ethelron was gone in Sula, and then while they had other business here in Eloas. And as the time came for him to return to his position as El's Second, there was not even a moment of misstep.

Ryo appeared with Erin and Melody and another small group of warriors. Ryo took up a protective stance at the door while Erin and Melody came to her side. They acted as a silent comfort for her. She was surrounded by all those she cared for. She was surrounded by *home*.

"One is by the far courtyard, the other is near the armory. There are teams at both, but they need assistance."

Ethelron nodded. "Take the breach at the armory. We will cover the courtyard. The king and queen will be tending to the wounded in the infirmary. Sio can go with them to make sure no stray erebi get to the wounded." No one argued, so Ethelron looked at each of them in turn. "The best course of action is to take out as many erebi as possible before killing Zepar. He is keeping them contained, for all intents and purposes. Once he is dead, they will likely swarm. Be careful, and good luck."

As the elves around the table parted ways without further conversation, Ana took a moment to consider her mother and father. In the few moments that she and Ethelron had been able to have with them before Aeron and the other warriors arrived, they'd given their blessing for Ana and Ethelron to be together. The princess hadn't expected the relief that came with it; there had been little doubt for *her* that they would accept El as her choice, but she knew how important it was for *him* to hear it. Especially on the precipice of battle, as they were. Ana hugged her parents quickly, relieved that they would not be in the middle of the chaos, where she would be worrying about them constantly. Ethelron gestured for the others to follow him, and they did so without hesitation. Once they turned a corner, he stopped. The others followed suit immediately. "El?"

"We could end this war today. *Free* this realm. Erin and Melody...thank you for fighting alongside us, for a realm that is not yours. I fear that this battle will take more lives than the others. Zepar will be desperate to finish what his sister started. We need to be more aware and alert than ever. *Please* be careful."

"Aww, you *do* care," Erin teased, winking at him. Ethelron shook his head with an exasperated smile.

Everything about him froze when his eyes fell on her. Ana felt his gaze covering her like a protective shroud. In one step, he was directly in front of her, and he overwhelmed her with a deep, intense kiss. Though brief, it spoke volumes to her. *"I love you,"* he whispered across her mind. Tears jumped to her eyes, and she found herself wondering if he somehow knew the future.

"This is not goodbye, Ethelron."

He kissed her forehead without responding and began moving again. "The breach will be down this corridor. We need to be careful to contain them as much as possible. The infirmary is not far from here. The farther we can keep them from the wounded and the monarchs, the better off we will be."

A loud crash startled them, and an elf tumbled through what had once been a large door. An erebus stepped out behind him and hissed at the group now standing in its way. Ethelron held out a hand to stop the others, and Ryo ducked around the women to come alongside him. "It looks like the fight is coming to us whether we want it to or not." The silver-haired guard drew his blades and crouched into a fighting stance. Ethelron drew his own sword, and the women immediately followed suit.

Ana took a deep breath and cast a brief glance over the men and women surrounding her, all determined and willing to lay down their lives. She sent a silent prayer that it would not come to that, for *any* of them, and geared herself up for the fight of her life.

Chapter Twenty

Doyle kept his body between Briar and the door that Lyra would come through. It still amazed her just how tender and loving he could be while he stood like he'd rip apart anyone who looked at her the wrong way. His shoulders were tense, and she almost reached out to place her hand between them, but decided any outward show of affection would not be a good idea when Lyra could walk in any second.

When they'd woken that morning, Doyle tried to talk her out of going to Lyra again. She was not about to stand aside and let Lyra think she broke her, however, and once she said as much, Doyle nodded his acceptance in silence. Briar was pulled from her musings when the door opened. Lyra's eyes fell on her immediately, her lips turning into a snarl. "Ah, the observer returns to my presence. I thought my *loyal follower* was going to keep you locked away forever.

"He wouldn't have any reason to, would he? You swore not to hurt me again, so it should be safe for me to work with you once more."

"While this banter is as entertaining as ever," Doyle cut in as Lyra made a move towards them. "We are here because Briar had a vision."

"Hmmm, I can only imagine what the two of you spend your time doing locked away in your room, but if it provides me with information, then don't let me get in the way of such... *intimacies*."

Briar did her best to school her features, but her thoughts instantly went to the night before, and her fingers itched to reach out for Doyle's hand. "Lyra, do you want to hear what she has to say, or do you just want to keep throwing verbal daggers?"

"You were never one for an enjoyable conversation. Always to the point. Fine."

She breezed past them. "What news do you bring me?"

"In order to kill your sister, you will have to cast a spell on a weapon. The vision did not reveal the spell itself, but I believe Doyle knows someone who might have some information."

"And this group we did so much for? I thought we supposedly needed them, but now we just need a spell?" Briar took a calming breath as her annoyance spiked.

"We do still need them. They create a distraction to keep attention off you long enough to get to her. You wouldn't be able to win on your own. The group will help you."

"And when might that be?"

"I'm not sure. I haven't seen the pieces fall into place yet."

"Well, maybe the two of you can take a break from your favorite pastimes and try to focus on that information. Doyle, leave me the name of whoever I need to speak with and we will get started moving toward the end."

Doyle placed a hand at the small of Briar's back and started moving her toward the door. Lyra's gaze burned into her, making her both want to run toward the door and turn around and meet fiery gaze with fiery gaze. Doyle seemed to sense the change in her, some foreign part that wanted to go toe to toe with Lyra, and pushed her a little more firmly. As soon as they left the room, he sped up, dragging her along with him. They turned a corner and lost sight of the guards. He stopped to lean against the wall. Worry flooded her, and she reached up to cradle his face in her hands so that she could get a good look at him.

"Doyle? Are you okay?"

"Yes, I just wanted to get us out of there while it was still relatively peaceful. I feel like putting the two of you in a room is asking for the building to burn down around me." She wasn't sure what to say to that, so she remained silent and let him gather whatever thoughts he was working through. He finally seemed to calm, so she wrapped her arms around his middle and rested her head against his chest. The steady *thump* of his heart was soothing, and when his arms came around to hold her, she felt safe and whole. Like she was meant to be there all along.

"I just keep seeing everything that has been done to you. I'm not sure how you can even look at me. So much of this is my fault. I brought you here."

"We can't keep having this same conversation, Doyle. I've forgiven you for bringing me here, and you've *never* hurt me. In fact, you've done everything you can to keep me safe, and..." She paused and looked up at him. When she was a girl, she never would have seen the danger in his gaze and thought of him as the man who would steal her heart - hard lines and jagged scar, dark eyes that seemed to pierce her - but here she was. "I don't regret being here with you." His gaze warmed at her words, and he drew her closer to press a soft kiss against her lips.

$$.\wp .\wp .\wp$$

Before long, the crowd of erebi that had taken over the courtyard began pouring into the corridor in front of them. Ethelron and Ryo had already begun engaging - and dispatching - the first wave, but Ana, Melody and Erin took up the second defense. Erin and Melody fought back to back, slicing, ducking, and stabbing, but still getting edged back by the influx of erebi. Ryo gradually moved back to join them, and Ethelron made it to Ana's side. The five of them could defend themselves, but the horde was succeeding in pushing farther and farther towards where Ana remembered the infirmary to be.

"We have to get them back!"

"You poor, foolish girl, so sure that you can win." The voice, that could only belong to Zepar, sounded from her right. Ana spun to the source of the deep, menacing sound, and gave a strangled yelp. Long clawed fingers wrapped around her throat and lifted her off of the ground. The massive erebus straightened to his full height, having apparently used the chaos to his advantage to sneak into the center of the fight. He *was* the son of an ancient chaos erebus, after all.

"Aina!" Ethelron shouted, fighting desperately to reach her.

"Don't worry, I don't want to kill your precious princess. She killed my sister...I want her to watch as what is left of her pathetic little kingdom *burns*. Her parents, on the other hand? Entirely different story. I am sure, with their daughter only rooms away, they can feel the danger right now. Oh, won't you come out and *save* her?"

Ana kicked out at him and tried to hit the key pressure points to force him to let her go, but nothing worked. Dots danced across her vision, and she fought to drag in air. Her friends remained occupied by relentless attacks, and Ethelron was getting pushed farther away from her.

"Stop!" The single word echoed around the hall, sounding louder than the cacophony of fighting.

Unprepared for Zepar to release her, Ana dropped to her knees ungracefully. The princess dragged in air before looking up to see her mother standing in the doorway to the hall. "No," she breathed, her voice ragged. Ethelron slid to a stop beside her, hands grabbing her shoulders and pulling her to her feet. "No, I'm fine...he was using me to draw my mother out..."

Zepar moved easily through the erebi to reach the queen. Ana wanted to run to her, but the erebi pushed in behind Zepar, cutting off any route she could use to get to them. "*I have to get to my mother!*" Ana didn't even send Ethelron another glance as she began slicing through the erebi before her, attempting to get through. She was only alone in her fight for a moment, however, before Ethelron was at her side. Even together, it didn't seem like they were making a dent. Ana kept her eyes forward, trying to keep her mother in view.

.℮ .℮ .℮

"How are you doing, Mel?" Erin could hear the witch groan in frustration, but couldn't turn to see her.

"I broke a freaking nail!" Melody's voice was laced with sarcasm, and Erin had to laugh at her.

"You have spent too much time with me!" Erin pushed an erebus back and was glad she spent so much of her free time working out the last few months. Even with a trained body, she dripped with sweat and she could feel her muscles growing weaker with each infection erebus she took down.

"How's my hair?" Ryo called out, taking a moment to look back at the girls and flash them a wink. It didn't seem like he ever stopped moving. Both blades cut through the air in a delicate dance that seemed to only belong to elves.

Erin really wanted to yell out an obscenity to him, but settled on hurting his pride instead. "It's been better. And that erebi blood is really ruining your complexion."

"Dammit," Ryo sighed, "thanks for your honesty, though. You are a loyal friend."

The banter cut off when Melody was thrown into them, a throng of erebi pushing through to cover Zepar. Erin fell forward, knocked onto her knees, and threw her dagger upwards just in time to catch an erebus coming for her. Then she felt it: the water moving under the ground. She had used her magic on water before, but it was hard to master. Water was such a powerful force of its own, she found it hard to control. Even so, she *had* to try something.

"Ryo, cover us!" Erin yelled up before grabbing Melody and pulling her down next to her. "Can you feel the water beneath us? There must be an underground stream!" Melody nodded. "Together, we might be able to use it to flush out the doorway to stop more from coming in!" Ryo stood over them and tried to keep them protected, so Erin took Melody's hand, and together they touched the earth. Looking straight ahead, Erin tried to focus on the stream and draw it up. If they could get it to break through the ground, they could force it toward the erebi filing in.

Finally, she felt the pull, the rush and gurgling, making its way upward. "Now!" Together, they watched as the water bubbled up through the floor. Melody's grip tightened in her hand, and then the earth shook under them. Ryo glanced down at them, but Erin kept focused on the water ahead of her. Finally, they gained complete control and sent a wave, knocking erebi to the ground and forcing them to move back from the doorway.

Melody's grip loosened, but Erin refused to let go. She could feel the magic pulsing in the witch's palm, and used the power to strengthen her own. She pulled at nature and wound vines across the broken doorway, forming a new barrier. It wouldn't last forever, but it would hopefully allow them time to clean out the erebi that were now trapped inside with them. Erin turned with a smile and found that Melody's eyes were dancing, bright from the strength of their magic. With a laugh, they high-fived and got to their feet. Ryo reached out a hand and pulled Melody up before looking between the two. She thought he was going to compliment them; instead, he rolled his eyes and muttered, "show offs," before stabbing another erebus.

.℘ .℘ .℘

Ana watched in panic as Zepar met her mother. The wispy black of the infection erebi surrounded them, but none moved toward the queen. Instead, they all worked as a shield to keep anyone from getting to Zepar. Like his sister, he had long horns protruding from his head, but his skin was the color of sandpaper and his horns a smokey gray. He looked as though he had been burned head to toe. His nose was missing, leaving only two holes at the center of his face. His eyes were like Kali's however: solid black with the depths of the sea encased within.

"Aina, stop!" Ethelron grabbed her hand and pulled her back. A claw dug into the air in front of her, and she realized he'd stopped it from hitting her. He pulled her to his other side and quickly dispatched the erebus that had nearly struck her. She was so focused on the fight happening in front of her, she'd almost forgotten that she was surrounded by the infection erebi. His eyes narrowed toward her in warning, but she was already moving forward again, heart pounding so loudly in her chest it was making her head swim. Her mother dodged claws and kicked out at Zepar. She hit him, but he didn't fall. Instead, he grabbed her wrist and twisted with a growl.

Ana and Ethelron were almost to them, but at the very center stood infected elves, clad in armor. They moved as one. When Ethelron tried to push forward, they all shifted, beginning to crowd around him and Ana. She lost view of her mother's fight as one of her fallen kin towered over her and tried to knock her back. She pivoted quickly to dodge the attack and sliced her sword toward him. It took three hits before the infected elf finally fell to the ground. Ethelron had two at his feet, and only one more in front of him before he could reach her mother.

"Help her!" she screamed into his mind. He was closer, and she still had three more enemies delaying her. She grabbed the one closest to her and pushed him into another, trying to slide past. She stabbed at the one in front of her, but the other two regained their footing and came at her from both sides. A quick spin saved her from getting hit, but a fourth elf joined the fight and knocked into her. With a yelp of surprise, she fell to the ground. Ethelron stopped and started back toward her, seeing her fall. The erebi quickly closed in on her, so she kicked out to knock them back. Deftly, she found her footing and took down the one nearest her.

Ahead of her, Ana watched Zepar get a solid punch into her mother's stomach. *"Ethelron!"* He was fighting off another enemy, but looked toward the queen when he heard Ana's voice. In her moment of distraction, she took a hard hit to the back of her armor and struggled to take in her next breath. She saw Ethelron's eyes lock on her once more. She felt his hesitation, but she could do nothing to stop him. The next breath was a wheeze as she rammed her side into the infected elf coming at her, but she couldn't straighten enough to put strength behind her attack. Ethelron dispatched his opponent and was running toward her, seeing the danger she was in.

While he was looking at her, she was looking past him to her mother. The queen's eyes found hers, and their gazes locked, the rest of the fight fading away. With a war cry, Faervel dug her sword into Zepar's chest. Relief washed through Ana - her mother had won.

Ethelron crashed on top of her and pressed her to the ground, shattering her focus. An infected elf landed beside her, and once again it took her a moment to realize Ethelron had blocked its attack and killed it while she was watching her mother's struggle.

"Mama!" Ana rasped, trying to catch her breath with Ethelron's weight resting on her. Thinking the fight was done, Faervel released her sword, leaving it lodged in Zepar's chest. The queen's eyes remained on her, making sure her daughter was safe. She moved towards them, but Ana watched in slow motion as Zepar pulled the sword from his chest and plunged it into her mother, before he finally collapsed.

The erebi began to hum in chaos as their remaining leader died, his control over them falling away. Ana didn't see them anymore, though, her eyes locked on her mother's body. She pushed free from Ethelron and ran toward her at full speed. "Mama!" She fell to her knees beside Faervel's body, her blue eyes already glazed with the vision of death. "No!" Ana couldn't believe what she was seeing. "*Erin! I need you!*" Her eyes searched the battle and found the halfling in the midst of her own fight.

Erin turned and found Ana. "*Coming*," was all she answered.

Ethelron gained his footing and reached her first. "Aina?" he questioned, trying to see the damage. Ana couldn't move from her mother, though. Instead, she glared back at him, rage filling her so she wouldn't have to accept what was happening.

"You should have protected her!" He reached out to touch her arm, but she jerked away. Once again, it was *her* fault one of her loved ones was dead. He had turned away from going to her mother because he was worried about *her* getting hurt.

"Aina, let me see. Can I help her?" His voice had an edge that she couldn't quite place.

"I told you to go to *her!*" Ana ignored his question.

"She looked like she had the fight handled! You were surrounded! I wasn't going to let you die!" He moved closer, even as Ana tried to cover her mother with her body. Once he saw the queen, he'd know she was gone. Until then, she had a few more moments of hope. Hope that her mother wasn't truly gone.

"So you let my *mother*?" Her voice turned sharp. "You had a choice, and you chose wrong! *She* is the queen." Her voice finally broke then, the truth crashing down around her. Erin was fighting, trying to get to her, but there was nothing she could do. Her mother was already gone.

"Aina, *please*, at least tell me. Are *you* hurt?" His voice was suddenly demanding, but the way his breath caught at the end gave her pause. She finally allowed herself to *look* at him. Ethelron was pale, dangerously so, and his mouth was pressed into a grim line. "Aina?" Her heart leapt into her throat as she watched his hazel eyes roll to the back of his head just before he collapsed.

Chapter Twenty-One

Erin was finally able to get through the erebi and reach Ana's side. Her barrier of vines was still holding, but it was growing weak. Soon the remaining erebi on the outside would break through, and they would have more problems on their hands.

"Ana?" Erin gasped when she finally saw what was waiting for her. The sight of Queen Faervel lying dead had her freezing in her spot. Everything stopped as her mind tried to make sense of it. The woman who had so quickly taken her in like a daughter, who accepted her simply because her son had loved her. But just like her son, she was gone. It took Erin a moment to realize that Ana wasn't with her mother. She was standing off to the side, another body at her feet. Kicked back into motion, Erin ran forward and found Ethelron, pale and still in a pool of blood. *His own* blood.

"I was yelling at him!" Ana was frozen, staring down at Ethelron, eyes wide with shock. "He was dying, and I was yelling at him!"

"Stop!" Erin fell to her knees at his side and found a weakened pulse. "He's alive, Ana." Quickly, she searched for any sign of infection. "Help me!" Erin finally found the source of the blood, but his armor was covering the wound and Erin couldn't see. She needed to know if it was infected, or if he'd been injured by something else.

Her order seemed to break through Ana's shock, and the elf quickly leaned down to help undo the straps of the armor. She pulled it away, and Erin could finally assess it. There was no sign of blackness around the wound; his veins looked perfectly normal. "One of the elven erebi must have stabbed him in the side. He's not infected!" She spoke with relief, but Ana still looked doubtful.

"Erin, I was yelling at him. I was blaming him..."

"Shh." Erin closed her eyes and tried to concentrate on her center of energy. In desperation, she grappled for the power that had been so lost to her since Gabe's death. She thought of Gabe's smile, thought of how his mother had kissed her forehead as though she were hers. Erin remembered how Ethelron had watched Ana with longing in his gaze in the memories, and how he had doted on the young prince. Finally, she felt the warm ball of power. She focused on Ethelron's wound, keeping her hands steady over it. His body slowly started to work with her magic to heal. "Go to your mother." Erin's eyes turned up and found Ana looking between two of the people she loved. "I've got him. This is going to take some time, but I have him. Go to her." Ana gave a small nod and sent one last tear-filled look to her guard. She pulled her mother into her lap, letting the queen's head rest on her thigh.

The elves within the building had managed to take out most of the erebi. In their chaos, it seemed the elves actually had an easier time killing them, since they were without orders, leaving them unsure of what to do; whether to attack, run, or simply destroy. With a quick glance, Erin located Melody and Ryo hovering near the doorway covered in vines. Many of them were breaking away, and soon the rest of the erebi would be through. She needed to hurry and heal Ethelron before she was forced to leave his side and fight again.

"Erin, how close are you?" Ana called to her, seeing the same thing she was. The fae only shook her head in answer, trying to will his body to hurry in its healing. She was already weak from using so much magic in the fight.

"Come on, Ethelron!" She could feel his muscles knitting back together, her magic working to re-make blood cells, and then finally, his skin came together, leaving behind a thin scar across his side. The light faded from her fingers and her head swam. She hadn't paid attention to how much she was draining her own energy; now that Ethelron lay healed under her palm, she felt how weak she was. His eyes opened and landed on her in confusion. He looked down and realized what must have happened. "Aina?"

Erin couldn't talk just yet, so she nodded behind him. He sat up, turning to make sure the princess was okay.

"You idiot!" Ana yelled at him, surprising Erin. "You should have said you were hurt! You could have died!" Erin still couldn't move, in fear she would be sick if she tried. Taking several steadying breaths, she watched Ethelron quietly gather Ana into his arms. The elf was lashing out at him, but he didn't say a word. Instead, he kept his hold on her until she burst into tears. "You could have died!" She sobbed again, both grieving for her mother and releasing the worry she had for him.

"I'm right here, I'm right here."

The vines chose that moment to give out completely, and Erin realized she'd left Ryo and Melody at the front lines. "Ana!" Erin called the elf to draw her attention. Ethelron was on his feet as the erebi burst through.

"Erin, take the queen into the infirmary!" That was the leader of the guard speaking, but she shook her head firmly.

"You need all hands to finish this fight! If anything, Ana should be with her!"

Ethelron placed a gentle hand on her cheek and leaned down so he was at eye level. "You are weak after healing me. *Please*, take the queen to her husband." *Damnit*. That was her *friend* imploring her, and she couldn't refuse.

"Ana?" Her gaze darted to the princess, the elf's features warped in grief.

"I've got her, I swear it." His voice was determined. Erin nodded, knowing if Ana was unable to fight, he would keep her away. She also knew Ana and knew she wouldn't leave the fight until it was done.

"I've got her," Erin repeated his words as she gently took the queen from Ana's lap. The elf gave a sorrowful nod and quickly kissed her mother's forehead.

Before Ana could stand, however, a large blast echoed like fireworks within the castle.

.℘ .℘ .℘

Melody thought she and Ryo made a good team. Erin had been called away to help Ana, and Melody just hoped her friend was okay. Too much was happening for her to get a view of anything other than the press of erebi. Ryo never stopped moving at her side, never rested. She knew she wasn't as good at the hand-to-hand combat, but she held her own, keeping his back covered. The erebi were in a frenzy now, their uncoordinated movements making it easier to take them out.

She shot off bursts of fire as she was able, making sure to keep her energy in reserves. Her magic didn't seem to be waning, though. She'd let Erin drain from her in order to control the water, and she'd been sending shots of magic to keep the erebi from crowding around them too badly, but she still felt as strong as she had when she woke that morning.

"The vines!" Ryo nodded his head towards the doorway. A flood of erebi waited on the other side for them. *Fantastic.* They needed to back up, regroup, before those vines finally gave up their fight. As well as she and Ryo had been doing, they wouldn't be any match for that many. He grabbed her arm, yanking her against him to use his body as a shield. She fired a few more bursts of magic to make room for them, but it was too late. The vines gave way, and with a roar, the erebi flooded in. They were wild, not even trying to fight, just slashing their claws in every direction.

Her gaze connected with Ryo's, and she noticed a small crease of worry on his brow. He moved to push her further behind him, closer to where their friends had gone, but when he released her, she dodged back around him. "Melody!"

She ran away from him and towards the invasion. Her magic was a live wire, twisting in her gut, begging to be let out. This was a challenge she was ready to accept. She might not be good at dating, she might have to return to Sula alone after all of this is done, but she could *end this war*. She could take down the last of the invading infection erebi. The power to do so was humming right at her fingertips. She closed her eyes, the smoky scent of the erebi burning her nostrils as they drew closer.

Ryo was closing in at her back; she could feel the energy of him there, just as she could feel each individual infection beast in the room. Where everyone else was giving off a glow of magic for her to draw from, the erebi were black holes in her inner eye, trying to draw all the magic into themselves. They existed to consume, to *destroy*.

With a confident exhale, Melody released the buildup inside of her. The gentle buzz of her energy balls was *nothing* compared to the shock that rushed through her veins as she let out a battle cry. Magic flowed into her *and* from her, bursting forth and barreling towards each of those black holes in her vision. The magic struck each of them, burning them with the shock of magic, too strong for them to consume or fight against.

Her mind drew deeper into itself as she continued to seek out each of those black holes, ignoring the bright flashes of others with magic. Something tickled at her spine, but she was too consumed with ending this, saving them. *This* was something she could do. She might be destined to be alone in this world - well, *whatever* world - but she could also make the world safer for those she loved. Intrusive thoughts of her parents caught her off-guard, threatening to derail her. Memories of their hate and abandonment chipped away at her confidence, and her magic faltered in response. As her grip on her powers loosened, she realized just how weak she'd grown, how detached she'd been from her own body.

Melody knew she needed to stop, so she drew the specks of magic still hunting for targets back to herself. She was aware of her knees giving out, and the fact that she never touched the ground, but everything else was foggy. She was back in her body, but still disconnected.

"Hey there, I've got you." *Ryo was holding her, that's why she didn't hit the ground.* "That was some trick. Like a bomb going off. I like your new hair too, looks like you were trying to match me." There was a softness against her temple, a slight brushing behind her ears. Melody tried to open her eyes, but it was like her spirit was trapped, wide awake from the shock of power, while her body took a rest.

"Melody! Mel!" Ana's cries of worry made Melody want to fight to regain control of her body. She pushed, trying to reach the surface of whatever this blackness in her mind was, but there was nothing there for her to reach.

"I have her. I think she drained too much of her energy. She just needs some rest."

"That was crazy. She took out all of them. *Just like that.*"

"Do you need me to take her?" Ethelron's deep voice was close.

"What happened?" Ryo seemed to ignore Ethelron's question, something else drawing his attention.

"Zepar...they killed each other." Melody tried to understand, but everything was growing foggy. Their voices seemed farther away, even though she could still hear Ryo's heart pound under her ear. She really hoped she wasn't dying. She *shouldn't* be; Melody could still feel magic swirling inside her, so she hadn't fully drained herself. Ryo was probably right, she just needed rest...

.℮. .℮. .℮.

Panic seized Ana's chest anew when Melody sagged against Ryo. There was an ashen tone to her skin and a shocking white strip in Melody's hair that revealed just how much energy the witch had expelled. Ryo tensed as well when Melody went limp, but relaxed when his fingers settled under her jaw. His relief was shared by all of them, but the dark shroud of grief sank into Ana's bones again immediately.

"Your Highness?" She tried to answer the unspoken request for clarification about who was fighting Zepar, but it hurt too much to *breathe*, let alone give voice to the truth.

"The queen is dead," Erin murmured, and tears burned Ana's eyes. *Her* mother *was dead*. "We need to take her to the king...we need to tell him it's over."

Nausea rolled in her stomach. The king. *Oh Papa...*

Out of the corner of her eye, Ana noticed Ryo glancing between Erin and Ethelron until the latter shook his head. She closed her eyes in a desperate attempt to push back her tears. Straightening her spine and squaring her shoulders, Ana hurried to Erin's side. She refused to allow herself to look at her mother's too-still form as Ethelron gently lifted her; instead she focused on supporting Erin, who was swaying on her feet. Ana allowed muscle memory to take over her feet as her mind shut down. Erin leaned on her as they made their way to the infirmary, and Ana kept a tight grip. The thought of letting go felt far too much like risking the loss of someone else, and that wasn't something that she was going to be able to handle.

It didn't take long for them to reach the infirmary, but Ana couldn't bring herself to cross the threshold. A glance around showed that she wasn't the only one. Doing so would mean revealing the truth to the king...not only telling him that his wife had been killed, but also that he would eventually succumb to his infection, as she could no longer help him.

The doors opened from the inside, however, and removed that responsibility from them. Brannor stood before them, grief etched into every line of his face. Ethelron stepped forward, and they were all ushered inside. The din of conversation among the handful of elves in the infirmary fell silent as Ethelron brought the queen in and laid her down on the nearest bed. Ryo settled Melody onto a bed nearby, and

Ana eased Erin into a chair beside the queen, still refusing to look directly at her mother's body. Brannor dropped to his knees beside his fallen wife, his healthy hand cradling her face tenderly and silent tears streaming down his face. Ana stood behind him and squeezed his shoulder, and the breath caught in her chest when he shuddered under her touch. As her father fell apart, Ana's devastation was finally given room to breathe, and the tears she'd been fighting back finally spilled over her lashes.

Erin. She reached out her hand towards the woman slowly curling in on herself in the chair beside the bed. Erin looked at her hand, seeming dazed, before turning her eyes up to Ana's.

"No matter the length of time, my mother saw you as a daughter. You need to allow yourself to grieve, Erin." The halfling stared at her a moment longer before taking her offered hand and joining her standing behind Brannor. Ana did not let her hand go, and instead leaned into her until their shoulders touched. She didn't know how long they stayed like that; when she finally turned back to Ethelron, his own grief was clear on his face. She threw her arms around his neck and clung to him like a lifeline.

"I'm so sorry, El."

"Hush, Princess," he soothed. He pressed a kiss to her temple, and she remembered how close she'd come to losing him.

"I love you. I'm so sorry for shouting at you for protecting me."

"I know. It's okay, I know."

"Sir?" A soft voice interrupted the solemn moment, and Ana pulled away from Ethelron to see Myriil watching the leader of the guard anxiously. "F-forgive me for the interruption, but the General sent me to request assistance. They still struggle with some remaining untethered erebi."

Ryo stepped up behind Ethelron and placed a hand on his shoulder. His eyes met Ana's, and she was grateful for the resolution in his silver gaze. "We will help clean up the last of the mess Zepar left behind, and I will bring him right back, your Highness."

Myriil bowed to Ana, and then to Brannor, who had silently turned to watch the exchange. Ryo bowed to the king as well and then sent a grin that didn't quite meet his eyes to the rest of them as he followed the scout. Ethelron stole Ana's breath with a deep, intense kiss.

"Please…don't make me say goodbye to anyone else today. Come back to me, El." He didn't respond, simply pressed his lips to her forehead and stroked her cheek with his thumb, and then he was gone. Fear tangled itself into the grief constricting Ana's chest, and she covered her face with her hands to force tears back.

The battle lasted late into the night, and Ana could tell her father was taking on more guilt with each passing moment over not being able to join them. To remind him of why he couldn't, would have been a knife to the chest for both of them, and she couldn't bring herself to consider what was to come. The return of the guard was a welcome distraction, brief though it was; the war had finally been won, and would be honored as such...but at such a devastating cost.

Chapter Twenty-Two

Doyle woke to Briar thrashing in his arms and his head pounding. Knowing there was not much he could do, he sat up to gather her against him and waited for whatever vision she was having to end. It was never easy to see her this way; to be helpless while she suffered something he couldn't fight off. A sharp pain shot down his spine, and then she woke with a groan. If she wasn't suffering, the unladylike groan would have made him chuckle. Instead, he started massaging down her spine and waited for her to settle.

Finally, Briar turned her colorful eyes on him and gave a small smile. "Things are falling into place." Chaos erupted outside his door, and he was on his feet with a dagger in his hand before he'd drawn in two breaths. He opened the door, and found people moving about, shouting over one another. He turned back to her and found her sitting on the edge of the bed, clearly already knowing something he didn't.

"What did you see?"

"The elves have won their war. Erebi are retreating. The queen is not happy about the loss, but Lyra just might be." She massaged her neck and gave a small smile. "The group is ready for her now."

His heart-rate spiked at that. He knew bringing the group in was the true beginning of the end for their queen. Everything they had been working toward was finally coming close to an end. Once Lyra took the crown, Briar would be free to return home, though that thought made his gut twist. He wouldn't be able to go with her. He would stay to help make sure the right decisions were made, so that his realm and people could actually have a chance to thrive instead of continuing to war with everyone else. He wouldn't be able to leave, but there was no way he could keep her there with him. Her eyes met his, and he thought of just how bright they had been before he'd brought her back here. She wasn't built for this realm. Even if he could make Skia better, it still wouldn't be Loinnir.

He loved her, but there was no way he could keep her for himself. "What are you thinking?" she asked quietly, standing to move closer to him. Her touch was cool against his skin, but it set his nerves ablaze. No one else had ever made him feel that way before. It was like she turned on a light inside of him that he hadn't realized was there.

"Just thinking that it is almost over." He touched her face, her soft cheek, her chin, the little smile that pulled at her lips. "We should go to Lyra, tell her about the group." He said the words, but made no move toward the door. He'd always known his time with her would be limited, but now it seemed more real. Who knew how long they would have before she had the freedom to run home? He claimed her lips before she could move away from him. He drank in the small moan she made and put his hand at the small of her back to draw her flush against him. Briar's hands grasped at his shirt and when he lifted her into his arms, she wrapped herself around him, clinging to him like he was to her. Lyra could wait a little longer to hear about Briar's vision.

When Doyle and Briar went to Lyra, it took some time to locate her. By the time they did, she was in a foul mood. She'd spent most of the afternoon with her sister trying to calm Skia after losing their stand in Eloas. So many resources had been used over the years, only for them to get pushed out completely in the end. The ancient ones were not happy; if Zepar had not been killed in the end, he would be suffering a far worse fate at their hands.

"What do you two want? And am I ever to see you without your new tagalong?" She shot at Doyle as she moved swiftly down the corridor.

"I could certainly come to you on my own, but Briar had another vision." He expected her to stop at that, but she just kept moving.

"Oh really, did she see our *whole realm* going to shit, because that's what I'm seeing as our current future?"

"Actually, I saw you going to retrieve the group we've been waiting for." Briar spoke up from behind him. Her voice was no longer timid as it had once been around Lyra; instead, she became all sharp edges. It still threw him off to hear the tone in her voice when he mostly just saw the soft glow that seemed to surround her.

"Really?" Lyra stopped at that and turned, her eyes darting between them.

"The queen is weak now, after such a loss. The ancients are unhappy with her. Skia is in chaos, and the amulet is about to be activated, making our group ready to collect."

Lyra moved before he even blinked. She stood before Briar, the fae's face between her hands. His heart faltered in his chest to see Lyra's hands on her. Briar didn't cower, though; her spine stayed straight, and she didn't blink as they held each other's stare. He wanted to move between them, but Lyra grinned and gave a small shake of her head. "I guess you have proved somewhat useful."

"You'll want to go to where the amulet is. They'll all be together, and you can give them your terms. But first, I'll need to tell you everything about what the amulet did and why they are in your debt."

"Having the queen as a sister has finally come in handy, it seems." Lyra twirled a ring on her finger. "This will help me travel through the portal and land where I want. So, fill me in, and let's get this thing moving along."

Doyle noticed a dark flash in Briar's gaze. "I didn't know what the amulet would do. I only saw that we would need it. If I had known, we could have moved this along sooner, and the group may not have suffered as greatly." Her purple eyes flashed to him and there was a well of sadness there. But then she tucked away her emotions and turned to tell Lyra what they had actually done in giving that group the amulet.

.℘ .℘ .℘

Melody and Erin walked solemnly behind Ana and ahead of Ethelron and the king through the wounded elven forest. Melody could feel the grief radiating from both the princess and her father, and desperately wished she could ease their pain. Only a day had passed since the war that had been plaguing this realm for years finally ended. Melody and Erin had watched in awe as the elves worked together to gather their dead and care for their injured to prepare for this moment. Ana had explained the significance of funerals for their kind, since aging was so much slower, and an elf could easily live for hundreds of years before their death. Typically, these events took days to prepare as family and friends of the fallen would weave boats from twigs and vines, a true labor of love.

But with the war, they'd lost so many. Some families were left with nothing to hold on to because the bodies had been taken by infection. Children who had never lived a peaceful day within Eloas were gone before they'd ever seen the light. So many were mourning their own personal losses, but it was evident to Melody that the loss of the queen weighed heavily on *every* heart. In just the day that they'd been processing, she'd heard stories of how Queen Faervel walked amongst her people, healed their pains, and spent time at the bedsides of the injured. How, together, she and her husband worked to keep their people safe, and allowed all the elves a haven.

Queen Faervel, in the end, gave her life to save her people. She killed the leader of their attack and finally released their chains. Cleared of the erebi, the world was already coming back to life. It would take years before the forest was truly alive and full of magic once more, but the colors were already a little brighter. With care, they could revive their realm. They could rebuild, but they could not bring back their dead.

Many families wanted to wait to send off their loved ones. They wanted to stay as true to their traditions as they could. But the king knew his time was short. After only a day without his wife, he was declining rapidly. Walking beside Ethelron now, he limped and wheezed with every step. So the kingdom gathered to give the queen a final farewell.

Donned in white robes, the elves moved through the forest as one. A quiet hum hung heavily in the air, taking on a life of its own. Even with the world drained of magic, nature seemed to join in, the tree branches swaying out of the way to allow the mourners an easy journey.

"You have to promise me you'll take care of her." The king's voice was soft, but still possessed a quiet strength that reminded Melody so much of his daughter. The finality of his words brought tears to her eyes, and with a surreptitious glance at Erin, she confirmed that she wasn't the only one. It wasn't fair for Ana to be reunited with her family after so long, only to have them systematically ripped away from her all over again.

"I shall protect her with my very soul. Her side shall never be left unguarded for as long as I am alive." Ethelron's voice left no room to question his devotion, his determination to do what little he could to shield her from the pain bearing down on her clear in his tone.

Melody was drawn from her thoughts when they reached what Ana had explained was a mourning stone in the middle of the forest. A large stone circle rested a few feet off the ground, carved with an elven prayer. The procession that walked ahead each held a flower for the dead. Taking turns, they circled the stone, leaving a flower behind. The queen's body, wrapped in elvish silk, was placed in the center, and room was made for the king and princess to stand at her side.

Ana's face was solemn, but watching her, Melody could see her inner fight. Tears continued to threaten, but she was trying to keep up a brave face in front of those she would now have to rule. Ana was well aware that soon she would stand at that stone again, alone. Her blue eyes, so much like her mother's, stared at her father. Mel didn't need her to share her thoughts like Ana could with Ethelron; she knew the princess was counting down the moments before Brannor joined his wife. She was memorizing the details of his face, and comparing them to the happy father she once knew.

The hum rose in the forest as the elves began to sing. Sorrow filled each note, but there was also a celebration. Celebration of Faervel's life, her family, her sacrifice. Erin and Melody stepped back from Ana and moved to stand at Ethelron's side. The witch could feel that her face was wet with tears, and Erin held her, her own face carefully contorted to hide away her pain. Melody wished that her friend would allow herself to grieve with the rest of them. It was hard enough to deal with this loss from where Melody stood; she could only imagine the depth of agony it caused to lose one of the few remaining pieces Erin had of the *love of her life*.

The elven song slowly lowered, growing quieter until it returned to the low hum. King Brannor placed his healthy hand over his wife's body and Ana followed suit, placing her own over his. Old elvish whispered from their lips as they repeated the prayer carved into the stone. "Time is without beginning, without end." Ethelron whispered the translation for Erin and Melody. "A journey well traveled will forever leave a light, never to wane, never to decline. As we leave this world, our magic remains, to join in nature, and become forever part of time. Until we all meet again in nature, farewell."

Light appeared under the palms of their hands as they called forth part of their inner light. Slowly they lowered them until they touched the silk, and it took to flame.

The elven song rose high into the air once more, following the smoke. Ana and Brannor held hands as they watched the queen become forever part of time.

.℮ .℮ .℮

Ana's trance-like stare into her mother's now-fading funeral pyre was only broken by her father's gesture to begin the recessional back to the castle. She wasn't sure how long they'd stood there, but she would have remained indefinitely if it meant that she didn't have to face the fact that time would continue to march on without her mother.

Her father was fading quickly beside her without his wife's healing gift, and his ability to hide the truth was disappearing even faster. He was going to be taken from her as well. Her entire family - the family she had already mourned once - would really and truly be gone, and she would be left standing alone.

"Aina?" *Ethelron.* His presence was warm and steady at her shoulder, and the walls that she'd built up to get her through the funeral crumbled. Tears burned her eyes and blurred her vision.

"I couldn't do this for Toron. I said the prayer, but I had to bury him. I wasn't able to give him a true elven farewell." Finally, she turned to face him, and his openness nearly undid her completely. "How long until I stand here again? Days? How many more goodbyes do I have to give? How much can one lose until the heart simply shatters?" *How am I supposed to lead these people when I've been living in Sula for the past eighteen years? How will they ever trust me when my entire family is dead because of* me? *How-*

"Come here." He pulled her tightly against him, silencing the spiral of intrusive thoughts threatening to drown her. The firm pressure of his arm around her waist and his hand against the small of her back grounded her, and she took a shuddering breath. "Do you wish to return to the castle? You can be around your friends?" He tipped her chin up so he could look into her face, but she shook her head.

"Not yet," she sighed, burrowing deeper into his hold.

"Okay." He kissed the top of her head. "Let's walk for a bit. This is your first chance to really breathe in elven air without the erebi." Keeping an arm tightly around her, he led her deeper into the forest. With each step, those walls fell away more, leaving her emotions more raw and exposed, until she couldn't hold back the dam on her grief any longer. Nearly falling into his arms, her knees gave out and Ethelron supported her, resting her head against his chest as she covered her face with her hands. The steady stroke of his fingers through her hair and the massage of her ears helped to soothe her frayed nerves while she sobbed, and Ana was reminded that while she was grieving her family, she was *not* going to be left standing alone.

"El…" Her voice was hushed. His touch and her heightened emotions left her reeling, aching for a more tangible reminder that he was *hers*. An escape, however brief, from the pain was an enticing thought as well. She looked up at him and could immediately read his confusion and concern. "Help me to forget. Just for a moment." She couldn't bring herself to care that she was pleading with him, and a visible war of emotion raged across his features. Finally, he shook his head with a sigh.

The sting of rejection threatened to overwhelm her, but Ethelron took her face between his hands tenderly and kissed the tip of her nose. "*Never,* my love. Pain is not to be forgotten or pushed to the side. It will make you stronger and heal your soul. But I *will* stay by your side and help you through it. You shall not be alone in this for even a moment. I wish I could tell you that you would suffer no more loss. You deserve nothing but happiness. But I am here for all of your moments, regardless. I will be here when your heart fills with joy, and I will be here when it breaks. My strength is yours." He took her hand and kissed the palm, "my *heart* is yours," he kissed away a stray tear racing down her cheek, "my very breath is yours if you need it." Softly, his lips found hers, and she melted against him.

Chapter Twenty-Three

Erin came around the corner in time to catch Ethelron pulling Ana against him. She knew she should turn away, let the elves have a moment of privacy, but she found she couldn't tear her eyes away. The two looked at each other with such love it made her heart hurt. She couldn't hear what they were saying, but their actions spoke volumes. Even in her grief, Ana looked at Ethelron with adoration. They had each other and they would make one another stronger.

They kissed, unaware of her spying. Ethelron, such a hardened warrior, held her like she was a delicate flower, something precious to care for. Erin finally had to turn away; the pain from watching them became overwhelming.

After all their group had been through together, they would be separated. Erin would have to return to Sula, but Melody might choose to stay with Ana. Here she could perform her magic without other humans hindering her. Ana had taken in the witch and treated her like a daughter. Erin would completely understand if they chose to stay together. And she would be alone. *Again.*

She wasn't sure she could do it. Not after knowing what it was like to have friends like them. Not after knowing how it felt to have true love. She'd gained a family, only to have them all taken away. Erin couldn't stay, though; she didn't belong here. Here, in the eyes of the other elves, she would be the halfling holding on to a love long gone. She would be the one that the queen and king took pity on, only to join their son in the afterlife. At least in Sula, her home, she was unknown. She could become lost and forgotten in the crowd.

Erin rested her back against an old tree and let a buildup of tears finally fall. After all this time, she'd opened herself up to people other than Gabe, and now everything she'd *always* feared would happen, was coming to pass. She would be alone, broken from her losses. She would have to go the rest of her life knowing what she could have had, if Gabe had lived, if the queen hadn't been killed. Her hand gripped Gabe's amulet like her life depended on it. A sharp pain pricked her palm as her grip became too tight, and Erin looked down in shock to find that the metal had cut her hand. A few drops of blood slid off her skin onto the ground before the wound healed itself and the pain vanished.

But then, the air shifted. A feeling of darkness and light seemed to battle the air around her. Erin scrambled to her feet, wondering what was going on. A flash lit up the forest before her. For a moment she thought she was growing dizzy, but realized the world in front of her had actually grown fuzzy as the elements collided with something *other*. She'd only just made the connection of it being a portal when something fell from it and it seemed to zip shut, the air smoothing out once more.

The naked back of a man was shivering on the ground, and Erin leapt forward to help. "Are you okay?" She was wondering where he came from, and how he made a portal appear, when his head lifted. Her mind blanked. *Very* familiar green eyes stared at her with obvious confusion. He was having trouble focusing, but instead of supporting him, she dropped his arm and scrambled back with a scream, kicking dirt as she tried to get away.

"What…*Erin*? What happened to your hair?" His voice, *oh that voice*, that only came to her in dreams, spoke out as he tried to gain his bearings. "Erin, what's wrong?" He stopped to cough and realized he was naked. "We were in a battle. Where am I? Are *you* okay?" His eyes scanned her, looking for injury. Finally, he gained his balance and went to her side. She couldn't move, couldn't speak. Her heart thumping loudly in her chest blocked out all other sounds. "Erin, *tell me what is happening!*" His hands suddenly on her arms seemed to wake her up. He was *real*. He was *touching* her.

"Gabe!" She threw her arms around him, pulling him against her, his homey forest scent filling her senses.

"Please, tell me what is happening. Is Aina okay? She was about to get…" He trailed off as he tried to remember.

"Gabe, just *shut up* for a minute!" She pulled his face to her and drew him into a kiss, needing to know for sure he was there. Needing to feel him, taste him. She wasn't sure what was happening, but if she was dreaming, she was going to take full advantage of it.

"Erin, are you ok-" The sound of Ryo's voice had Erin regretfully pulling away. She turned and found the silver-haired elf taking in the scene. She *was* standing in the middle of the forest, kissing a naked man. He had a sword at the ready and seemed to be debating if he should use it. "Sorry to *interrupt*. I heard you scream." He didn't seem like he was planning on leaving her alone with the naked man.

Gabe's hands came around her protectively, but sh laid a hand on his chest to calm him. Then Ryo stared into Gabe's face and suddenly straightened, recognizing the mixture of royal features. "Prince Toron?" His eyes flitted to Erin, and she could only imagine the myriad of emotions he found on her face.

"Ryo, get Ana."

"And," Gabe spoke up, still visibly confused about what was happening, "can you bring me something to wear?" Ryo glanced between them again, his sword still in hand, before he finally nodded and went off to do as they'd asked.

"Erin, are you going to explain what is happening?" Erin turned from Ryo's retreating figure and tried to make sense of it all herself.

"What do you remember last?" she asked instead.

His hands left her and she nearly grabbed for him, afraid if he let go she would lose him again. "I remember that you were taken; we were coming to rescue you. Then Kali…she was about to attack Aina."

"Gabe…that was *months* ago."

"What?" Color drained from his face.

She grabbed him again and laid her head against his chest. She felt his warmth, heard his heart beating. "Gabe, we *buried* you. You were *dead*." Erin fought against the tight ball of emotions in her throat. He was *here*. He was *real*. Once as much of her body was pressed against his as physically possible, acting like a shield against anything that might try to take him away again, she told him about the end of the battle in Loinnir, and everything that had happened since.

.℮ .℮ .℮

"I see why my daughter loves you so much. Not everyone would volunteer to accompany an old, grieving man."

"She just kept me around because I understood how she liked her tea." Melody teased, trying to ease the tension. She wasn't ready to talk about Ana right now, not when she knew everyone and everything would be changing. Ana wouldn't be coming home with her, and while she and Erin were getting along, they didn't have the same closeness. Now that Eloas was saved, Melody didn't even know if Erin would want to keep in contact. She also was well aware the man holding her arm, Ana's *father*, only had days left to live. If he was lucky. She wished there had been time to get to know them. Ana needed more time to get to know them again; she needed that family connection she'd been missing for so many years. Even with their makeshift one, it wasn't the same, she knew. Melody still felt the hole left behind by her own family. She still felt their rejection like a thorn in her side.

"It will be okay, Melody." The king gave her hand a small pat, their height difference not as noticeable as he hunched in pain. "I will join my wife soon, and Ana has been fine all these years. She's grown into the kind of leader Eloas will need, and she'll have her friends at her side. Even if you and Erin return to Sula, now that the war is won, you can freely travel to each other. All will be well."

"It shouldn't have been like this for any of you. None of this is how it should be." The ball of grief in her throat made her voice tight.

Brannor settled himself in a chair and tugged her down into the one next to him. He turned his body, his face pulled in a grimace. "My wife used to reassure me that everything is as it should be. Our children were separated from us. There was no way for us to know if they were safe. Our best chance to protect them was to get them away from here, but every day felt like we were missing limbs. Even thinking they were safe. Then there was this never-ending war, and I was injured. Even still, Faervel always insisted we were where we were supposed to be. There are other forces outside of us. Our threads of fate were connected to others, and we just had to trust our place within it. I believe she and I did what we needed to do, and now others are ready to take our place. All will be well. You should go enjoy the fresh air. You used a lot of magic in that last battle, let the realm fill you again now that the infection erebi are gone. It is safe once more. I'll just rest for a bit." He patted her hand again, giving it a small squeeze, before sending her on her way.

Melody left the king to his rest and made her way through the castle. There was a buzz of activity as everyone seemed to have their own jobs to accomplish. She longed for a mug of hot chocolate and a TV show to get lost in. Since they didn't exactly have Netflix in Eloas, she thought sitting outside would at least give her the space to settle her mind.

She *had* used an extravagant amount of magic, but after she'd rested, she'd felt fine. She didn't feel weak, or tired, as she sometimes did in Sula if she pushed herself. Instead, she'd woken up to find Ryo sitting by her bedside, teasing her about showing off and making him look bad in battle. He'd teased her about the streak of white that was still in her hair. He'd asked her about that display she'd put on, but it wasn't something she could explain. She'd only said that she felt stronger here; her magic felt almost separate from her.

He'd said something similar to Ana, that she was probably pulling in magic from the realm, and that her reserves must just be really deep. Sula hadn't had enough magic for her, but in Eloas, she could fill those reserves, and she was starting to feel just how strong she truly was.

Then he'd told her that she'd saved them with her little magic trick, and while he'd deny ever doing so, he thanked her. It had been an odd moment, having a warrior like him *thank her*. Melody knew she was powerful. She knew she could hold her own in a fight, but to get that level of recognition felt like something else. Knowing she'd done something good with her powers, powers her parents had hated her for, gave her a new kind of strength she hadn't realized she was missing.

"Woah!" Just as Melody stepped outside, she bumped into a wall of muscle. Ryo caught her easily.

"Sorry, I was distracted." His tone was odd and made her look closer.

"Everything okay?" Melody asked. His hands dropped from her, and he was already looking back towards the woods.

"Yes...no..." He shook his head. "Yes, I just need to find the princess."

"Ethelron was taking her to get some space in the woods when I left them. I'll come with you." Ryo didn't respond, just gave a sharp nod and took off at a fast pace. Melody had to jog to keep up with his longer strides. "Want to tell me what's wrong?"

"I don't know."

"You don't know what's wrong? Or you don't know if you want to tell me?" He glanced at her then, and his lips lifted in a small smile. His gaze fell to her legs, noticing how she was working to keep up with him. His strides shortened without comment. She wanted to appreciate the gesture, but also worried about slowing him down when she didn't know what was going on.

"I'm not sure exactly what's wrong, or if it is *wrong*. It'll be easier once everyone is together. There's no reason to go over all of this multiple times...you'll have to see it to believe it." He tilted his head like he was listening for something, and then turned to the right, heading deeper into the trees, before coming to a full stop. "Oh, come on! You accuse me of debauchery, but no one in the woods today seems to realize we have a castle full of rooms *right there*!" Melody made it to his side just in time to catch Ethelron block Ana from view. Not before Melody caught the flaming red of Ana's cheeks and her well-tended lips. She smothered a smile. Hey, she's not one to judge. Everyone grieves differently.

"I need everyone to meet in the sitting room."

"What's happened?" Ethelron's demeanor changed, visibly growing tense, but he kept Ana half blocked behind him. She stepped around him, however, and looked between Ryo and Melody.

"I'll tell everyone together. Can you and Ethelron get your father and meet me there?"

"Okay, what about Erin?"

Melody glanced at him when he didn't answer right away. "I'll...I'll bring her. Just meet me there."

Ethelron looked like he might argue, but Ana must have seen something in Ryo's face, and simply nodded. "Okay, Melody, are you coming with us?"

"She'll come with me," Ryo answered before she had a chance. Melody didn't argue, simply looked at him oddly. The moment Ana and Ethelron started back towards the castle, Ryo gestured to Melody for them to get going as well. He stopped at a small outpost building, leaving her outside without a word. She was just starting to wonder if it was all some kind of elaborate prank when he returned with a set of men's clothing tucked under his arm.

"Ryo-"

"Listen, everyone is about to get quite the shock. I still think you need to see it to believe it, but I'm not sure what happened or if it can be trusted. So even though you are going to be surprised, I need you to be alert. With your powers, if something is wrong, I believe you can shield us from it."

"Did something happen to Erin?" It was the only explanation that made any sense, but even that didn't quite fit. Ryo didn't answer.

Instead, he slowed and stepped in front of her so that his body was blocking hers as they approached their destination.

"Where's Ana?" Erin's voice seemed normal enough, if not a little...emotional.

"She's getting the king and meeting us at the castle. I brought clothes," Ryo responded.

Melody stepped out from behind him, replaying Ana doing the same thing with Ethelron only moments before. Erin was sitting on a fallen tree, looking normal, but then Melody caught movement beside her. Ryo's body was still blocking the view, so she had to side-step further. With that extra step, everything changed.

"Erin, what did you do?" Melody glanced back at her friend, but that only lasted a second before she had to look again. *At Gabe.*

"Nothing, I was just sitting here-"

"Let's talk about this all together back at the castle," Ryo broke in, tossing the clothes at Gabe. Melody turned back to Erin to find her watching Gabe carefully, looking as confused as Melody was feeling. Clearly, whatever happened, Erin hadn't done it on purpose.

"Thank you, Ryo."

"Okay…" Gabe stepped in front of Erin and shot a dark look towards Ryo. "I know I've been…*gone* for months now and everything, but I *need* to know. Is there something between you two?" His voice was harsh, and Erin physically jerked back at the sound.

"Gabe!"

380

"I get it, okay? And I won't judge you for it, Erin. I was apparently *dead*. So if you found comfort in someone's arms, I'll have to accept that. But I deserve to know," his voice rose with anger when no one answered him, "if you were *fucking* someone while I was gone!" Ryo stepped in and grabbed Gabe's arm to take his attention off Erin. Melody felt her magic rise to her fingers in defense.

"Listen, I'm not going to lie." Ryo leaned in close, his eyes flicking to Erin. "I've offered it a time or two. But Erin never once stopped thinking of *you*. I know you must be going through some shock right now over what she's told you. You can just know that she never stopped loving you or thinking about you. Focus on that for the time being." Erin pulled herself together and took Gabe's hand in hers.

"Come on. We should go to the castle and talk to everyone. Your father will be there."

Gabe didn't move at first, but his gaze softened on Erin. "I'm sorry, Erin. I don't know what came over me." He ran a shaky hand through his hair before turning to apologize to Ryo, too.

"Hey, Ethelron punched me over you once, so I'm just glad my nose is still intact. I can't even *imagine* what you are going through right now, so no worries. We should get going; everyone will be waiting to see why I summoned them together." With a shrug, he took the lead. Melody watched Erin and Gabe move to follow him, their hands clasped together.

Gabe had been dead, and as far as she knew, only very dark magic was capable of bringing him back. They would have to get to the bottom of it, and quickly.

Chapter Twenty-Four

Ana silently watched her father from across the room. Ethelron and a few other more practiced healers tried to take his pain away, but no one had been strong enough. Her mother had just barely been able to do it, and she'd been the best healer in the realm. Now the king was hunched in his chair, his eyes barely focused. She wondered how long the infection would take to kill him. After being repressed for so long by her mother's magic, it seemed the infection was at least weak and taking time to spread, but it *would* eventually take over.

"Do you think Ryo and Erin are now secretly having an affair? Maybe they are getting us all together to announce it?" That was the last thing Ana would believe, but she wanted to ease the tension in the room, and she thought Ethelron would have a few things to say about *that* comment.

"What?" he asked when she turned to look at him, one eyebrow raised. "All you ladies are too good for him. He's lucky one of you hasn't thrown him out a window."

"I think you should be a little more grateful toward him." Ana leaned back in her seat, feeling a little better while giving him a hard time.

"How so?" Ethelron raised a brow, his voice dropping to a dangerous tone.

"Maybe I was worried his relentless flirting would eventually wear you down, and that's why I fought so hard to get you to stop being so stubborn about us."

He leaned closer, his large body invading her space. He moved to whisper in her ear, but first he brushed his lips against the sensitive skin at her jaw. Her entire body reacted to the small touch, and she could tell from the deep rumble in his chest that he hadn't missed it. "If you are ever worried about me even *noticing* the existence of another, then I'm not doing my job correctly, and I would expect you to let me know immediately, so that I can rectify my mistake...*thoroughly*."

Okay, point goes to Ethelron. He leaned back in his seat with the ease of someone that knew he'd won.

Finally, the door opened and Melody came through first, taking up a seat next to Brannor. She took the king's hand in hers, and Ana watched as her father gave the young witch a small smile. She didn't miss the fact that Melody carefully avoided her gaze.

Then Ryo stepped through, leaving the door ajar but blocking the hallway from view. He took a deep breath. Ana shifted in her seat, growing nervous. "So, we don't know how it happened." Ethelron sat up a little straighter and reached over to take her hand in his. "This will be a bit shocking, so please try to stay calm, okay? We need to work to figure this out, and if everyone goes *crazy*, that will be hard to do."

"Just tell us what is going on all ready," her father spoke up, his voice shaky and impatient. Ryo gave a nod and finally pushed the door open. Erin walked in, her face pale, and pulled *Gabe* in beside her.

Ana tried to make sense of what she was seeing. It *was* Gabe. It *was* her brother, alive. He searched each of their faces and tightened his grip on Erin's hand for support.

"Toron!" Brannor rose to his feet and had his son held tightly against him in the span of a heartbeat, while everyone else continued to stare in shock.

"Aina?" Ethelron spoke quietly beside her, and she realized he was watching her carefully, his own eyes wide with surprise. His voice seemed to pull her out of her daze, and she found her feet. Her eyes connected with Erin's, bright with fresh tears, and the truth hit her like a freight train. He *really* was alive and standing there. Ana ran to him and joined the impromptu family hug. She would ask for answers later.

She would worry about the meaning behind it *later*. Right now, she had her brother back.

"How very sweet, a family reunion," a cool voice spoke from behind her. Ana turned to find a woman standing at the center of the room, appearing out of thin air. Ethelron was on his feet, his sword at the ready before she could even react. She could feel his unease over being separated from her, the intruder situated in the center of the group.

"You!" Gabe moved away from his family and stepped up to the stranger in recognition.

"I told you I was a friend," she answered with a smile, revealing pointed teeth. "My name is Lyra."

"Gabe?" Erin stepped to his side and watched her carefully. With long copper-brown hair and sharp yellow eyes, she made for quite a sight, standing in a room full of people who had killed their fair share of erebi.

The yellow eyes cut to Erin, and Gabe stepped forward to block her with his body. The movement drew her attention instead to the amulet. "You must have made a blood sacrifice. And in his home realm. Just the ingredients it took to bring him back."

"She showed up right before we went into battle. She pricked my finger with that," he gestured his head toward the amulet, "and told me to wear it. Then I was *killed*."

"Well, don't blame me! *I* didn't kill you. I gave you a way to come back. It's not my fault it took your girlfriend so long to figure it out. Maybe if she stopped looking at all these handsome men around her," the erebus' eyes flitted between Ethelron and Ryo, "she would have been more desperate for answers. I wouldn't blame her though, she got around to it."

"Erin?" Ana questioned softly.

"It pricked my hand. I was holding it." She touched the amulet now, realization dawning on her face. "I didn't know." Erin turned to Gabe. "We tried to figure out what it was, but we couldn't. No one had ever seen a stone like this before. You," she turned back to the stranger, "did *you* send that erebus after me?"

"What?" Gabe turned his attention back to Erin, concerned. "What erebus?"

"That dragon half-breed? No, he wasn't mine. I *wanted* you to get your man back. But let's just say, the amulet was not mine to give. I should tell you I went through a *lot* to get it. Now, the way I see it, I'm owed a little payment in exchange for his life."

"What sort of payment?" Erin stepped forward, but Ana rushed to stand at her side.

"You let my brother die when you could have warned us. Clearly, you wanted to use him against us all along. Why should we help you?"

"He is forever bound with that amulet." The erebus stepped closer and stroked the rock lying around Erin's neck. Her yellow eyes were taunting yet almost seductive. "It uses blood magic. When I gave it to him, I pricked his finger. *Erin* cut her hand on it to bring him back. They are *both* connected to the amulet now. If I were to destroy it," the erebus looked to her with a triumphant smile, "or return to Skia and tell interested parties where to find it, both of them would die"

Erin jerked away from the erebus' hand and grabbed Gabe's arm. "What is the payment?" The question sounded like quiet resignation, and Ana looked at her. She was happy to have her brother back, but she also knew the erebus could not be trusted. Erin's eyes were hard as she stared at Lyra, and Ana realized she would do whatever it took.

"Fortunately for you, the offer I have is mutually beneficial. The master of Skia needs to be taken out. You are the '*good guys*' who kill *bad* erebi. You don't even have to wrestle with your *morals*."

"Why do you need the erebus gone?" Gabe's voice was deathly calm, seeing that he didn't have a choice. Ana could feel their brief moment of peace slipping away. She found Ethelron's hard stare facing her from across the room. He was quietly considering their options.

"This really isn't the time for questions. But I'm sure you can all understand living under the reign of an unfair ruler. I simply want you to take her out. A very small price to pay to have a loved one back.

Also, she is the one I stole the amulet from. So once you take her out, you will no longer be in danger."

Gabe's green eyes fell on Ana. "You don't have to come with us-"

"Don't even finish that sentence, Toron. I lost you twice already. I'll not do it again."

"Wonderful, lovely. Shall we go?" The erebus clapped her hands together, looking around the room with a too-wide smile.

Ethelron stepped forward, the tip of his sword hovering centimeters from Lyra's throat. "No. This realm has been at war for seventeen years. *We* just ended that war *days* ago. You expect us to do your bidding? Give us time to recover before expecting us to dive into a new war."

The erebus chuckled, pushing the blade away with her index finger without concern. "Down, boy. Go, do your little elf thing. Sleep, screw, say your goodbyes. I really don't care. I'll be back, and you'd better be ready to go." Just as suddenly as Lyra appeared, she vanished, her chuckle echoing long after she was gone.

.℘ .℘ .℘

Lyra seemed to be happy over her visit with the group, and Briar itched for a stronger vision about the people Lyra would be working so closely with. Instead, Doyle led her to sit with Malux while he and Lyra discussed plans. Now she sat picking at a thread that was starting to fray from the bottom of her shirt while Malux watched her in silence. They had to start planning. She could feel them running out of time, but she was no closer to knowing who to put on the throne instead of Lyra.

She was also still worried over Doyle. There hadn't been more visions of him choosing to kill her for Lyra, but that didn't mean that future wasn't still *there*. She'd seen a change in him, in how he stood up to Lyra over and over to make sure she was protected, but how would he feel once he found out she'd been working to betray him and his vision for Skia?

"You are going to leave here without a shirt if you keep pulling at that." Malux finally broke the silence, claiming her attention. "I really don't want to explain why you are shirtless when Doyle returns."

Her hand dropped away. "We have a week, then the group will be here." She sighed heavily. "And after a short march through erebi-infested land, they will be at the castle, and they will help Lyra fight against her sister. That is all the time we have to find someone more suitable for the crown."

"You told Lyra about the spell to put on her blades?"

"Yes, she's going to Horace. He should be able to give her everything she needs to ready her weapons in time."

Malux nodded silently. "And how is your relationship with Doyle?"

"With, at best, two weeks to find a ruler for this realm, are you *really* asking about that?"

"You are planning to overthrow the person *he's* been planning to put in power. I'd like to know how strong his bond is to you, so I know how big of a fight we will have on our hands." He spoke aloud her own worries. She started picking at the thread of her shirt again.

"I'm in love with him, Malux. But I'm afraid. He wants to protect me, but I'm not sure if he'll choose me over Lyra, and I feel awful even trying to force that choice on him. As horrible as Lyra is, she still helped him, and if she takes the crown and then gets overthrown, she will die."

"If she takes the crown and keeps it, she'll keep you enslaved. She won't let Doyle stand in her way, and she'll be too powerful then. You've seen a future where she was more than willing to kill him. She won't need him once she's queen. But she won't be willing to lose someone as powerful as you. You *must* know that."

"I do, I just...I just know Doyle is going to get hurt in this, and I wish I could spare him."

"Well, I'd keep focusing on trying to get a vision of the right ruler. We have to just hope that everything will fall into place." Malux reached forward and pulled her hand from the thread of her shirt when he caught her pulling at it again. "And Doyle loves you; I can see it. You should have seen him when I told him they'd taken you that day. He was ready to burn the whole place down around us in order to save you. A man who feels that strongly is not about to raise a hand toward you, no matter what you've done."

She nodded, but didn't quite feel it. Her vision blurred as she blinked back tears. She wanted a lifetime with Doyle, but she wasn't sure exactly what that would mean, or what that would look like, *if* it was even possible. Ever since her first vision of the love they could share, some part of her had fallen for him. Some part of her felt that tenderness that was an undercurrent in everything he did, and it just kept drawing her closer and closer to him. Now, she'd had a small taste of what they could have, and she wasn't ready to let it go. But she was *also* well aware he would not truly be hers until he knew everything. It would be wrong of her to ask that of him when she was still hiding such a secret.

"Is there a reason you two are holding hands?" Doyle's voice jerked her from her thoughts of him.

Malux's grip tightened as he flashed Doyle a grin. "I think Briar here has decided a half-dragon being is more interesting and would like to leave you for me."

"Oh, is that so?" Doyle crossed his arms, but his gaze was soft as it shifted between them.

"Well, it *is* tempting." She picked up on the teasing attitude as Malux released her hand. "Maybe you should show me the benefits of being with you." She could feel the flush spread over her cheeks as his gaze changed. His brow rose at the challenge and her breath caught in her throat.

"Oh, great. I get to watch this lovely display." Malux rose with a groan and disappeared into the shadows, but Briar hardly noticed him move.

"I leave you alone for a few hours and you start causing all kinds of trouble. What am I to do with you?" He kissed the corner of her mouth, and she still couldn't find words. Her worries melted away as he drew her into his arms and followed the line of her neck with his lips.

A vision suddenly washed over her like a wave pulling her under. She didn't even have time to fight it; she just fell against him as her body gave over to it.

Chapter Twenty-Five

"So you were lying to me this whole time?" Doyle watched her with a predatory glare. It was so different from the looks she'd grown used to from him that she drew a step back with a small gasp of surprise.

"It's not like that, Doyle. You've seen how she is. You know she won't let me go, and she won't let you stand in her way. She'll do anything she can to get more power. You want the best for your realm, Lyra is not it!"

Doyle stepped toward her, and she wanted to scramble back out of reach. There was danger in his gaze. All the good she'd seen in him was gone. It was like the Doyle she knew was no longer there, and a stranger stood before her instead.

"Lyra will bring this realm to its full potential. I'd kill you for your betrayal, but she wants to keep you around, to use your powers to continue to help the realm." His hand shot out and grasped her arm. Struggling was no use; he didn't even budge against her attempts to escape.

"Doyle, don't do this! I love you." Her words did nothing, and she realized that somehow she'd lost him. Her Doyle was no longer there. "What did Lyra do to you?" She choked on the words as he dragged her behind him. He brought her to the erebus in question, whose eyes danced at the sight of Doyle's painful grip on her.

"What did you do to him?" Briar spat at her, struggling to free herself once more so she could scrape her nails down Lyra's face.

Lyra just grinned, sharp teeth glinting and eyes gleaming. "Not all of my sister's ideas are terrible." Doyle shoved her to the floor and when she turned to him, she saw just a flash of his old self. It gave her just a little hope that he was still there, somehow. That he could beat whatever Lyra had done to him.

"It's overpowering right now; it will fade a bit, and he'll be more himself until I order differently. But he's fully under the spell."

Briar's heart fell as she understood. The dark magic that the queen had used against Malux...she looked to Doyle again and her heart squeezed with loss. He wouldn't be able to ignore a direct order from Lyra...and the only way to break it would be to kill him. "Doyle..." He just tilted his head in response.

"Go, put her in chains. We'll see if we can get some visions from her."

"No, Doyle, don't do this!" His hands gripped her and pulled her up to her feet, dragging her behind him to the other room, where he could chain her from the ceiling. Something inside her broke, and she spiraled down into darkness.

℘ ℘ ℘

"I don't like this, Aina."

"None of us do, El. But Toron...he died right in front of me. I *buried* him. I don't trust her. I don't trust that it's as simple as she would like us to think. This whole situation has me on edge, but I cannot lose him again." She sighed heavily, stepping up to Ethelron and settling her hands on his chest. "I have to follow my brother and Erin into this fight. You do not. I need someone here to protect my father, in the event someone gets the bright idea to attack the realm while we are still rebuilding."

His response was immediate and intense. "Absolutely not!" Anyone less attuned to Ethelron might have cowered away at his barked answer, but Ana didn't even flinch. "How many times do I have to tell you I am with you? I said I do not like this...not that I am blind to the reality of the situation."

Ana wondered if they would get to experience a life together without war. She yearned for peace, and the kind of life that could bring them. She leaned up and pressed a tender kiss to his lips. "We have survived this far, El. We will make it through this. Together."

He pressed his forehead to hers and took a deep breath. "There is something that I need to do before we leave. I'll be back." Ana drew back and gave him a confused look, but he simply kissed the tip of her nose and strode away, leaving her alone in the corridor. With a frustrated groan, she threw her hands up in the air and headed for the library.

Since the erebus left, everyone discreetly cleared the room to give Gabe some time with his father. When Erin tried to leave the two alone, however, Gabe grabbed her hand and asked her to stay. He hadn't let go since. He clung to her like a lifeline as Brannor told him about Faervel. The last time Erin talked to him, he hadn't had his memories back. As far as they'd both known, he didn't have a family. While she was captured, he remembered them, only to believe that they had died along with his realm. Now, in a sick twist of fate, he was sitting beside her - back from the dead himself - hanging on every word his father told him of how his mother *actually* died.

The memory of him as a small boy, running up to his father, love written all over his features, broke her heart. He never got the chance to be reunited with his mother, and the time with his father would be short-lived.

"This is some girl you found for yourself, Toron. Your mother loved her dearly." Brannor's eyes fell on her, so she gave him a weak smile.

Gabe pulled her to his side and kissed her temple. "She is. I've been lucky to have her. It's hard to believe so much time has passed...I wish I could have been here to help end the war." A soft knock at the door drew their attention. Brannor gave a small grunt as he moved in his chair and called for them to enter. Ethelron noticed Gabe and Erin still sitting with the king and started to apologize. "It's fine. We should let you get some rest, anyway." Gabe kissed his father's forehead and held his shoulder for a moment.

Brannor patted his hand. "Erin told us we would have been proud of the man you became. I never doubted her, but I'm glad I got to see it for myself. I'm so sorry we sent you and Aina away. We just wanted to keep you safe."

"I know, Papa." Gabe turned to Ethelron and paused, recognition from his childhood flitting across his face. "Ethelron? I saw you earlier but so much was happening...wow! It's so good to see you again! I hope you didn't let Erin meet Siofra."

Ethelron glanced at her in amusement. "Actually, I think they have come to tolerate each other nicely." Erin sensed his unease and noticed his eyes flitting to the king.

"Yes, but I didn't handle our introduction very well. We'll give you two some time." With a smile, she led Gabe from the room.

"That man was like my father's shadow. I don't think this place would feel like home without him here. I don't think he ever knew it, but I hero-worshiped him a little. He got to spend all this time with my father, learn how to fight, plus the cool wolf for a pet."

Erin chuckled. "I could see that. We didn't exactly get along at first, but I almost see him as a brother now. And, you should probably know, he's involved with your sister."

"What?" That stopped him in his tracks. Erin shrugged with a smile and led him to the room she shared with the others. No one was inside, which made her wonder where Ana and Melody were. She laid down on a bed and Gabe quickly followed, pulling her against him and letting her rest her head on his shoulder.

"Erin, I'm really sorry for what I said to you in the forest. That was really out of line."

"You've been through a lot. There is a lot of information to process. There is nothing to forgive. I have you back. That's all that matters." Erin ran her fingers over the stubble on his jaw. She couldn't stop from touching him, needing the constant reassurance that he was there. He was truly alive and hers once more.

"But at what price, Erin? We are both now tied to this stone. You're in danger now because of me." His hand fell on the stone around her neck, and she could almost feel the hate for it rolling off of him. She propped herself up on one arm so she could look at him better.

"You have no idea what it has been like for me, being without you...Knowing the last time I really talked to you, you found out you are elven and I'm a fae halfling. I've spent *months* wondering if we would even be together if you had lived. I lied to you and hid who I really was. I'm so sorry. I should have told you the truth about me right away; I just didn't know how..."

The feel of his fingertips in her hair had her melting. "We are two parts of one soul, Erin. I wouldn't be anywhere else other than by your side. I guess now, that's even more true," his fingers again fell to the necklace, "connected by blood magic and all."

"I guess I should call you Toron now. Your mother told me it means forest. A bit of a coincidence after all those times I teased you about being a lumberjack." She teased, but his face was serious as he held her face between his hands.

"No, I was Gabe when I met you. I was Gabe when I fell in love with you. I'm still Gabe. *Your Gabe.*"

"But you know now. You know you are elven. Would you rather have the name your parents gave you, or the name some random person picked out for you when you didn't know who you were?"

"It's not a choice between the two. I spent most of my life being Gabe. I came back to life and heard *your* voice calling me *Gabe.*"

"I don't want you to feel like you have to give up something for me. You *are* elven and-"

"Erin," he cut her off, "shut up, will you?" Then he rolled, pulling her on top of him and dragged his teeth over her lips, sending away any thoughts she might have that didn't involve kissing him.

"Why didn't you heal this?" He pulled away and his fingers followed the line of her scar, her reminder that Gabe died because she got caught up in revenge. She pulled away from his touch, not wanting him to look at that part of her. She tried to roll off his lap, but he grabbed her hand and held her still. He seemed to read her thoughts and didn't allow her an escape. Instead, Gabe leaned forward and pressed his lips to the scar. Warmth filled her at his show of affection, and when he pulled back, he grinned at her.

"What?"

"You healed it. It's gone." She reached up to touch the small line of raised skin, but it was smooth. Then his hands were on her thighs and his lips wandered, erasing all thoughts of grief and loss from her mind with the heat of his touch.

.℮ .℮ .℮

Doyle was sharpening his dagger, trying to ignore the pressure at the bottom of his skull and the sad noises coming from Briar's throat. He'd carried her back to his room when the vision took her, and laid her down on his bed so she wouldn't hurt herself on the stone floor. She didn't seem to suffer in the vision, but the sound she kept making was ripping his heart out. It was like someone was tearing *her* heart into pieces, and he was once again left on the other side to watch with no power to do anything to help her.

He noticed signs of her coming out of it, so he sat at the edge of the bed next to her. She blinked slowly at the ceiling, coming back to herself after fighting through her vision. "Hey there. You should stop doing that while I'm kissing you. I'm going to get some sort of complex." He tried to go for a teasing tone, but when her eyes landed on him, her features filled with fear. She gave a small gasp and shot herself across the bed, nearly landing on the floor.

Something inside him twisted at her fear. Raising open hands, Doyle backed away from the bed slowly. "Briar, it's just me. Are you okay?" He tried to keep his voice even so he could find out what she'd seen without startling her more.

"Doyle..." His name sounded broken on her lips.

"Briar, what did you see?"

She moved quickly. First she was on the other side of the bed, and then she was flinging herself into his arms. He nearly missed catching her, but the moment she was in his embrace, her scent surrounded him, calming him. Then he felt her shaking and heard the small sob escape her; he could only guess that she'd seen another possible way he'd die.

"I'm right here, Blue." He carried her back to the bed so he could sit down and hold her close. It took a few minutes, but finally she calmed. After wiping away her tears, she looked up at him, and he felt something in her was broken. Maybe there wouldn't be a way to save him, maybe his end was drawing close. If that was true, then he had to make sure she'd be safe after he was gone. His mind had already started working to solve problems he wouldn't be around to deal with when she swiped a thumb over his scar.

"Doyle, I'm sorry. But we can't trust her. You have to believe me...We have to stop Lyra."

.℮ .℮ .℮

"I should have known you'd go to the library." Ana smiled when Ethelron's low voice echoed in her mind. As she waited for him to find her, she looked over the pictures she'd gathered of a time when her family was whole. Before they'd been separated. Before war had ravaged Eloas and torn apart everything that they'd known.

"It is secluded here, a perfect place to think." *Amongst other things*, she added to herself. Despite everything they had lost, would still lose, Ana counted herself blessed to have Ethelron by her side. He was her source of light and hope, her constant; his presence helped to ground her when everything else in her world was upside down, and she realized she needed to make sure that he knew it. Even for their kind, they had learned all too well that life was too short to withhold the truth.

A strong arm corded around her waist, palm covering her navel to press her back against his warm, broad chest. His free hand caressed the side of her neck as he drew her hair away from it, and Ana hummed in contentment when his lips found the newly exposed skin.

"Did you get done with your urgent business?" Though she'd attempted a light tone, it came out somber as her eyes fell on a picture of her with her mother. Ethelron seemed to follow her gaze and smiled sadly against her neck.

He lifted a picture reverently, and she wished desperately that she could read what he was thinking. In reality, she did not know how close he'd gotten to the king and queen in the years that separated them; he'd been close to them long before she'd left, seen the royal family as his own…it stood to reason they'd bonded even more in the time of war and isolation that they experienced. Ana filed that thought away to confront more directly when the time came. "Part of it. We will finish the rest tomorrow."

"Is that so?" She turned her head to trace her nose along his jawline. Ethelron shuddered, the hand over her navel twitching and pressing her into him again. He dropped the hand that had been in her hair to her waist, tracing patterns in the cloth of her dress over her abdomen. Ana's pulse quickened under his lips, and he nipped the skin of her neck lightly. She couldn't hide the breathy sigh in response as every nerve in her body came alive, and she was sure if she could *see* the grin that she could feel on his lips, she'd be done for.

"Oh, you know. Acting on the feelings I should have admitted long ago."

Ana stilled before she turned in his grasp. "El?"

Taking advantage of her new position, Ethelron reached around her easily to gather the pictures and set them to the side, out of their way. The movement forced her to lean against the edge of the table and pressed their bodies together briefly. Ana had to tilt her head back to look up at him, and he took the opportunity to drag his lips slowly up the line of her neck. It took everything she had to keep herself from arching up, trying to mold herself against him, and by the smirk on his face, *he knew it.* She narrowed her eyes at him. That smirk morphed into open affection, and he kissed the tip of her nose before becoming serious.

"I told you that my heart is yours, Princess." He settled a hand over her heart and braced himself against the table with the other, towering over her and holding her wide gaze steadily. "And I know yours belongs to *me* as well. Clearly, our lives were not meant to be simple...and so I refuse to wait until after we've gone and risked them again." He lifted her easily by the waist and slid her back to sit on the table before he stepped between her legs. "I told your father of my intentions with you...and he agreed to marry us tomorrow. If you will have me, my Princess."

Ana gasped and then surged up to meet him for a heated kiss. *"Through this lifetime and the next..."*

The following morning felt like an entire lifetime later to the elven princess. So much had changed. She'd lost so much, and gained some of it back, but she couldn't be more thankful that she had Ethelron by her side through so much of it. He'd been her rock when they were children, and it took no time for him to become so again once he found her. Now, she fought off butterflies in her stomach as Erin and Melody secured ceremonial Elanordis, white flowers native to her realm, into her hair.

"You ready for this, Ana?" Melody murmured, a smile tugging at her lips as she took in her friend's nervous energy.

"I think I have been waiting for this day since the moment I met him," Ana whispered. She watched as Melody carefully sectioned off her hair to tie it into a tight bun that she then circled with flowers. A soft knock at the door drew their attention.

"Are you ladies ready? Your Highness, you look stunning. Ethelron will be beside himself." She blushed at Ryo's compliment and glanced at her dearest friends.

"Thank you for standing beside me today. I love you both." Before they could say anything that might make her emotions get the best of her, she pulled both of them in for a hug.

"Yes, yes, very sweet. Erin and Mel, you both look lovely as well. Someone is getting anxious out there and might come in here himself if we don't hurry." All three of them rolled their eyes good-naturedly at the warrior, but complied nonetheless. Ana stopped just before leaving the castle and grabbed Ryo's arm. He looked at her to make sure she was okay, and Ana gently kissed his cheek with a smile. He just stared at her in surprise, making her laugh.

"This could all be because of you. So, thank you." Ryo's eyes flashed to Melody with a silent question, but the witch just grinned and shrugged.

As soon as they stepped out of the castle and into the beautifully-decorated courtyard, all that Ana could see was Ethelron, standing tall beside her father. Siofra rested at his feet. Gabe, waiting by the door for her, offered his arm. She took it and followed her friends down the path, each step bringing her closer to her destiny. It felt like forever before they'd finally reached the end, and tears were swimming in her eyes as she turned to face her soon-to-be husband.

Brannor began the ceremony, speaking in Old Elvish. Erin and Gabe each handed them a single Elanordis flower. Ethelron took her left hand and tied the stem of the flower around her ring finger, and then Ana did the same to him. As Brannor read in elvish once more, they raised their hands and pressed them together, palm to palm. The flowers seemed to vibrate with magic, and Ana knew a new rune was being imprinted into their skin. Ethelron held her gaze steadily, his emotions utterly unrestrained as he opened his soul to her. A tear slid down her cheek, and he caught it with the pad of his thumb. *"Not regretting your decision are you, Princess?"*

"Never."

Brannor completed the ceremonial reading and then took their hands to remove the flowers. He then pressed their hands back together, guiding them to lace their fingers together. "You are now bound to one another. You are of a shared heart, soul, and mind, and are held to your promise by the runes on your fingers." His hand settled over their joined fingers. "Protect and love one another unreservedly, and present a unified front in all things." He looked to Ethelron. "Continue to protect and cherish my daughter, as you have all of your life. I could not have asked for a better partner to share her life." He nodded to his new son and released their hands. Ethelron bowed to the king and then turned his attention to Ana, a broad grin spreading across his features. *Wife.* He sent the thought to her, and then without further hesitation, he pulled her close and kissed her deeply. Ana grinned against his lips and hugged him close to her. *Husband, I am yours.*

Chapter Twenty-Six

Briar watched Doyle pace and massaged at her neck while she waited for him to calm down enough to speak to her. Maybe it would have been better if she had said nothing, but after seeing him that way, she couldn't bring herself to hold back. She couldn't stand aside and let Lyra put that spell on him. In the visions she'd had before where he'd killed her, he'd still been *him*. He'd made the choice, even though it hurt him to do so. In this last vision, he'd had no control. It was like darkness had infected him and forced him to hurt her.

"She really cast that spell on me? The same one that was done to Malux?" He stopped walking and turned to her. She nodded, but didn't bother to speak. This had been going on for some time now, and she couldn't really do more than sit and let him process. He started pacing again, so she sat back and waited for his next question.

Someone knocked at the door and both of them turned to stare at it. Doyle held out a hand to motion for her to stay back, but she was already as far away from the door as she could get. She'd long since noticed no one ever came to his room, though. He usually checked in with Lyra in the morning, and if there were things she needed done, he'd go off and get them done. From what he'd said, even Lyra stayed away from his space.

Doyle opened the door, and she got a small glimpse of one of Lyra's guards on the other side before Doyle moved to block her from view. "Lyra would like to speak with both of you." The guard started off with a demanding tone, and Briar watched Doyle's spine straighten before he leaned against the doorway and crossed his arms, making himself appear completely at ease.

"And why would that be?"

"I didn't ask. She rarely sends for you, so I would guess it's important. It sounded like she expected you to come without question."

"Come now, Lyra knows me better than that."

"Doyle-"

"We'll come, but I'm not ready at this moment. I'll be up shortly." Briar could hear the long pause stretching out between them. She wished she could see the guard's face, but had an idea just what it would look like. "Run along now. You can let her know we are coming." Doyle shut the door before the guard could argue.

"What do you think she wants?" Briar asked quietly when Doyle didn't turn around right away.

"I'm not sure." He finally turned so she could see his face. It was paler than it had been a moment before. "Briar...if she really plans on doing this to me...how do we stop her?" When his gaze caught hers, she felt like he was silently begging her for an answer that she didn't have. At least not yet. She stood and walked to him and took his hand, as he had done so many times for her.

"We'll figure it out. Together."

"If she does this, what happens to you?" He hadn't asked her until then, and her heart tumbled a little. She wasn't ready to tell him that Lyra would turn him against her, that she would use him to enslave her. She tried to look down, to break their contact, but he moved to tilt her chin back up. "Come on, Blue, this doesn't end well for either of us, does it?"

"Not if Lyra does this spell, and," she swallowed and made her decision, "not if she becomes queen." His sharp breath hurt her. She knew everything was coming down around him. He released her and started his pacing again. "Doyle..."

"How long have you known? How long have you known we couldn't crown Lyra?" She'd hoped they wouldn't get there. The walls suddenly felt too close, and Briar wanted nothing more than to escape.

"A while," was all she could manage through her tight throat.

"So all this time...have you just been planning to work around me? You were just going to keep this from me until the end?"

"No...I just needed more answers. I needed you to trust me..." Doyle's eyes flashed, and she realized she'd said something wrong.

"So you *knew* I'd grow to have feelings for you. I mean, I'm sure you saw that...and what, you were just biding your time to make sure I was on your side before you told me about Lyra?" The hard edge in his voice gave her an uncomfortable reminder of the visions she'd had, and it took everything in her not to cower away from him. Her most recent vision was still too fresh to ignore the fear that spread through her. "Well?" At his harsh demand, she *did* take a step back. Pain flickered across his features and he stepped back with a shaky sigh. "Briar-"

"Yes. I had visions that showed the relationship we *could* have. I saw two versions of you finding out about Lyra; in both of them we shared love, but in one of those visions you killed me for betraying Lyra."

He noticeably flinched at those words and started shaking his head, but she pressed on. "I couldn't tell you because firstly, I knew that finding out about her true nature and what she was capable of would hurt you, and that's the last thing I want to do. And secondly, I knew from the beginning that there was some part of you that would always be loyal to the Lyra that saved your life and kept you safe all these years, and that you might choose to protect her. That you might kill me despite the feelings we have for one another. But this last vision...you didn't have a choice. You weren't *there*. She cast that spell on you, and you were gone. She took your choice away. I couldn't keep that from you. I'm sorry that I didn't tell you everything I knew, but you have to understand what it's like for me to have these visions of *every possible outcome*. I don't know what is really going to happen, or what choices people will make. I-" A sob tore through her so suddenly that it cut off her words, and she took a few steps back to gather herself.

"Doyle, I love you, but no, I could not trust you completely, because I've seen a future where you loved me but you stabbed me with the very dagger sitting on your desk right now. How could you expect me to trust you completely when I've seen that version of you, and I couldn't know which Doyle I would end up with until I stopped having split visions?"

"Blue..." He was still shaking his head, his features haunted. Then someone started pounding on his door, causing them both to startle. When the pounding came again, he moved swiftly and nearly tore it from the hinges. "What?"

"Sir, Lyra *demands* your presence immediately. She said if she has to come down here herself, she will, but one of you will pay the price." The guard on the other side sounded a little shaky, and if her and Doyle's conversation wasn't still playing in her head, she might have felt bad for the guy.

"Fine," Doyle barked before turning to her. His features softened just enough that she didn't feel the need to recoil farther back from him. Silently, he held out his hand, and she sensed a question there. There was still so much unsaid between them, but she could sense that he was asking if she trusted him, if they were still together in all of this mess. She wondered if she was crazy when she reached out and let him clasp her hand in his.

.℮ .℮ .℮

The light shone in through the windows, waking Ana from her deep slumber. Her body felt loose, all her muscles relaxed. She stretched and a small sound of pleasure escaped her lips. Ethelron rolled next to her, his arm draping over her stomach and pulling her close. Still half asleep, he kissed her shoulder and her neck, making her keenly aware they were alone in Ethelron's room instead of the shared dorm. Even Sio had left her master's side after the wedding, allowing them complete privacy for their wedding night.

"Good morning, wife." He was slowly waking himself up, exploring her body in a lazy way, like they had all the time in the world. In that moment, she saw what their lives could be if they lived through their next quest of danger. If they saved Erin and Gabe from the jeopardy the amulet now put them in.

"Good morning, husband." He hovered over her now, his all-too-rare smile shining on her. "I love you." Leaning up, she pressed her lips to his, desperate to drink in as much of the moment as she could before the erebus returned to take her payment. Ethelron didn't argue; he deepened the kiss and nothing else mattered but the two of them.

.℮ .℮ .℮

Erin woke to an empty bed, fully rested for the first time in months. A quick scan of the room revealed that she was alone. Panicked, she was on her feet and out the door in two breaths. Scenarios raced through her mind: the erebus returned, Gabe was gone again, more erebi attacked the kingdom while she slept. After asking a few passing elves about her friends, she was finally directed to the library where she found Melody and Ryo sitting on the floor, books spread out around them. It looked like Melody was doing the reading and sending Ryo to search for other volumes. But there was no sign of Gabe.

"Mel? What are you guys doing?" The witch looked up, her eyes clouded from her serious reading. "Trying to find more information about Skia, the amulet, blood magic." Melody huffed out a sigh, and Erin wondered how long they had been at it. "There is so much information, but none of it seems to be of much help. I haven't found anything about the master of Skia. I found some stuff about blood magic and amulets, but I'm not sure what it all means."

"What did you find?" Her curiosity piqued, and she reached up to touch the stone around her neck. The one that now controlled her and Gabe's future.

"Oh you know, blood magic is an extremely dark magic." Melody stood and stretched, and Ryo seemed to appear with a tray of food out of nowhere. Erin thanked him and took a piece of bread while he sat and picked at a piece of fruit, clearly enjoying the break from fetching books for Melody.

"There doesn't seem to be a way to break the connection once it's made, other than destroying the stone and killing you both," he added.

"Basically what Lyra said. We are stuck doing her bidding to repay her. We will have to take out the leader of Skia so she doesn't come after the amulet again." She thought of how easily the amulet could have been lost to them forever. They could have buried it with him, it could have been stolen or taken from her...she could have lost it so many times without realizing.

"Melody," Ryo urged quietly, nudging the witch's calf with his foot. Erin realized she had been chewing her lip, deciding whether to tell her something else.

"What is it, Mel?"

"It's unclear; everything in these books is cryptic. I had to do a spell on most of them so I could even read them so Ryo didn't have to translate elvish for me this whole time-"

"Mel, it's fine. Just tell me."

"It brought Gabe back from the *dead*, using dark blood magic. That's not a light thing, and magic has consequences..."

"Other than us now being at the beck and call of *Lyra?*"

"Gabe's soul was contained in the stone until you released it. The whole time it was surrounded by the dark energy of the amulet."

Erin grew cold at Melody's words, a strange foreboding hitting her.

"The dark magic may have...imprinted on him. Left a mark of its own on his soul. There's no way for us to know other than wait and see if something happens. There's nothing we can do if it did. He would simply have to fight it on his own. But like I said," Melody rushed on as Erin's head grew light, "the books are unclear. And even then, he may be fine."

"Okay...thanks Mel." Her eyes flashed to the oddly quiet silver elf. "What spell did you do on *him* to get him to help *and* stay quiet at the same time?" She teased, needing to change the subject and lighten the mood.

"I'll have you know, I am a very nice person...plus I've seen what this girl can do with her magic, so she asked for help and I obeyed." He shrugged with a grin, and Melody flashed him a threatening look.

"Do you guys know where Gabe went this morning?" Erin asked, even more anxious than before to find him.

"He got up early to go to the king." Ryo's voice softened then.

"How is Brannor?" Fear gripped her when she saw the looks on their faces.

"It's spreading fairly quickly now. The infection is gaining strength now that it's been awhile since the queen healed him. He lost consciousness early this morning for a while but came back. The pain..." Erin nodded, able to imagine.

"Has anyone told Ana yet?"

"We thought they should be allowed a bit of a honeymoon. I think Gabe wanted some time alone with him, anyway. When they come to get food, we are going to tell them." Erin nodded in agreement and let them know she was going to peek in to see if there was something she could get them.

She quickly realized just how serious the situation was when she found three guards standing outside, clearly waiting for orders to fetch the princess at a moment's notice. When she saw them, she paused, not wanting to interrupt their private moment. But one guard saw her and stopped her.

"Prince Toron asked us to send you in when you arrived." She gave a solemn nod and stepped inside the room. The relief that washed over Gabe's face was immediate. He left the bedside and gathered her in his arms, and she realized he was shaking.

"You should have gotten me up," she whispered, hugging him tightly to her.

"You needed rest." He kissed her cheek and when he pulled back, she saw the pain clearly in his eyes.

"You needed me." Erin was grateful when he reacted to the words - it was a skill she hadn't really practiced - but he didn't respond. Instead, he took her hand, and the two walked together to sit by the king's bed. Through the night, he'd clearly turned a corner. The black infection was taking over his veins, spreading slowly over his face. His good hand was also turning black, the skin hardening. He was almost out of time.

"Hi, Brannor." She placed a hand on his chest and wished she could heal him. His eyes opened, still as green as ever, but washed with pain.

"Please, get Ethelron. I need to speak with him." His voice was weak. Erin started to rise, but Gabe placed a hand on her arm. He rose instead and stepped outside the door to ask the guards to fetch the others. "Thank you for bringing me my son, for loving him."

"I never had much of a choice. He's far too easy to love," Erin replied. She placed a soft kiss on the king's cheek and had to fight back tears when she felt his skin burning with fever. Gabe was behind her once more, a shaky hand resting on her shoulder. She reached up to tangle their fingers together and give him as much comfort as she could. They listened to each raspy breath, waiting for Ethelron and Ana to join them.

.℮ .℮ .℮

"Your stomach is growling," Ana whispered in amusement, looking up at her husband.

"Guess we should rejoin the world once more. I need nourishment." With a reluctant nod, Ana rose and began to dress for the day. Ethelron dressed more quickly and came behind her to silently braid her hair back, the moment intimate as his fingers brushed over her neck and touched the back of her ears as they went. When he was done, he pressed a kiss to her neck, and she had to stop herself from turning in his arms and returning the kiss.

"Let's go, you need food." She took his hand and kissed his new rune gently before they left the room. They'd only made it down the first hallway when a guard rushed toward them and stopped in his tracks to bow to Ana. "Your Highness, I've been sent to fetch the two of you."

Fear and anticipatory grief clenched around her heart. She already knew, but she still had to ask: "What is it?"

"The king, ma'am..." Ethelron gripped her hand tightly, and the two took off at a run to the king's chambers.

When they arrived, Ana knew her moment of light was now over. Ryo stood alongside a guard and gave a small bow as they approached. Ethelron kissed her hand before leading them through the doorway. The air was warm, as though her father's fever was high enough to heat his entire chamber. Melody came to her side, taking her free hand and giving it a reassuring squeeze before releasing her to approach the bed. Erin turned to her and gave her a sad smile. Toron didn't move, his back stiff and his eyes on their father. She went to his side and touched his shoulder in reassurance before taking in the figure on the bed. Brannor's eyes lit at the sight of his daughter. She saw he wanted to reach out to her, but both hands were now taken over by the infection, and he looked frozen in place.

His gaze searched those around his bed and when it landed on Ethelron, his mouth fell into a grim smile. "Ethelron, I have a grave favor to ask of you." Ana looked at her husband in question and watched some unspoken realization sink in. She still wasn't sure what the favor would be, but it seemed El understood. He gave her father a short, solemn nod and her father sighed in relief.

"Papa?"

"I love you, my children. My family has grown, and I couldn't have chosen better mates for you if I'd searched for a thousand years.

Make each other happy, and know that Faervel and I will always be with you. You must leave us now."

"Us? Papa, what are you talking about?" Ana looked to her husband again and froze when his eyes finally met hers. Suddenly, the grim look in her husband's eyes made horrible sense. "No!"

"Aina, my bell, *please*. I shall not ask this of you or Toron, but I cannot bear it. I am dying. Please let me go in my own way. *While I'm still me.*"

"*Aina...*" She looked up at the sound of Ethelron's voice in her mind and saw how heavy the weight was for him. But he would do as his king asked, and she knew he was being kind in doing it.

"No." Her voice was softer this time, and her hands shook. Ethelron loved her father as his own, had followed him without question for years, even to the point of denying himself her love in fear of disappointing the king and queen. She could not allow him to make this sacrifice. "I'll do it Papa. If that is what you wish, let me do it."

Chapter Twenty-Seven

Ana spoke a cleansing prayer over her dagger after the arguing finally died down. Her father didn't want one of his children to carry the burden, but she knew it didn't matter who he asked, they would *all* carry it. As the eldest, it only seemed natural that she be the one to do it. Everyone had a quiet moment with Brannor to say their goodbyes, then stood around the bed together to share his final moments. Ethelron came to stand by her side, and Toron and Erin stood across from them. He was surrounded by loved ones, his children.

"Aina, you don't have to do this."

"I love you, Papa." She ignored her husband's voice and kissed her father's cheeks. The infection was moving more quickly now, and his skin was beginning to harden in more than just his arms. She didn't want him to finish the transformation, she wanted to end his suffering while he was still *himself*. A few deep breaths, and she held the dagger over his heart. She envisioned herself plunging her blade into his chest…but she couldn't actually make the movement to do it. She stood frozen over him as all her childhood memories came rushing back to her. All the love he had for her. Sobs racked her body, and her hands fell helplessly to her side.

After all her father did for her, *sacrificed* for her, and she was now unable to take away his pain. "I'm sorry," she managed through her tears, and read the understanding in his eyes. Ethelron reached to take the dagger from her, to take the heavy burden for himself. Before he could, the sound of a blade sliding from its sheath filled the room.

Her father was still looking at her, but the light faded from his eyes quickly. She looked up to see Toron standing over him, a dagger in his hand dripping with blood. Erin's eyes were wide as she stared at the king's body and tried to make sense of what just happened. Toron didn't move, his face devoid of emotion of any kind. His eyes were empty as they stared at their father.

"What did you do?" She fell to her knees by her father's body and laid her head against his shoulder. Only a moment before he had been alive, looking at her, and now both her parents were gone.

Ethelron moved from her side and slowly took the dagger from Toron's grasp, his eyes worried as he watched the prince. "Prince Toron?"

"Gabe! My name is Gabe," her brother snapped, startling most of the occupants in the room. His outburst even surprised himself, it seemed, because Ana watched the fire in his eyes douse as quickly as it had flared. He reached for Erin's hand and practically dragged her from the room without so much as a backwards glance towards his father.

.℘ .℘ .℘

Erin watched Ana approach and knew what was coming. The last day and a half had passed in a blur as the kingdom held a funeral for their king and crowned Ana and Ethelron as their new rulers. Quickly, the royal duties were placed on the newly appointed head guard, Aeron, as they knew that soon the erebus would return to summon them away.

"Erin, we need to talk."

"Ana, we talked about it already. Mel, back me up!"

"I only know what I told Erin about blood magic, and that the king was asking for his suffering to end." Melody had been trying to avoid getting pulled into the middle, but after she told Ana the same thing about dark magic possibly imprinting on Gabe's soul, Ana clung to the information as the only explanation for Gabe's actions.

"Ana, he was in shock! His father was suffering, and he did what had to be done! I'm not talking about this anymore! You can't put the blame on him! He simply did what you could not! He kept your husband from having to do it. Thank goodness too, because otherwise you'd be standing here wondering if *Ethelron* was some kind of psycho!"

"Erin, it's not the fact that he killed him, it was his *expression*. There was *nothing* there! He didn't cry, he didn't look pained at his actions. Nothing. *That's not normal*!"

"You've seen him, he's been *normal* since then. Don't you think if something was actually wrong with him, there would be more signs? He was grieving at the funeral, and he's been in pain over the loss. Stop doing this, Ana!"

"Erin, I've been looking for you." Gabe called out, his strides long and even, and his gaze only for her. It still took her breath away to see him. He was actually alive. He was *there*. All of Ana's worries were pushed to the side as Gabe reached them and wrapped his arms around Erin, placing a soft kiss on her cheek. "Aina, I'm glad you are here. I haven't really had the chance to talk to you with so much going on. I wanted..." he drew in a ragged breath that Erin could feel against her back, "I wanted to apologize for how I acted. I know I snapped at you in a very emotional moment, and I really am sorry. I don't even know *why*. I think everything was just too much. And I know I'll always be Toron here, and I don't want you to think I'm trying to erase that part of me. Just, *I* know myself better as Gabe. I met Erin when I was Gabe, I have spent most of my life thinking of myself that way. I feel like *Toron* is just a reminder of all that we've lost. I don't *feel* like Toron anymore."

"It's okay." Ana reached out and squeezed his forearm. "I will respect your wishes to be called Gabe, and I will make sure the rest of the realm falls in line." She gave her brother a caring smile. As much as she and Ana were butting heads over this amulet and what it might mean, she knew Ana wanted her brother back just as much as Erin had. She knew Ana loved him, and that helped ease some of the anger she'd felt when Ana had tried to push this conversation about dark magic. "You will always be my family, whatever name you choose for yourself. I'm so glad you are back, and I'm so glad you and Erin have found each other."

Gabe released Erin so he could lean forward and pull his sister into a tight hug. Erin hoped it was the start of their healing. They had lost far too much, but they were both still here, still alive, and back together. "Thank you, Aina. Now, if you'll excuse me, I needed to steal Erin away for a bit."

They all waved to one another before Erin fell into step beside Gabe. "What did you need?"

"You." He grinned down at her, giving her hand a squeeze and pulling her so her side bumped into his. "I still find it very hard to believe I've been away for months. All that time feels wasted. I should have been at your side, loving you." He stopped walking and looked down at her, his emotions clear in his gaze. He was hurting, and he was hurting because he knew *she'd* been hurting from his loss. Gabe kissed her, his hand holding her cheek with a tenderness that nearly broke her heart. He took his time, tasting her slowly, and only pulled away once she was having trouble drawing breath.

"You look naked without some crazy hair style." His voice was gentle and teasing as his fingers tugged at her longer brown hair.

"You don't like it?" Her hair had been the least of her concerns the last few months. She couldn't really say if she looked odd or not without an ever-changing hairstyle, as she'd done her best to avoid looking at herself in the mirror.

"No, it's fine. It's your natural color...I'm just used to you having some wild color. This reminds me of when we were younger, before you chopped it all off." He tucked it behind her ear before giving her ear lobe a playful nip.

"Maybe Melody can do a spell on it for me, make it purple or something." He chuckled and pulled her against his chest. Warm reassurance washed through her as she heard the steady beat of his heart under her ear. He was *fine*.

.℘ .℘ .℘

Doyle was still holding on to Briar's hand like a lifeline when they entered Lyra's chambers. Briar's grip tightened when Lyra's eyes focused on their tangle of fingers, but he was not about to let her go. Not while he was still reeling over everything Briar had just told him. He couldn't understand how she had ever let him *look* at her when she'd seen a version of him that would...he shook himself to rid the thought of plunging his dagger into her. He'd watched her being hurt before, and *that* had nearly torn him apart, even before he'd grown to know her and have feelings for her. To imagine a version of himself that would be so tied up with putting Lyra on the throne that he would *kill* her seemed out of reach...*but.* He'd been so willing to do so many other things, to hurt other people in order to further their cause...

He gripped her hand tighter. He was angry with her for keeping so much from him, and still wanted to talk to her about it, but he understood. It had to be hard for her to have feelings for him, and to see that they could have a great love, but to know it could go so very wrong. He wanted to pull her aside and kiss her. To show her he'd never harm her, even if she made him mad sometimes. Even if she saw parts of the future that she did not share with him.

"I'll be going to our little band of misfits soon. I think we need some kind of plan," Lyra finally spoke, her eyes turning from their joined hands to meet his eyes. He felt the hatred brewing there, and wondered if she was already trying to figure out how to put him under the dark spell that held Malux for so long.

"After you see them again, if there is something small you can bring me, even just a hair, it will give me something to focus on. I can try to see more about their travels in the realm. Otherwise, I don't think you really need to stay with them the whole time. Just tell them where to head. It will take them a few days to reach the castle from the portal they will have access to, and once they do, we'll have to help clear the way so that you and the group can get to the queen. Have you had luck with the spell for your blades?"

Doyle listened to Briar and wondered what her ultimate plan was. If she knew Lyra could not take the crown, then he wondered if she'd seen someone in the group take over instead. There was so much he needed to speak with her about, and he couldn't while trapped in here with Lyra.

"I have a small list of some ingredients he did not have. Nothing too drastic to get a hold of. If I don't have to be with the group the whole time, then I should be able to get that taken care of with time to spare. Have you seen anything else since your last vision?"

He felt Briar's hand spasm in his, but she kept a straight face. "Nothing, but I shall try to keep focused on finding out all I can about the last steps. We are getting close to the end."

"Yes; and since we are close to the end of all this, I think we should start working out the plans for after you take the crown," Doyle cut in, wanting to test the waters. "Sending Briar home, for one; and what position you would like me to take after all this is over."

Her expression tightened, and her eyes darted between them again. "Well, I thought with how close you two have become, Briar thought of this as her home now."

"The deal was for her to help take down the queen and then she would be released to go back to Loinnir. My plan for her has never changed. I hope yours has not?" He watched Lyra carefully, but she closed herself off and he couldn't glean anything from her expression.

"It is certainly helpful having the observer around, but I will keep my word. It might be good to ask her what she wants, but that can wait until the crown is safely on my head. As for you, I planned on keeping you in much the same position you have been in for me all these years. I trust you are still loyal to my cause?"

"Of course." He gave a quick bow of his head.

"Good." She turned her attention back to Briar. "Then I hope to hear if you have any more visions. I will go to the group soon to bring them here." She dismissed them with a wave and Doyle was left feeling like he gained nothing from their brief conversation. Once they were free from prying eyes and ears, Briar turned to him.

"Doyle, about earlier-"

"I'm sorry," he cut her off. When she'd first gotten to the realm, he'd thought she was so weak. He thought it would only take a day or so to break her and get her to work for them without argument. She'd seemed so innocent and naïve to him then. Now she was this strong, vibrant being that had held her own in a different realm, surrounded

431

by people who could hurt her, many of whom were more than willing to do so in order to get their way. "You were right. You couldn't tell me everything before. And I know your visions aren't always easy to navigate. I...I can't understand how you could share a bed with me when you didn't know...when you thought I could-"

She put a finger over his lips to cut him off. "We are in this together now. And we have some plans to make...if you're with me?" Her eyes were wide with questions, and he felt torn between the life he'd always thought he'd have since the day Lyra saved him, and the life he could have with Briar. It only took a second for him to choose. He drew her against him and claimed her lips as his and dove into whatever the future would hold for them together.

.ℓ .ℓ .ℓ

"The erebus should be back tomorrow, right? Our respite is up?" Ana looked to Ryo as he walked beside them. He'd joined them in their discussion with Aeron, making sure everything would run smoothly in the absence of Eloas' new rulers. In their talks, however, Ryo hadn't mentioned his plan to join them in Skia.

"'*Our* respite?' And what does your mother have to say about you leaving for Skia when our home is finally at peace after all these years?" Ethelron asked with a raised brow. His arm brushed against hers as they walked, and the small touch almost distracted her from Ryo's response.

"She's not exactly jumping for joy at the notion, but I'm not letting you go without me. I want to have a little fun, too. No more erebi to fight *here*, you can't let my skills go to waste."

"You want to come with us?" Melody gave him an odd look as she met them in the hall.

"Sure, don't you think it will be a relief to have my dashing good looks around while in a realm "of hell" as I believe you called it while looking over the books?"

Ethelron snorted at Ana's side, draping his arm around her waist. He'd been all about keeping them touching in some way. While she wasn't going to complain, the affection was such a shift from the guard persona she'd always known that it kept surprising her.

Mel raised a brow toward Ryo. "*We* don't want to go. What kind of crazy person *volunteers* for something like this?"

"The kind who knows you are going to need all the help you can get. I was with you, Melody. I saw all the erebi in those books. You were trying to stay calm, but we all know what you are going to be up against."

"Let him come if he wants. He's right about needing help," Ana spoke up. "We should all stay together tonight and get some rest. I don't know when Lyra will show up. We have to be ready."

"I already sent Sio to get in a good hunt." Ethelron stated, his thumb making lazy circles at her hip. "We should get food, and pack supplies." He pressed a gentle kiss to her temple and led the group back.

They walked in silence for a while. Melody approached Ethelron from the opposite side, and Ana caught her tucking something into his hand before dropping back to walk with Ryo. Ana was about to ask what it was when Ethelron pulled her to a stop and turned to the others. "You two find Erin and Prince Toron. We will catch up with you in the main hall." She raised a curious brow at him, but he just shook his head silently. If he was planning on stealing her away for another quiet moment together, she knew she should argue that there was too much to do, but she wasn't going to. She wanted every second she could grab.

As soon as she realized he was taking her to the library, Ana began leading the way herself. She made it inside quickly, loving the quiet of the space. Her heart was still so heavy with her recent losses, and while she had much to celebrate, the weight still seemed overwhelming when she was surrounded by too many people. Ethelron followed her in silence, only stopping when their feet touched. He rubbed her arms, lifting her hand to kiss their matching rune. Then he leaned down and kissed her forehead tenderly, before turning her gently by the shoulders so that she faced away from him once more.

"I noticed that you no longer wore the necklace that your father gave you at your coming of age ceremony."

"I...I had to use the flower to bring back my brother's memories," she whispered, fingers unconsciously brushing against the skin where the jewelry once rested. Ethelron brushed her hair free of her neck, kissing the newly bared skin before reaching around in front of her. He took the item in his right hand and spread it between both hands, revealing a familiar white flower encased in glass shaped like a teardrop. Ana gasped, touching it with trembling fingers.

"May I, my queen?" She nodded silently. "This is the flower that your father removed from your finger during the ceremony. I had Melody enchant it so that it will remain alive in the necklace," he explained, securing the chain as she stared at the vibrant pendant. "I know it cannot replace what your father gave you, but-"

"It is beautiful...it's *perfect*," she murmured, spinning around and pressing her lips to his. Ethelron wrapped his arms around her and lifted her off her feet, giving her a twirl before returning her safely to the ground. She always felt safe with him at her side. "Thank you, El. I love you."

"And I you, my dear Aina." He gazed down at her with a look of wonder. Then he left soft kisses across her cheeks before resting his forehead against hers. "I wish I could bring back all that you lost, but I swear, I will do everything in my power to bring you happiness. Your love has brought me so much joy in such a short time, that is all I want to do in return." His thumb traced her bottom lip before he kissed the spot. "We should get back to the others, it will be time to go soon." He took her hand and turned towards the door, but she pulled him back with unexpected strength. She needed another moment with him. Their honeymoon was about to be spent in Skia, facing so many unknowns. They had a lot of things to take care of, but right now, she needed to focus on her husband.

Ethelron came back to her easily enough, and then their lips were crashing together, desperate to find peace in one another. He held her close and kissed her with everything he had. She hummed happily when his tongue slid between her lips. Her fingers tangled into his hair, drawing his head down, before nipping at his bottom lip. Her husband growled, the sound reverberating in his chest, and he turned her to press her back against the door. Ana grinned against his mouth, releasing his lip and tracing it with her tongue. "Is this a reaction to getting jewelry, or is there something else I did that I should be taking note of, my wife?"

"This is just how I say 'I love you' to my husband." She grinned at him, feeling so much lighter now than she had when she'd walked into the library.

"Ah, well, I'd like to show you how I say 'I love you' to my wife. If my queen will allow it?"

"Hmm," She tilted her head before her gaze fell to his lips again. Their time was slipping away, but she was going to take advantage while she could. "She allows i-"

His lips cut her off, which seemed to be a habit of his they should discuss. He couldn't just quiet her with a kiss - his hands moved and his body pressed closer and any thoughts she was having disappeared.

.℘ .℘ .℘

The next morning, Erin woke to find Gabe frowning down at her in worry. His finger was brushing down her cheek and then tracing her lips. He gave her a soft smile when she blinked at him, before he leaned down and pressed a soft kiss there. "Good morning," she whispered, sitting up and seeing that everyone else was still asleep.

"Erin, I love you. I want you to be safe, and I know we are in this together. But..." He looked around the room with a slow shake of his head. "We could go without them. Leave my sister the amulet and kill this erebus ourselves. She'll protect the amulet for us, and they don't have to risk everything..."

"Gabe," Erin placed a hand on his cheek, "we are *all* in this together. They would never stand for it, and you know it. I understand your worry, but we can do this. *Together.*"

Sio whined across the room and Ethelron sat up, alert. A moment later, Lyra appeared before them. Her cat-like eyes glinted as she took in the view of all of them camped on the floor.

"Hope everyone is well rested!" Her voice was too cheerful, and jolted the rest of them awake.

Ryo got to his feet with a groan. "I prefer to wake to much quieter tones. Sometimes my company doesn't use words at all..."

"Oh, I *like* him." Lyra showed her sharp teeth as she grinned towards Ryo. "Well, I gave you your play-time, and now it's my turn."

Gabe stood and helped Erin to her feet. They each gathered their packs and checked their weapons in silence. Erin caught Ana looking at each of them, a small frown pulling at her lips. "What will you have us do?" she demanded.

"I'll take us to Skia, you just have to hold hands. So hurry up, find your buddy!"

Everyone moved slowly to make a circle, and Gabe came to Erin's side, taking her hand in his. She squeezed tightly, fear gripping her heart as she tried to mentally prepare for what was about to happen. Gabe must have felt the slight tremor that was starting in her body, because he pulled her closer so their whole sides touched. How had she gone months without him? She couldn't lose him again. Whatever it took, she couldn't live through his loss again. Melody took her other hand, followed by Ryo, Ana, and Ethelron. Ethelron reached out to touch Sio's fur.

"At least if I have to go to *hell*, I get to hold a pretty girl's hand," Ryo said with a wink towards Melody.

"You're just saying that because your real crush, Ethelron, is married now," Melody shot back, which helped ease some of the tightness in Erin's chest.

Lyra said a few words, and then the world around them shuddered.

Acknowledgements

So much goes into writing a book, and writing a series just becomes more complicated and demanding. We receive so much support during our writing process, and without our friends and family, the Mystifying series would not exist.

To our parents: you guys have always been encouraging and allowed us to reach for the stars. To our spouses: we are both so blessed to have found men that love us for exactly who we are, who give us the time and space to write, and who believe in and support us all the way. We love you guys and we appreciate everything you do.

Thank you to all our friends that have read our stories from the beginning. It has always been so good for us to have people we could bounce ideas off of; people that would give feedback, and tell us they had to know what happened next. You guys rock and your love keeps us going.

Thank you once again to the wonderfully talented (and just all around lovely) Megan Moore (@GraphiteGeek on Insta) for a beautiful cover! And to Jackie and Mike, who take the time to help us with editing (including when Jackie leaves us low-key threatening notes to protect her favorite characters.)

As always, we are also beyond grateful for the support of you, reading this book. We might be super introverts, but we would still love to connect with you, to hear what you think, to talk about other fandoms (we set Moore loose on Dragon Con for the first time this past year…please, gush with her about it) or to just chat about life. You can find links to all our socials on our linktree:

Author Bio

The Dorian half of Dorian Moore works as a preschool teacher by day, but in her free time, she is a hoarding book dragon with a frozen coffee in one hand and a pen in the other. In school, it was believed she was an avid note-taker, but she was really writing stories in her composition notebooks and avoiding math like the plague. No character is safe, the death of characters was even mentioned in a toast at her wedding, but when she's not killing off characters, she's helping them find love. She lives in Delaware with her loving husband, two boys, and houseful of pets.

The Moore half of Dorian Moore is a therapist by day, writer by night. When she's not working with clients or writing, she's hanging out with her husband and young son in her hometown in Delaware (probably outside). She also enjoys recreational archery and finding new toys for her pretty purple Jeep (aptly named Hawkeye). Moore writes in the fantasy genre when writing with Dorian, and leans towards contemporary new adult romance (dabbling in the Christian fiction genre as well) in her own stories.

www.ingramcontent.com/pod-product-compliance
Lightning Source LLC
Chambersburg PA
CBHW021121260626
47169CB00005B/1392